"I LOVED Katie!"
—LUCY KNISLEY, *New York Times* bestselling author of *Stepping Stones*

...entrepreneurship, and excellent, pun-filled pet names."
—*The Bulletin of the Center for Children's Books*

KATIE THE CATSITTER

BEST FRIENDS FOR NEVER

"The new Feline Queen of All-Ages Superhero Comic Books. A . . . universal story about growing up."
—ComicBookResources.com

"Super fun and utterly delightful!"
—GENE LUEN YANG, creator of *American Born Chinese*

"A winner!"
—NICK BRUEL, creator of the Bad Kitty series

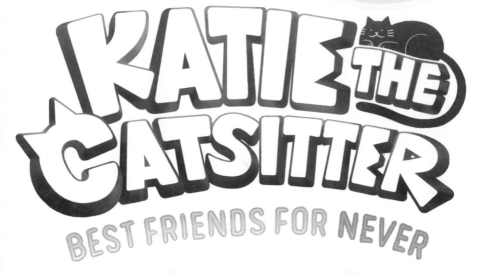

Read all the Katie the Catsitter books!

#1 *Katie the Catsitter*
#2 *Best Friends for Never*
#3 *Secrets and Sidekicks*

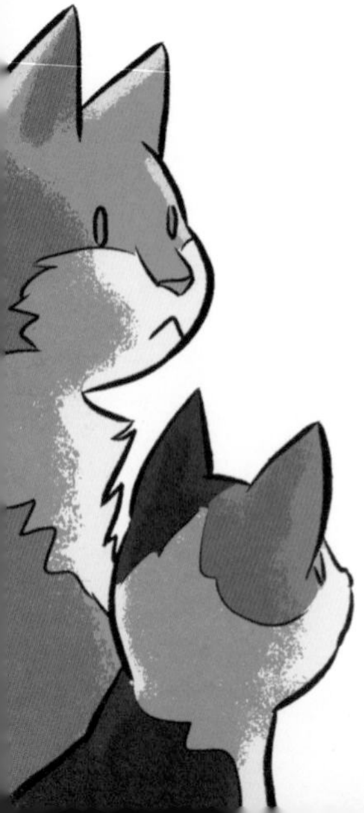

Random House New York

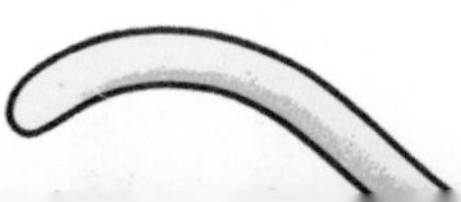

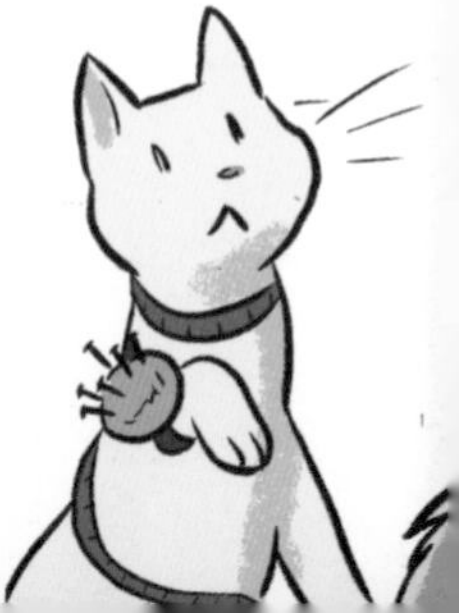

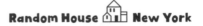

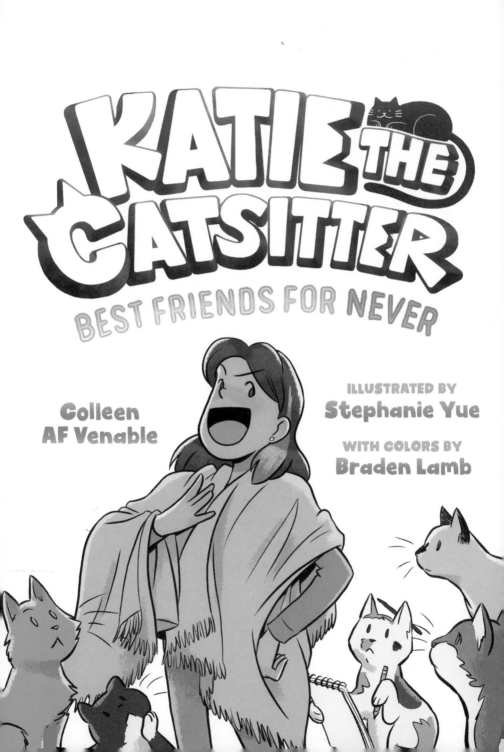

KATIE THE CATSITTER

BEST FRIENDS FOR NEVER

Colleen
AF Venable

ILLUSTRATED BY
Stephanie Yue

WITH COLORS BY
Braden Lamb

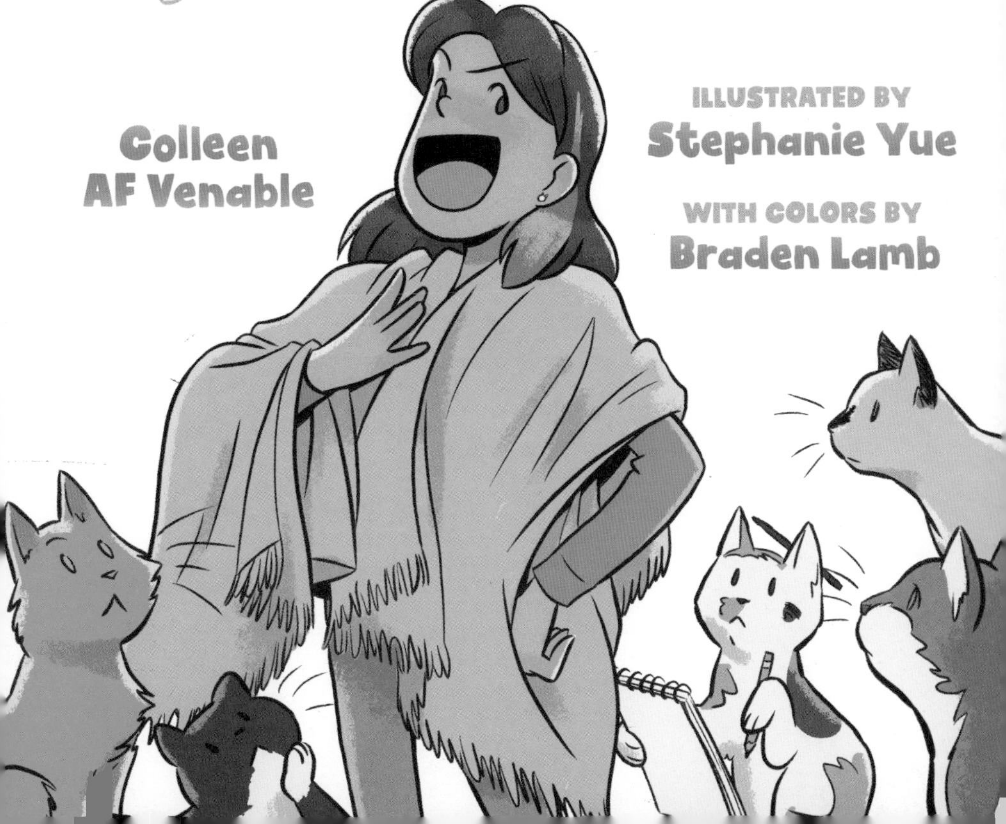

With grateful thanks to Shasta Clinch, Barbara Perez Marquez,
and Polo Orozco for their invaluable feedback.

Visit us on the Web! rhcbooks.com

Educators and librarians, for a variety of teaching tools,
visit us at RHTeachersLibrarians.com

Library of Congress Cataloging-in-Publication Data
Names: Venable, Colleen A. F., author. | Yue, Stephanie, illustrator.
Title: Best friends for never / Colleen AF Venable; illustrated by Stephanie Yue.
Description: New York: Random House Children's Books, [2022] | Series: Katie the catsitter; 2
Summary: Twelve-year-old Katie now knows her neighbor Madeline is also the Mousetress,
the city's most feared villain (or most misunderstood superhero), and she is ready to become
the super sidekick she always wanted to be.
Identifiers: LCCN 2021005451 | ISBN 978-0-593-37546-4 (hardcover) |
ISBN 978-1-9848-9566-0 (trade pbk.) | ISBN 978-1-9848-9567-7 (lib. bdg.) |
ISBN 978-1-9848-9568-4 (ebook)
Subjects: LCSH: Graphic novels. | CYAC: Graphic novels. | Supervillains—Fiction. |
Neighbors—Fiction. | Pet sitting—Fiction.
Classification: LCC PZ7.7.V46 Be 2022 | DDC 741.5/973—dc23

Book design by Stephanie Yue, April Ward, and Sylvia Bi

MANUFACTURED IN CHINA
10 9 8 7 6 5 4 3 2
First Edition

Random House Children's Books supports the First Amendment
and celebrates the right to read.

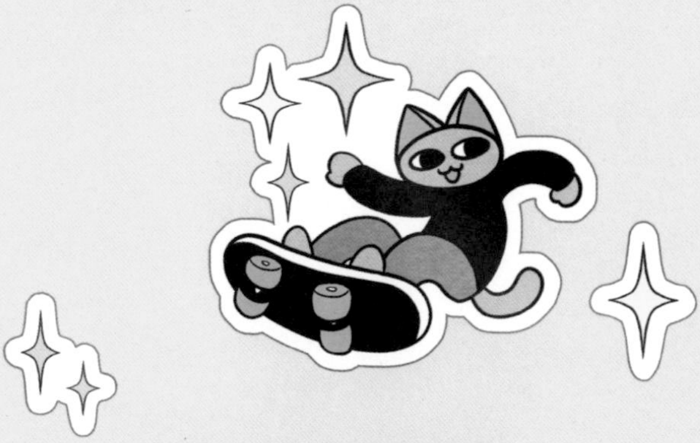

To my big sis, Kath,
who is stronger than Stainless Steel,
more brilliant than the Mousetress, and
smart enough to own only one cat

—C.A.F.V.

To Mendel, Salem, Olie, Poffie,
Mr. Puddinton, and friends around the
world, both two- and four-legged, who
kept me company from afar

—S.Y.

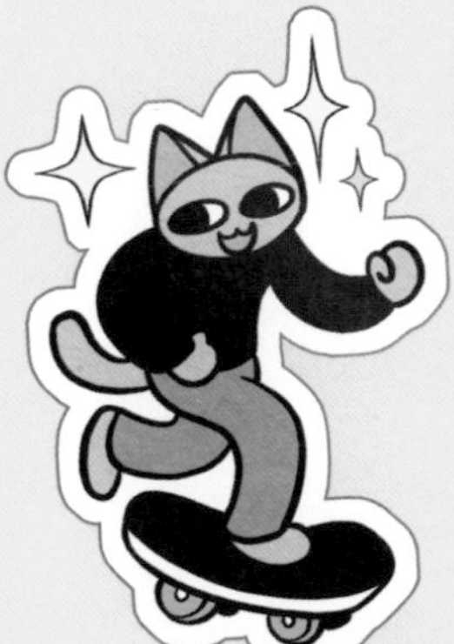

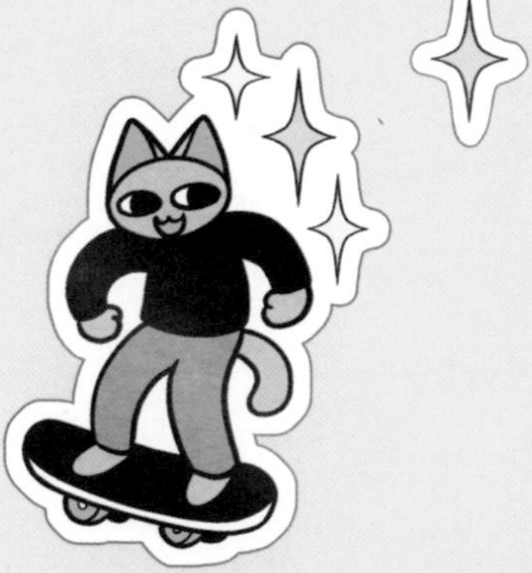

CHAPTER ONE

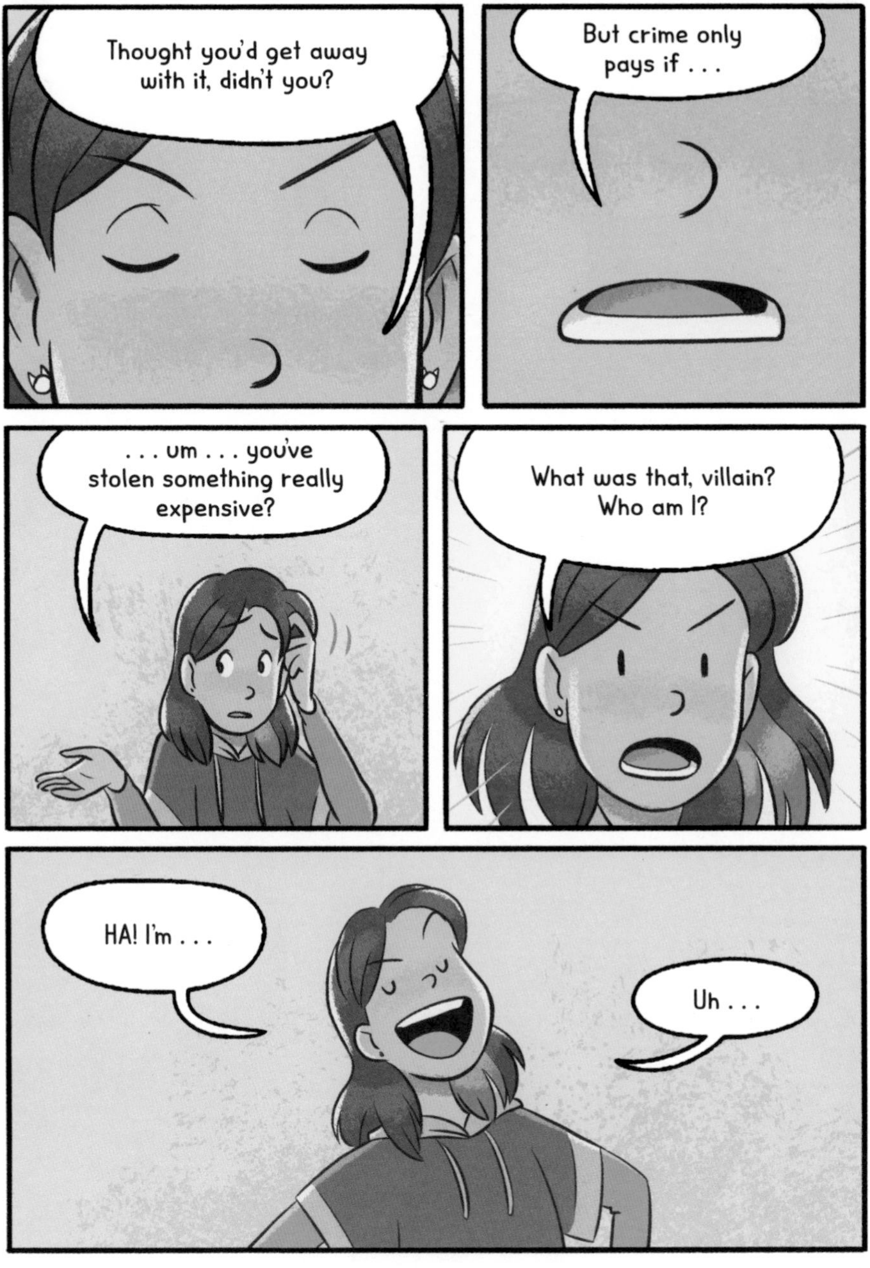
Thought you'd get away with it, didn't you?
But crime only pays if . . .
. . . um . . . you've stolen something really expensive?
What was that, villain? Who am I?
HA! I'm . . .
Uh . . .

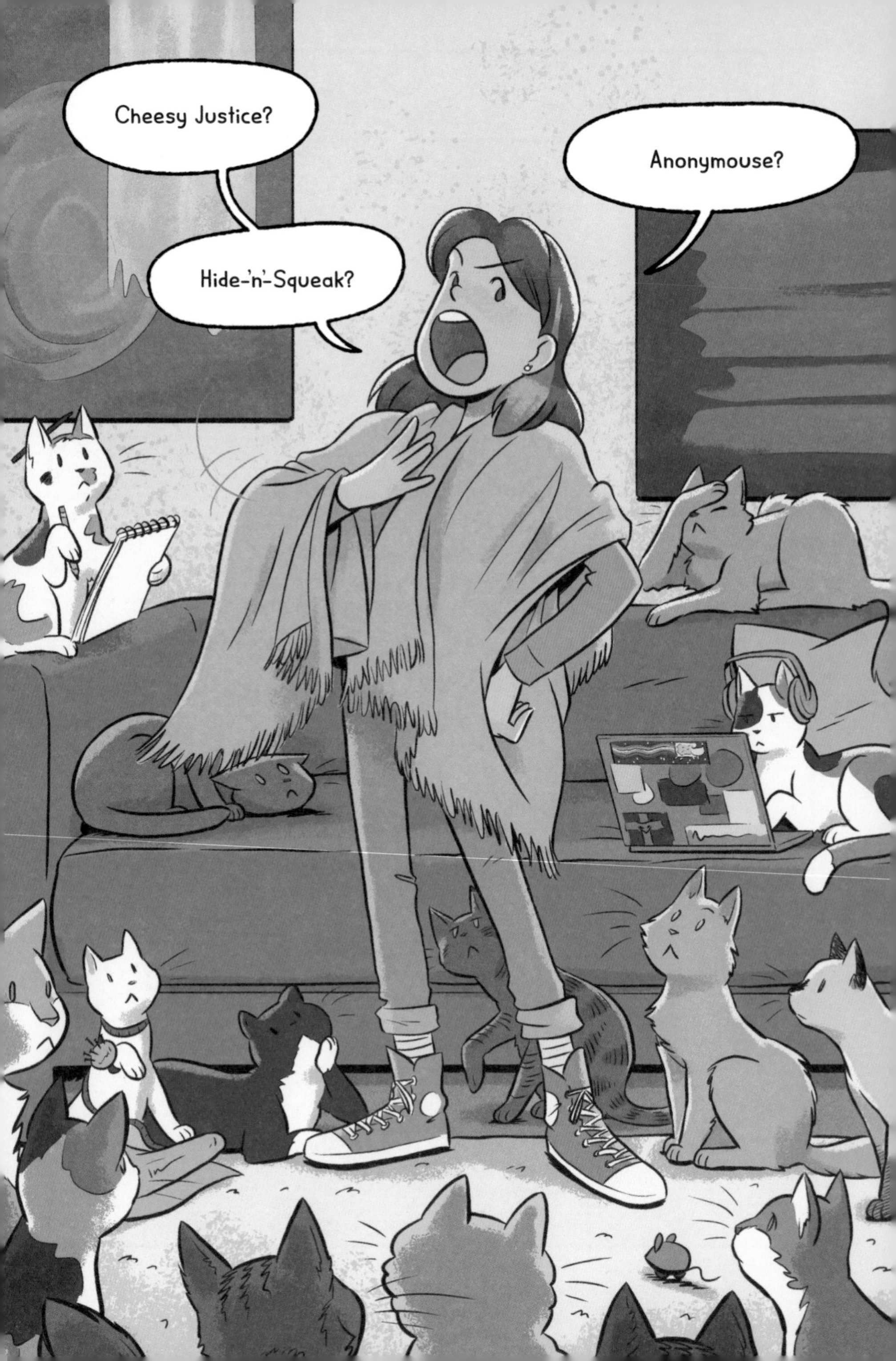
Cheesy Justice?
Hide-'n'-Squeak?
Anonymouse?

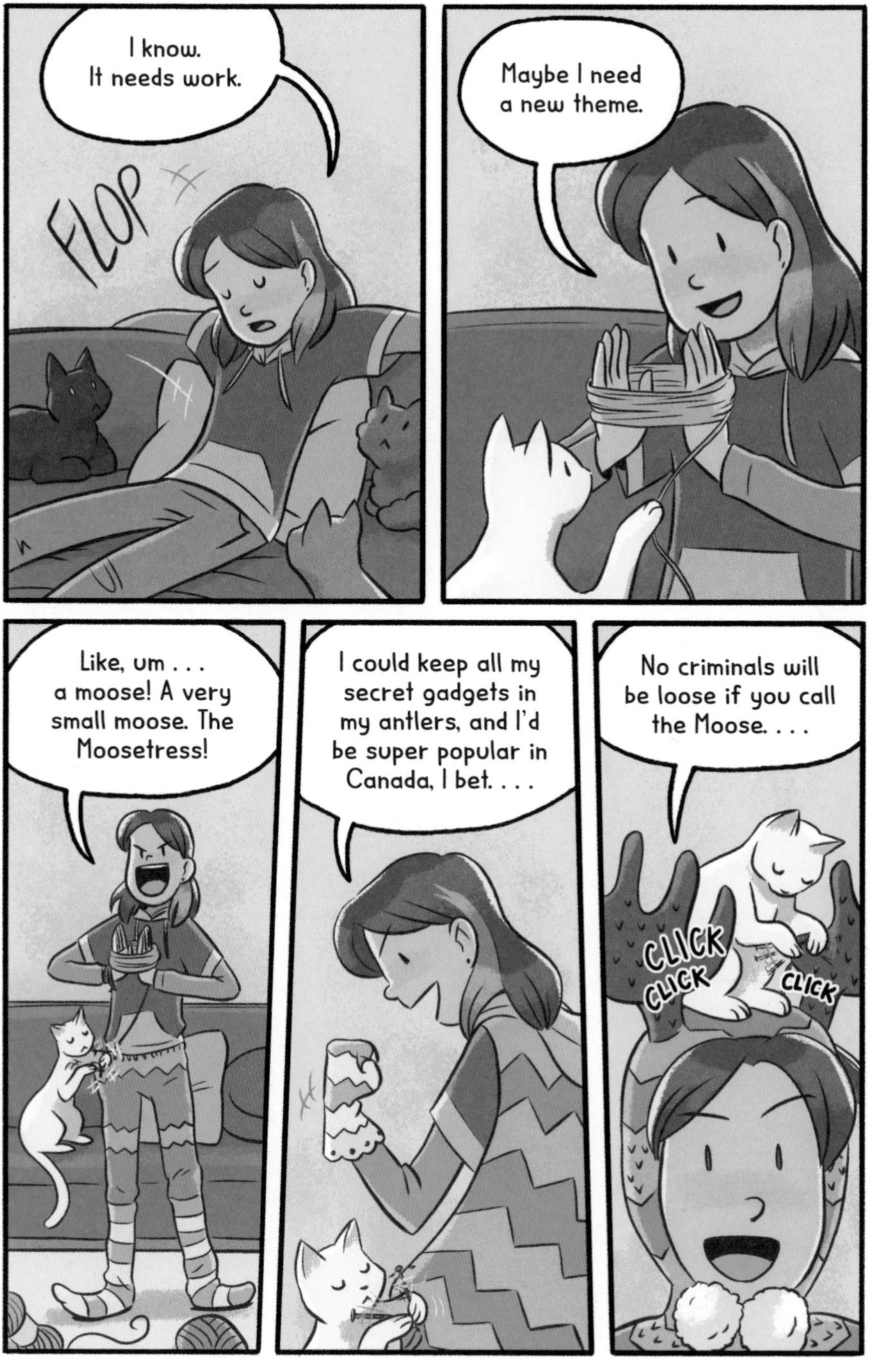
I know.
It needs work.
FLOP
Maybe I need
a new theme.
Like, um . . .
a moose! A very
small moose. The
Moosetress!
I could keep all my
secret gadgets in
my antlers, and I'd
be super popular in
Canada, I bet. . . .
No criminals will
be loose if you call
the Moose. . . .
CLICK
CLICK
CLICK

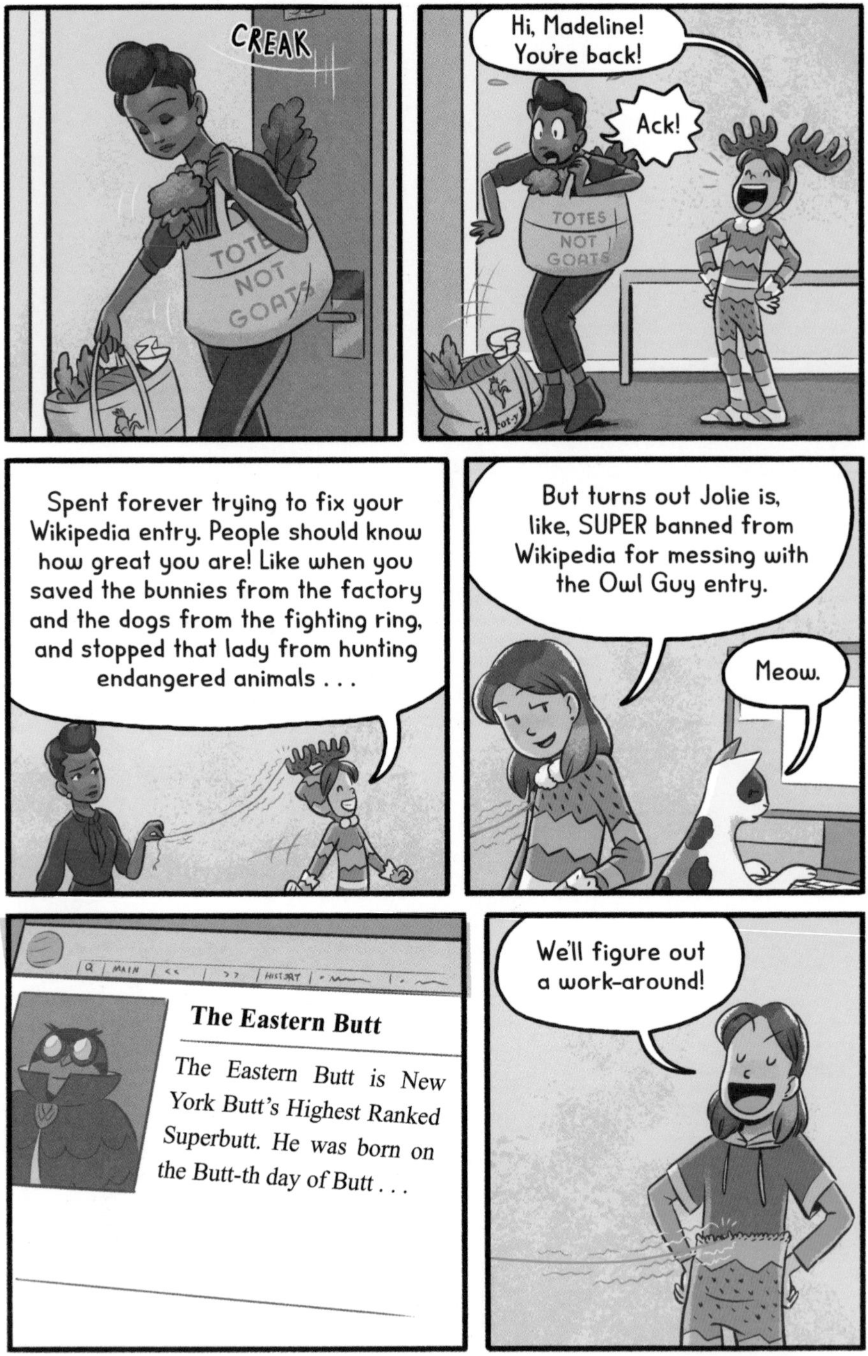
CREAK
TOTES NOT GOATS
Hi, Madeline! You're back!
Ack!
TOTES NOT GOATS
Spent forever trying to fix your Wikipedia entry. People should know how great you are! Like when you saved the bunnies from the factory and the dogs from the fighting ring, and stopped that lady from hunting endangered animals . . .
But turns out Jolie is, like, SUPER banned from Wikipedia for messing with the Owl Guy entry.
Meow.
MAIN
HISTORY
The Eastern Butt
The Eastern Butt is New York Butt's Highest Ranked Superbutt. He was born on the Butt-th day of Butt . . .
We'll figure out a work-around!

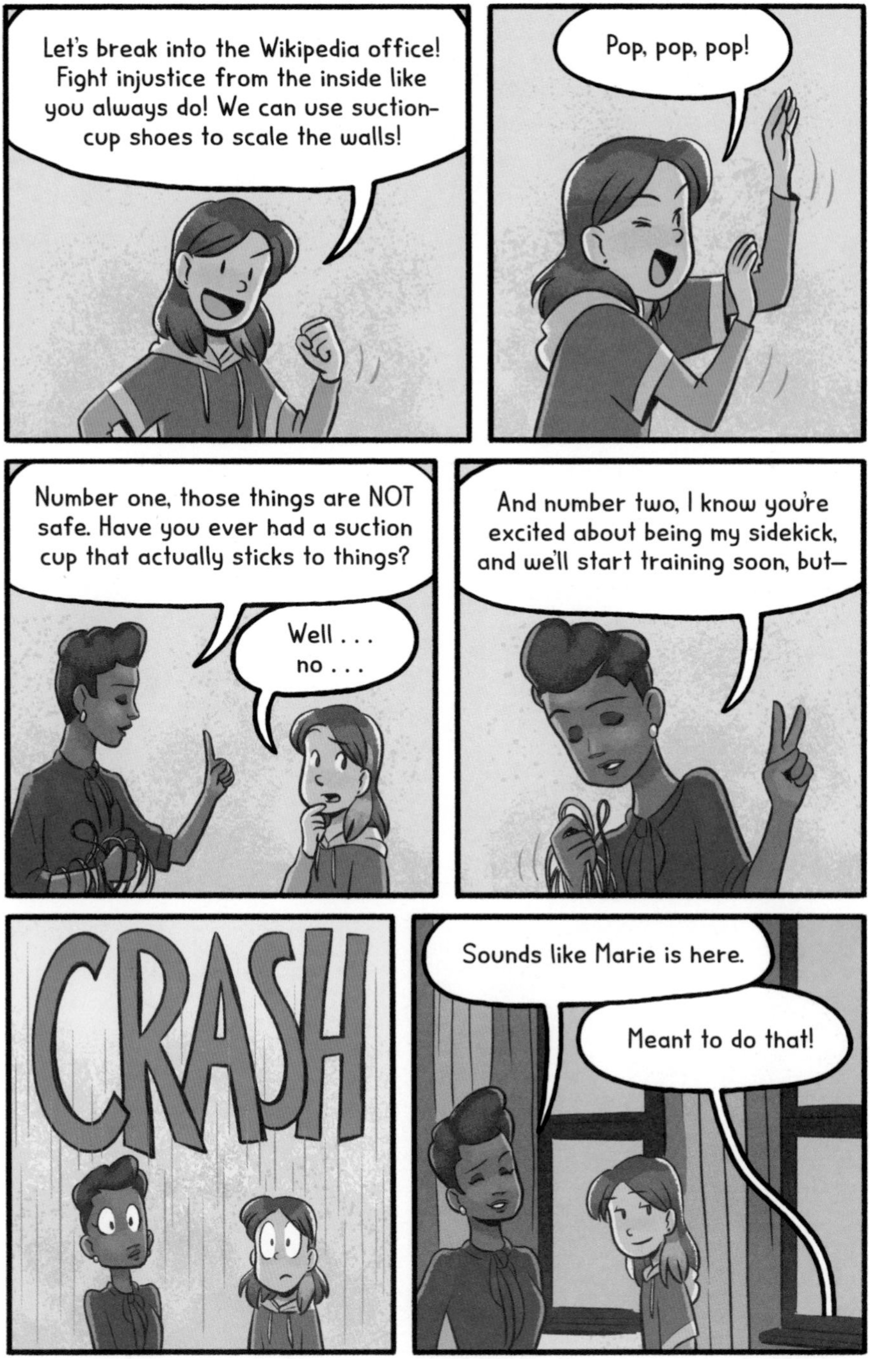
Let's break into the Wikipedia office! Fight injustice from the inside like you always do! We can use suction-cup shoes to scale the walls!
Pop, pop, pop!
Number one, those things are NOT safe. Have you ever had a suction cup that actually sticks to things?
Well . . . no . . .
And number two, I know you're excited about being my sidekick, and we'll start training soon, but—
CRASH
Sounds like Marie is here.
Meant to do that!

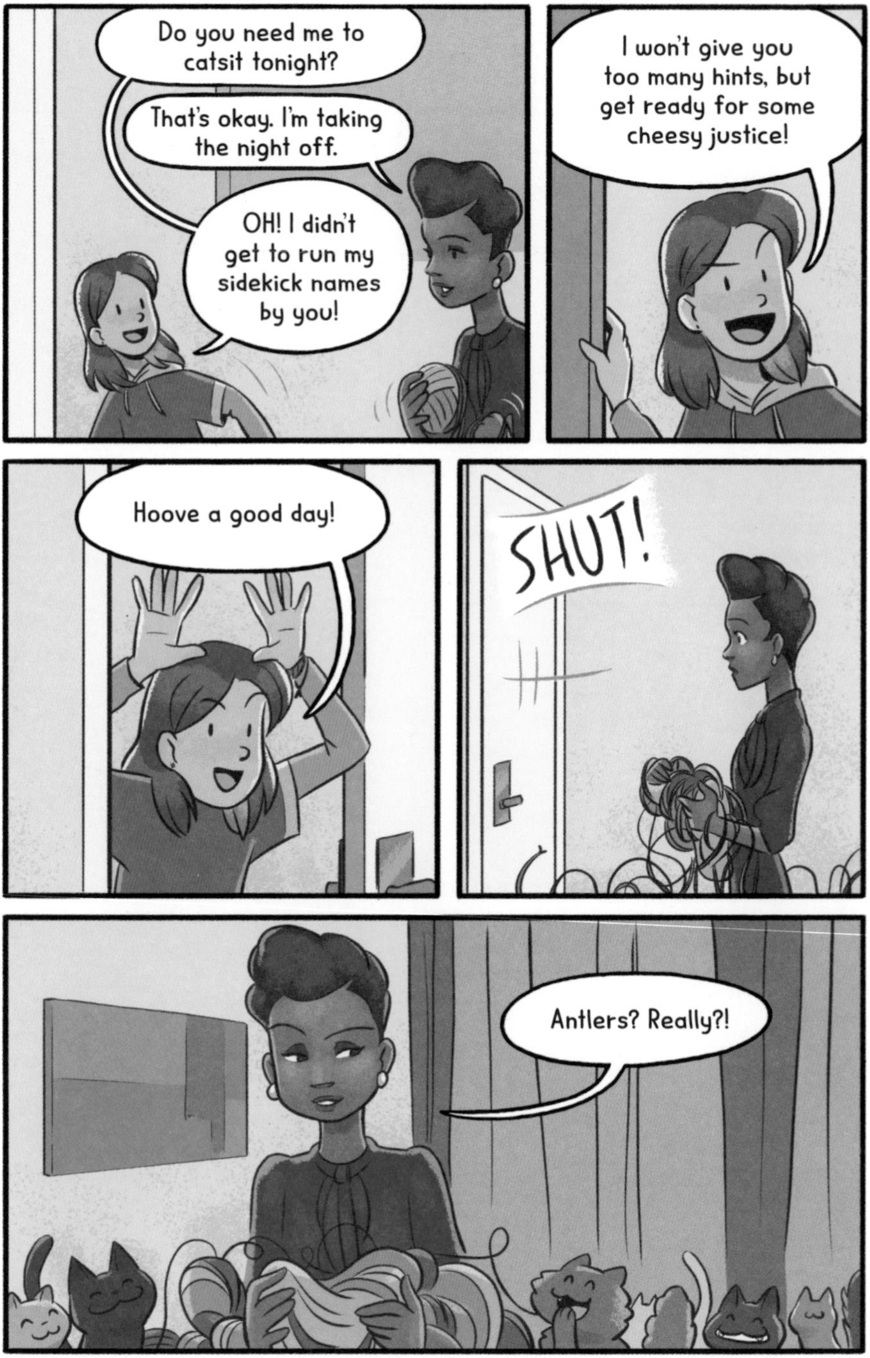

Do you need me to catsit tonight?
That's okay. I'm taking the night off.
OH! I didn't get to run my sidekick names by you!
I won't give you too many hints, but get ready for some cheesy justice!
Hoove a good day!
SHUT!
Antlers? Really?!

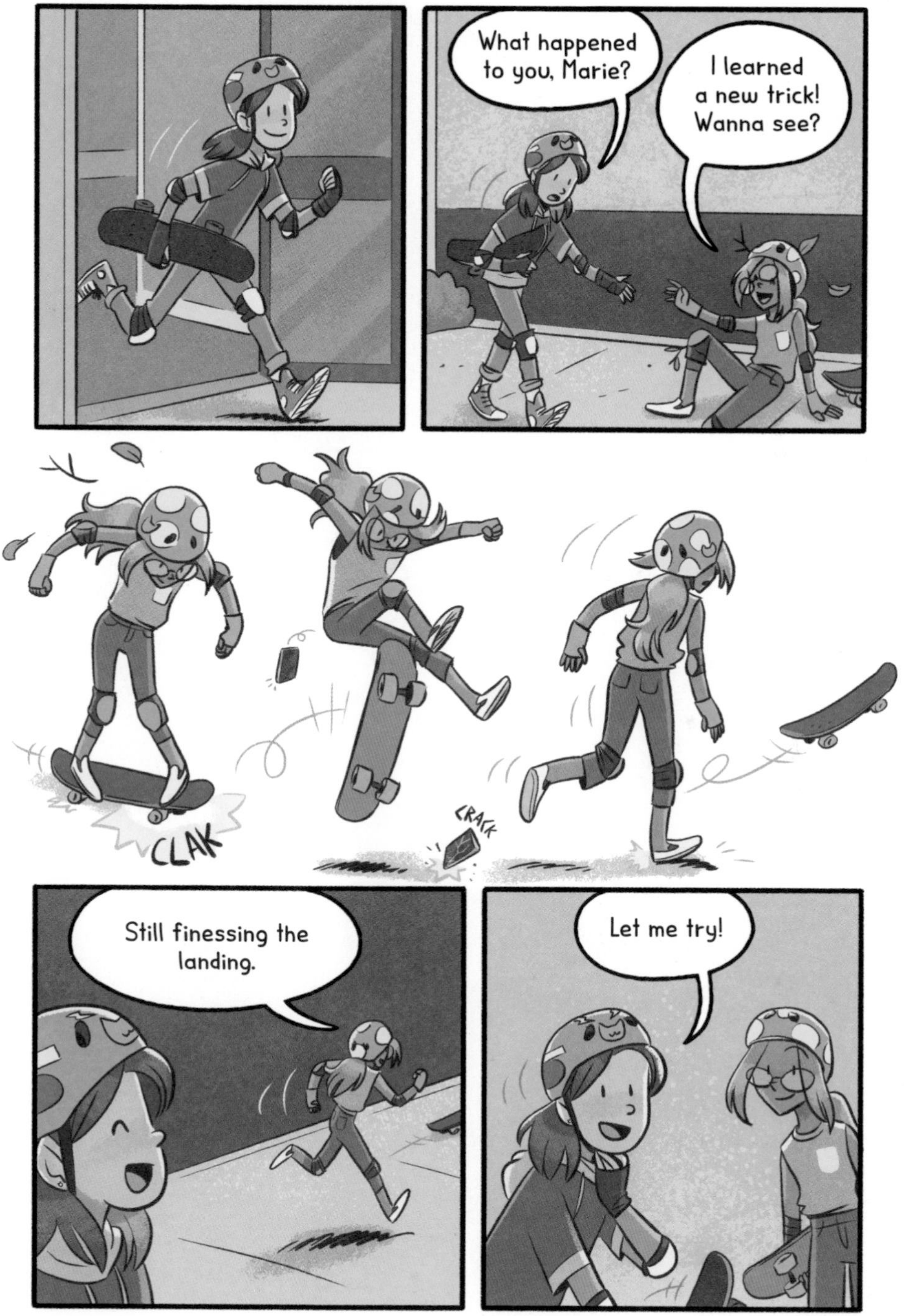
What happened to you, Marie?
I learned a new trick! Wanna see?
CLAK
CRACK
Still finessing the landing.
Let me try!

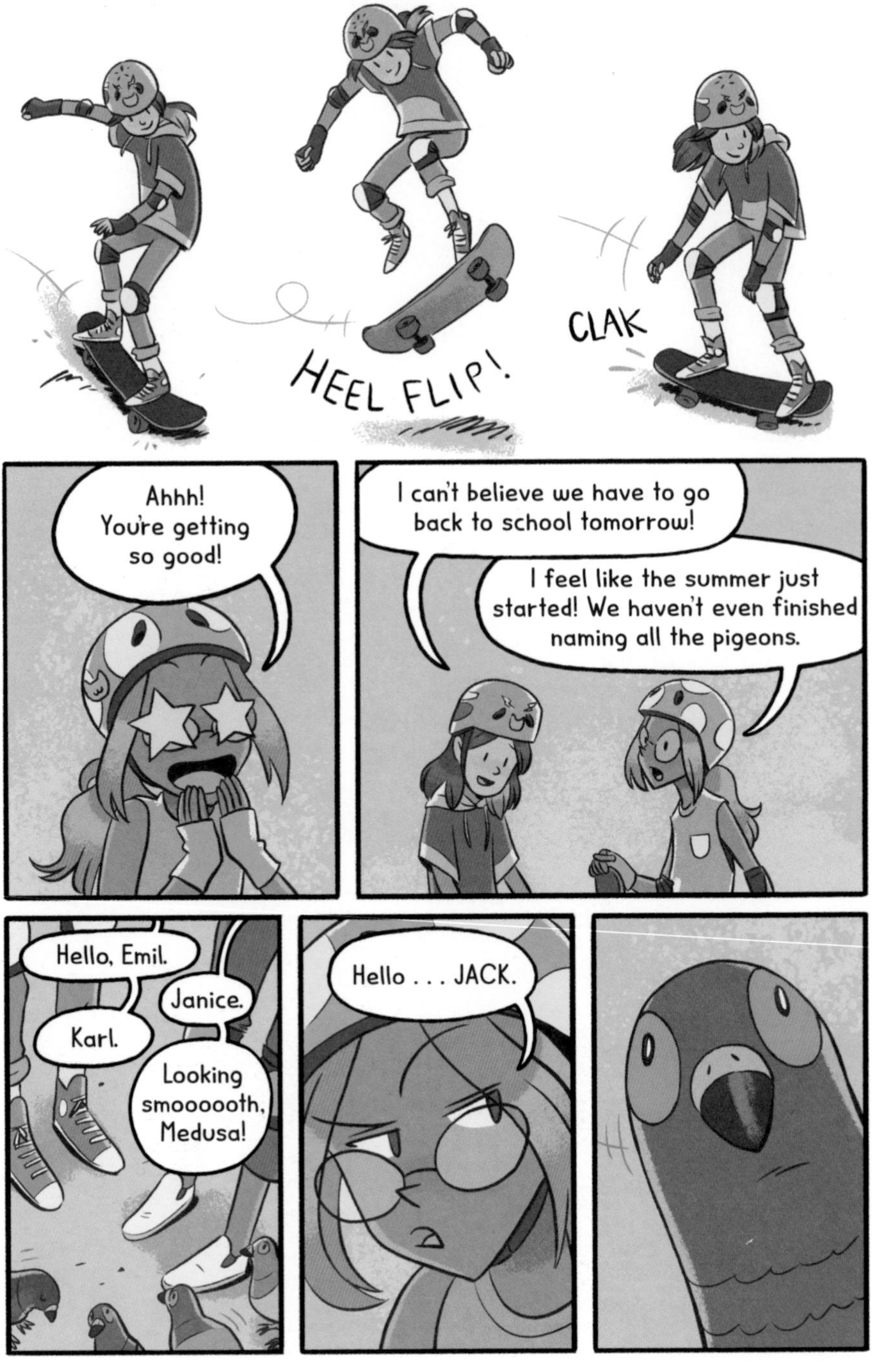
HEEL FLIP!
CLAK
Ahhh! You're getting so good!
I can't believe we have to go back to school tomorrow!
I feel like the summer just started! We haven't even finished naming all the pigeons.
Hello, Emil.
Janice.
Karl.
Looking smoooooth, Medusa!
Hello . . . JACK.

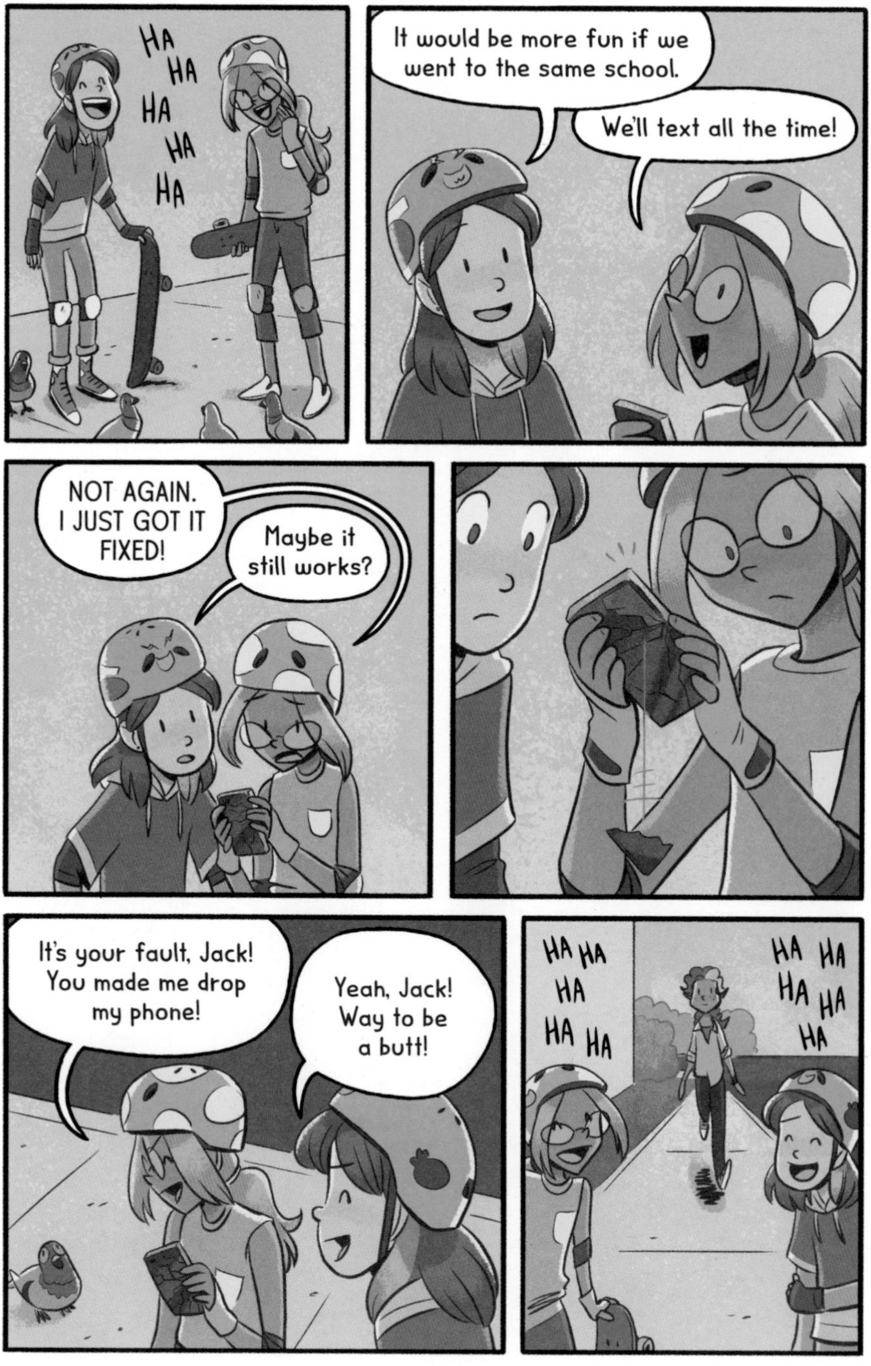
HA HA HA HA HA
It would be more fun if we went to the same school.
We'll text all the time!
NOT AGAIN. I JUST GOT IT FIXED!
Maybe it still works?
It's your fault, Jack! You made me drop my phone!
Yeah, Jack! Way to be a butt!
HA HA HA HA HA
HA HA HA HA HA

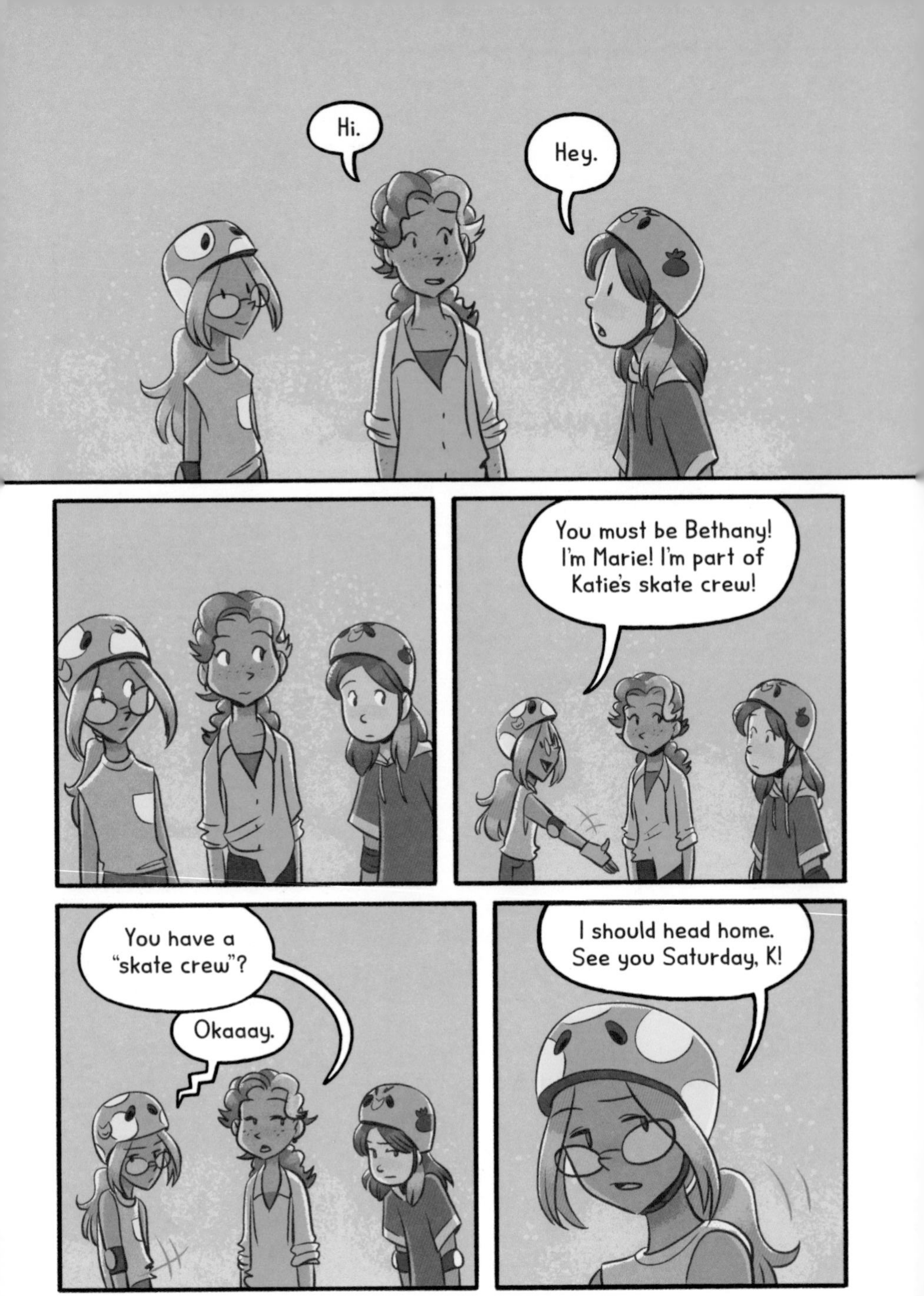
Hi.
Hey.
You must be Bethany! I'm Marie! I'm part of Katie's skate crew!
You have a "skate crew"?
Okaaay.
I should head home. See you Saturday, K!

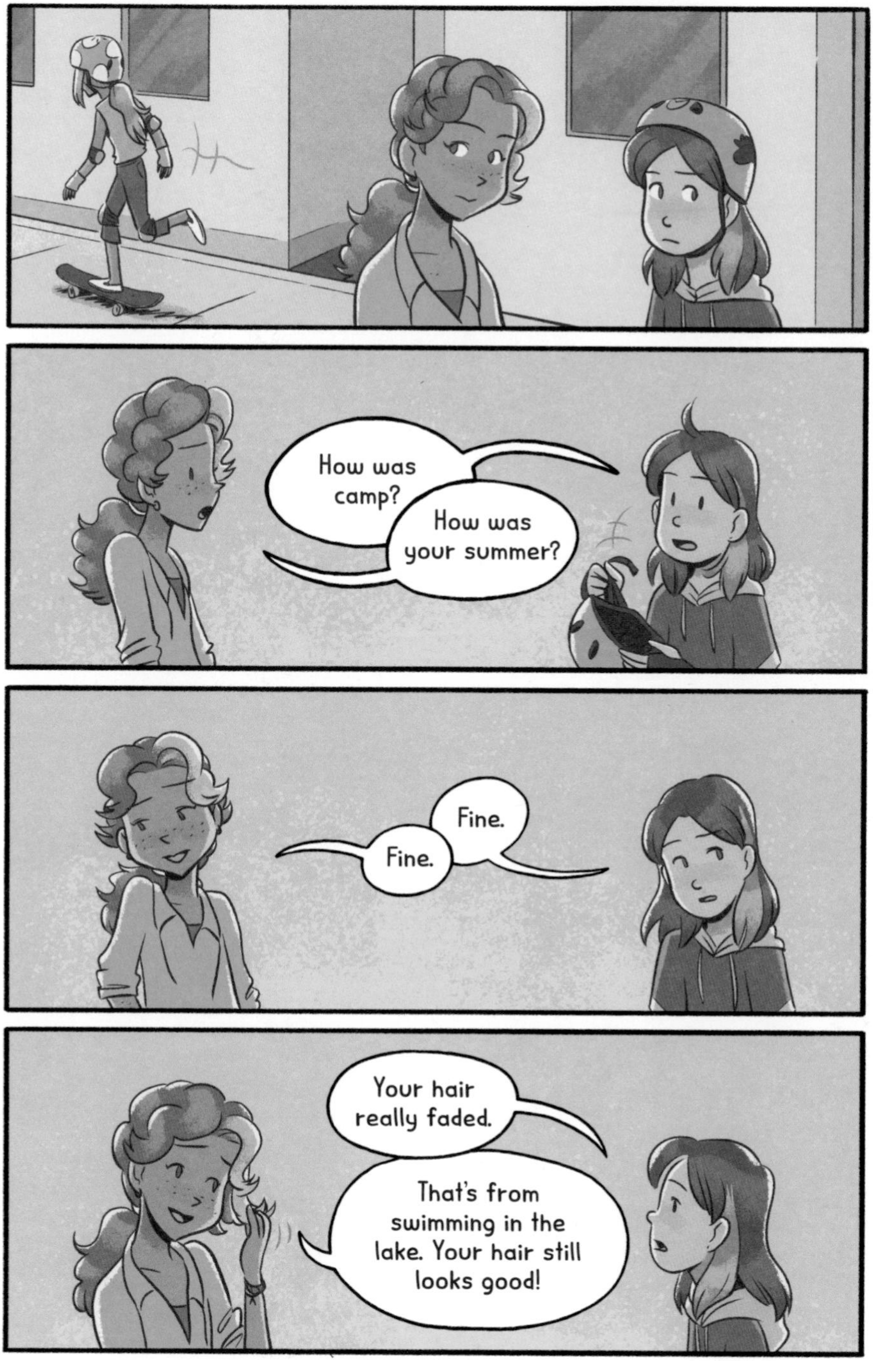
How was camp?
How was your summer?
Fine.
Fine.
Your hair really faded.
That's from swimming in the lake. Your hair still looks good!

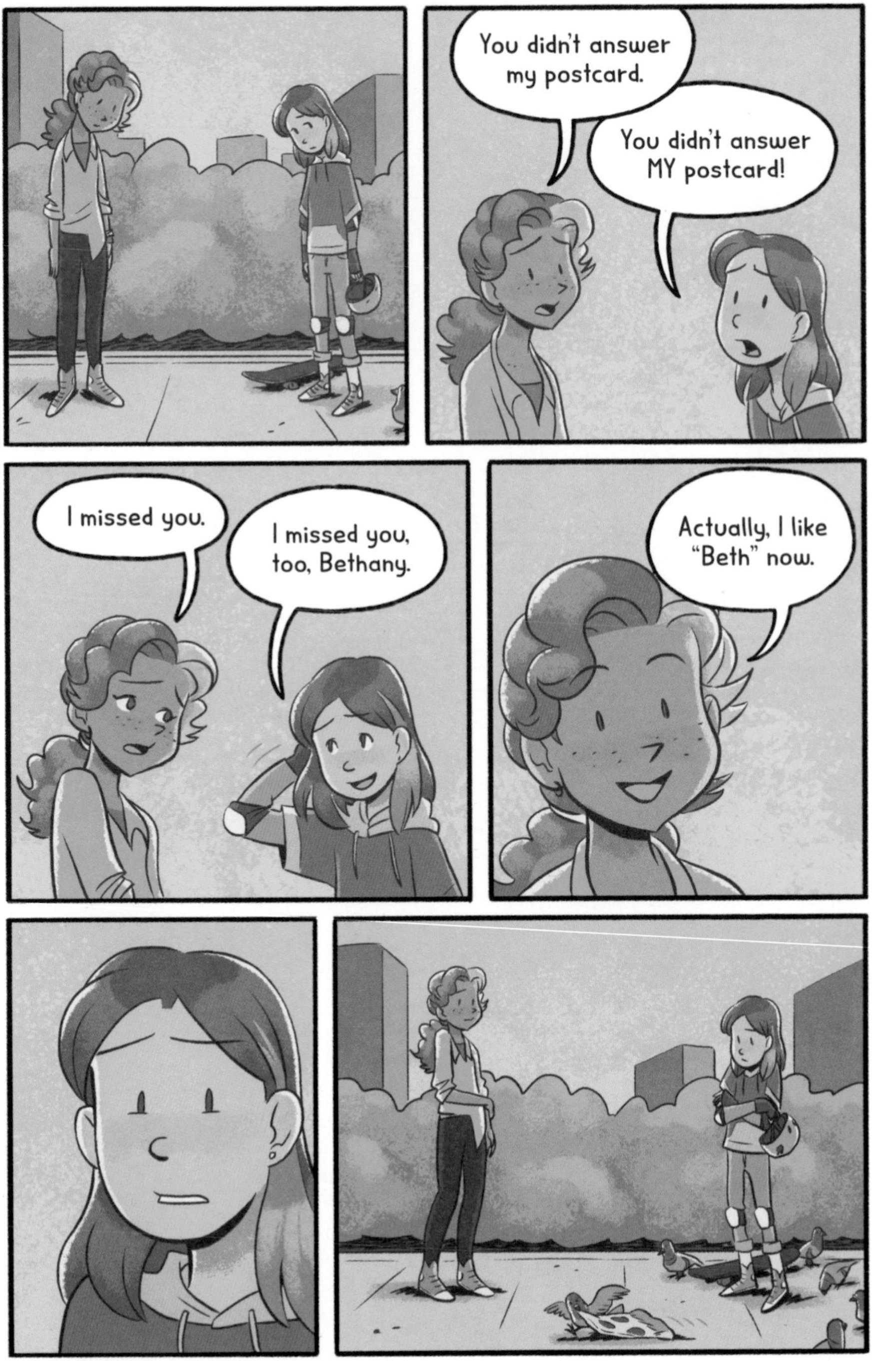
You didn't answer my postcard.
You didn't answer MY postcard!
I missed you.
I missed you, too, Bethany.
Actually, I like "Beth" now.

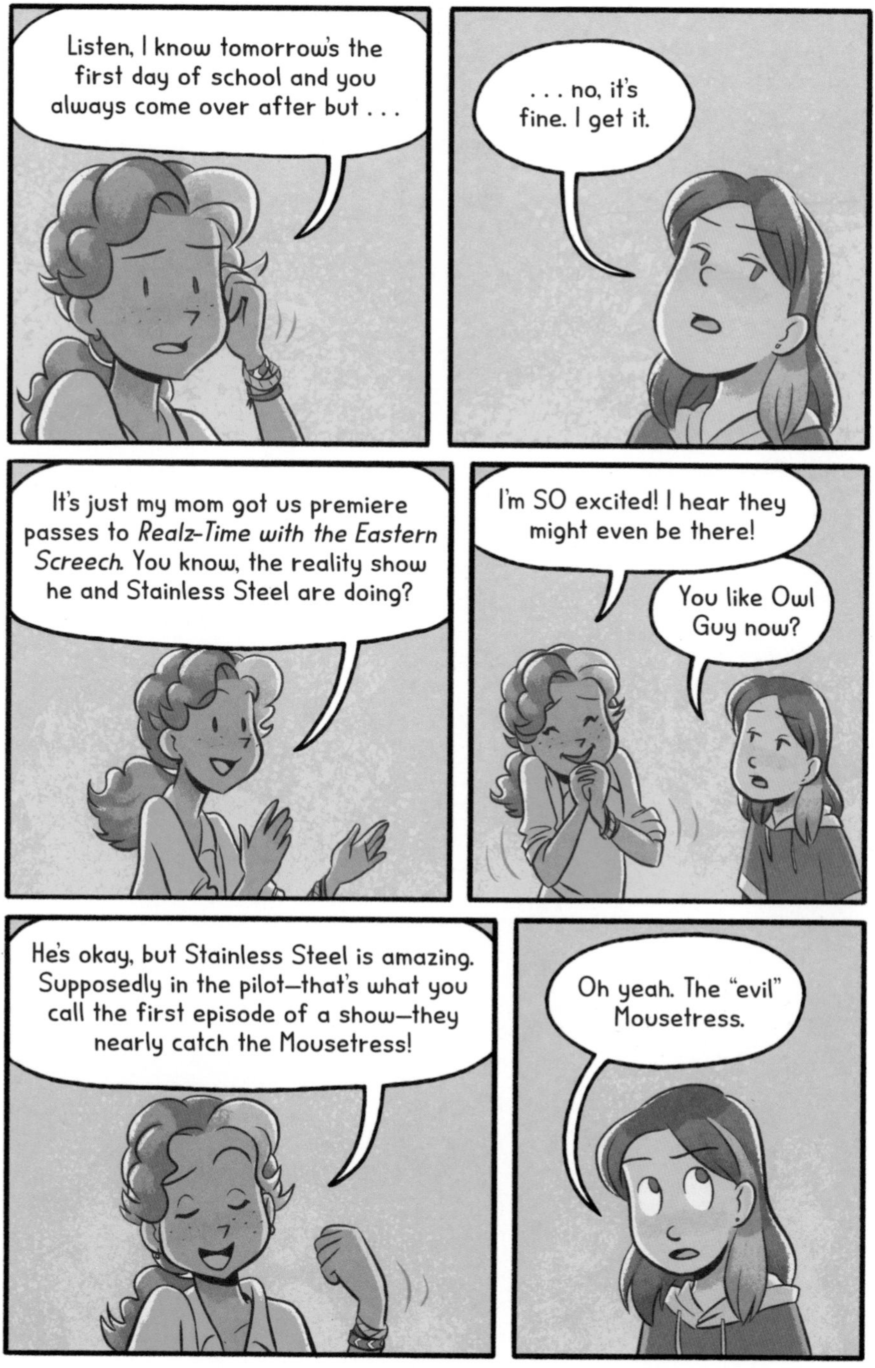

Listen, I know tomorrow's the first day of school and you always come over after but . . .
. . . no, it's fine. I get it.
It's just my mom got us premiere passes to *Realz-Time with the Eastern Screech*. You know, the reality show he and Stainless Steel are doing?
I'm SO excited! I hear they might even be there!
You like Owl Guy now?
He's okay, but Stainless Steel is amazing. Supposedly in the pilot—that's what you call the first episode of a show—they nearly catch the Mousetress!
Oh yeah. The "evil" Mousetress.

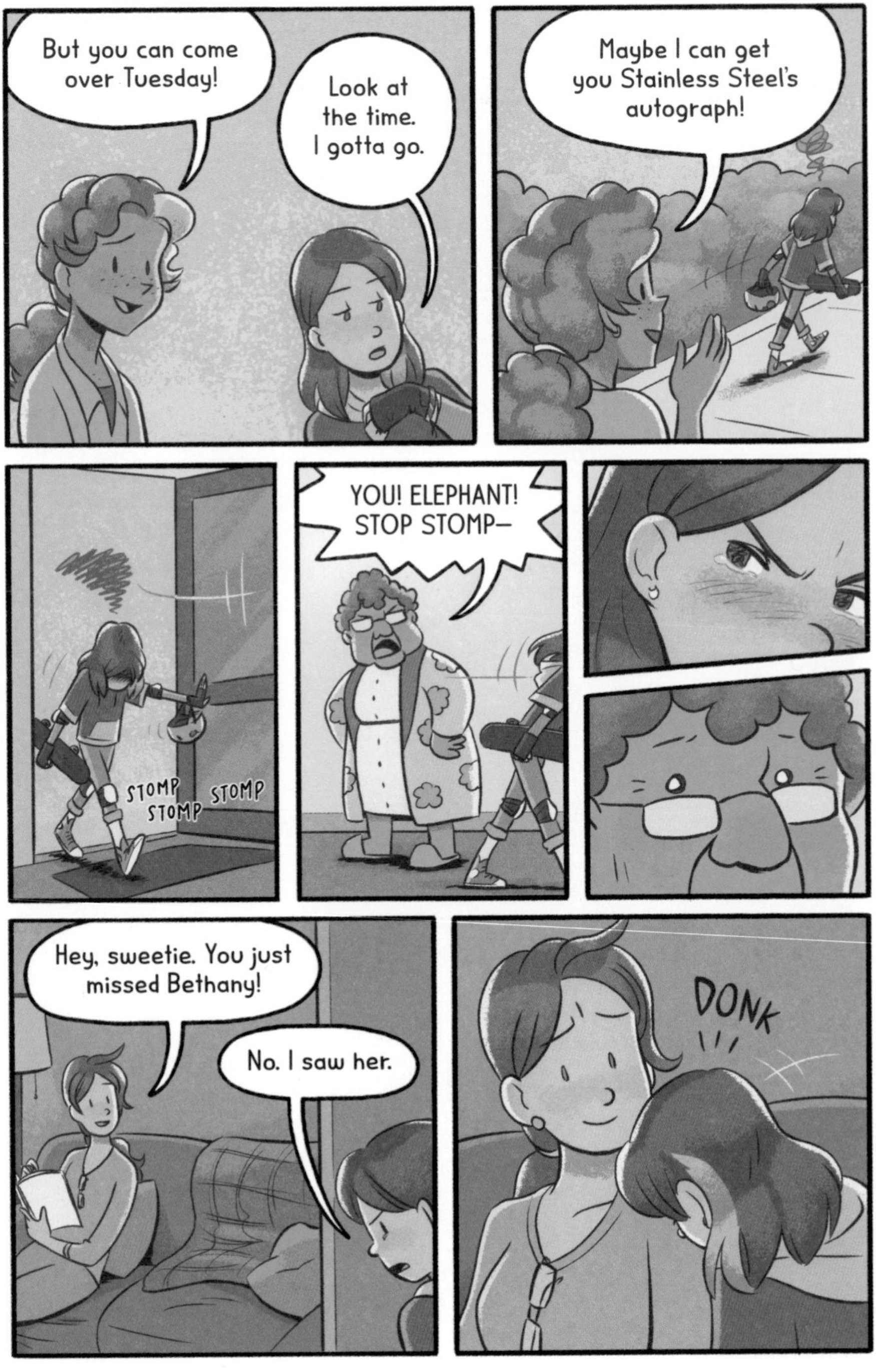
But you can come over Tuesday!
Look at the time. I gotta go.
Maybe I can get you Stainless Steel's autograph!
STOMP STOMP STOMP
YOU! ELEPHANT! STOP STOMP–
Hey, sweetie. You just missed Bethany!
No. I saw her.
DONK

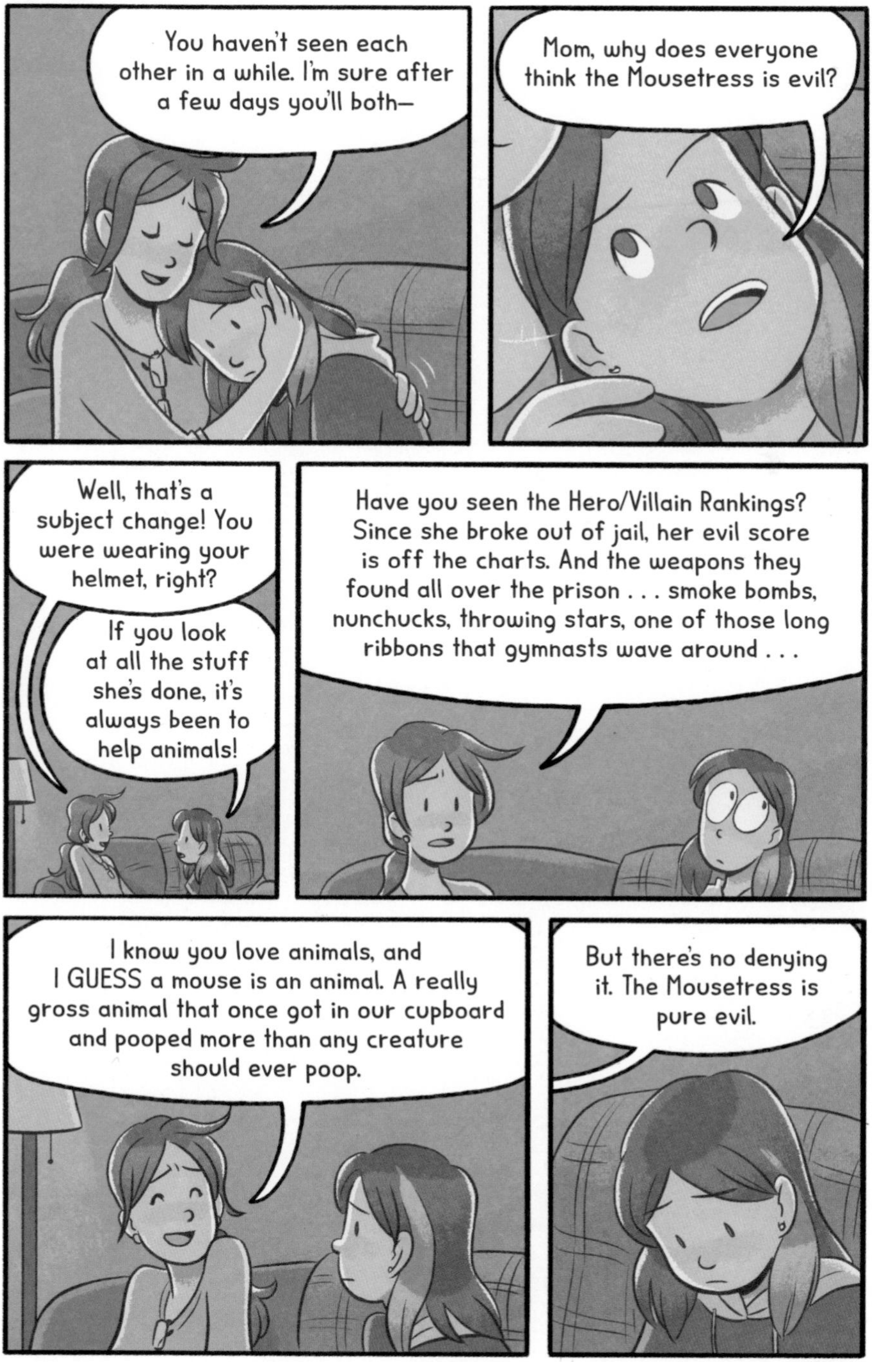
You haven't seen each other in a while. I'm sure after a few days you'll both–
Mom, why does everyone think the Mousetress is evil?
Well, that's a subject change! You were wearing your helmet, right?
If you look at all the stuff she's done, it's always been to help animals!
Have you seen the Hero/Villain Rankings? Since she broke out of jail, her evil score is off the charts. And the weapons they found all over the prison . . . smoke bombs, nunchucks, throwing stars, one of those long ribbons that gymnasts wave around . . .
I know you love animals, and I GUESS a mouse is an animal. A really gross animal that once got in our cupboard and pooped more than any creature should ever poop.
But there's no denying it. The Mousetress is pure evil.

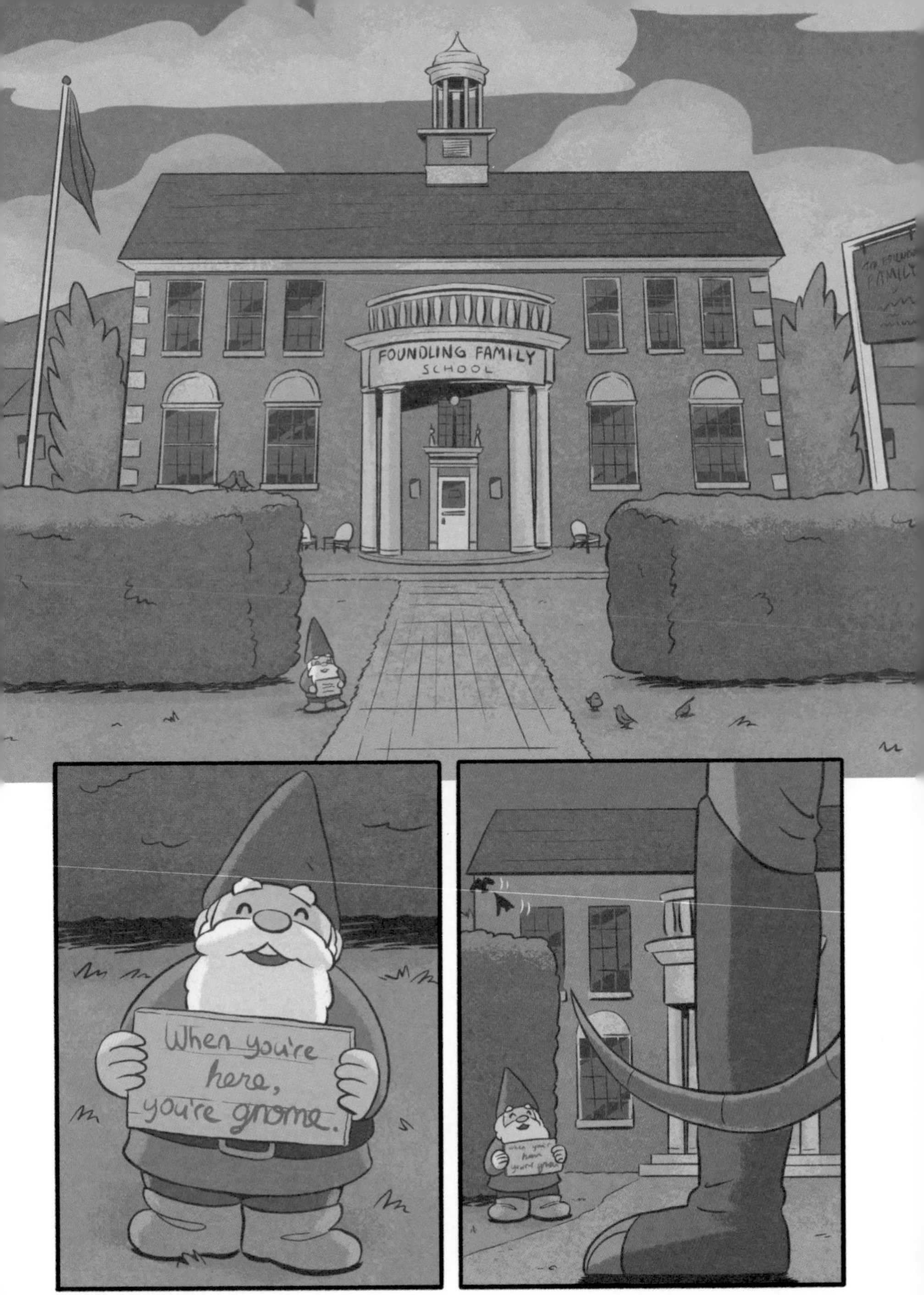
FOUNDLING FAMILY
SCHOOL
When you're here, you're gnome.

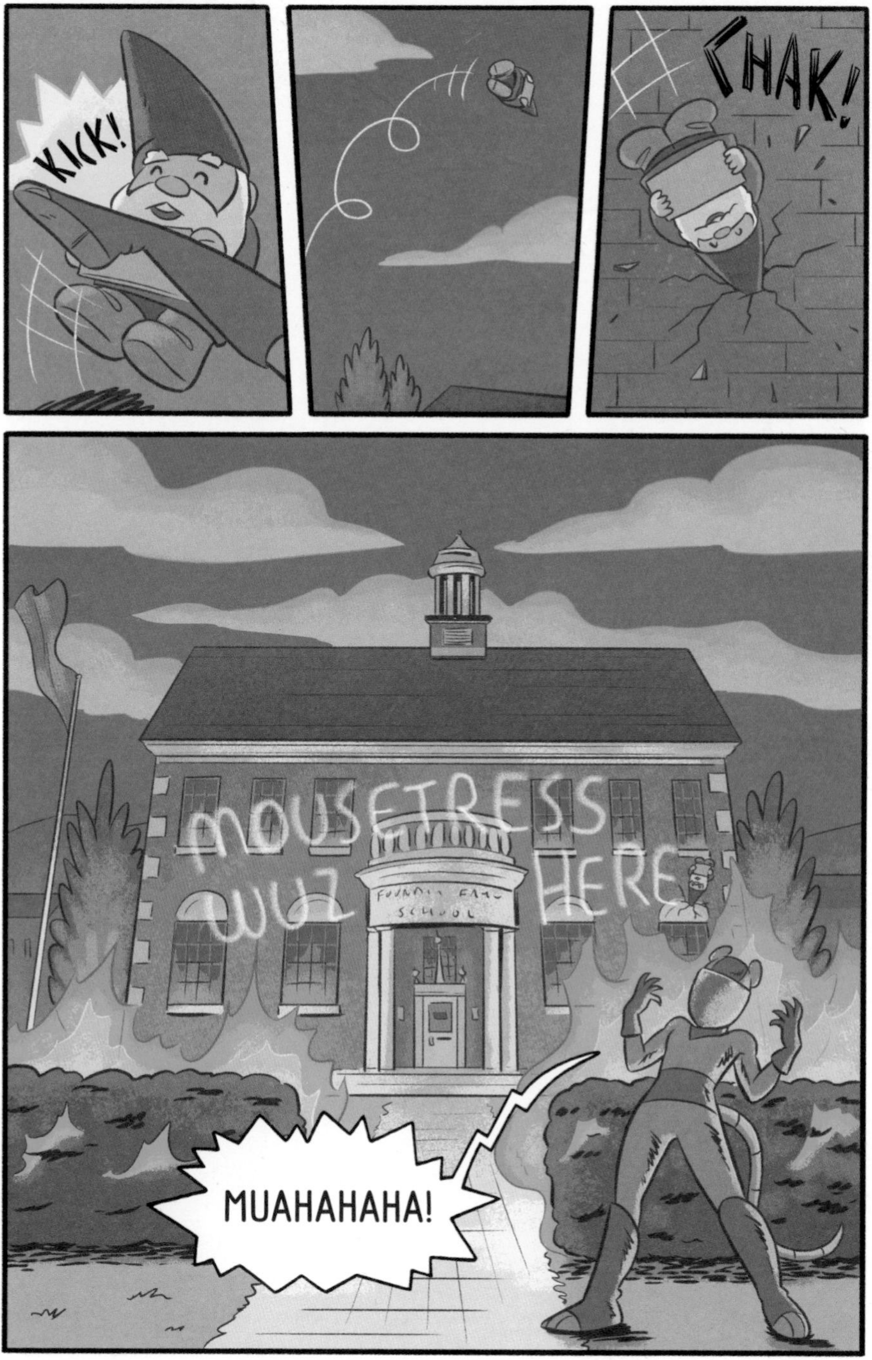
KICK!
CHAK!
MOUSETRESS WUZ HERE
MUAHAHAHA!

CHAPTER TWO

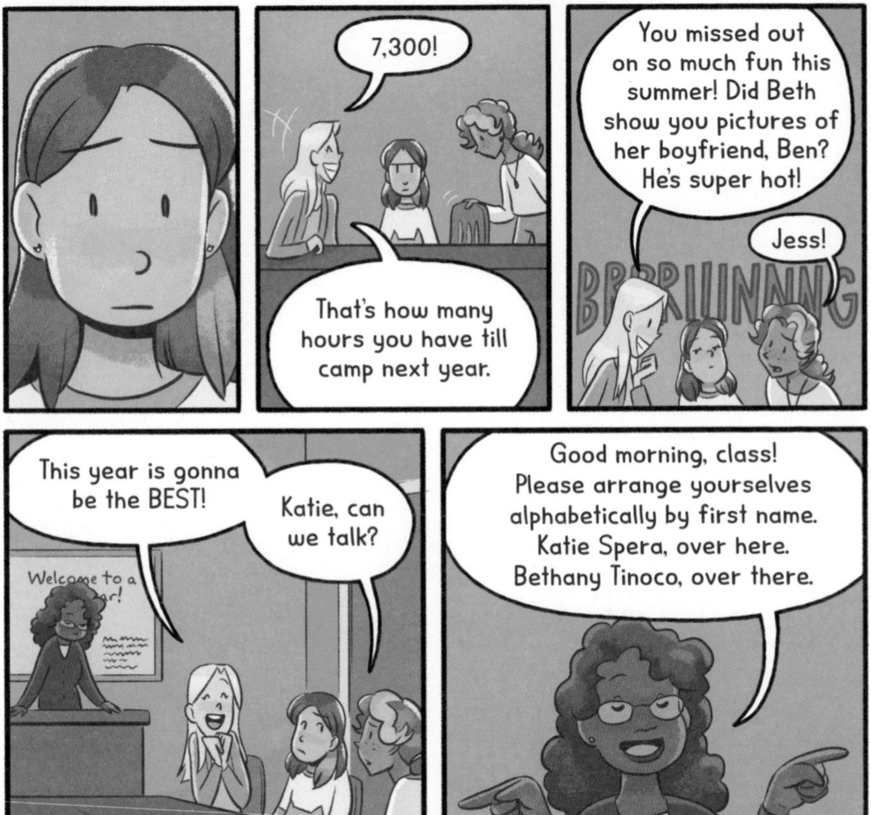
7,300!
That's how many hours you have till camp next year.
You missed out on so much fun this summer! Did Beth show you pictures of her boyfriend, Ben? He's super hot!
Jess!
This year is gonna be the BEST!
Katie, can we talk?
Good morning, class! Please arrange yourselves alphabetically by first name. Katie Spera, over here. Bethany Tinoco, over there.
DREAM BIG
Welcome to a new year!
BEE YOURSELF

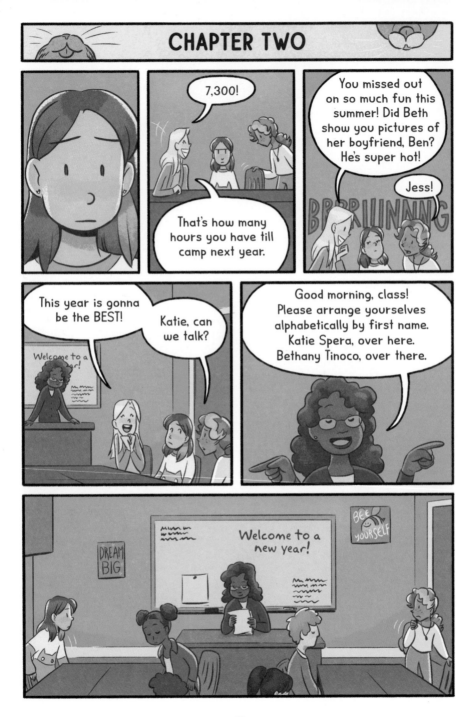

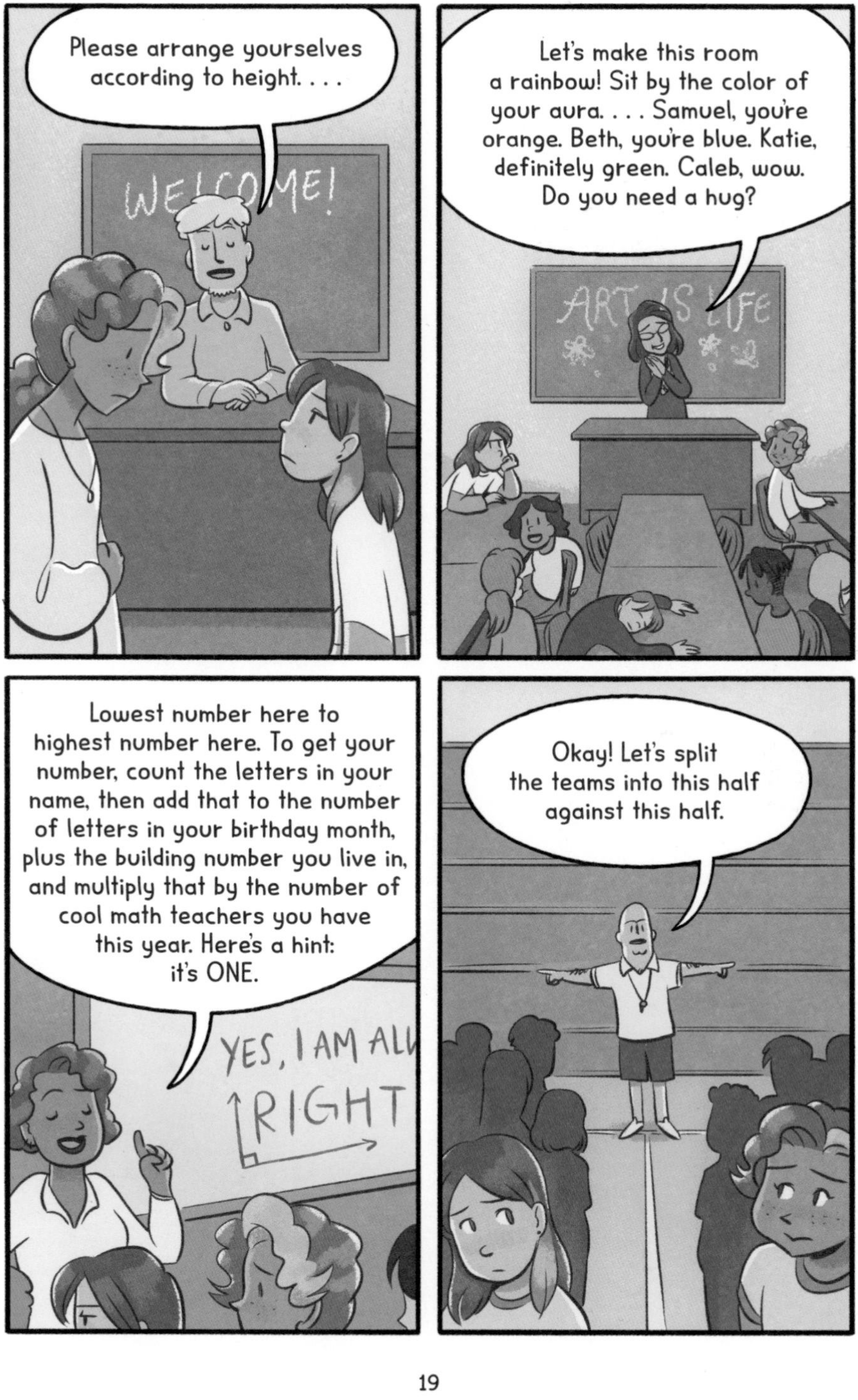
Please arrange yourselves according to height. . . .
WELCOME!
Let's make this room a rainbow! Sit by the color of your aura. . . . Samuel, you're orange. Beth, you're blue. Katie, definitely green. Caleb, wow. Do you need a hug?
ART IS LIFE
Lowest number here to highest number here. To get your number, count the letters in your name, then add that to the number of letters in your birthday month, plus the building number you live in, and multiply that by the number of cool math teachers you have this year. Here's a hint: it's ONE.
YES, I AM AL
RIGHT
Okay! Let's split the teams into this half against this half.

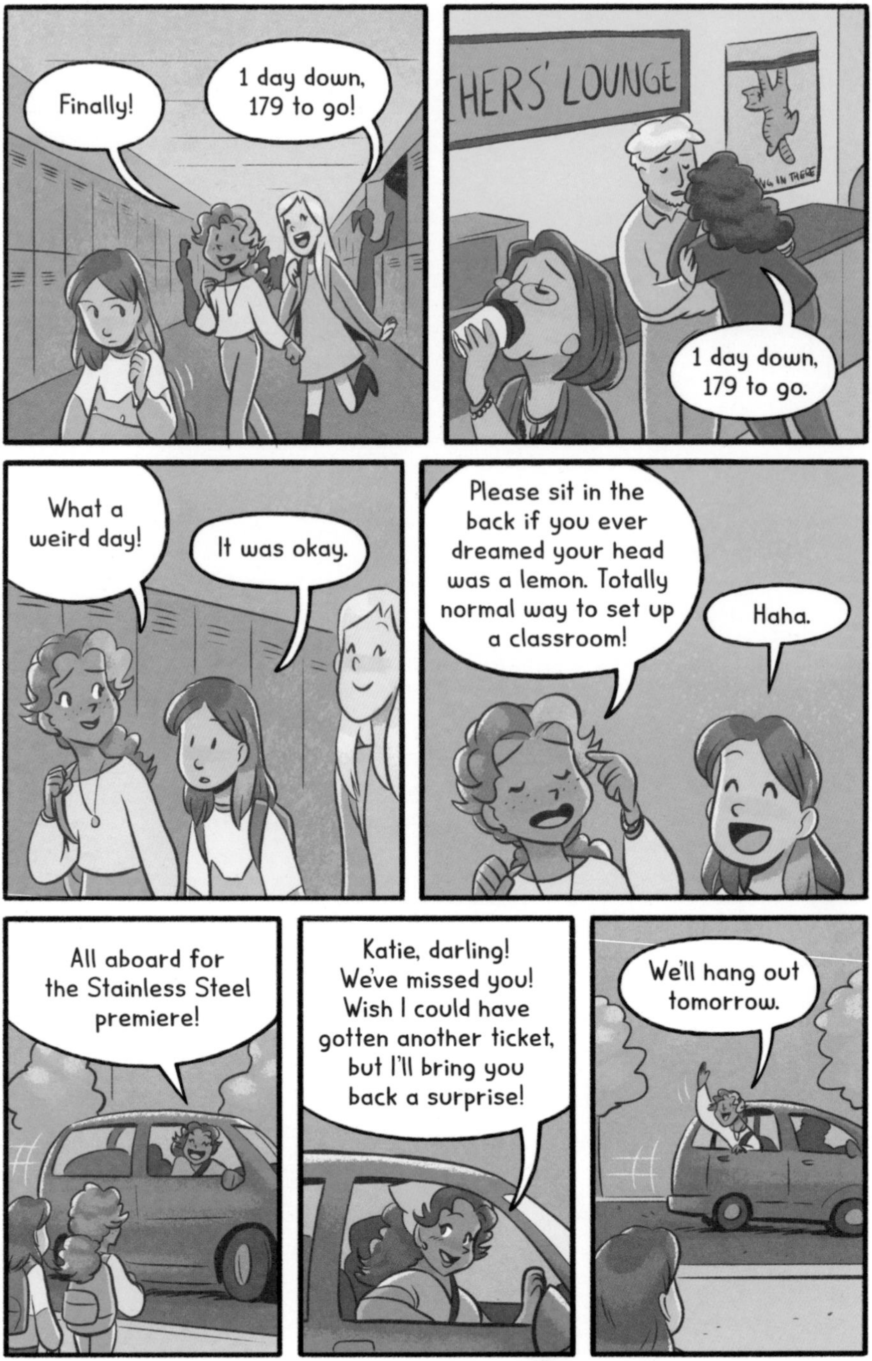
Finally!
1 day down, 179 to go!
1 day down, 179 to go.
What a weird day!
It was okay.
Please sit in the back if you ever dreamed your head was a lemon. Totally normal way to set up a classroom!
Haha.
All aboard for the Stainless Steel premiere!
Katie, darling! We've missed you! Wish I could have gotten another ticket, but I'll bring you back a surprise!
We'll hang out tomorrow.

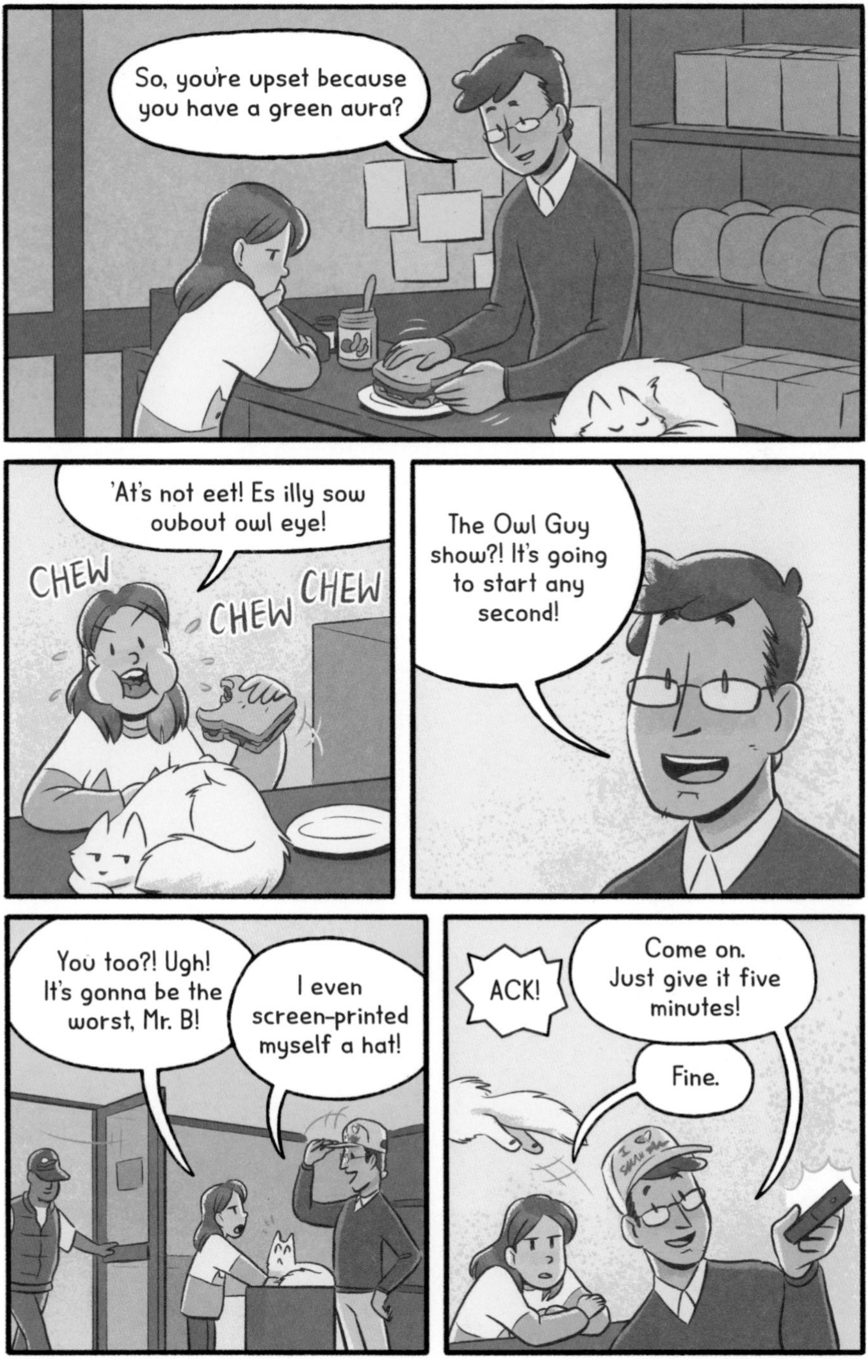
So, you're upset because you have a green aura?
'At's not eet! Es illy sow oubout owl eye!
CHEW
CHEW
CHEW
The Owl Guy show?! It's going to start any second!
You too?! Ugh! It's gonna be the worst, Mr. B!
I even screen-printed myself a hat!
ACK!
Come on. Just give it five minutes!
Fine.

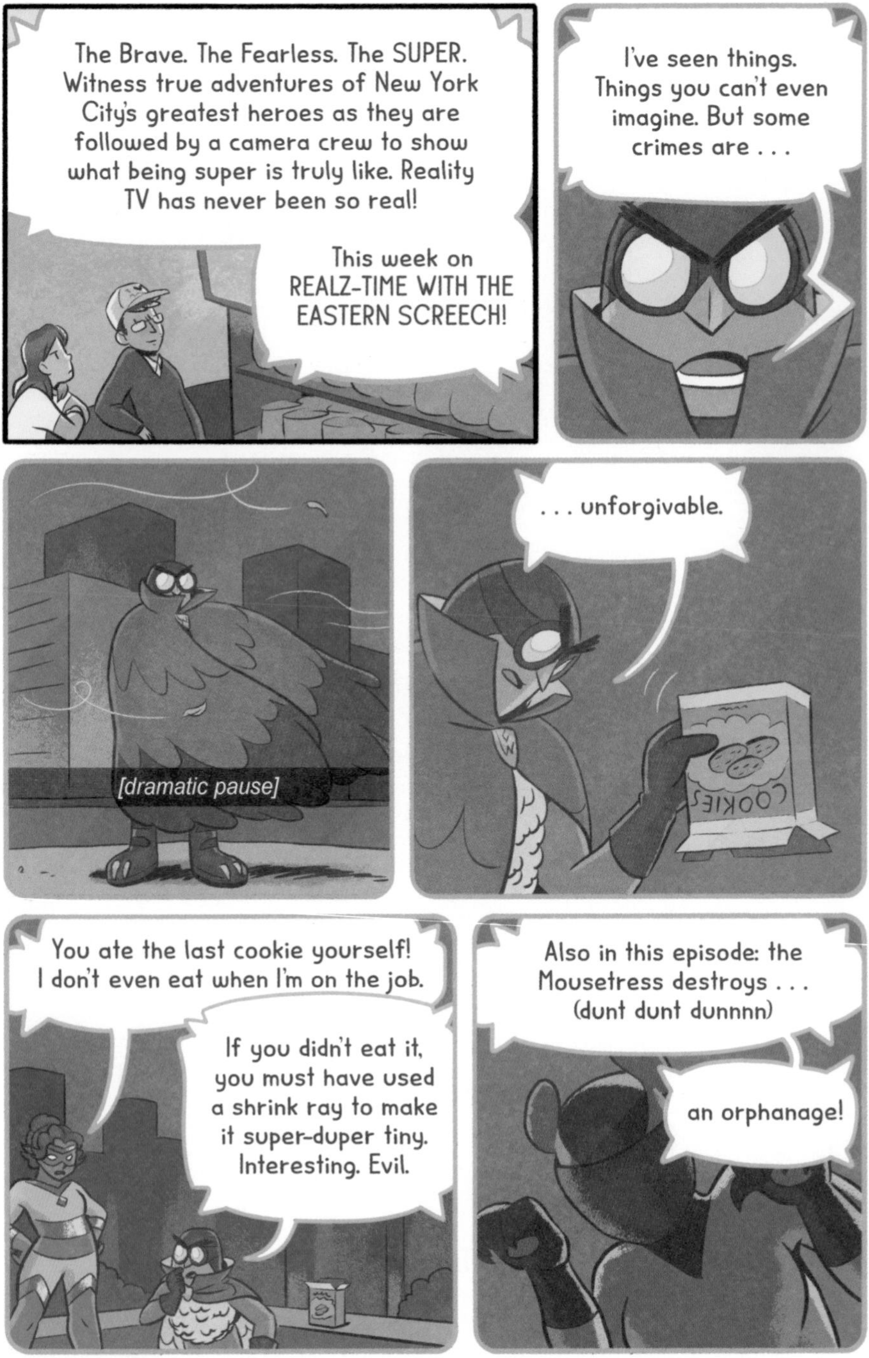
The Brave. The Fearless. The SUPER. Witness true adventures of New York City's greatest heroes as they are followed by a camera crew to show what being super is truly like. Reality TV has never been so real!
This week on REALZ-TIME WITH THE EASTERN SCREECH!
I've seen things. Things you can't even imagine. But some crimes are . . .
[dramatic pause]
. . . unforgivable.
COOKIES
You ate the last cookie yourself! I don't even eat when I'm on the job.
If you didn't eat it, you must have used a shrink ray to make it super-duper tiny. Interesting. Evil.
Also in this episode: the Mousetress destroys . . . (dunt dunt dunnnn)
an orphanage!

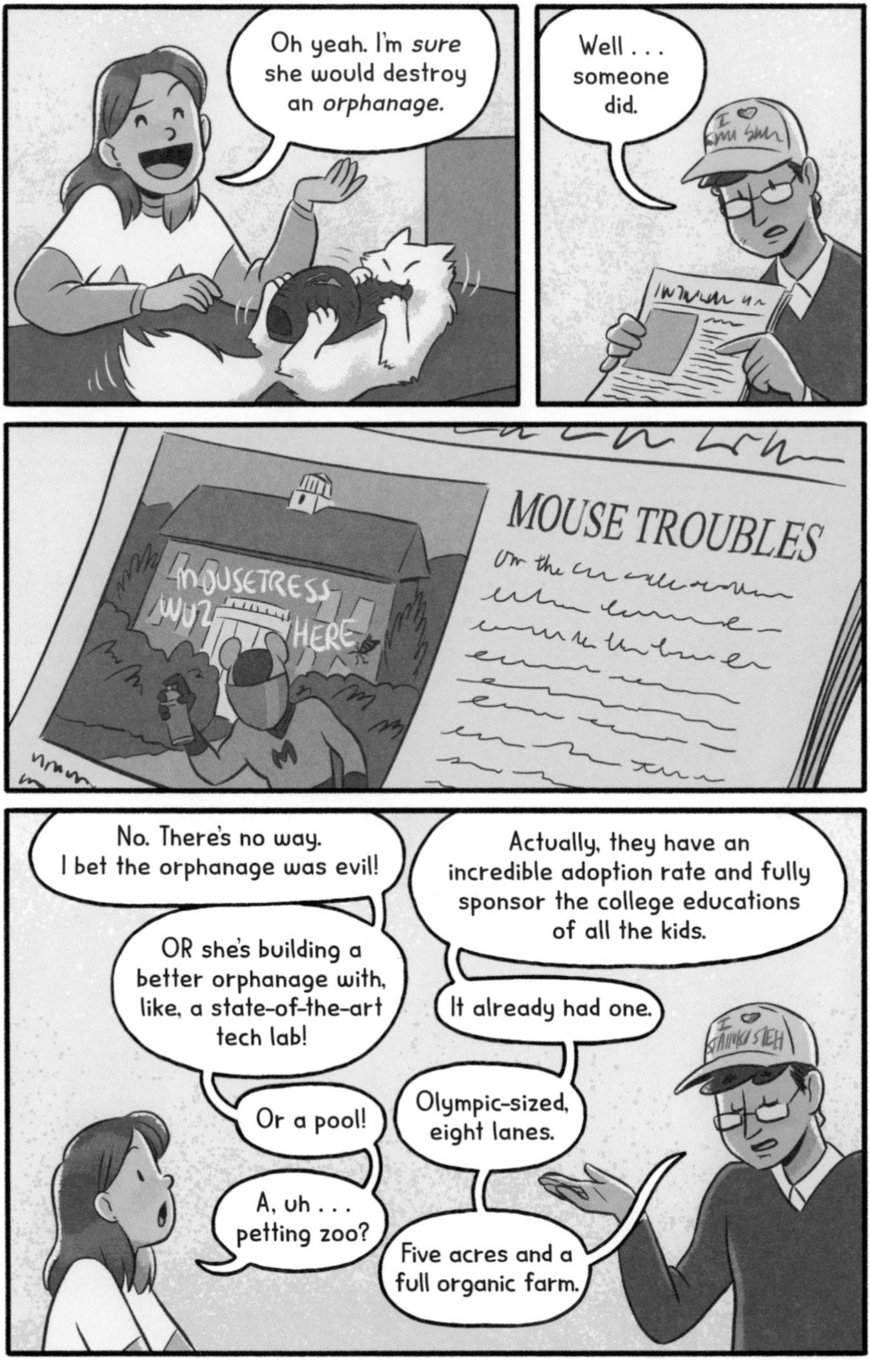
Oh yeah. I'm *sure* she would destroy an *orphanage.*
Well . . . someone did.
MOUSE TROUBLES
MOUSETRESS WUZ HERE
No. There's no way. I bet the orphanage was evil!
Actually, they have an incredible adoption rate and fully sponsor the college educations of all the kids.
OR she's building a better orphanage with, like, a state-of-the-art tech lab!
It already had one.
Or a pool!
Olympic-sized, eight lanes.
A, uh . . . petting zoo?
Five acres and a full organic farm.

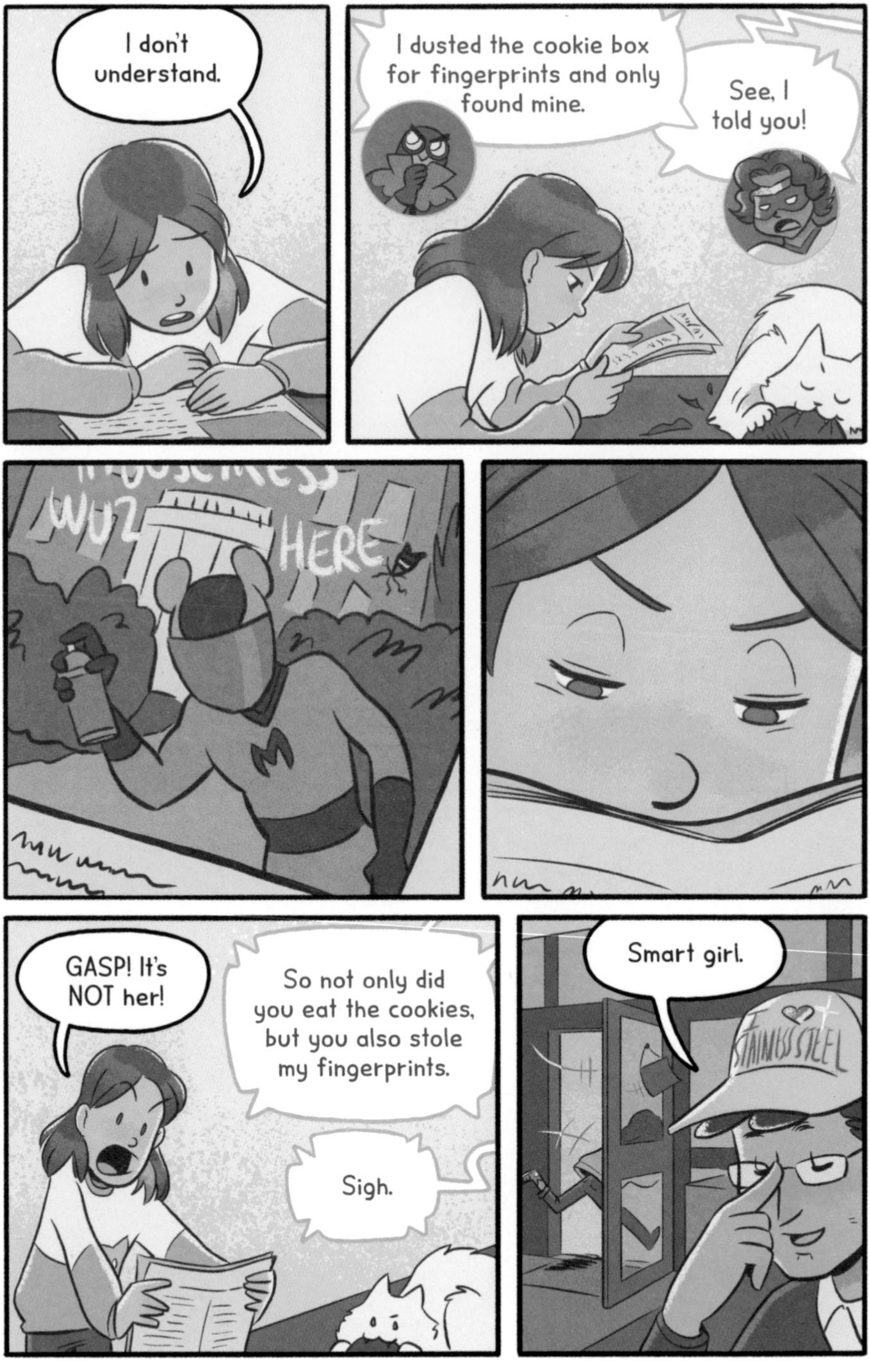
I don't understand.
I dusted the cookie box for fingerprints and only found mine.
See, I told you!
WUZ
HERE
GASP! It's NOT her!
So not only did you eat the cookies, but you also stole my fingerprints.
Sigh.
Smart girl.

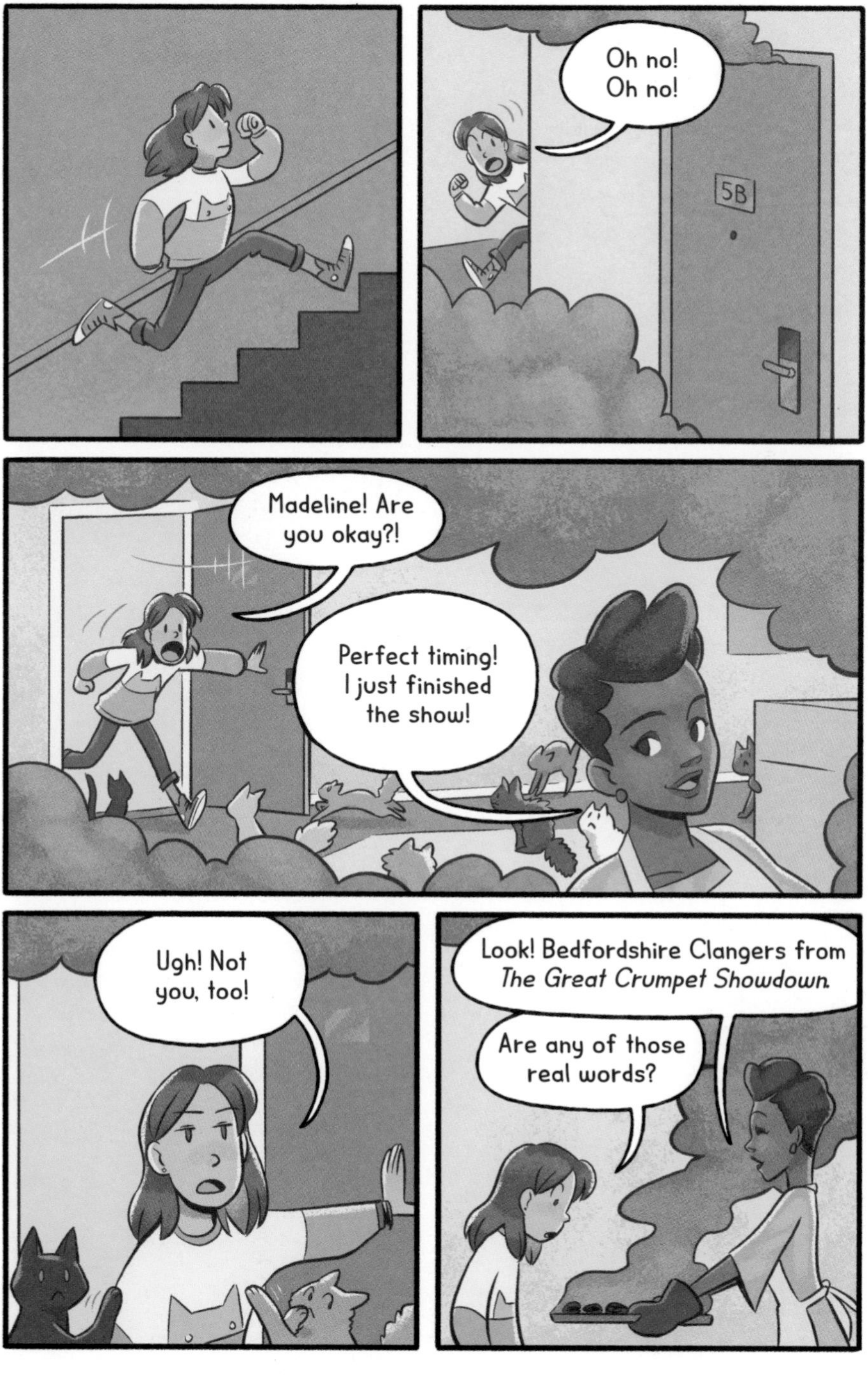
Oh no!
Oh no!
Madeline! Are you okay?!
Perfect timing! I just finished the show!
Ugh! Not you, too!
Look! Bedfordshire Clangers from *The Great Crumpet Showdown*.
Are any of those real words?

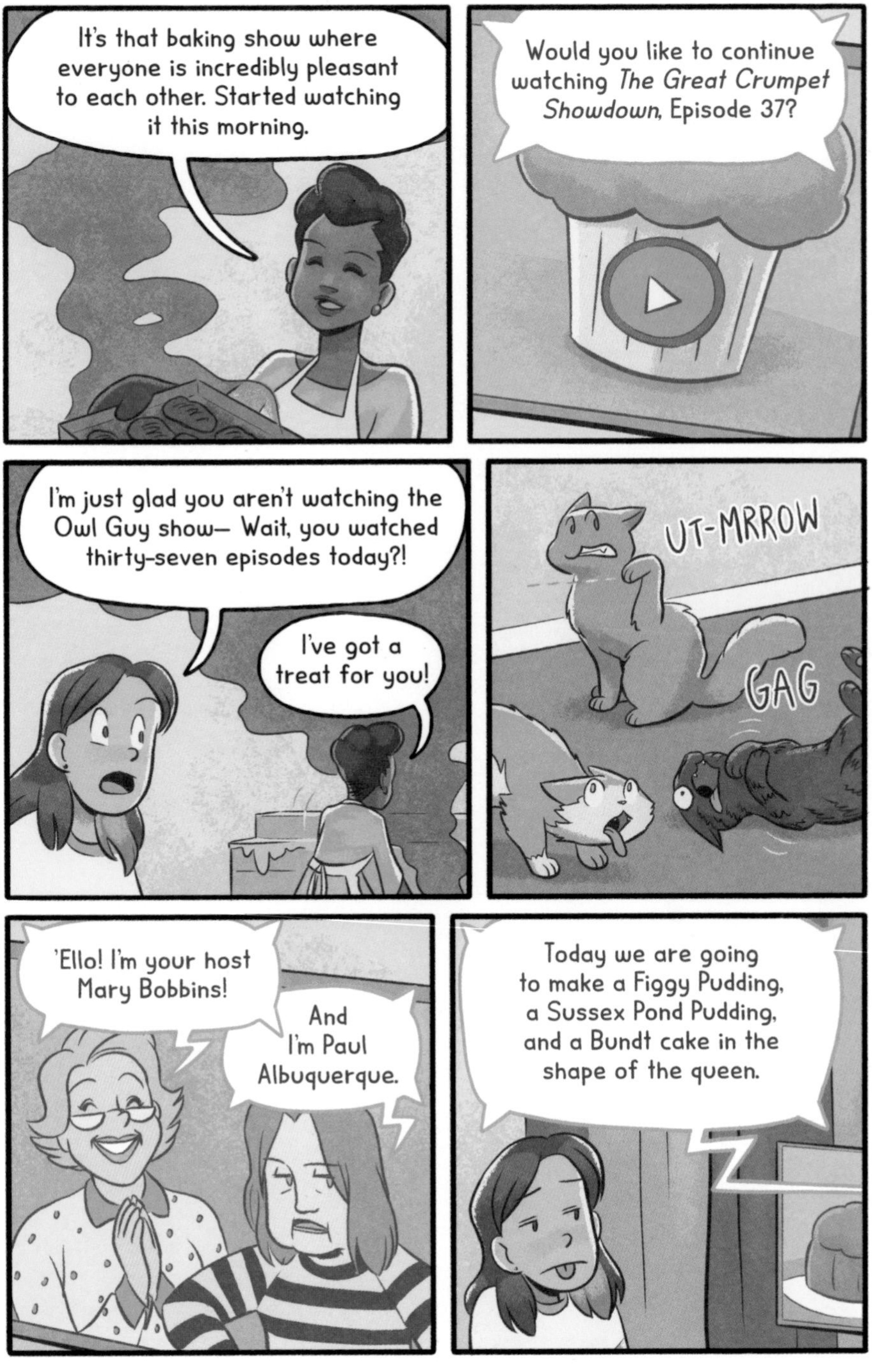
It's that baking show where everyone is incredibly pleasant to each other. Started watching it this morning.
Would you like to continue watching *The Great Crumpet Showdown*, Episode 37?
I'm just glad you aren't watching the Owl Guy show— Wait, you watched thirty-seven episodes today?!
I've got a treat for you!
UT-MRROW
GAG
'Ello! I'm your host Mary Bobbins!
And I'm Paul Albuquerque.
Today we are going to make a Figgy Pudding, a Sussex Pond Pudding, and a Bundt cake in the shape of the queen.

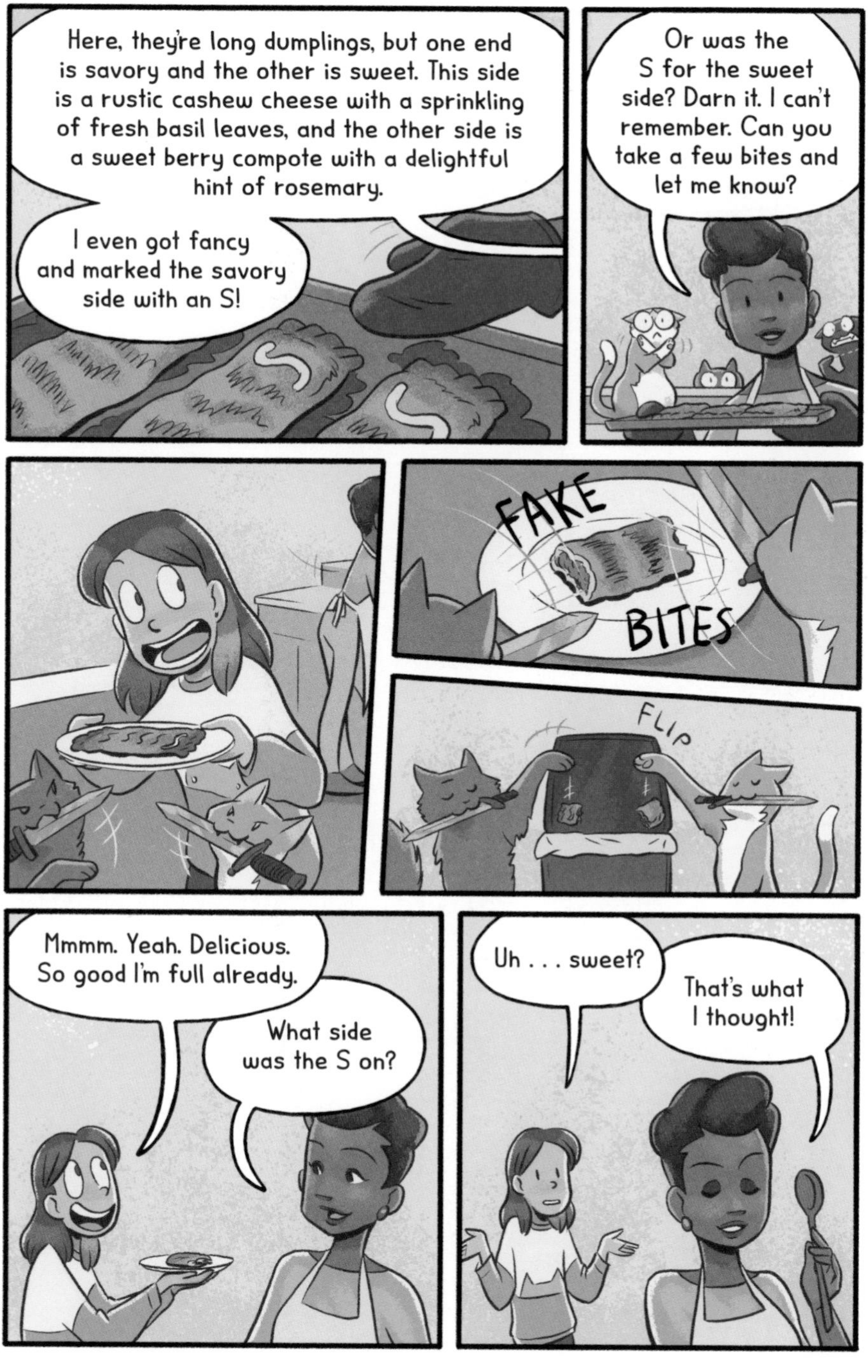
Here, they're long dumplings, but one end is savory and the other is sweet. This side is a rustic cashew cheese with a sprinkling of fresh basil leaves, and the other side is a sweet berry compote with a delightful hint of rosemary.
I even got fancy and marked the savory side with an S!
Or was the S for the sweet side? Darn it. I can't remember. Can you take a few bites and let me know?
FAKE
BITES
FLIP
Mmmm. Yeah. Delicious. So good I'm full already.
What side was the S on?
Uh . . . sweet?
That's what I thought!

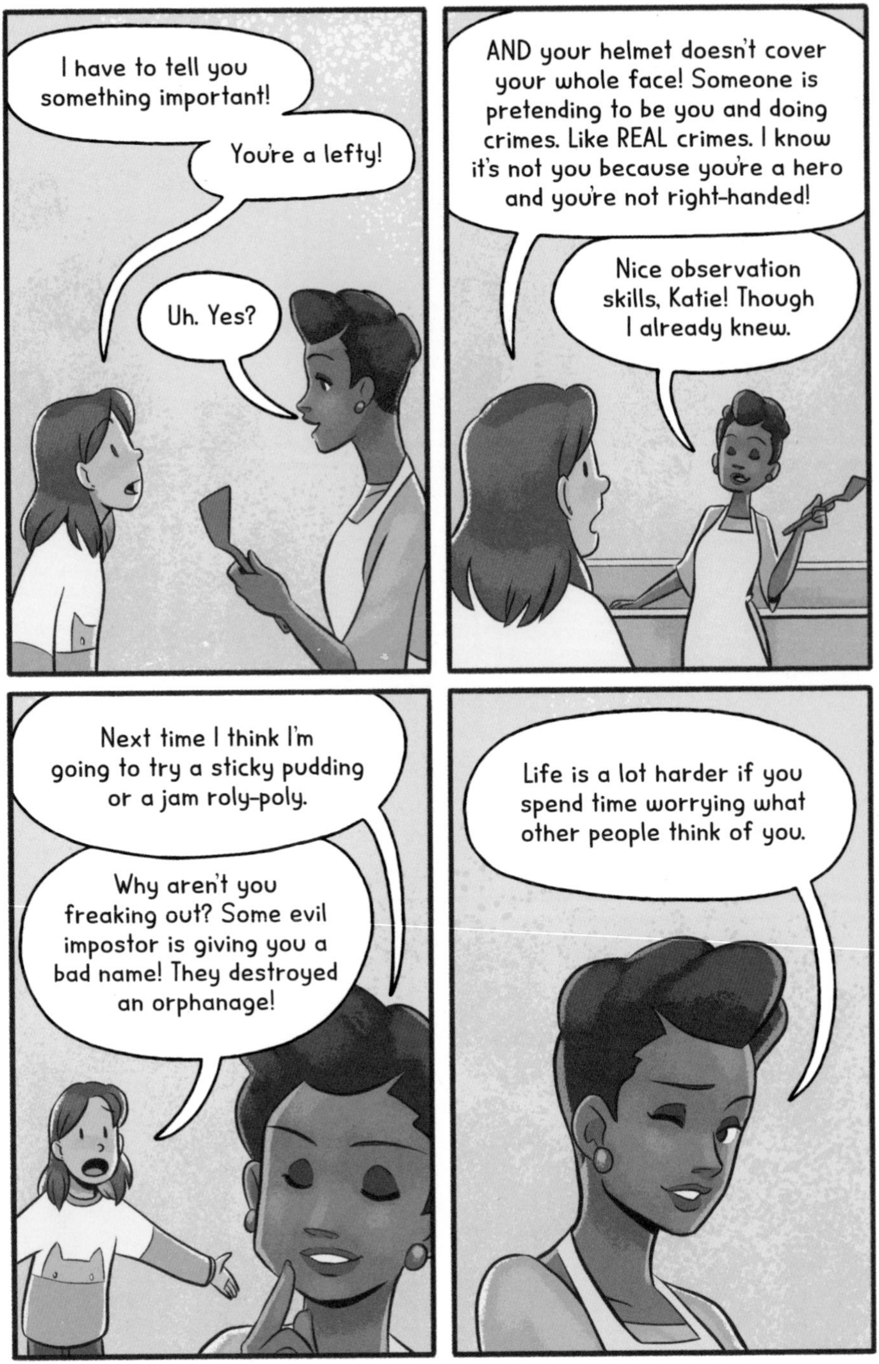
I have to tell you something important!
You're a lefty!
Uh. Yes?
AND your helmet doesn't cover your whole face! Someone is pretending to be you and doing crimes. Like REAL crimes. I know it's not you because you're a hero and you're not right-handed!
Nice observation skills, Katie! Though I already knew.
Next time I think I'm going to try a sticky pudding or a jam roly-poly.
Why aren't you freaking out? Some evil impostor is giving you a bad name! They destroyed an orphanage!
Life is a lot harder if you spend time worrying what other people think of you.

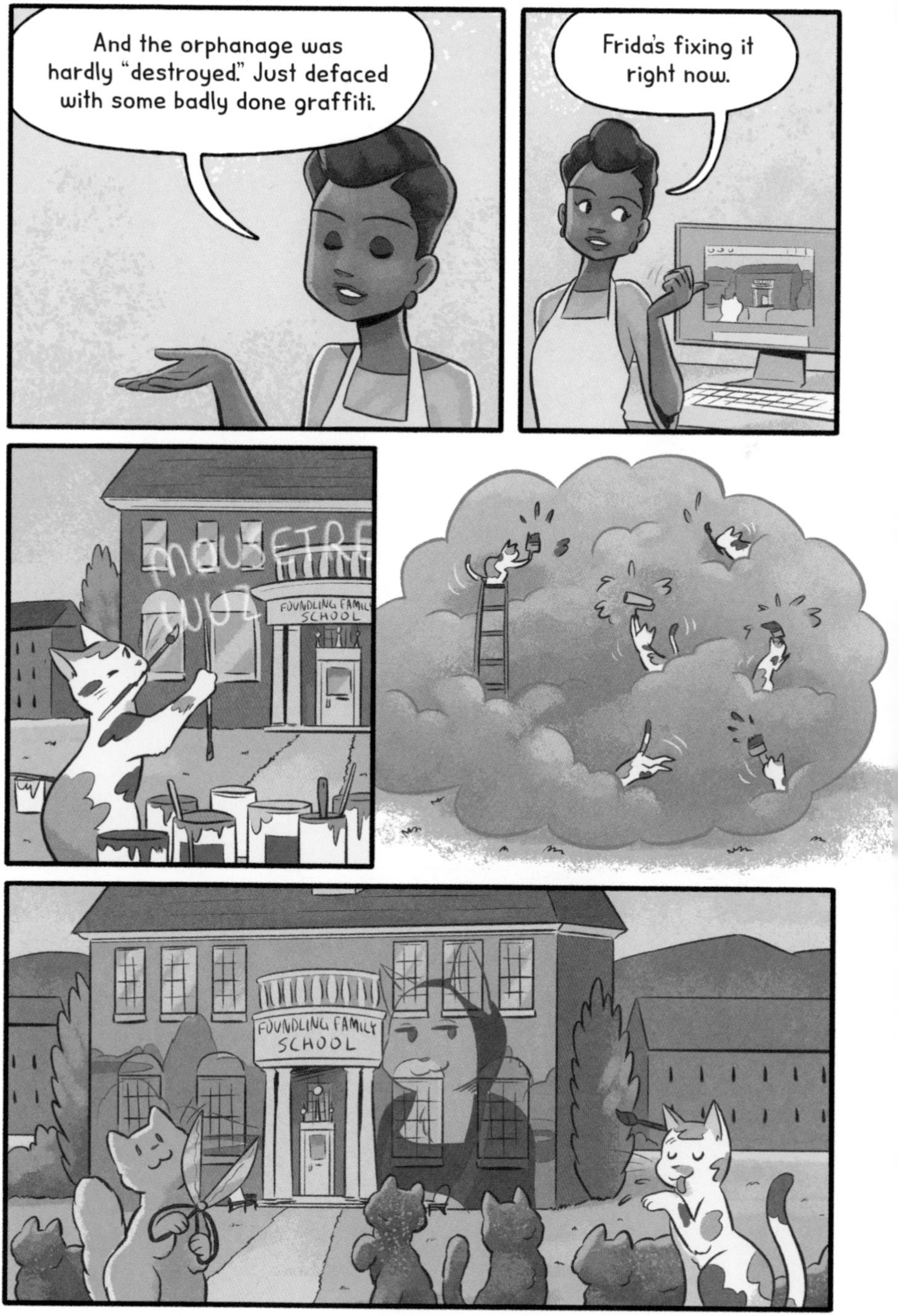
And the orphanage was hardly "destroyed." Just defaced with some badly done graffiti.
Frida's fixing it right now.
MOUSETRA WUZ
FOUNDLING FAMILY SCHOOL
FOUNDLING FAMILY SCHOOL

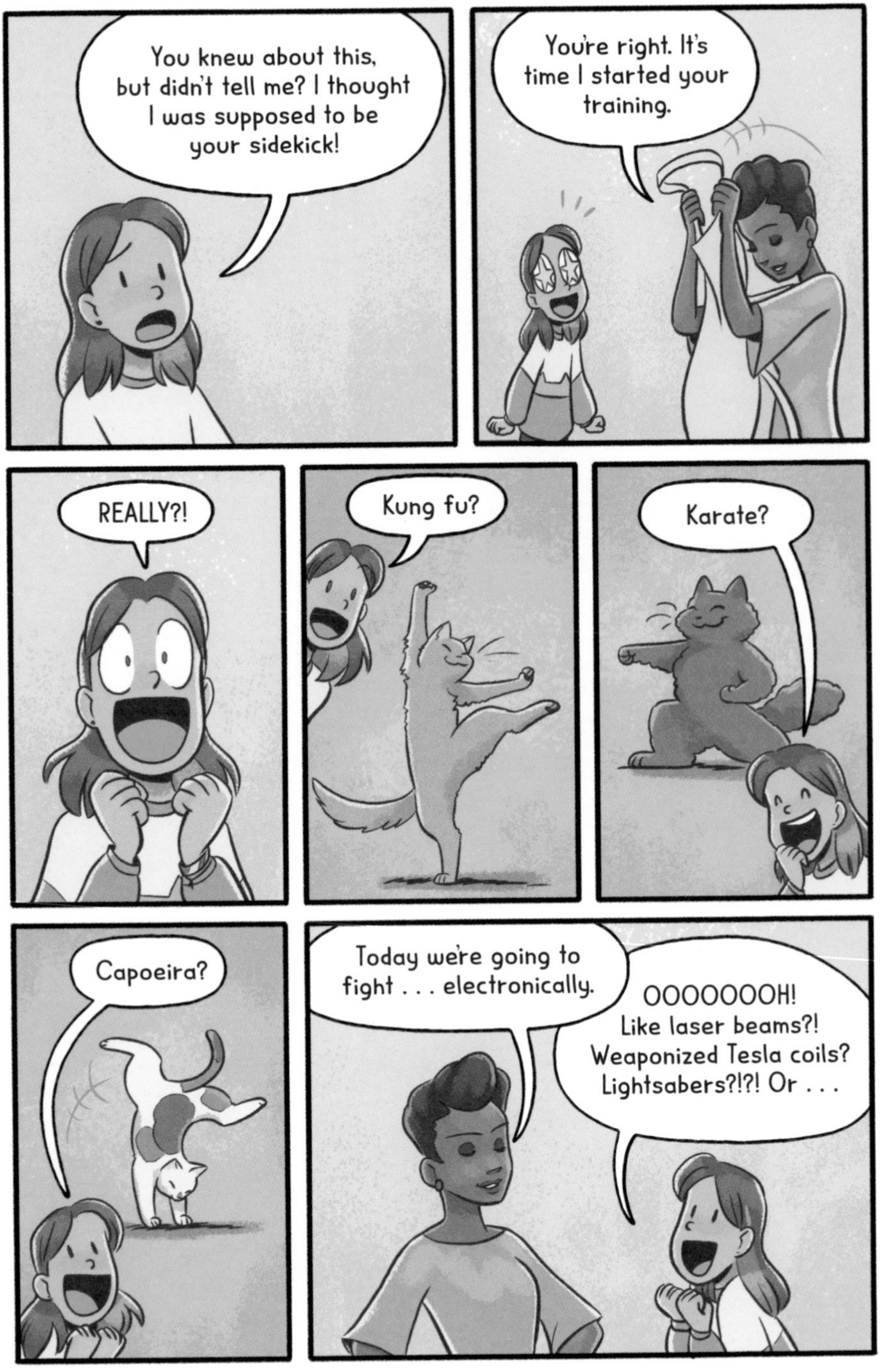
You knew about this, but didn't tell me? I thought I was supposed to be your sidekick!
You're right. It's time I started your training.
REALLY?!
Kung fu?
Karate?
Capoeira?
Today we're going to fight . . . electronically.
OOOOOOOH! Like laser beams?! Weaponized Tesla coils? Lightsabers?!?! Or . . .

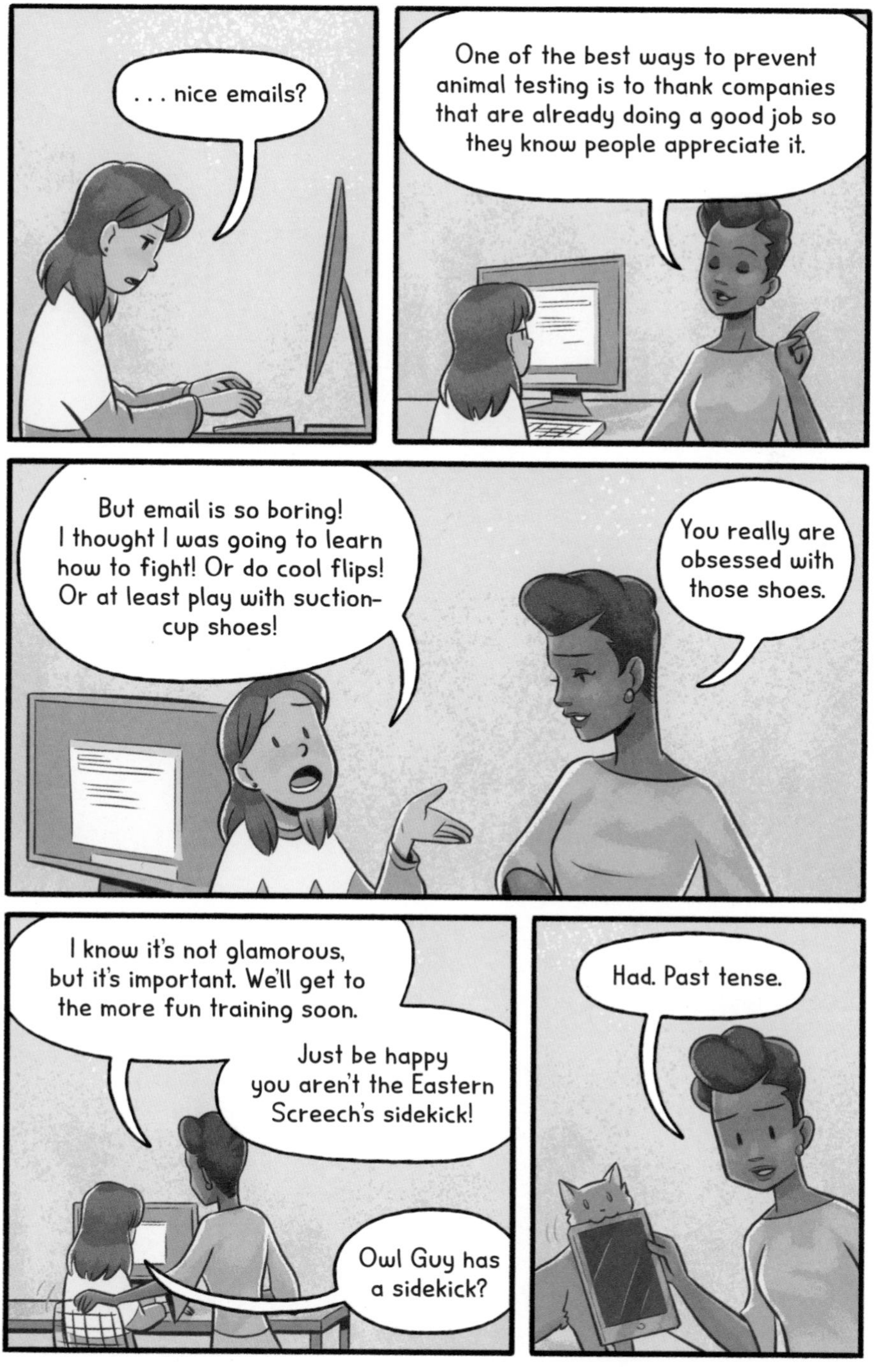
. . . nice emails?
One of the best ways to prevent animal testing is to thank companies that are already doing a good job so they know people appreciate it.
But email is so boring! I thought I was going to learn how to fight! Or do cool flips! Or at least play with suction-cup shoes!
You really are obsessed with those shoes.
I know it's not glamorous, but it's important. We'll get to the more fun training soon.
Just be happy you aren't the Eastern Screech's sidekick!
Owl Guy has a sidekick?
Had. Past tense.

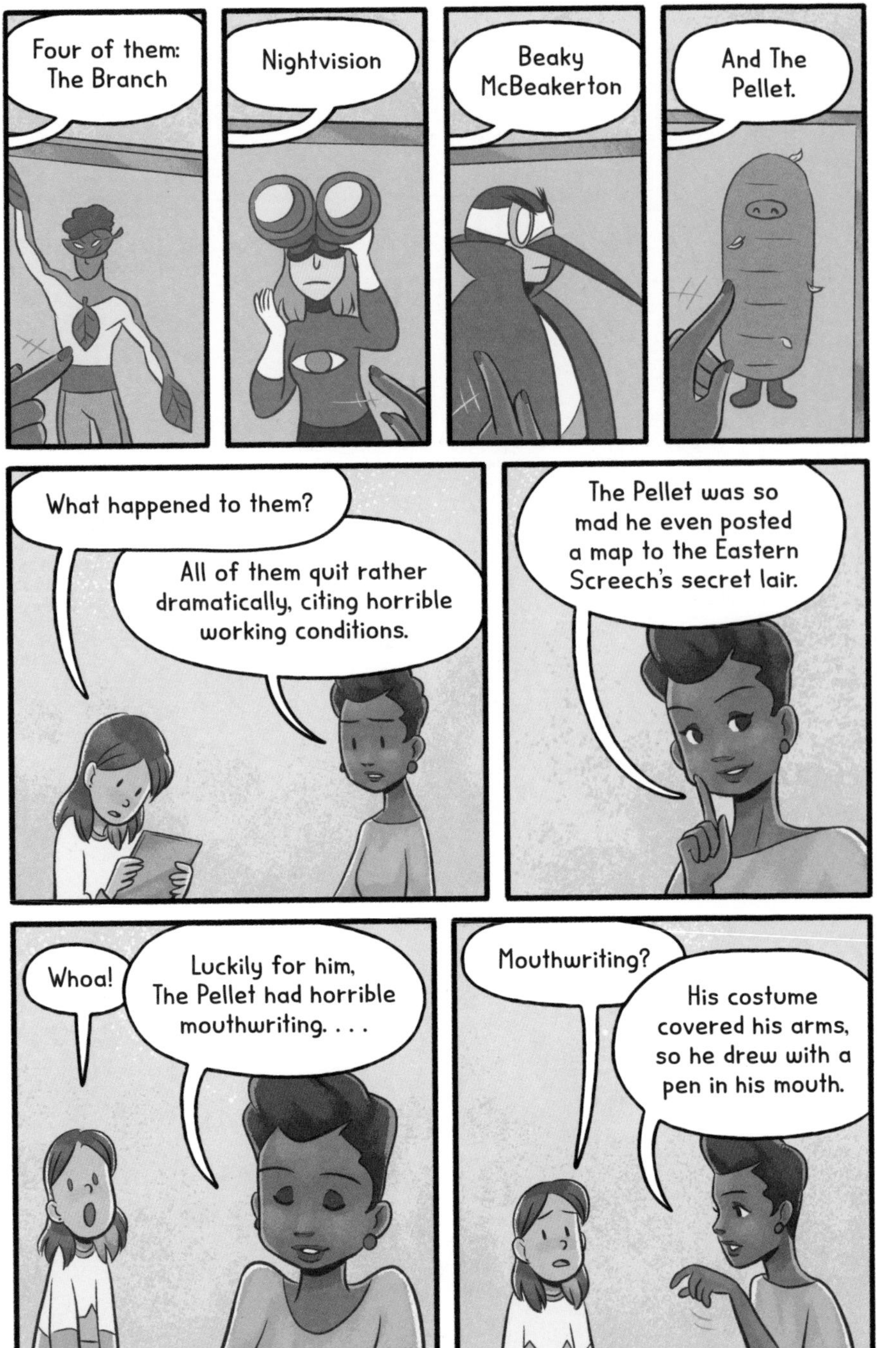
Four of them: The Branch
Nightvision
Beaky McBeakerton
And The Pellet.
What happened to them?
All of them quit rather dramatically, citing horrible working conditions.
The Pellet was so mad he even posted a map to the Eastern Screech's secret lair.
Whoa!
Luckily for him, The Pellet had horrible mouthwriting. . . .
Mouthwriting?
His costume covered his arms, so he drew with a pen in his mouth.

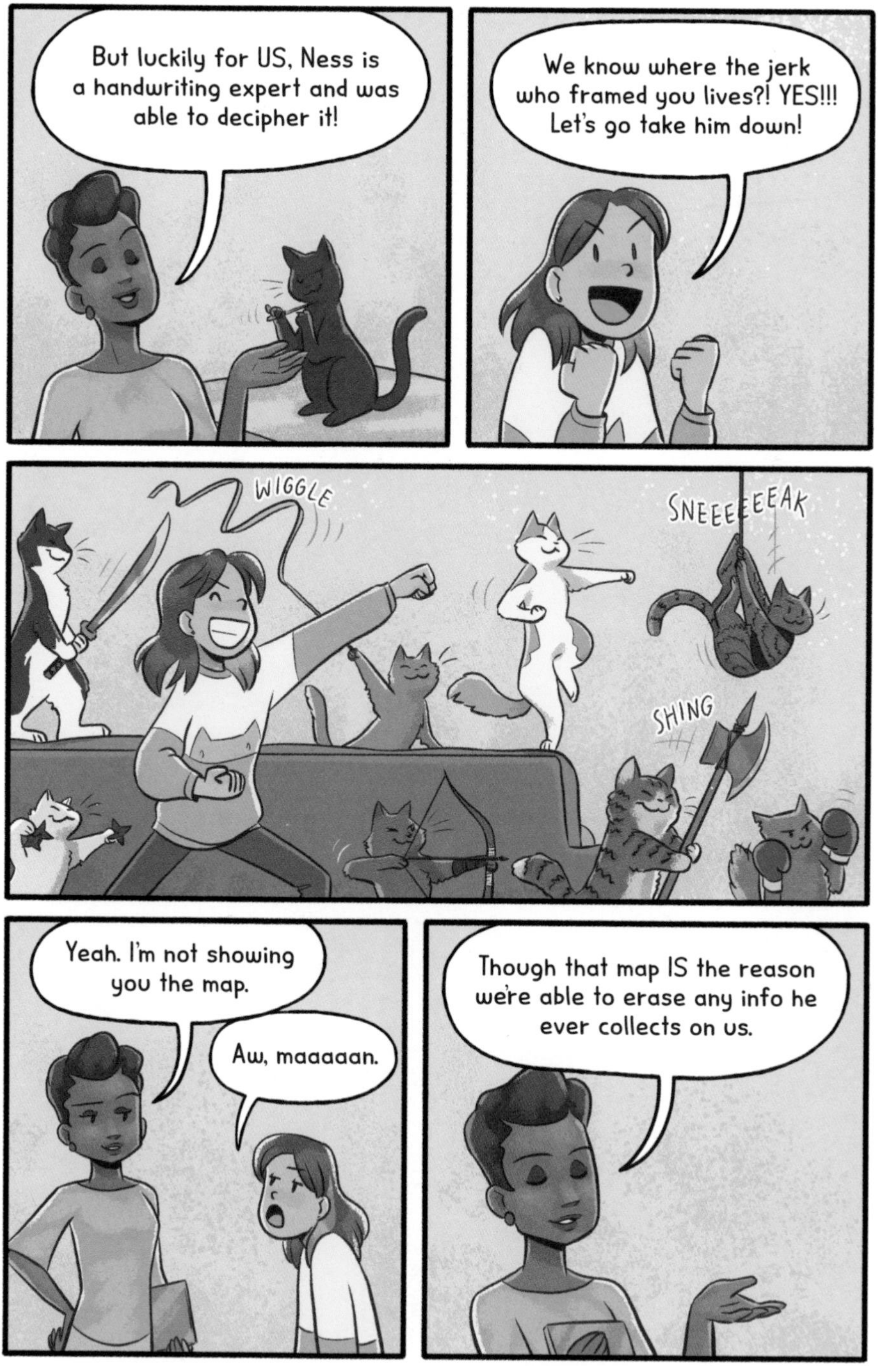
But luckily for US, Ness is a handwriting expert and was able to decipher it!
We know where the jerk who framed you lives?! YES!!! Let's go take him down!
WIGGLE
SNEEEEEEAK
SHING
Yeah. I'm not showing you the map.
Aw, maaaaan.
Though that map IS the reason we're able to erase any info he ever collects on us.

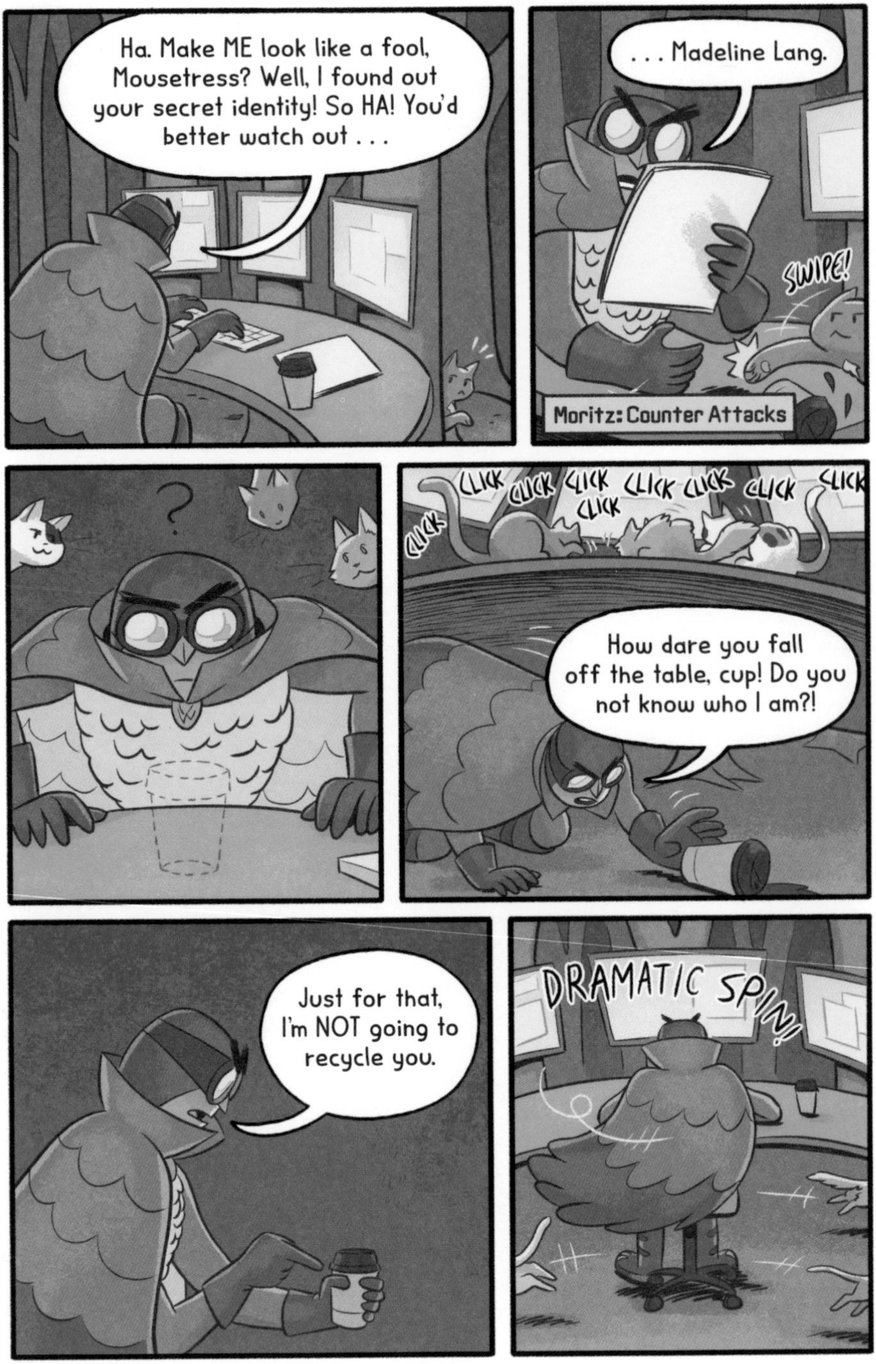

Ha. Make ME look like a fool, Mousetress? Well, I found out your secret identity! So HA! You'd better watch out . . .
. . . Madeline Lang.
SWIPE!
Moritz: Counter Attacks
?
CLICK CLICK CLICK CLICK CLICK CLICK CLICK CLICK CLICK
How dare you fall off the table, cup! Do you not know who I am?!
Just for that, I'm NOT going to recycle you.
DRAMATIC SPIN!

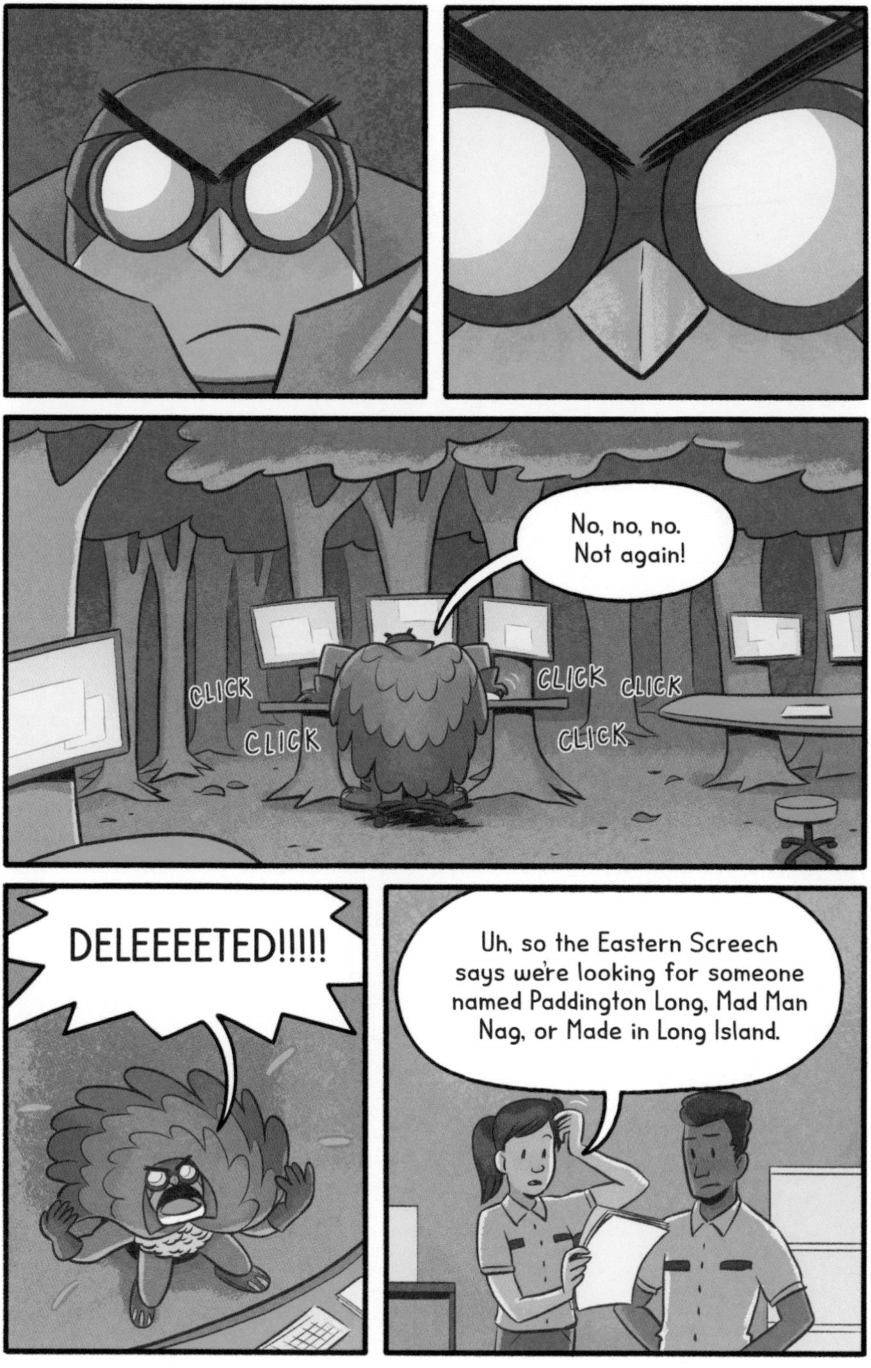
No, no, no.
Not again!
CLICK
CLICK
CLICK
CLICK
CLICK
DELEEEEETED!!!!!
Uh, so the Eastern Screech says we're looking for someone named Paddington Long, Mad Man Nag, or Made in Long Island.

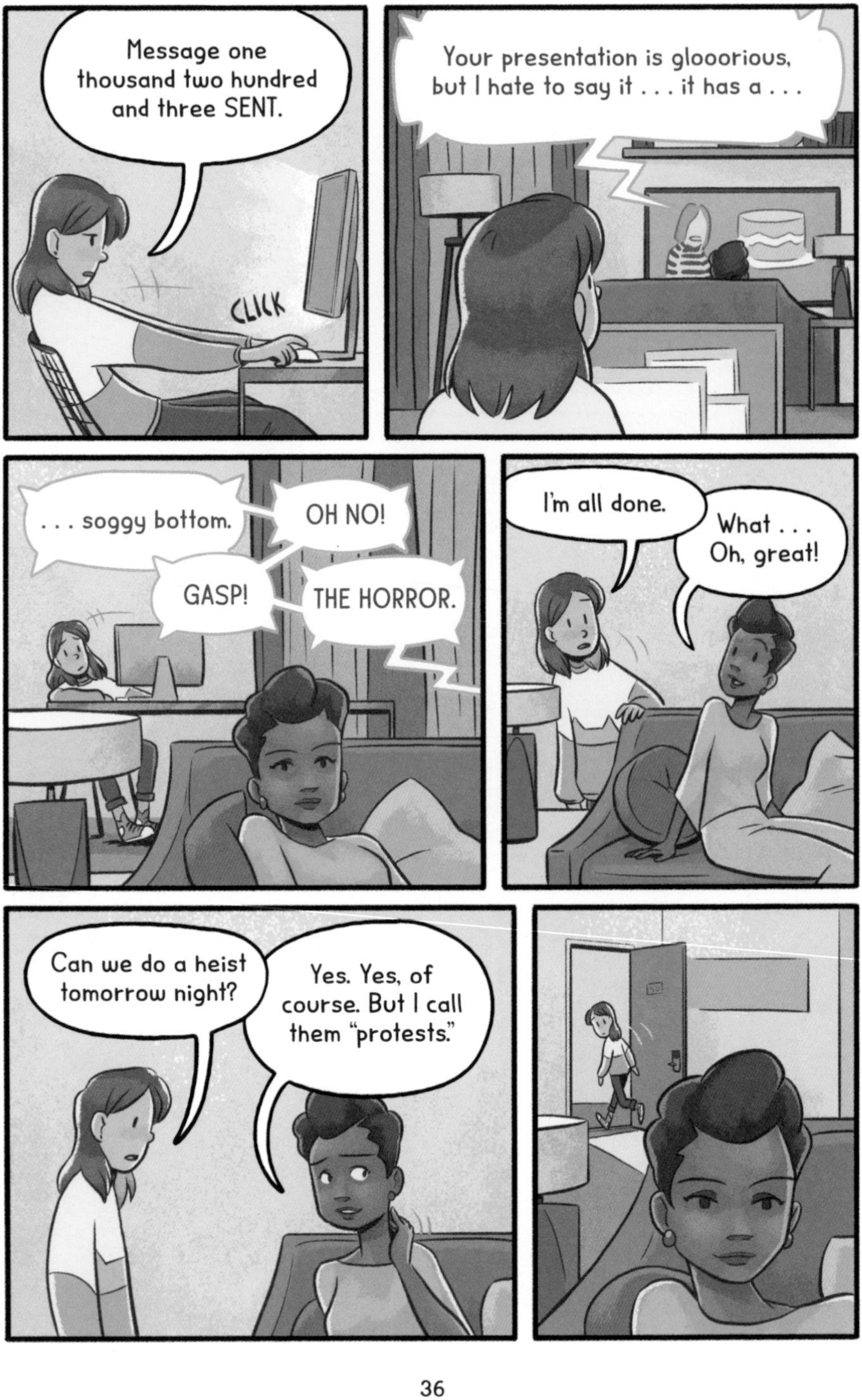
Message one thousand two hundred and three SENT.
CLICK
Your presentation is glooorious, but I hate to say it . . . it has a . . .
. . . soggy bottom.
OH NO!
GASP!
THE HORROR.
I'm all done.
What . . . Oh, great!
Can we do a heist tomorrow night?
Yes. Yes, of course. But I call them "protests."

CHAPTER THREE

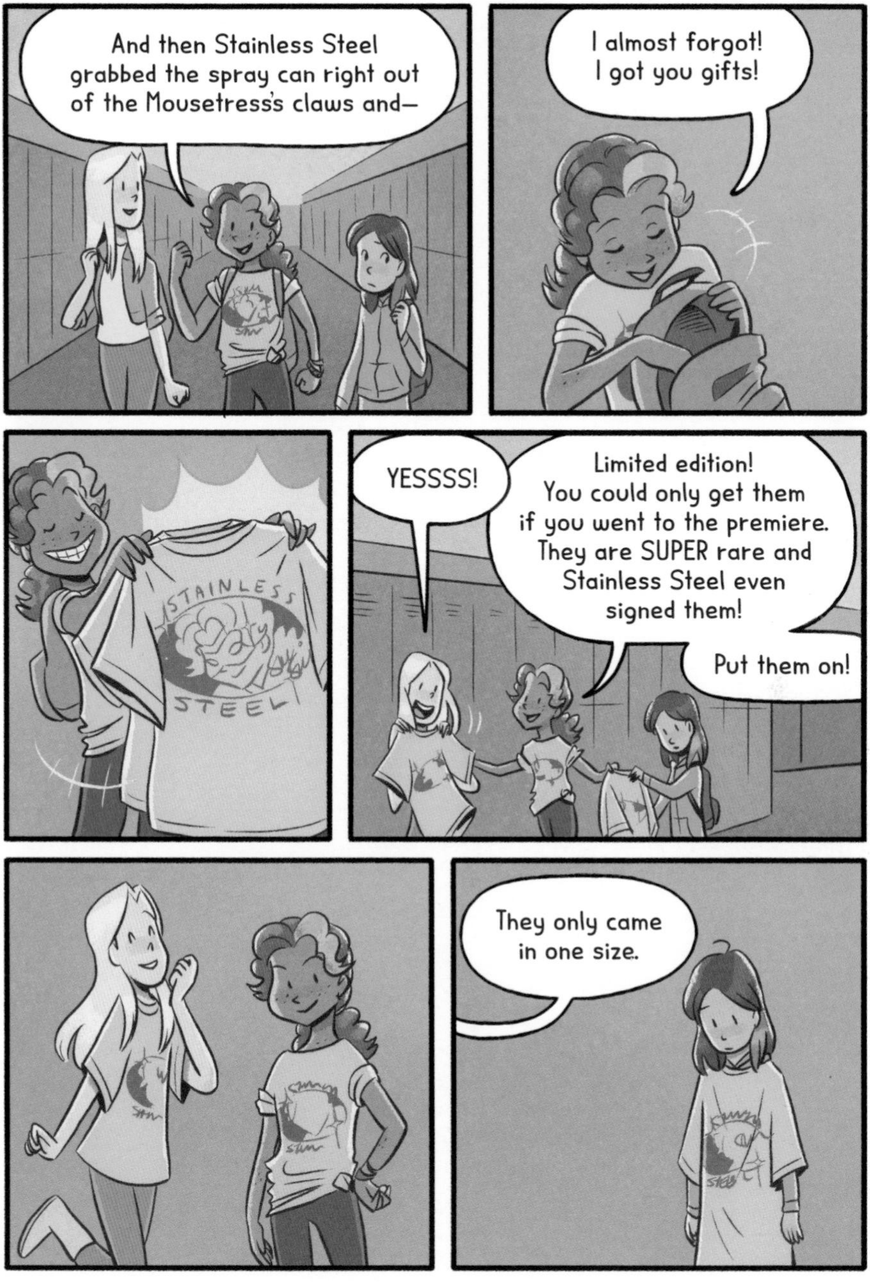

And then Stainless Steel grabbed the spray can right out of the Mousetress's claws and—
I almost forgot! I got you gifts!
STAINLESS STEEL
YESSSS!
Limited edition! You could only get them if you went to the premiere. They are SUPER rare and Stainless Steel even signed them!
Put them on!
They only came in one size.

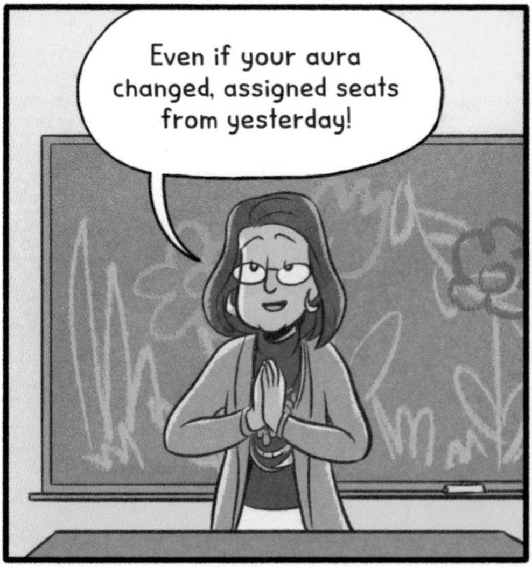
Even if your aura changed, assigned seats from yesterday!

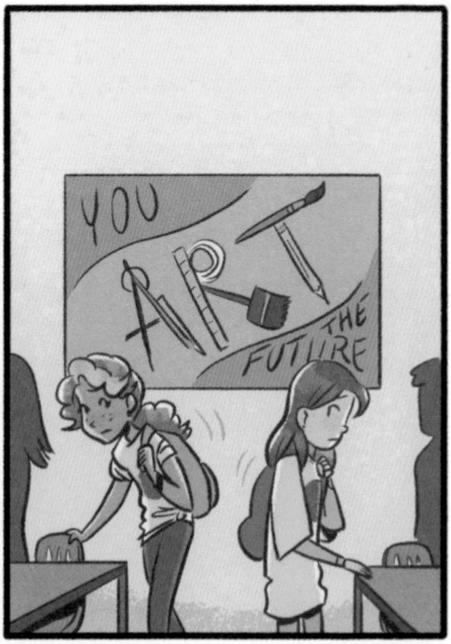
YOU
ART
THE
FUTURE

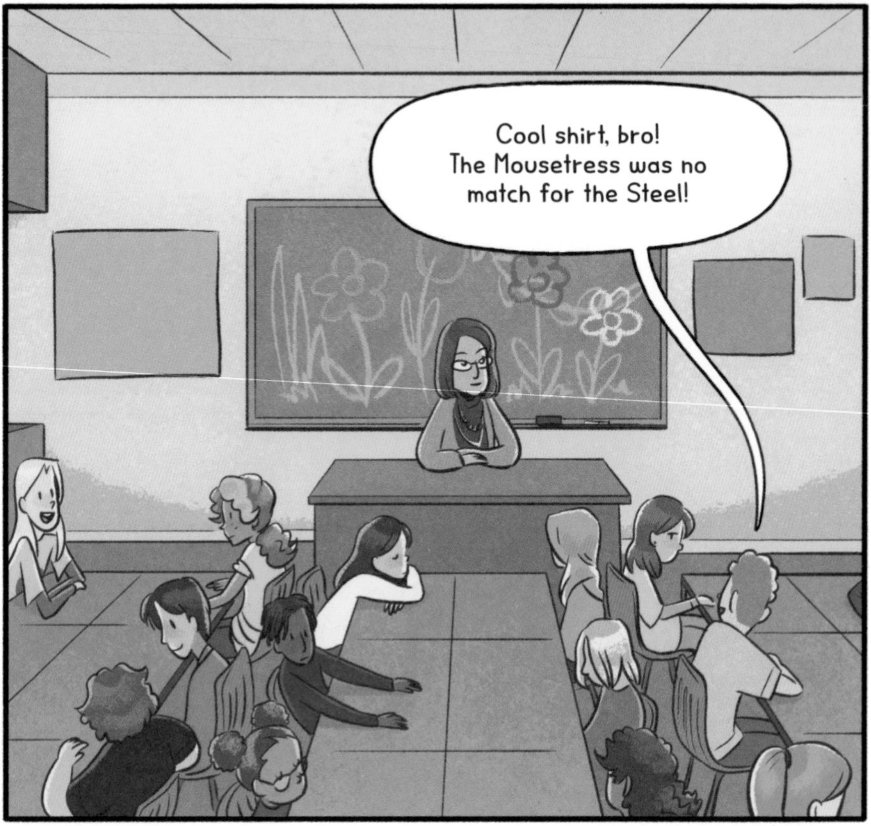
Cool shirt, bro! The Mousetress was no match for the Steel!

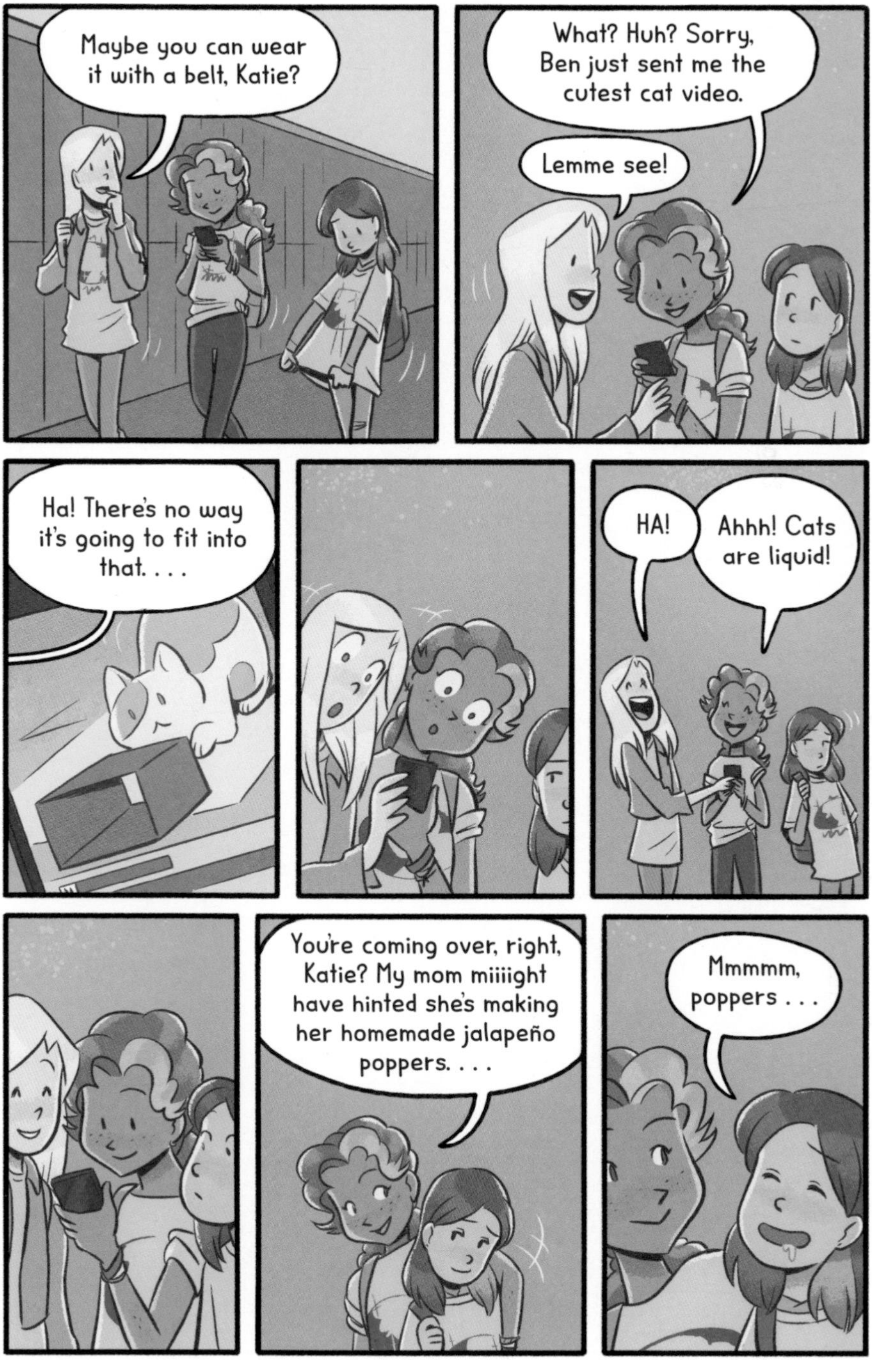
Maybe you can wear it with a belt, Katie?
What? Huh? Sorry, Ben just sent me the cutest cat video.
Lemme see!
Ha! There's no way it's going to fit into that. . . .
HA!
Ahhh! Cats are liquid!
You're coming over, right, Katie? My mom miiiight have hinted she's making her homemade jalapeño poppers. . . .
Mmmmm, poppers . . .

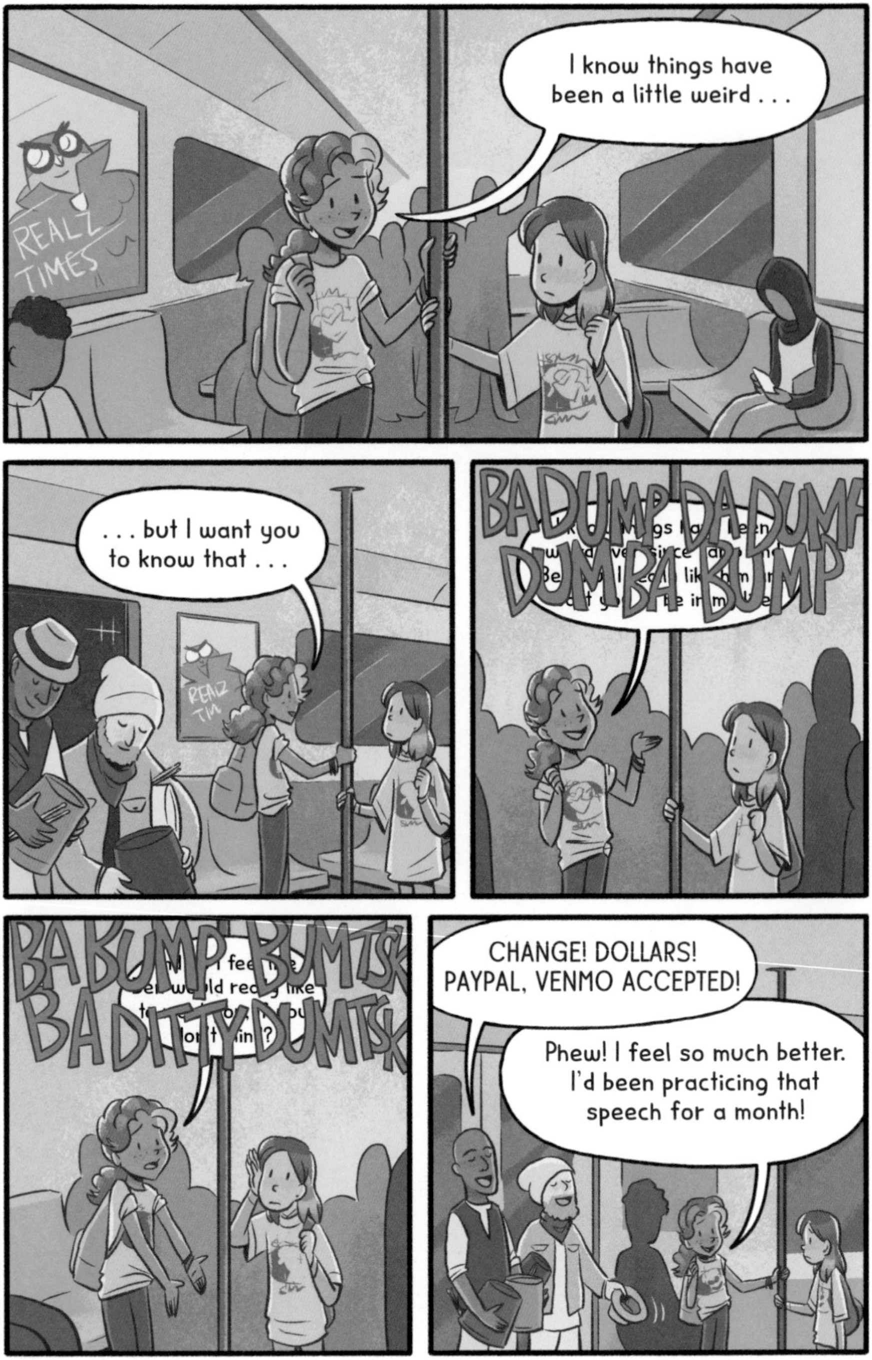
REALZ TIMES
I know things have been a little weird . . .
. . . but I want you to know that . . .
BADUMP DADUMP
DUMBA BUMP
BABUMP BUMTSK
BADITTYDUMTSK
CHANGE! DOLLARS! PAYPAL, VENMO ACCEPTED!
Phew! I feel so much better. I'd been practicing that speech for a month!

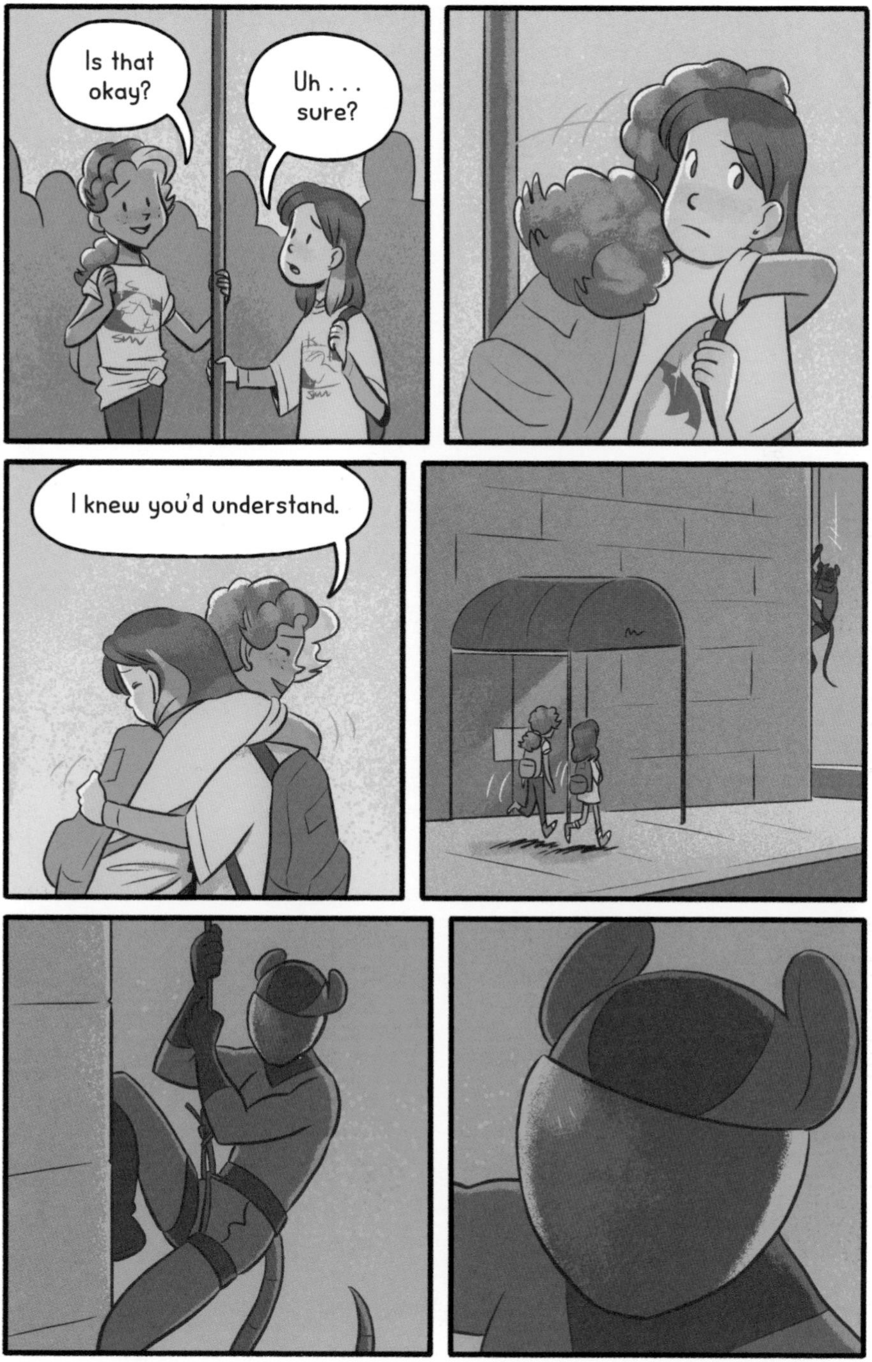
Is that okay?
Uh . . . sure?
I knew you'd understand.

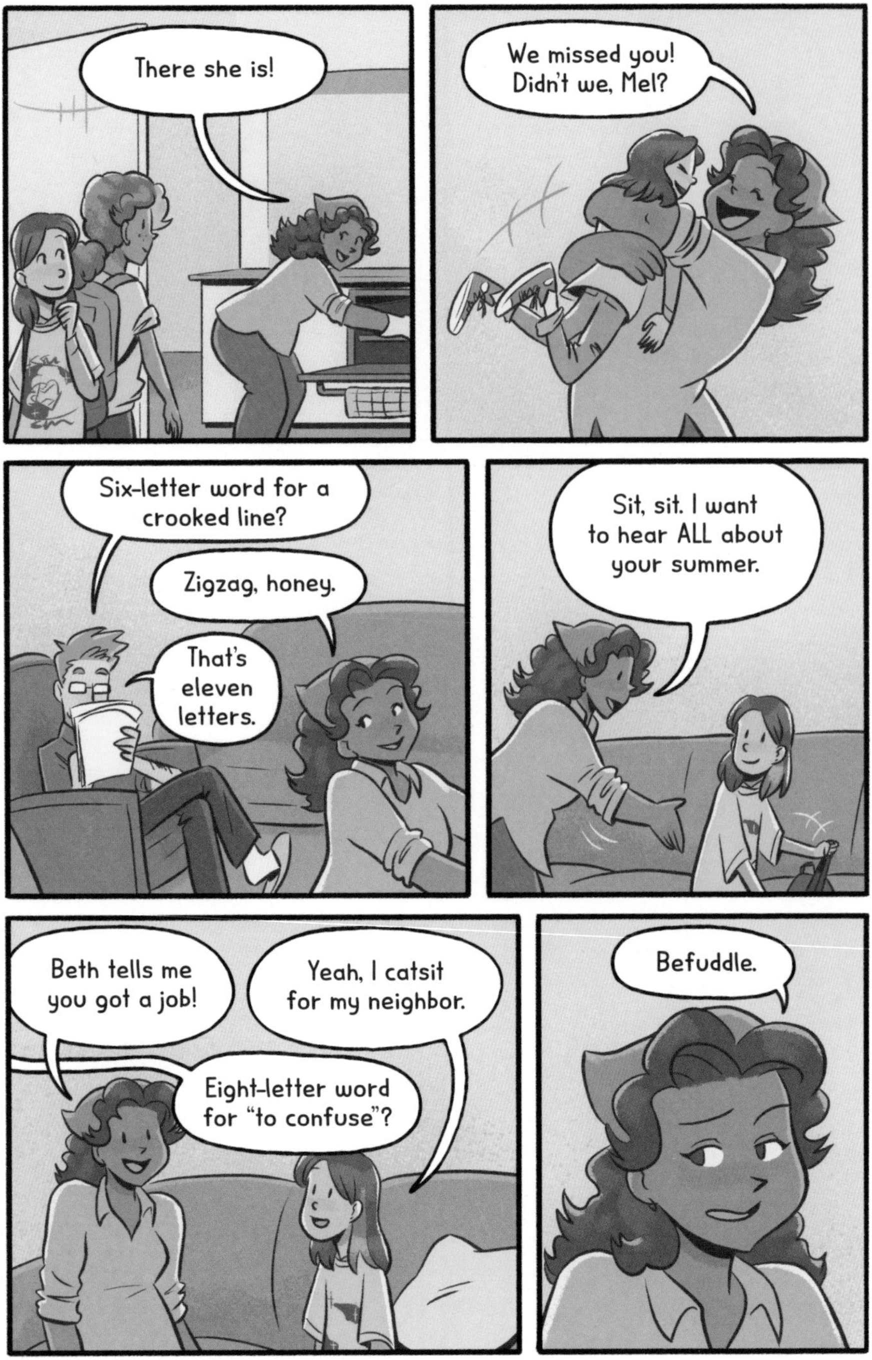
There she is!
We missed you! Didn't we, Mel?
Six-letter word for a crooked line?
Zigzag, honey.
That's eleven letters.
Sit, sit. I want to hear ALL about your summer.
Beth tells me you got a job!
Yeah, I catsit for my neighbor.
Eight-letter word for "to confuse"?
Befuddle.

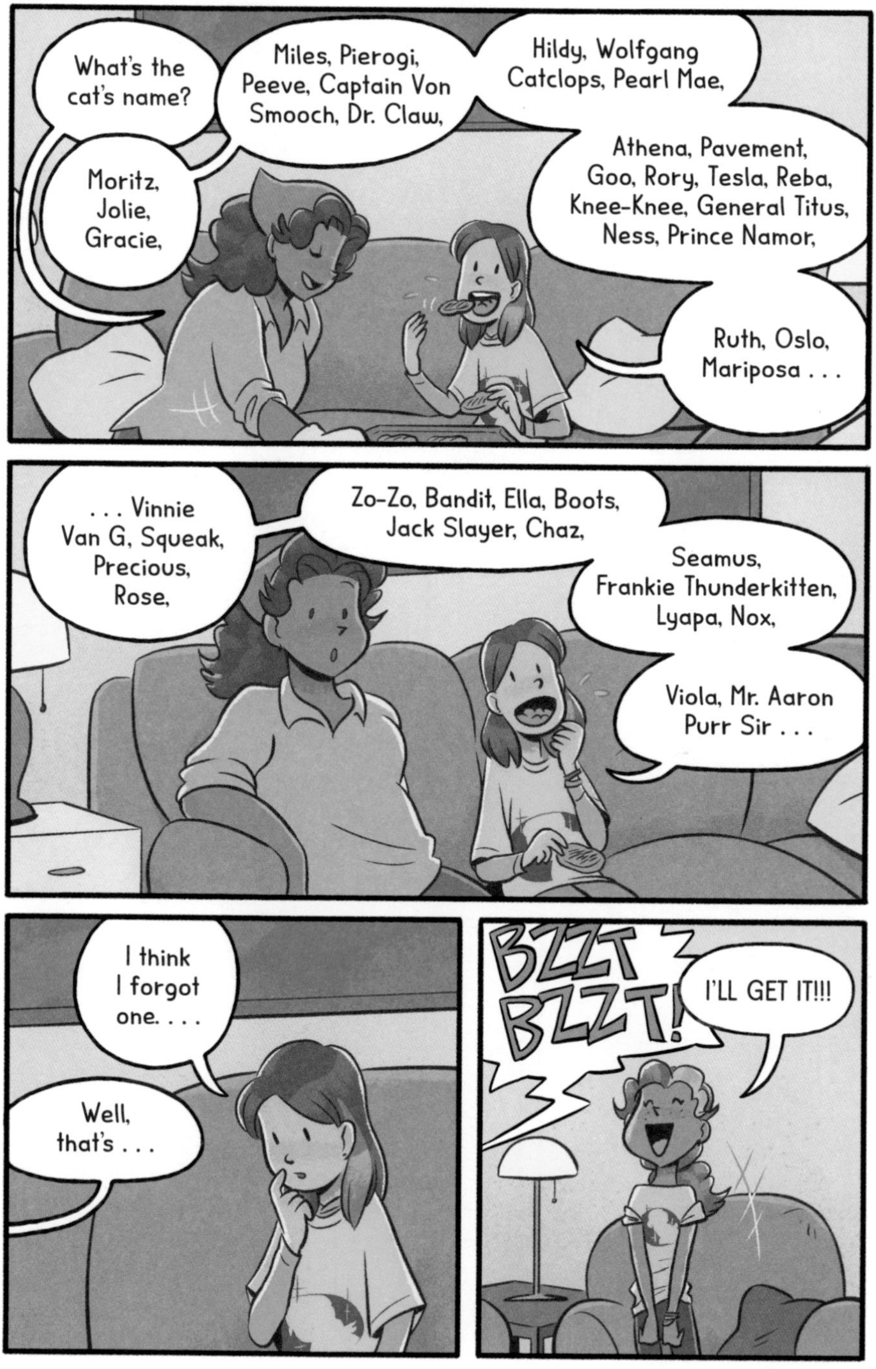
What's the cat's name?
Miles, Pierogi, Peeve, Captain Von Smooch, Dr. Claw,
Hildy, Wolfgang Catclops, Pearl Mae,
Moritz, Jolie, Gracie,
Athena, Pavement, Goo, Rory, Tesla, Reba, Knee-Knee, General Titus, Ness, Prince Namor,
Ruth, Oslo, Mariposa . . .
. . . Vinnie Van G, Squeak, Precious, Rose,
Zo-Zo, Bandit, Ella, Boots, Jack Slayer, Chaz,
Seamus, Frankie Thunderkitten, Lyapa, Nox,
Viola, Mr. Aaron Purr Sir . . .
I think I forgot one. . . .
Well, that's . . .
BZZT BZZT!
I'LL GET IT!!!

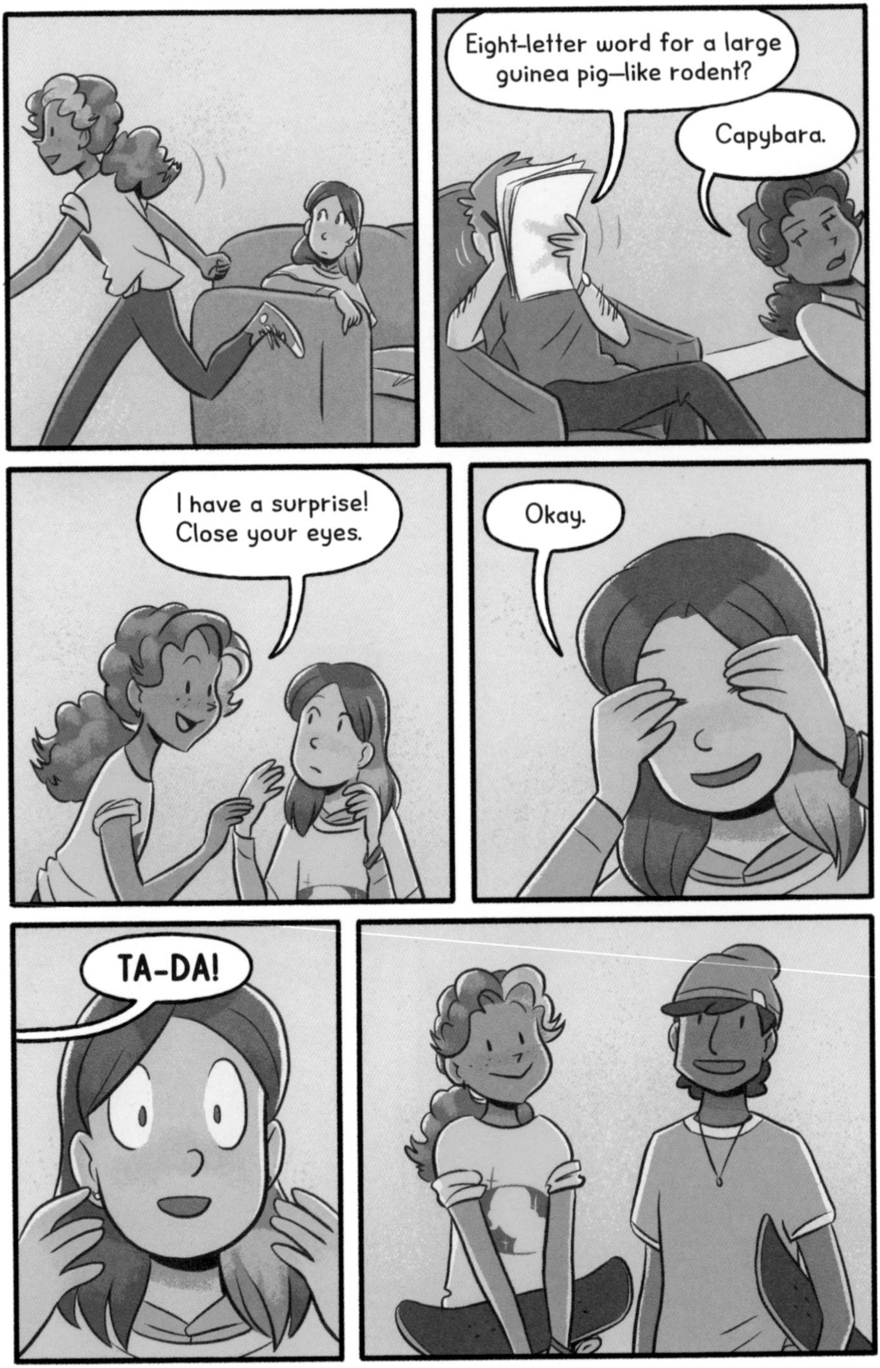
Eight-letter word for a large guinea pig—like rodent?
Capybara.
I have a surprise! Close your eyes.
Okay.
TA-DA!

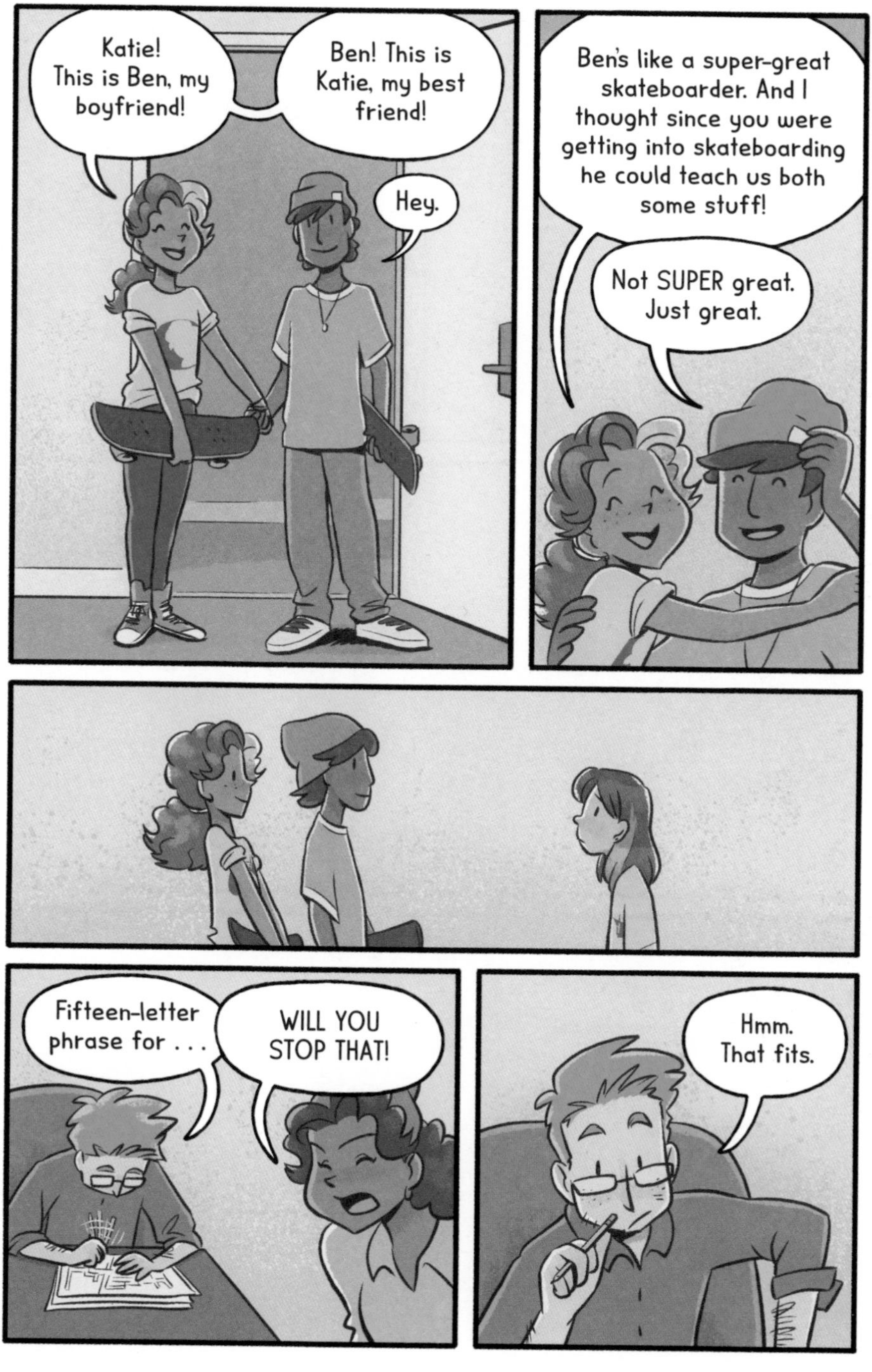
Katie!
This is Ben, my boyfriend!
Ben! This is Katie, my best friend!
Hey.
Ben's like a super-great skateboarder. And I thought since you were getting into skateboarding he could teach us both some stuff!
Not SUPER great. Just great.
Fifteen-letter phrase for . . .
WILL YOU STOP THAT!
Hmm. That fits.

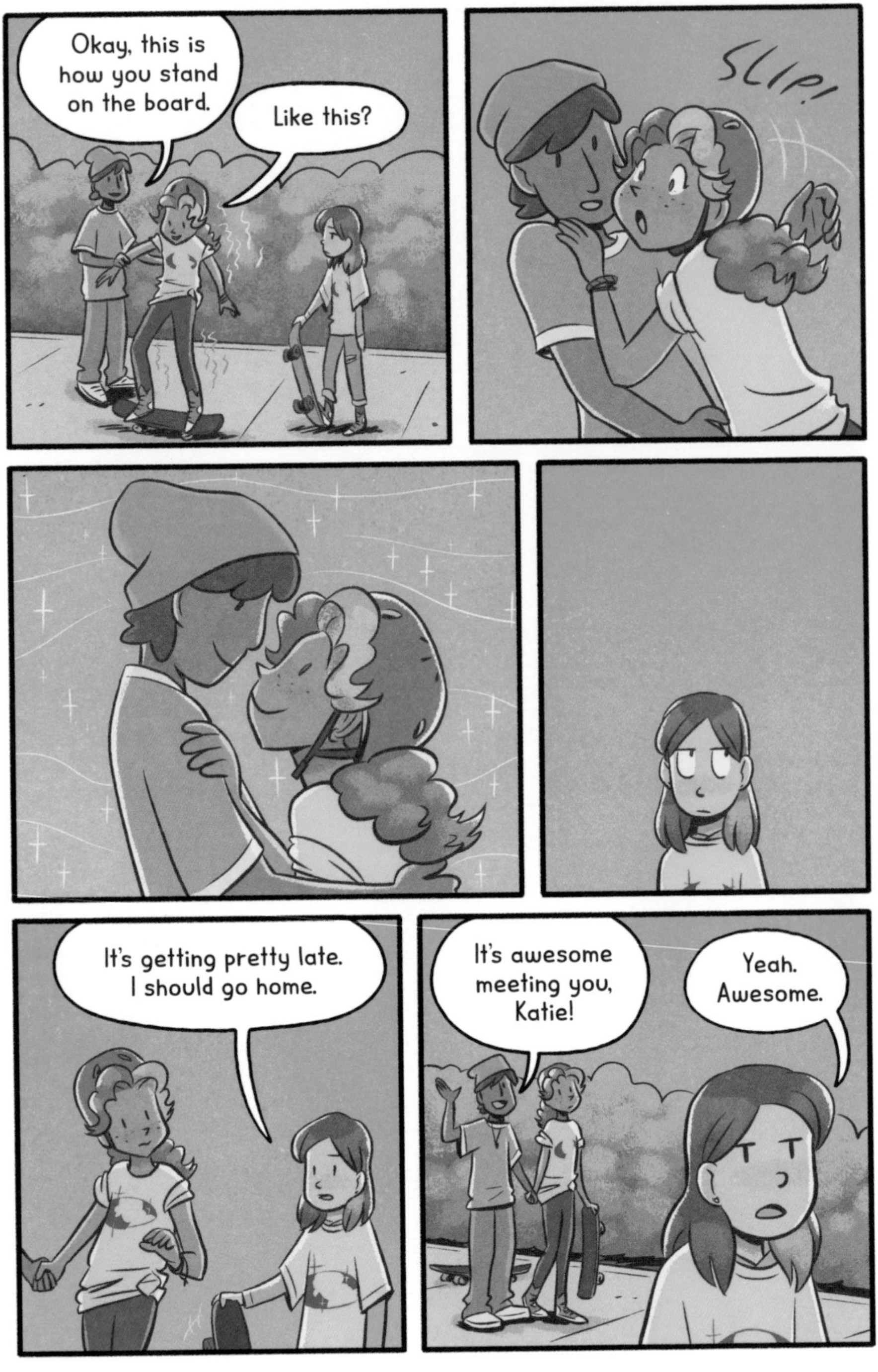
Okay, this is how you stand on the board.
Like this?
SLIP!
It's getting pretty late. I should go home.
It's awesome meeting you, Katie!
Yeah. Awesome.

CHAPTER FOUR

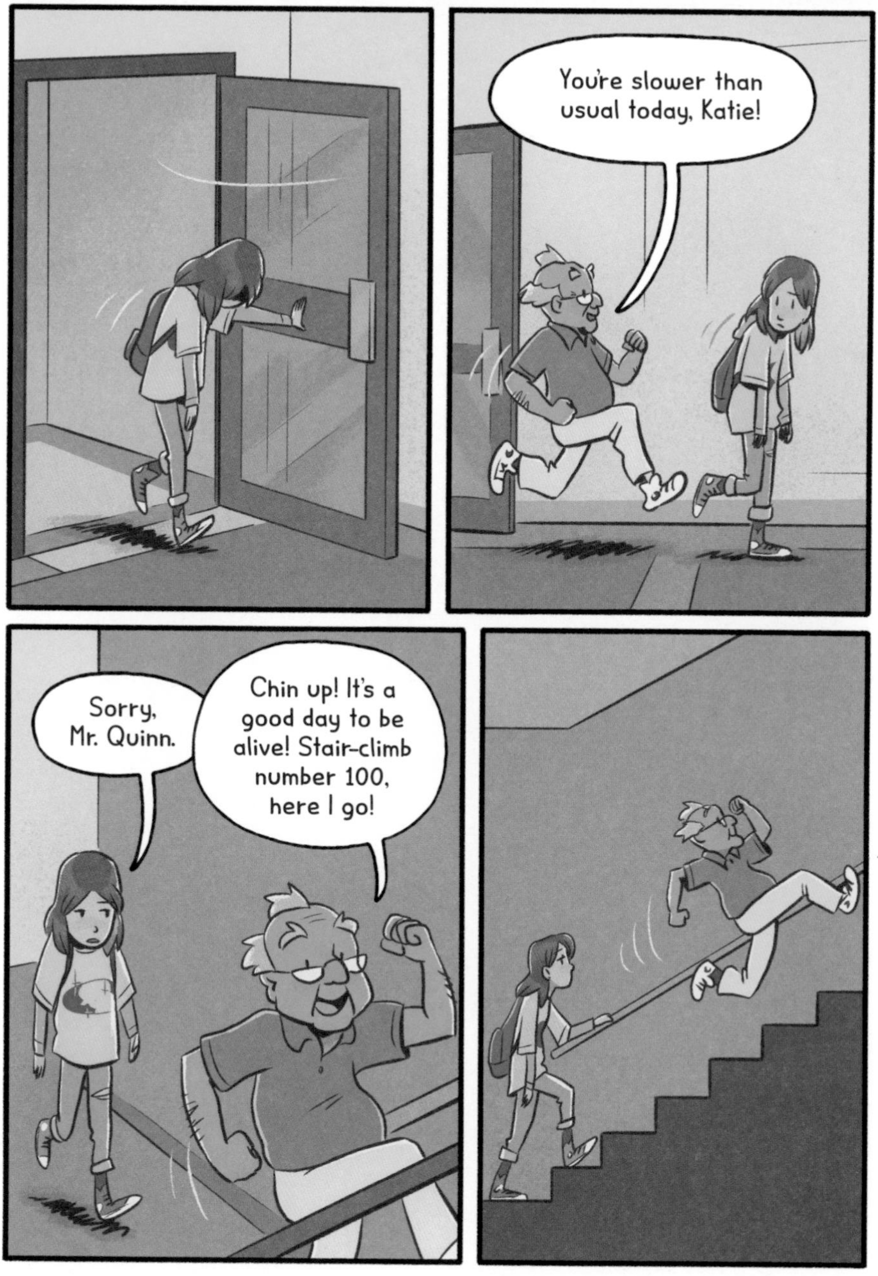

You're slower than usual today, Katie!
Sorry, Mr. Quinn.
Chin up! It's a good day to be alive! Stair-climb number 100, here I go!

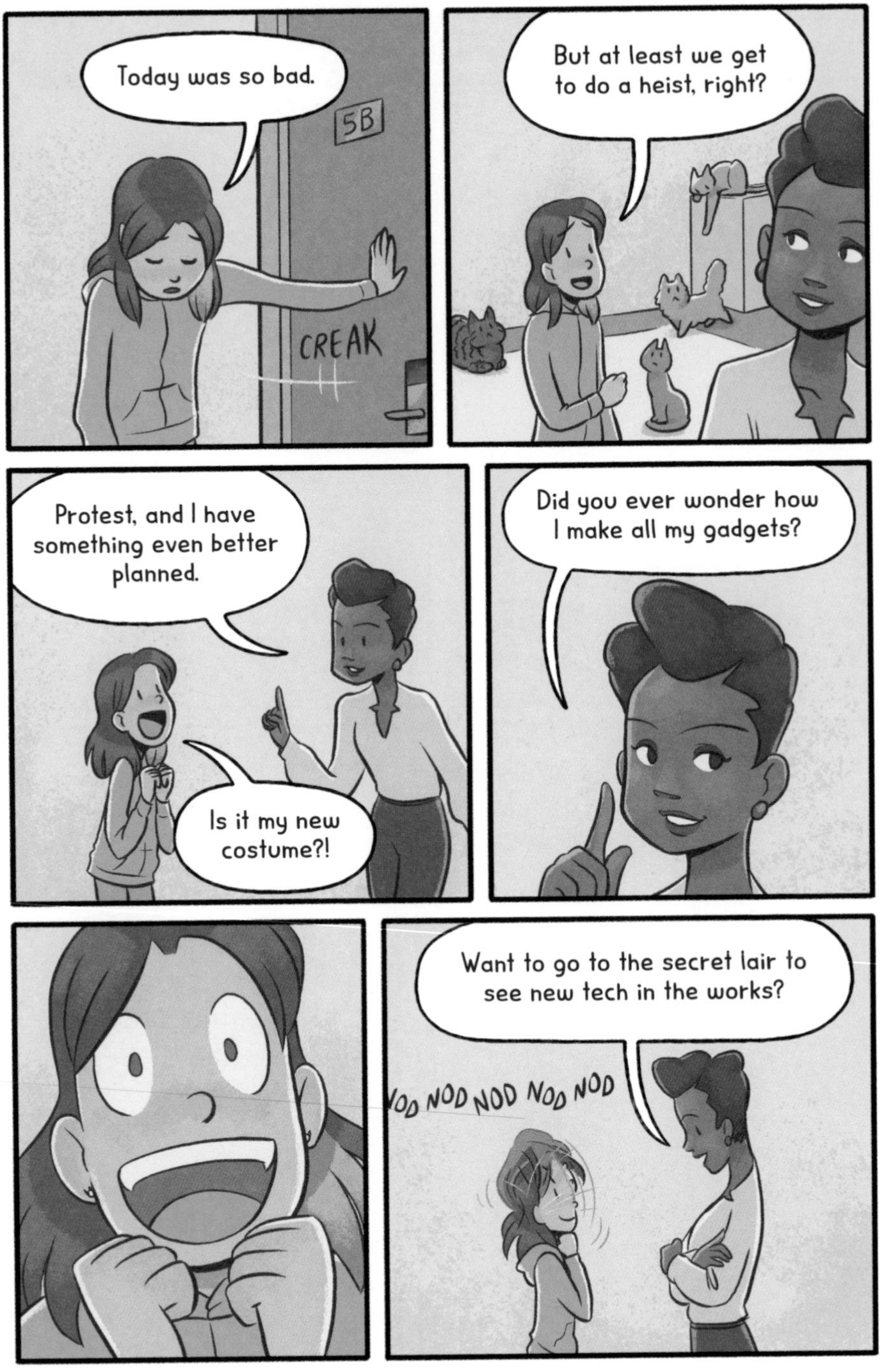
Today was so bad.
5B
CREAK
But at least we get to do a heist, right?
Protest, and I have something even better planned.
Is it my new costume?!
Did you ever wonder how I make all my gadgets?
Want to go to the secret lair to see new tech in the works?
NOD NOD NOD NOD NOD

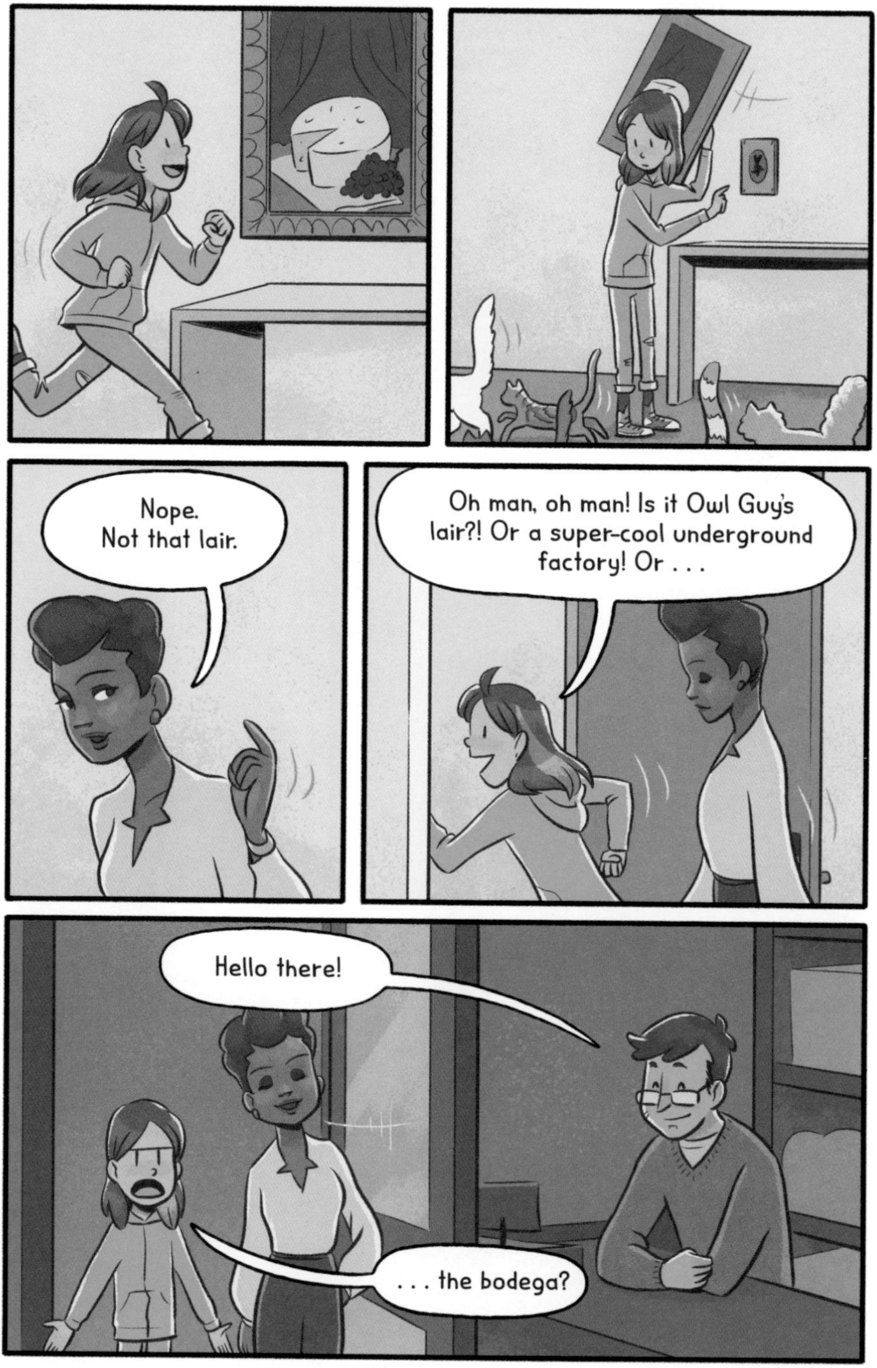
Nope.
Not that lair.
Oh man, oh man! Is it Owl Guy's lair?! Or a super-cool underground factory! Or . . .
Hello there!
. . . the bodega?

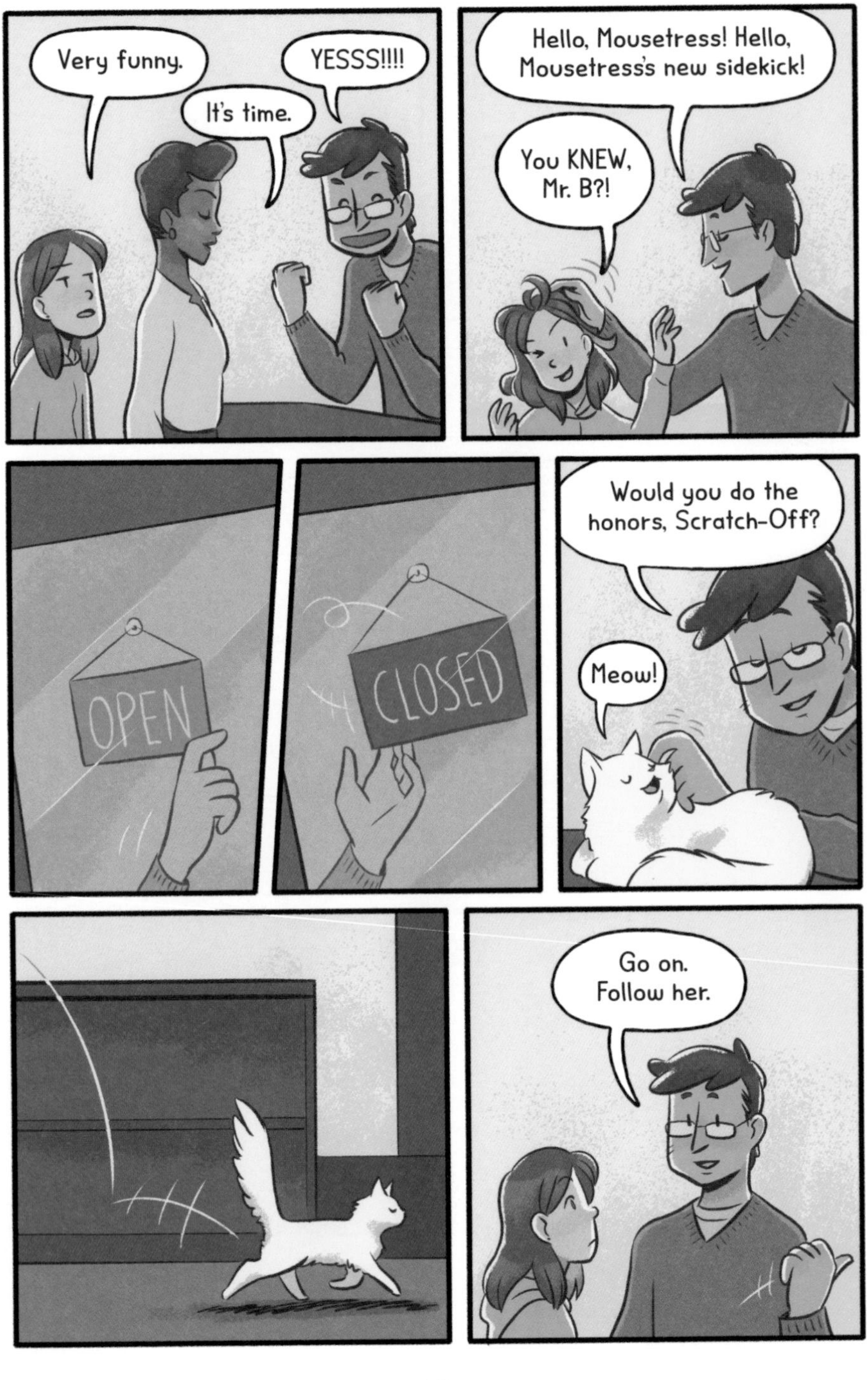
Very funny.
It's time.
YESSS!!!!
Hello, Mousetress! Hello, Mousetress's new sidekick!
You KNEW, Mr. B?!
OPEN
CLOSED
Would you do the honors, Scratch-Off?
Meow!
Go on. Follow her.

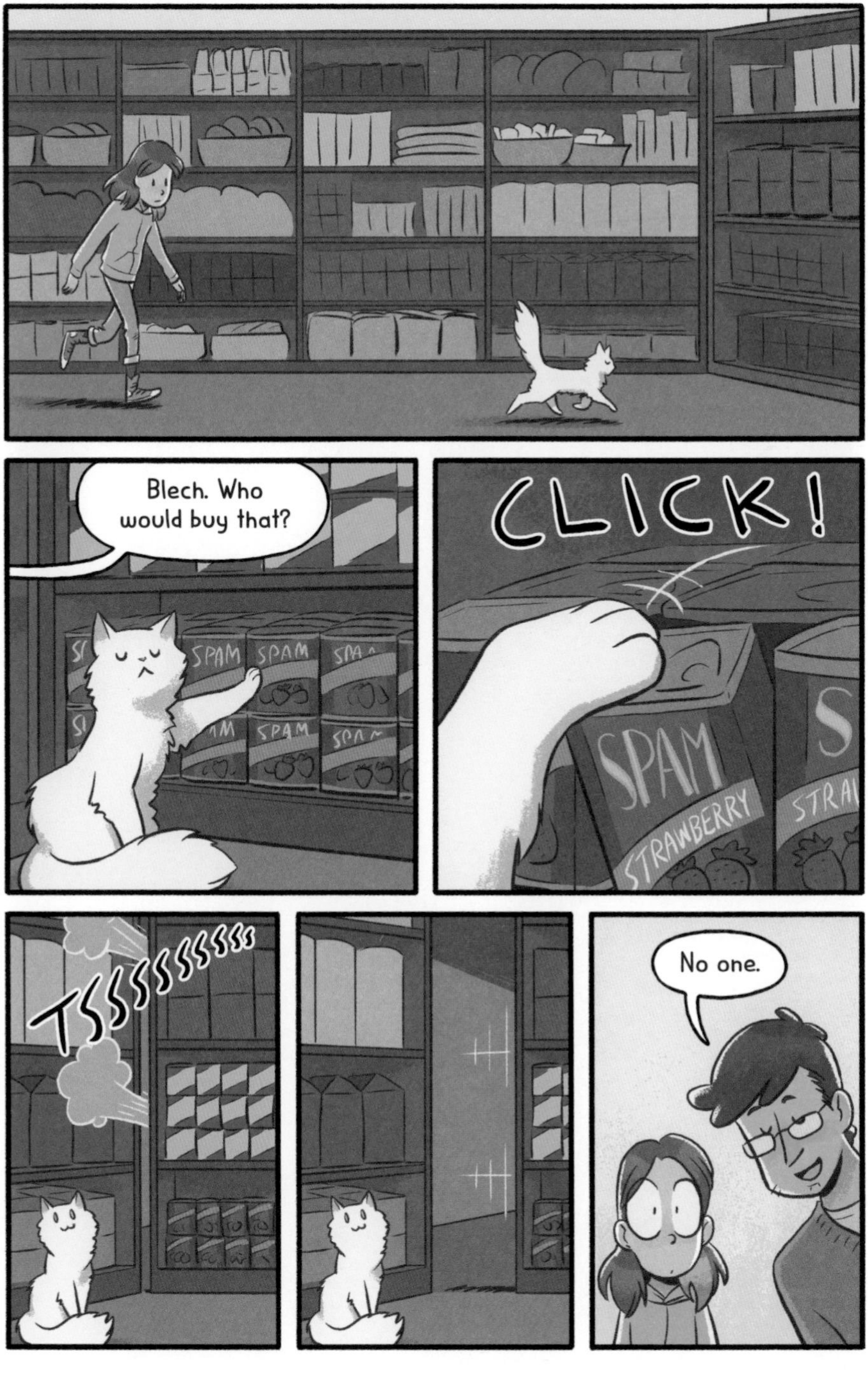
Blech. Who would buy that?
CLICK!
SPAM
STRAWBERRY
TSSSSSSSSS
No one.

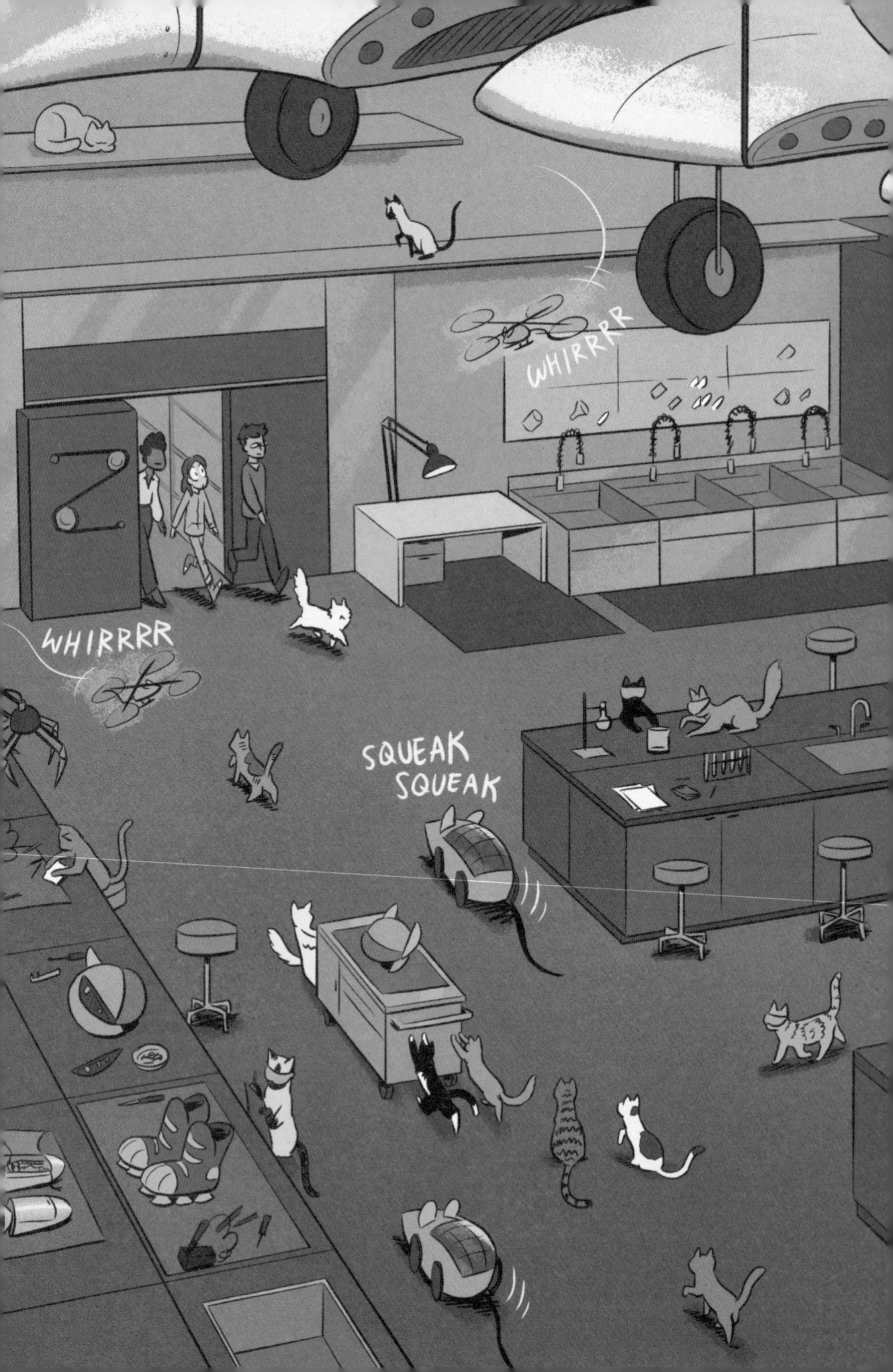
WHIRRRR
WHIRRRR
SQUEAK
SQUEAK

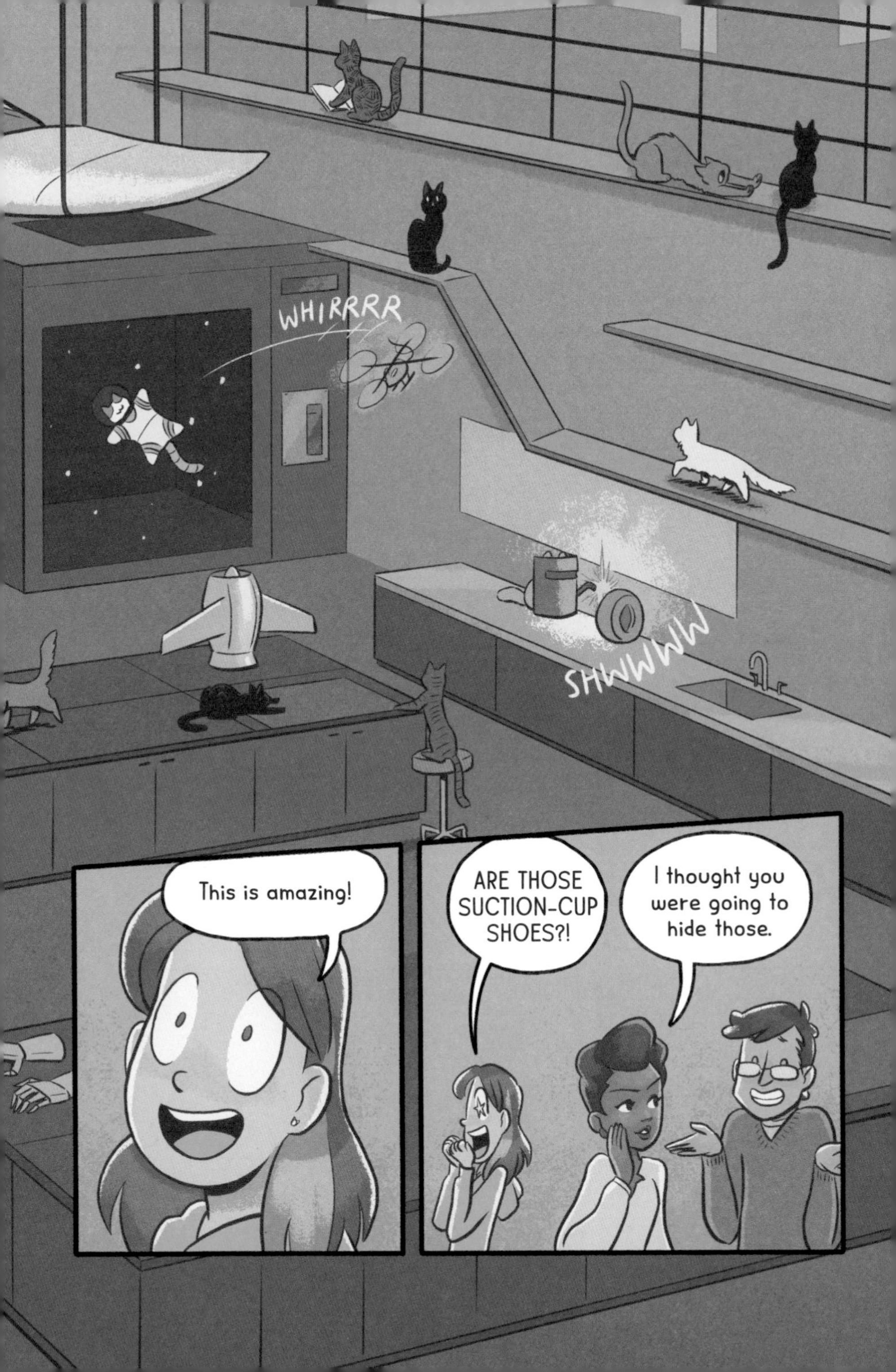
WHIRRRR
SHWWWW
This is amazing!
ARE THOSE SUCTION-CUP SHOES?!
I thought you were going to hide those.

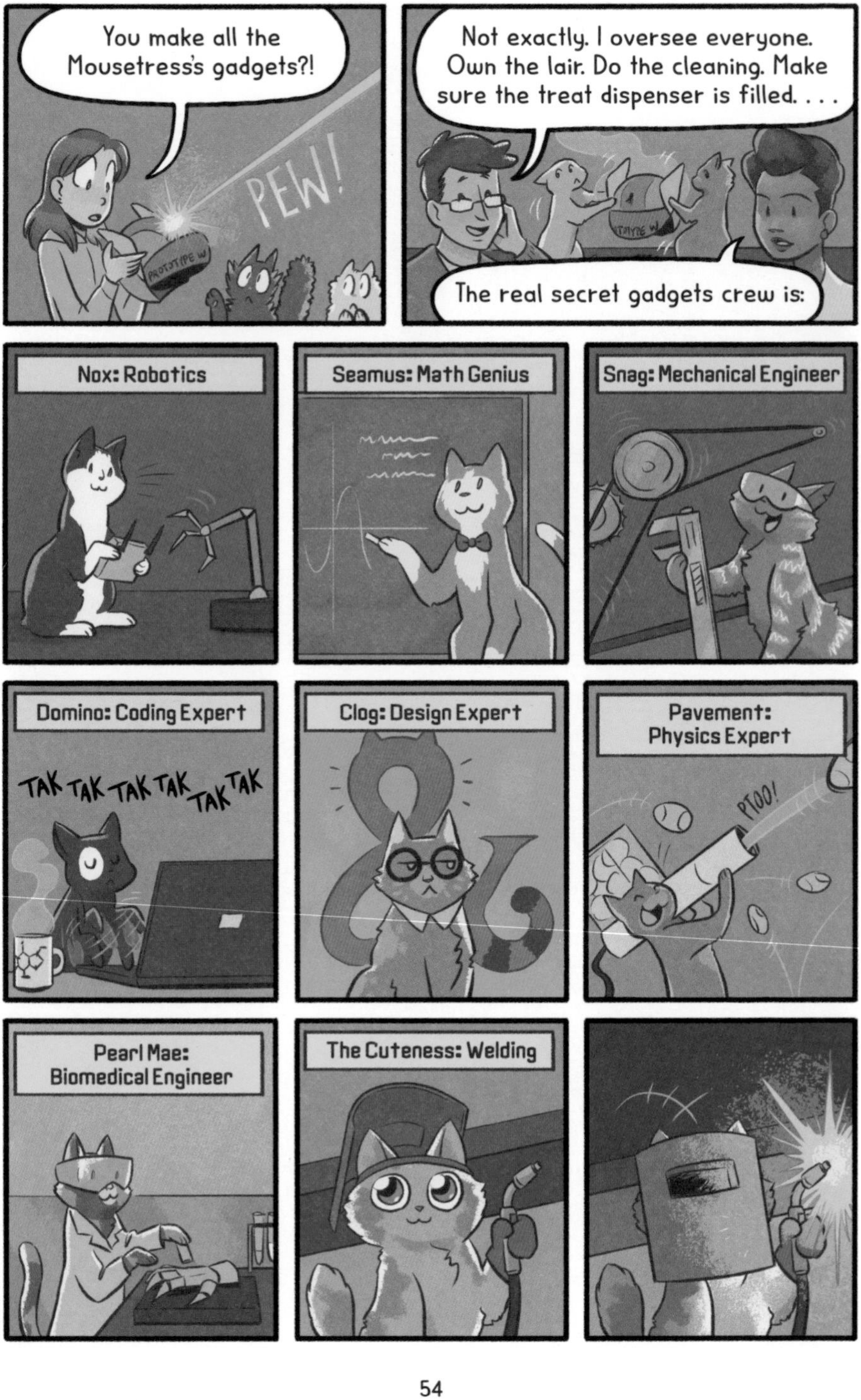
You make all the Mousetress's gadgets?!
PEW!
PROTOTYPE W
Not exactly. I oversee everyone. Own the lair. Do the cleaning. Make sure the treat dispenser is filled. . . .
The real secret gadgets crew is:
Nox: Robotics
Seamus: Math Genius
Snag: Mechanical Engineer
Domino: Coding Expert
TAK TAK TAK TAK TAK TAK
Clog: Design Expert
Pavement: Physics Expert
PTOO!
Pearl Mae: Biomedical Engineer
The Cuteness: Welding

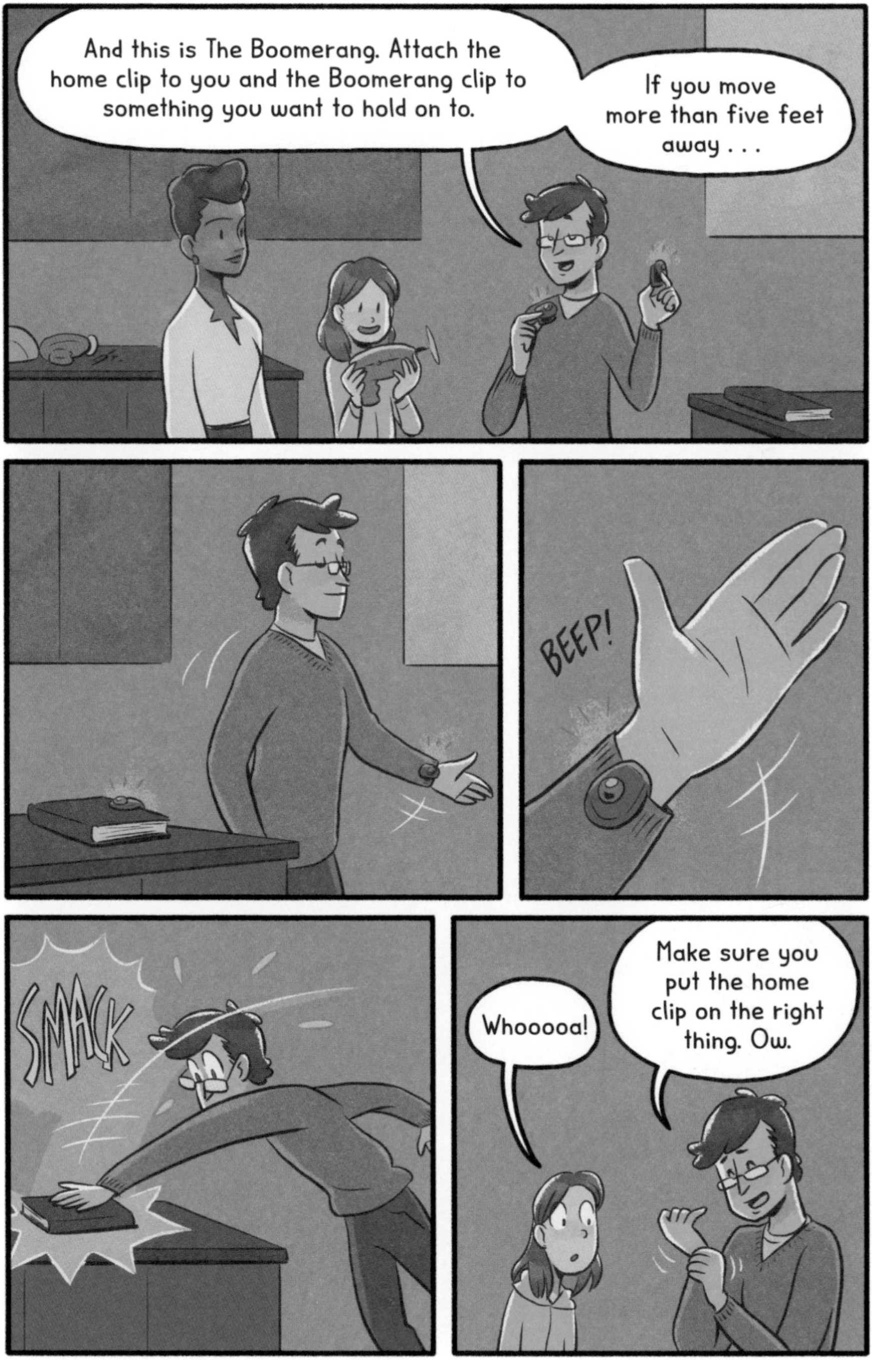
And this is The Boomerang. Attach the home clip to you and the Boomerang clip to something you want to hold on to.
If you move more than five feet away . . .
BEEP!
SMACK
Whooooa!
Make sure you put the home clip on the right thing. Ow.

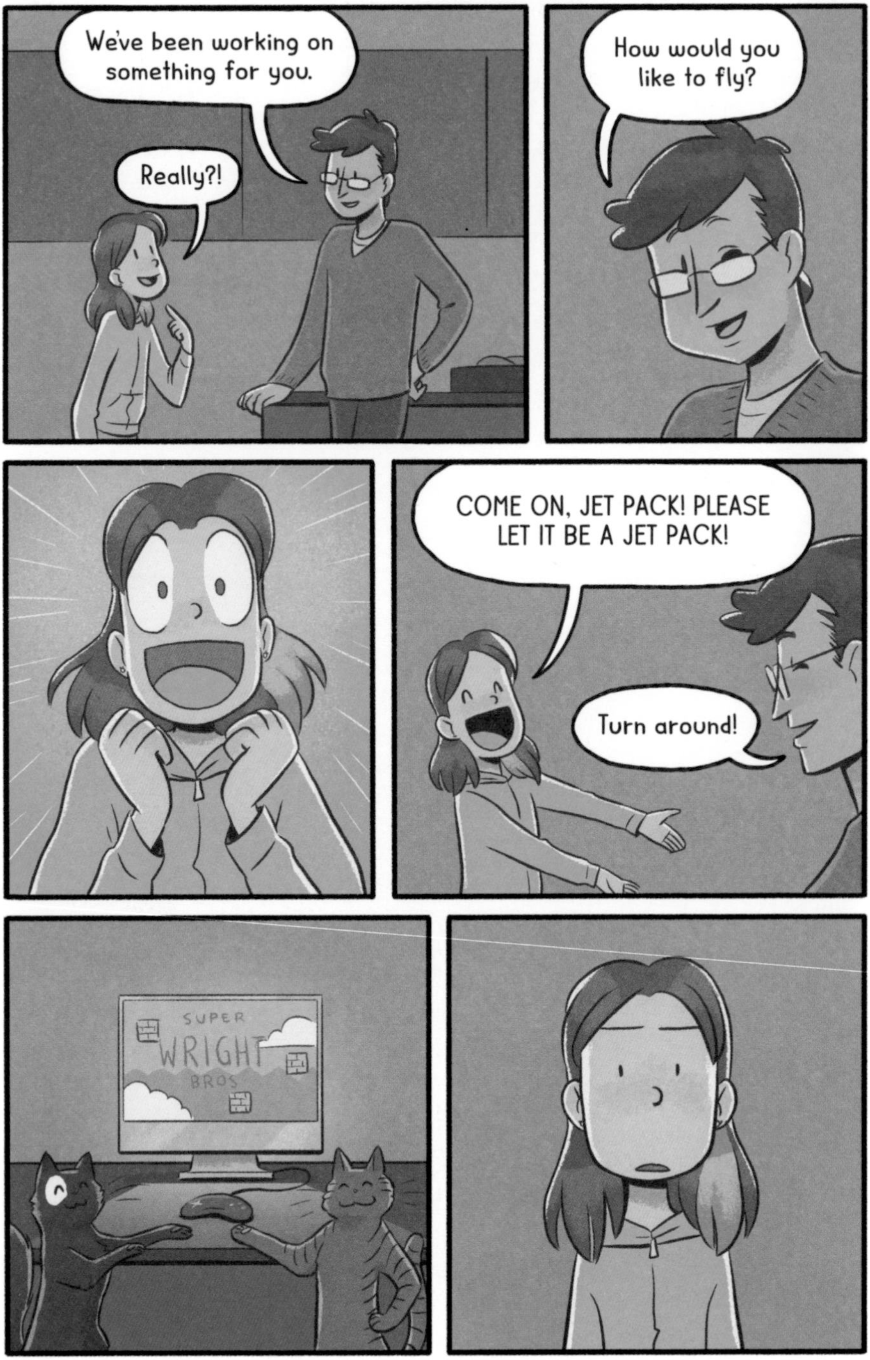
We've been working on something for you.
Really?!
How would you like to fly?
COME ON, JET PACK! PLEASE LET IT BE A JET PACK!
Turn around!
SUPER WRIGHT BROS

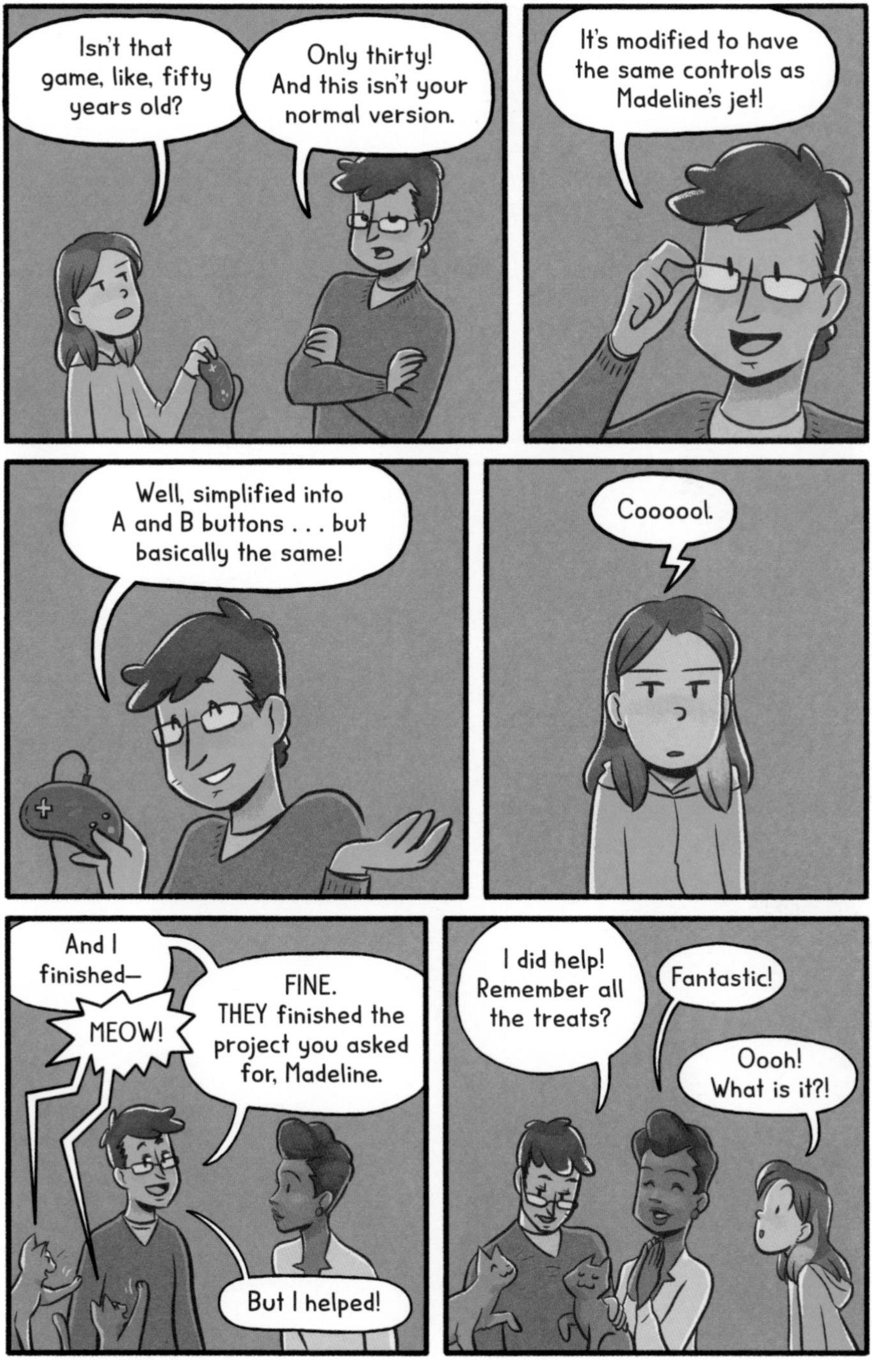

Isn't that game, like, fifty years old?
Only thirty! And this isn't your normal version.
It's modified to have the same controls as Madeline's jet!
Well, simplified into A and B buttons . . . but basically the same!
Coooool.
And I finished—
MEOW!
FINE. THEY finished the project you asked for, Madeline.
But I helped!
I did help! Remember all the treats?
Fantastic!
Oooh! What is it?!

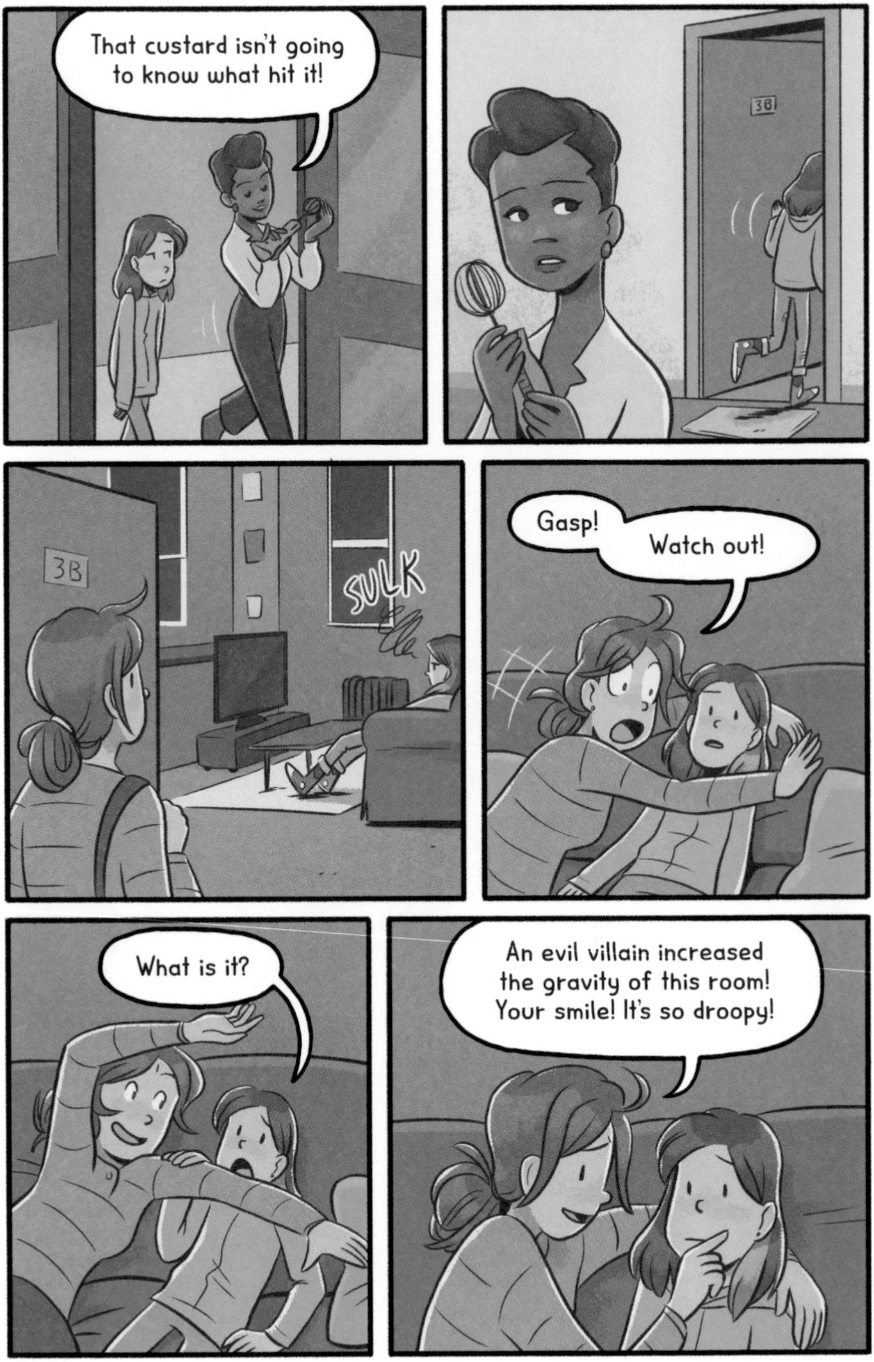
That custard isn't going to know what hit it!
3B
3B
SULK
Gasp!
Watch out!
What is it?
An evil villain increased the gravity of this room! Your smile! It's so droopy!

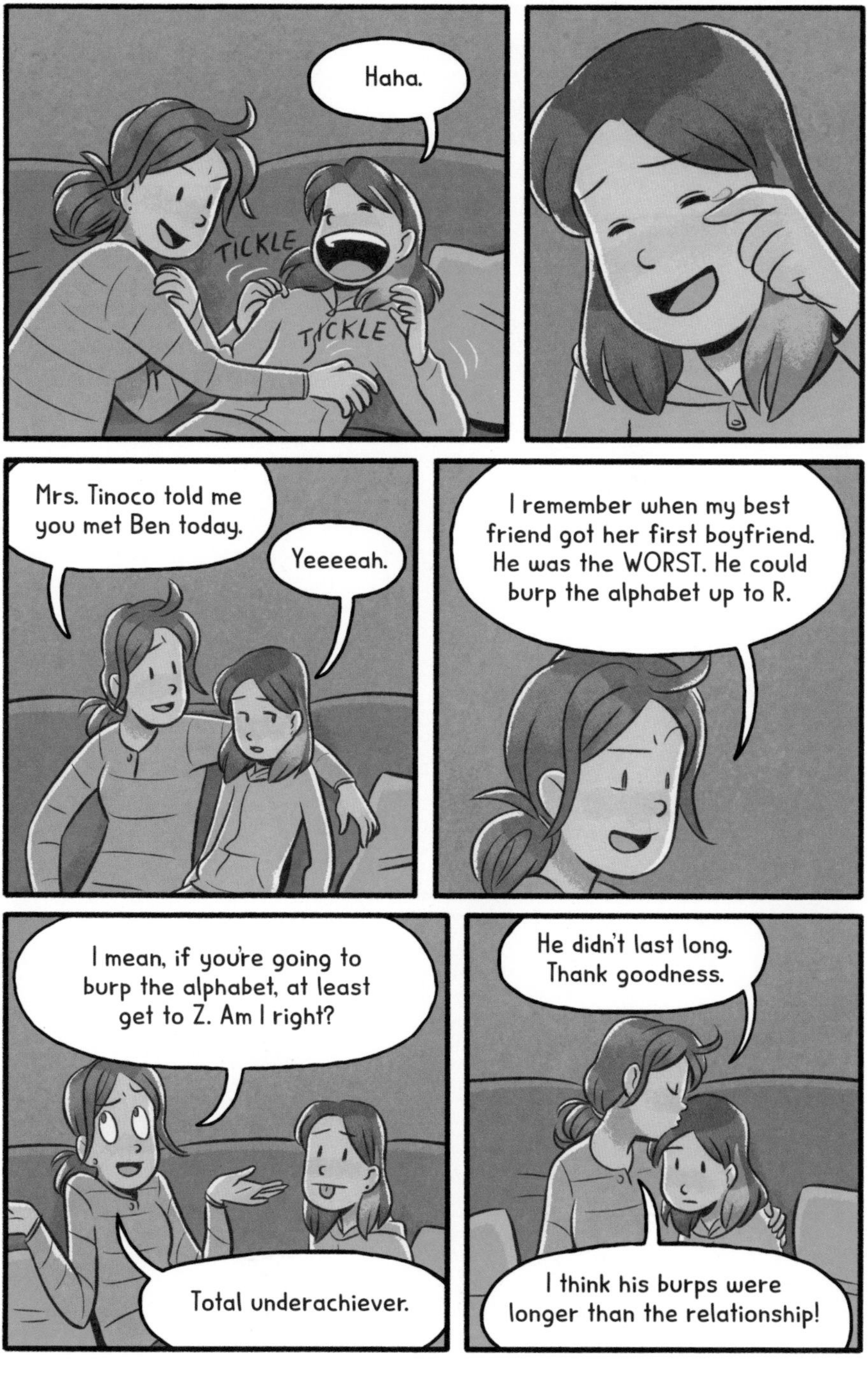
Haha.
TICKLE
TICKLE
Mrs. Tinoco told me you met Ben today.
Yeeeeah.
I remember when my best friend got her first boyfriend. He was the WORST. He could burp the alphabet up to R.
I mean, if you're going to burp the alphabet, at least get to Z. Am I right?
Total underachiever.
He didn't last long. Thank goodness.
I think his burps were longer than the relationship!

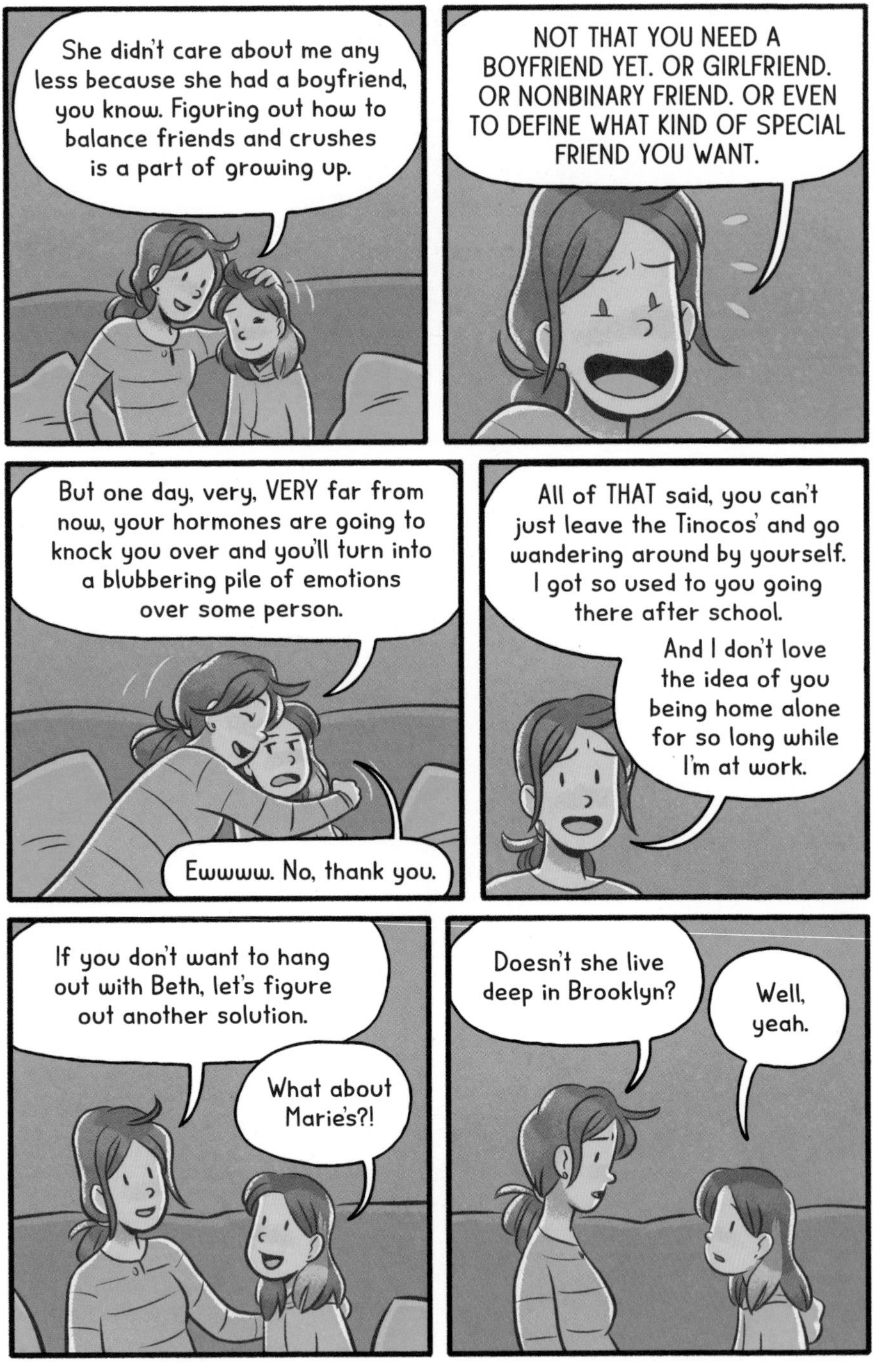
She didn't care about me any less because she had a boyfriend, you know. Figuring out how to balance friends and crushes is a part of growing up.
NOT THAT YOU NEED A BOYFRIEND YET. OR GIRLFRIEND. OR NONBINARY FRIEND. OR EVEN TO DEFINE WHAT KIND OF SPECIAL FRIEND YOU WANT.
But one day, very, VERY far from now, your hormones are going to knock you over and you'll turn into a blubbering pile of emotions over some person.
Ewwww. No, thank you.
All of THAT said, you can't just leave the Tinocos' and go wandering around by yourself. I got so used to you going there after school.
And I don't love the idea of you being home alone for so long while I'm at work.
If you don't want to hang out with Beth, let's figure out another solution.
What about Marie's?!
Doesn't she live deep in Brooklyn?
Well, yeah.

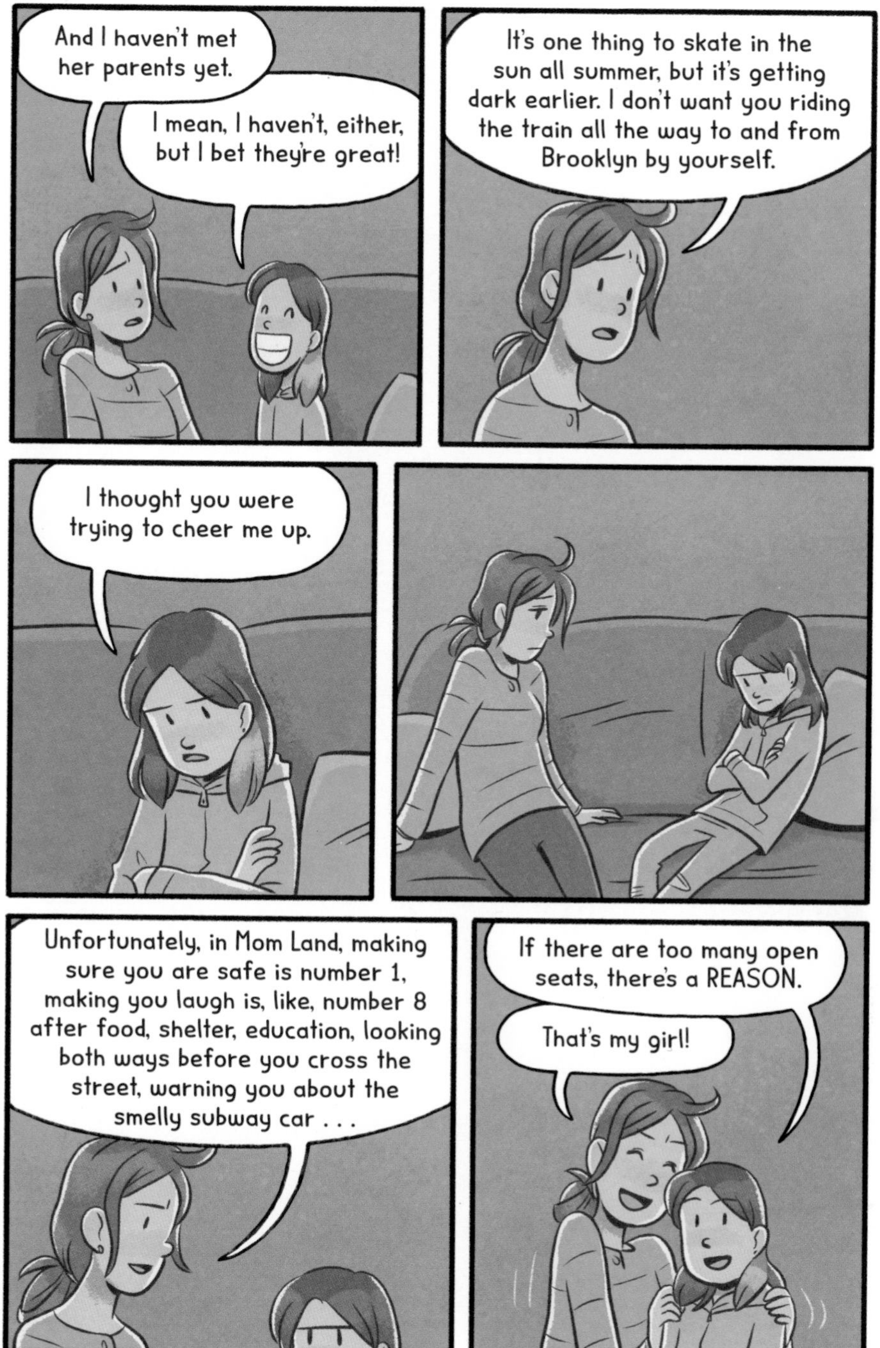
And I haven't met her parents yet.
I mean, I haven't, either, but I bet they're great!
It's one thing to skate in the sun all summer, but it's getting dark earlier. I don't want you riding the train all the way to and from Brooklyn by yourself.
I thought you were trying to cheer me up.
Unfortunately, in Mom Land, making sure you are safe is number 1, making you laugh is, like, number 8 after food, shelter, education, looking both ways before you cross the street, warning you about the smelly subway car . . .
If there are too many open seats, there's a REASON.
That's my girl!

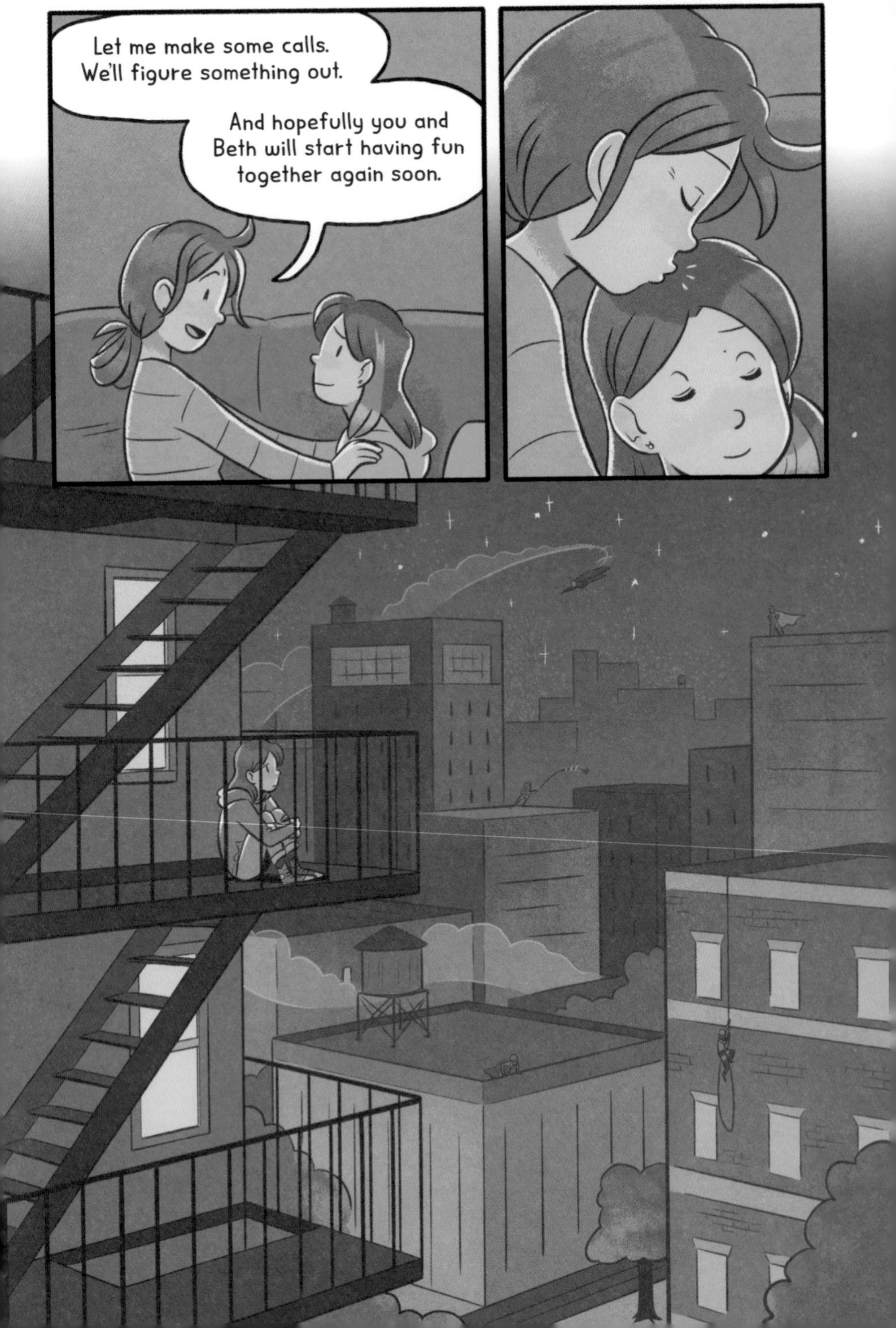
Let me make some calls. We'll figure something out.
And hopefully you and Beth will start having fun together again soon.

CHAPTER FIVE

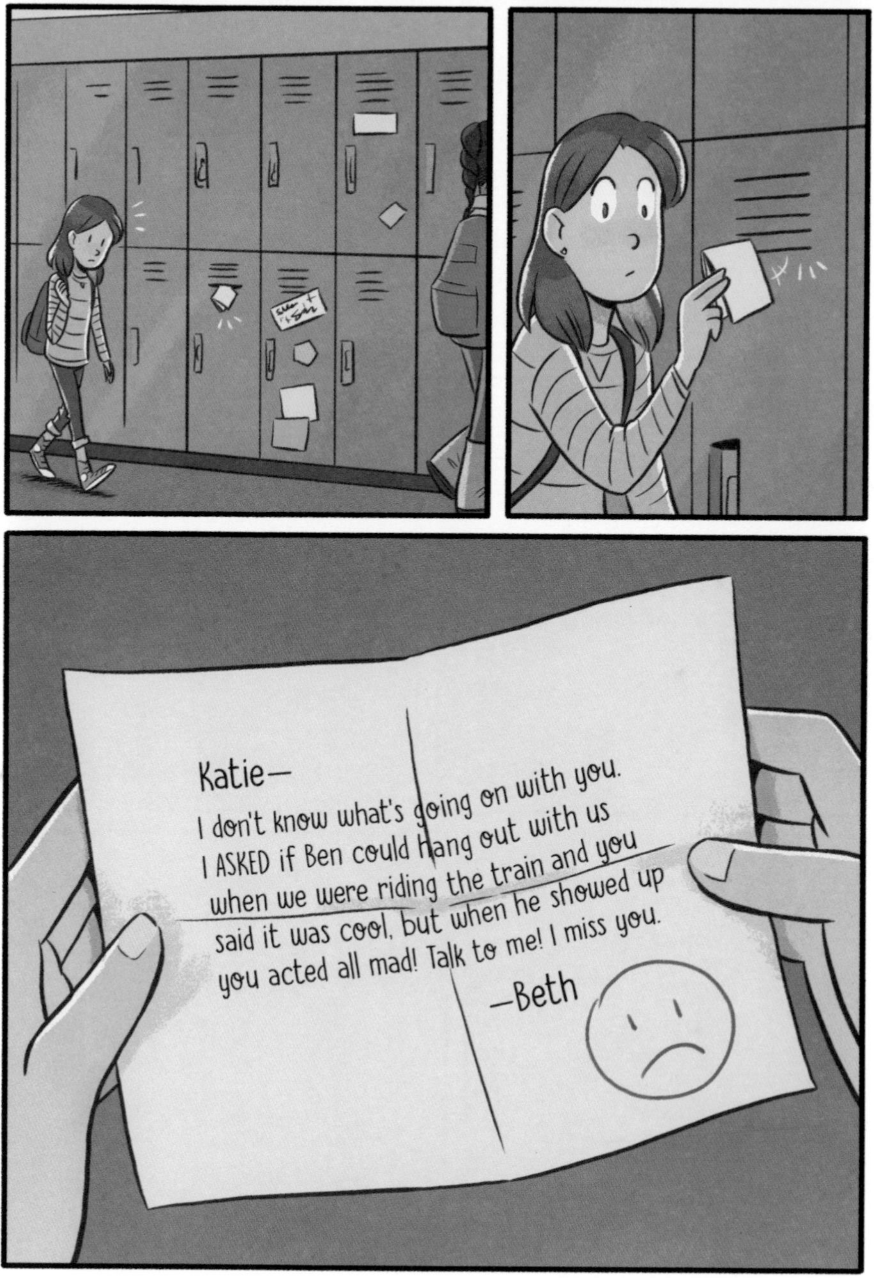
Katie—
I don't know what's going on with you.
I ASKED if Ben could hang out with us
when we were riding the train and you
said it was cool, but when he showed up
you acted all mad! Talk to me! I miss you.
—Beth

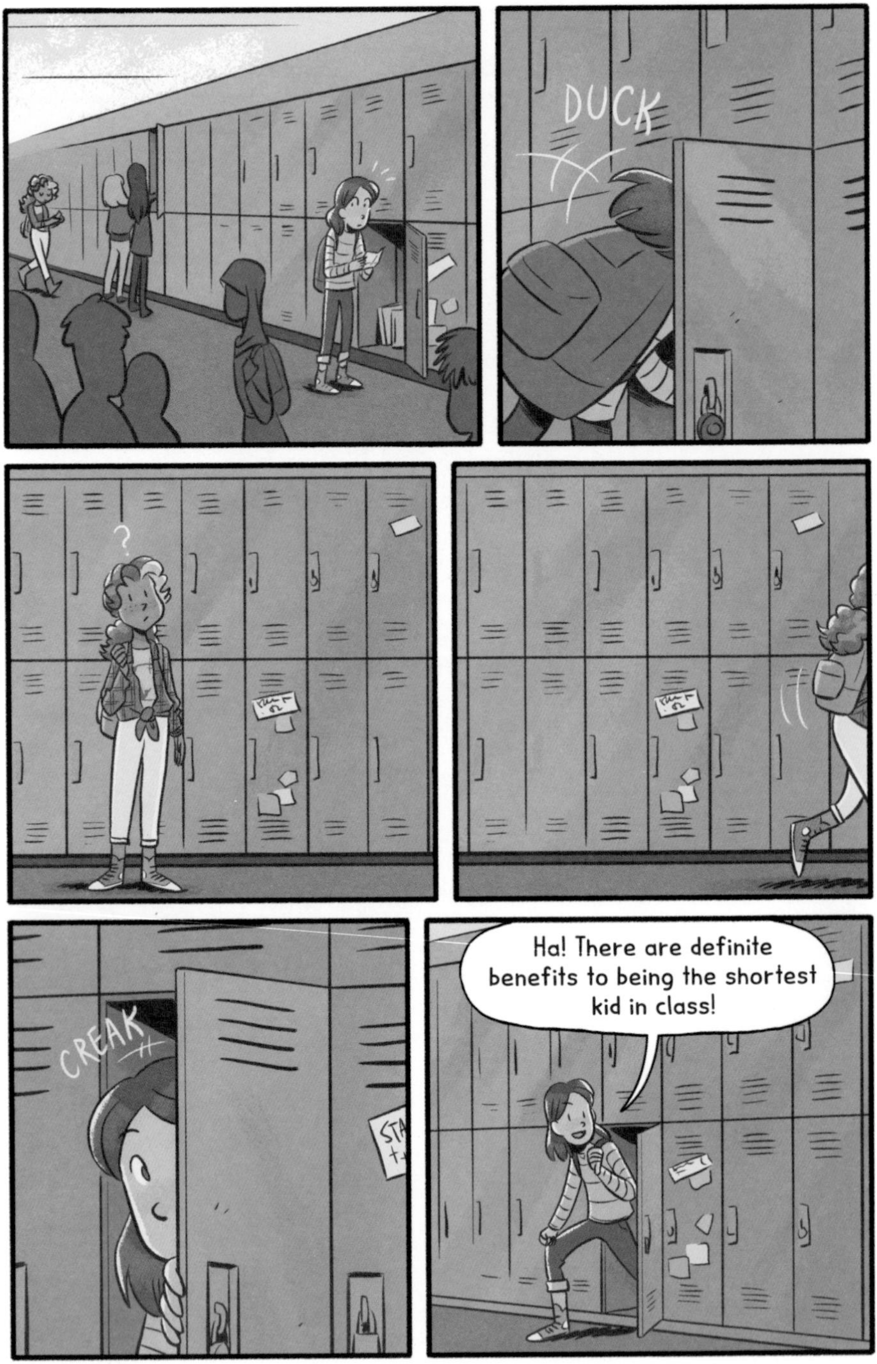
DUCK
CREAK
Ha! There are definite benefits to being the shortest kid in class!

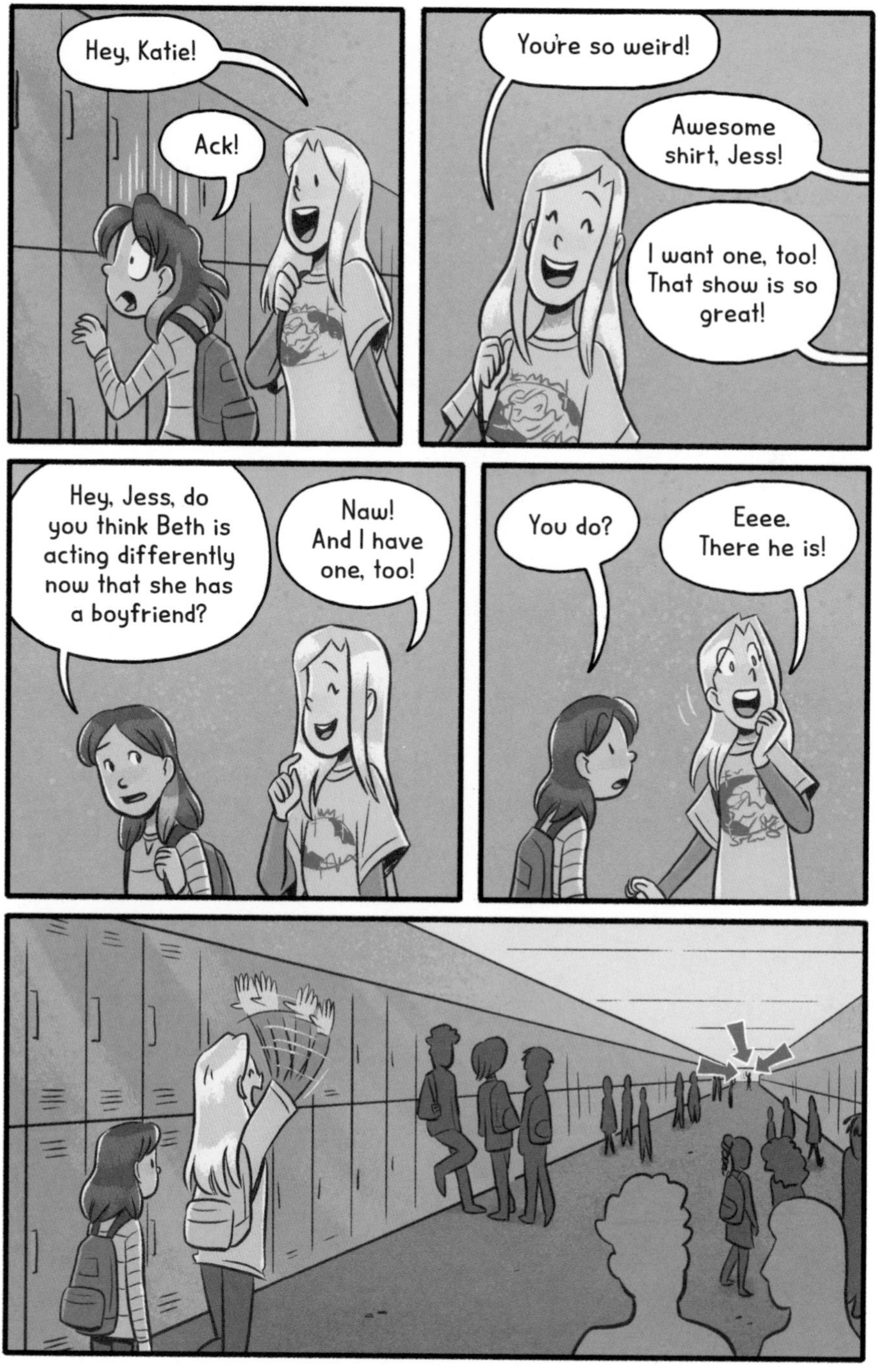
Hey, Katie!
Ack!
You're so weird!
Awesome shirt, Jess!
I want one, too! That show is so great!
Hey, Jess, do you think Beth is acting differently now that she has a boyfriend?
Naw! And I have one, too!
You do?
Eeee. There he is!

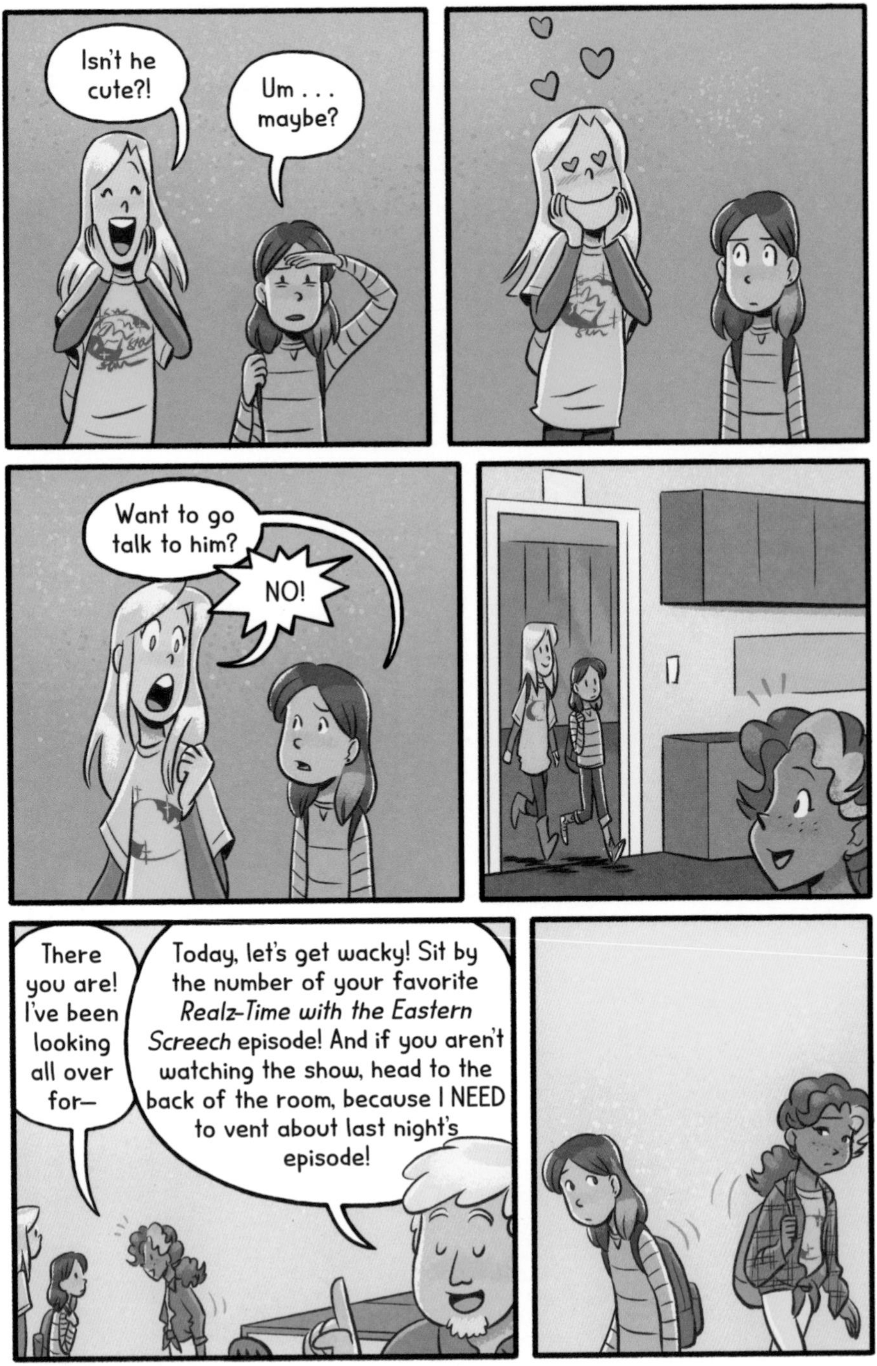

Isn't he cute?!
Um . . . maybe?
Want to go talk to him?
NO!
There you are! I've been looking all over for—
Today, let's get wacky! Sit by the number of your favorite *Realz-Time with the Eastern Screech* episode! And if you aren't watching the show, head to the back of the room, because I NEED to vent about last night's episode!

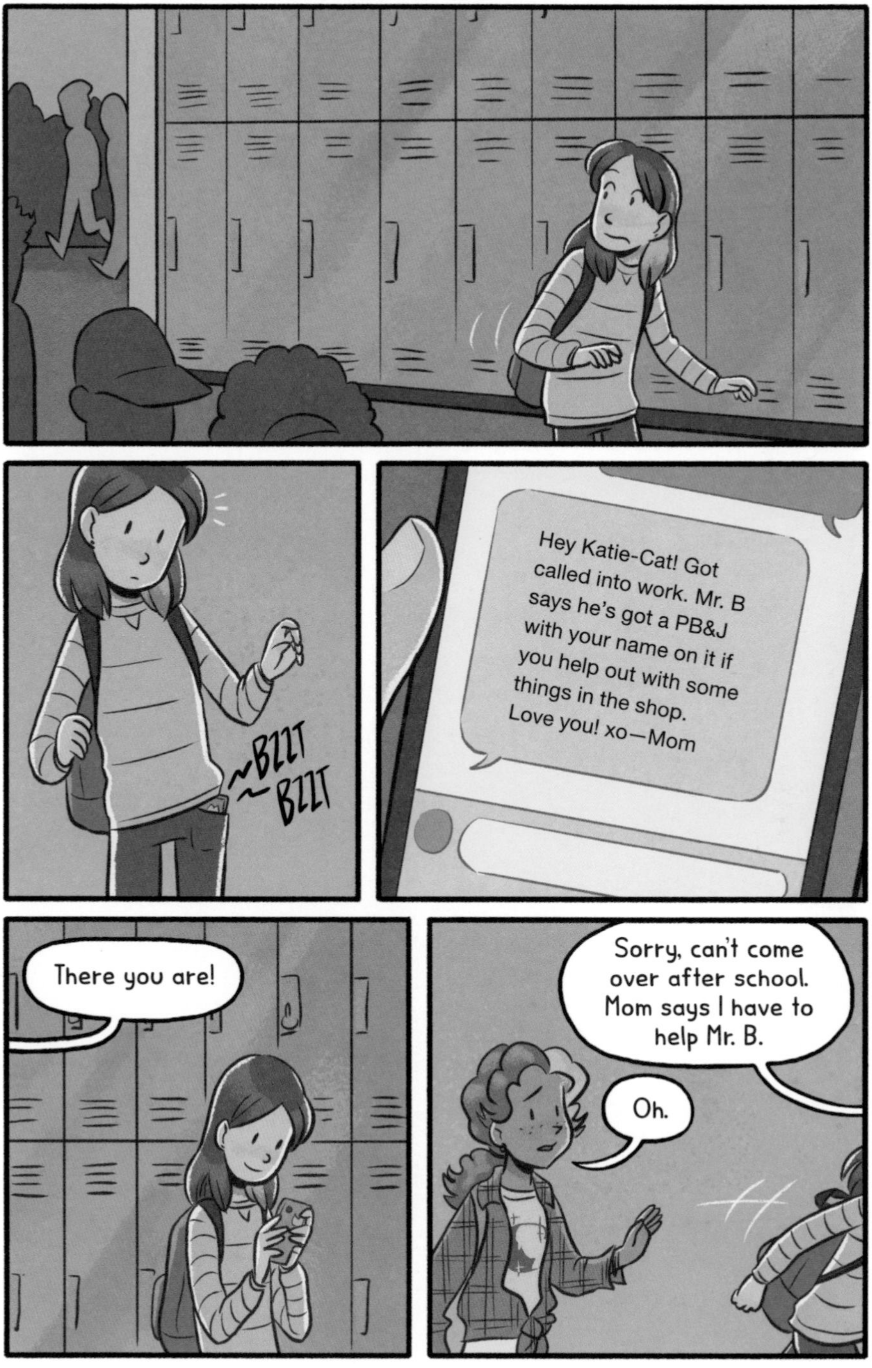
~BZZT
~BZZT
Hey Katie-Cat! Got called into work. Mr. B says he's got a PB&J with your name on it if you help out with some things in the shop. Love you! xo—Mom
There you are!
Sorry, can't come over after school. Mom says I have to help Mr. B.
Oh.

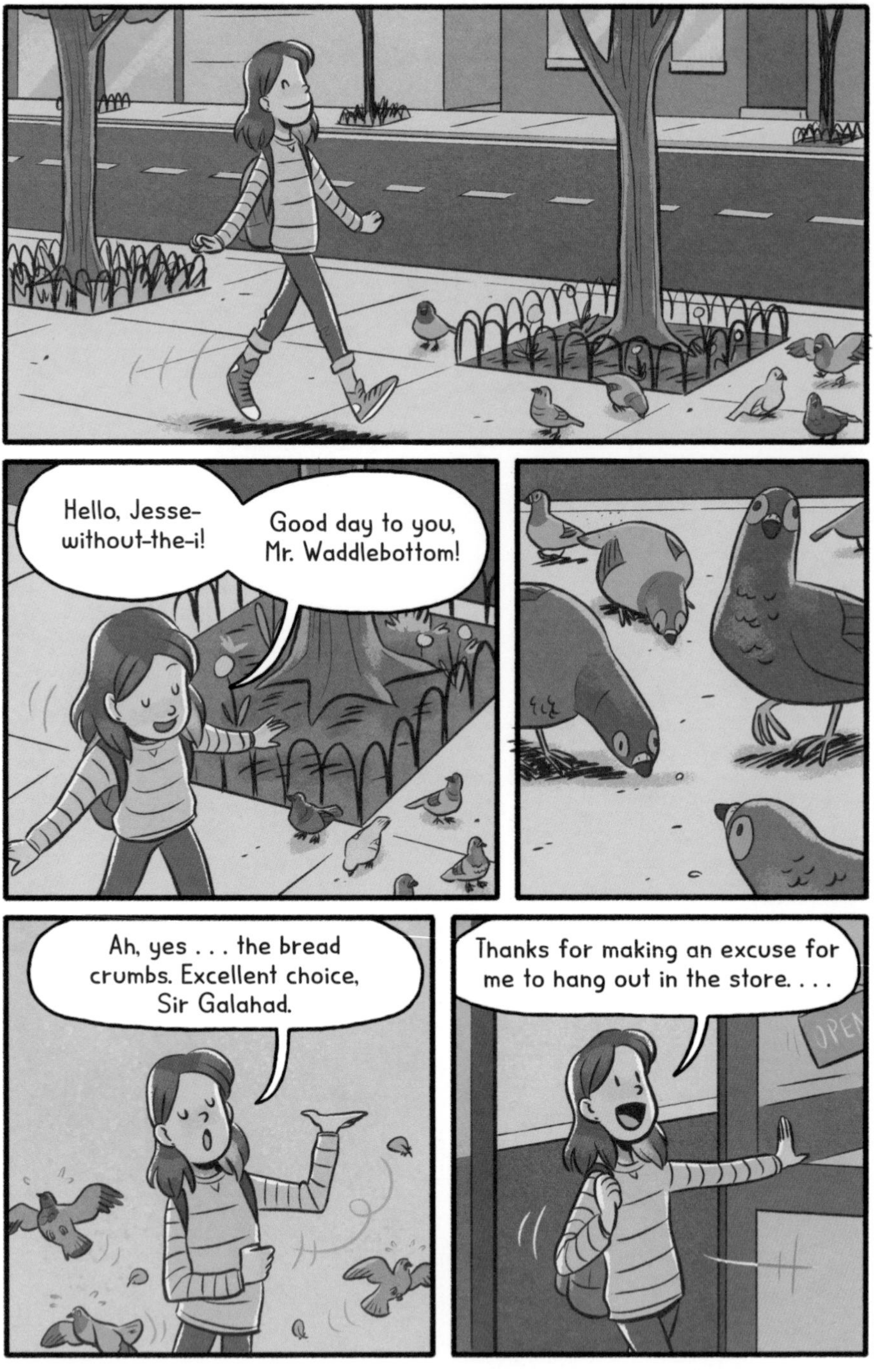

Hello, Jesse-without-the-i!
Good day to you, Mr. Waddlebottom!
Ah, yes . . . the bread crumbs. Excellent choice, Sir Galahad.
Thanks for making an excuse for me to hang out in the store. . . .
OPEN

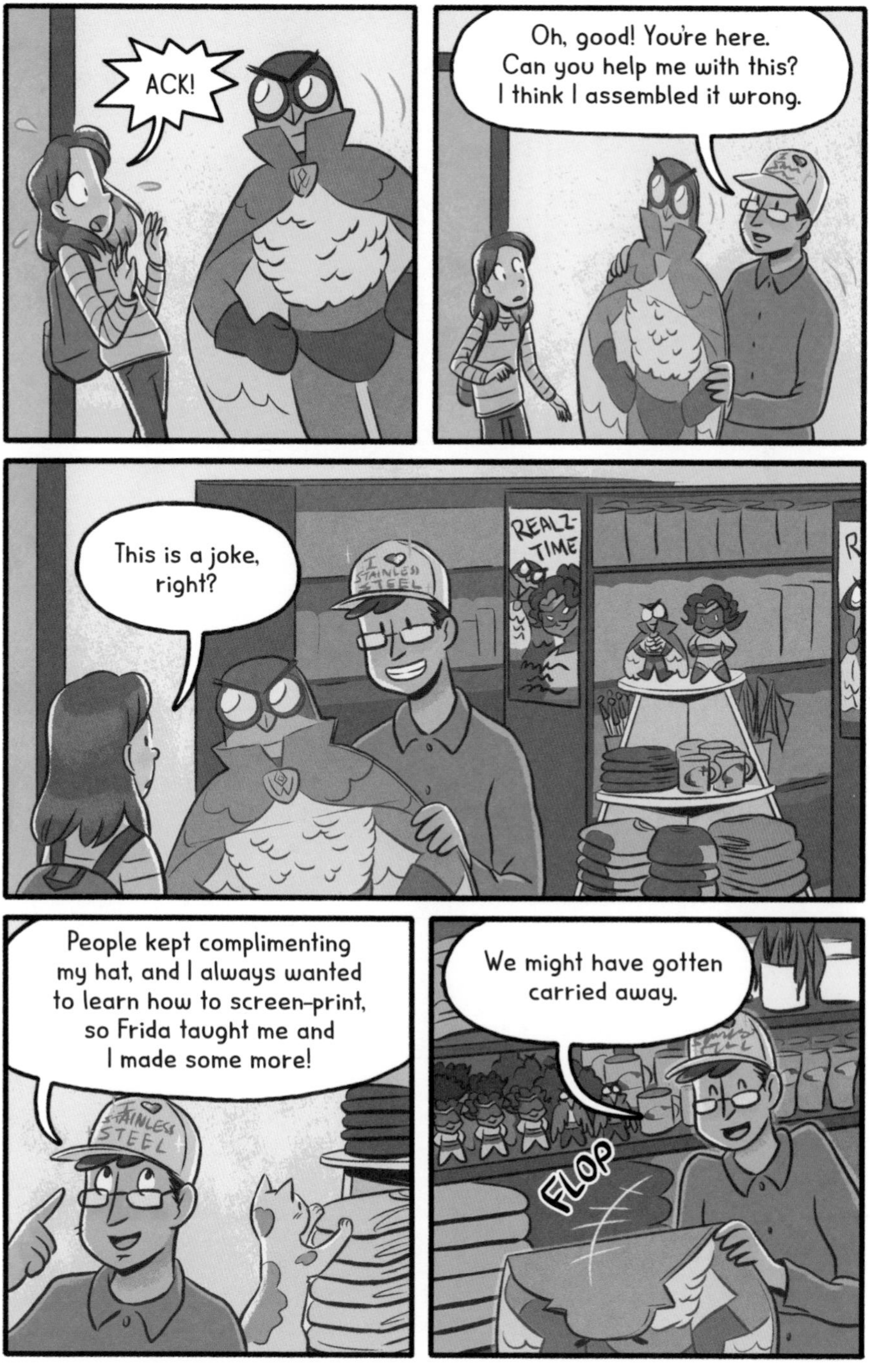
ACK!
Oh, good! You're here. Can you help me with this? I think I assembled it wrong.
REALZ-TIME
I STAINLESS STEEL
This is a joke, right?
People kept complimenting my hat, and I always wanted to learn how to screen-print, so Frida taught me and I made some more!
STAINLESS STEEL
We might have gotten carried away.
FLOP

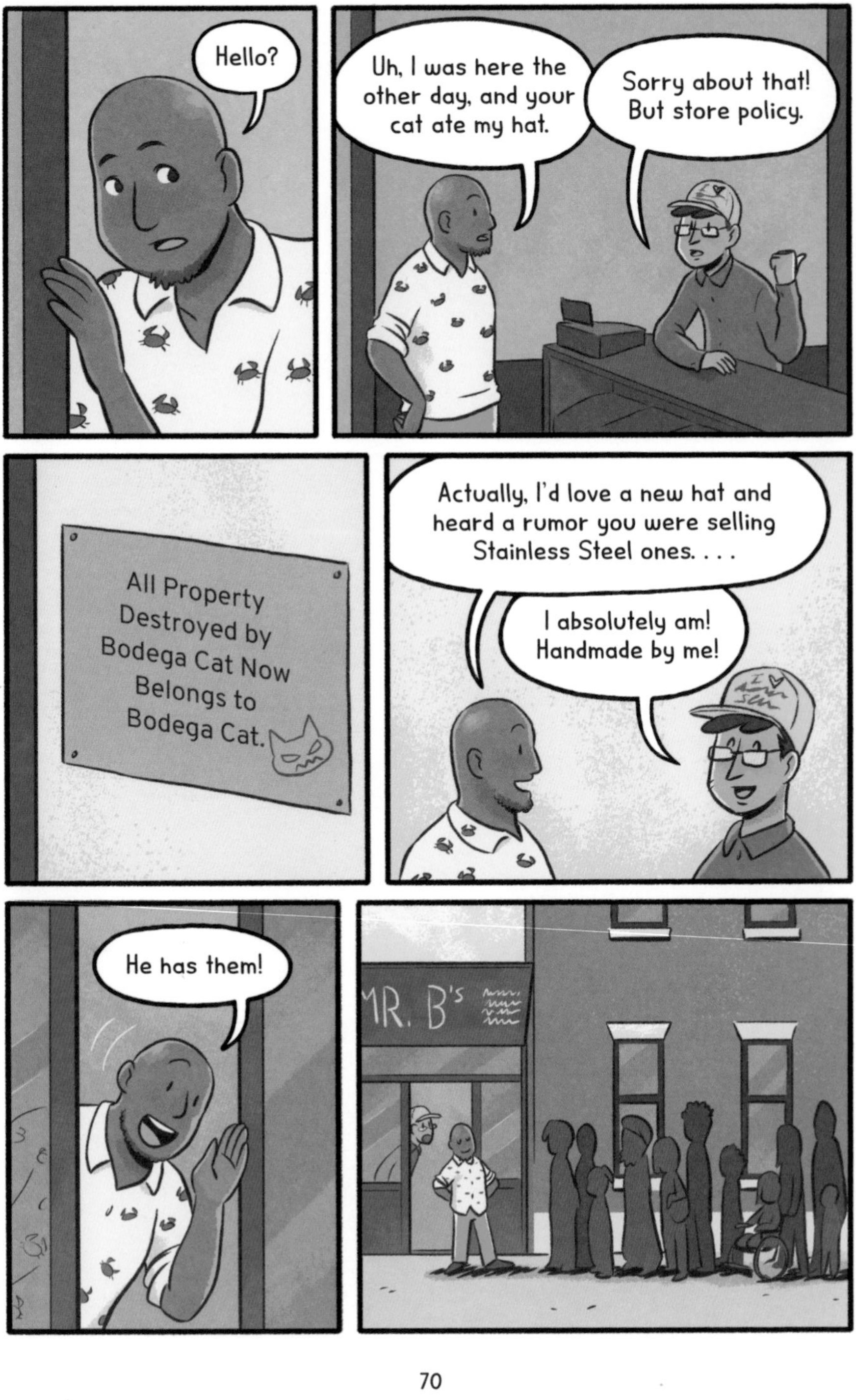
Hello?
Uh, I was here the other day, and your cat ate my hat.
Sorry about that! But store policy.
All Property Destroyed by Bodega Cat Now Belongs to Bodega Cat.
Actually, I'd love a new hat and heard a rumor you were selling Stainless Steel ones. . . .
I absolutely am! Handmade by me!
He has them!
MR. B's

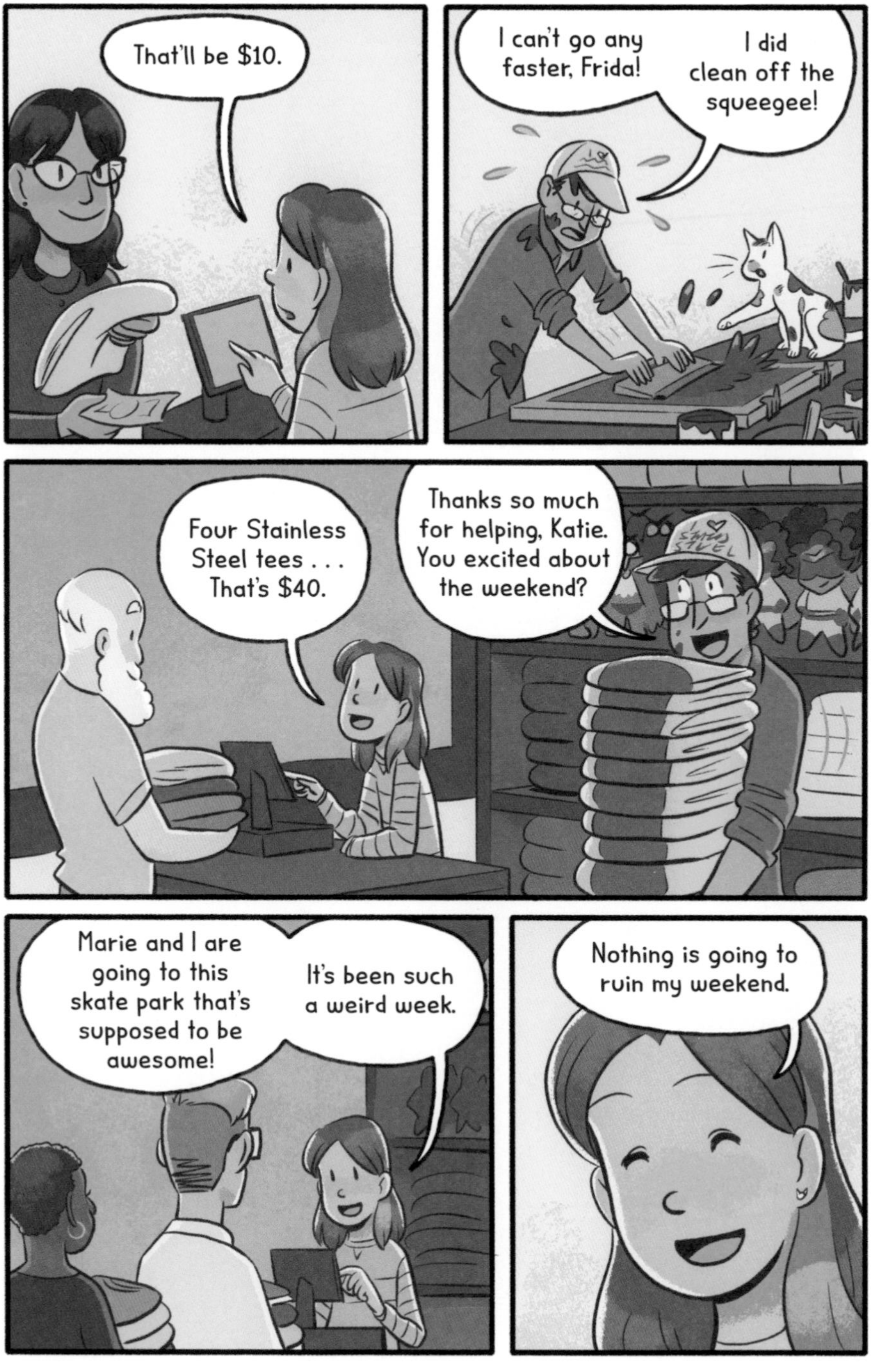
That'll be $10.
I can't go any faster, Frida!
I did clean off the squeegee!
Four Stainless Steel tees . . . That's $40.
Thanks so much for helping, Katie. You excited about the weekend?
Marie and I are going to this skate park that's supposed to be awesome!
It's been such a weird week.
Nothing is going to ruin my weekend.

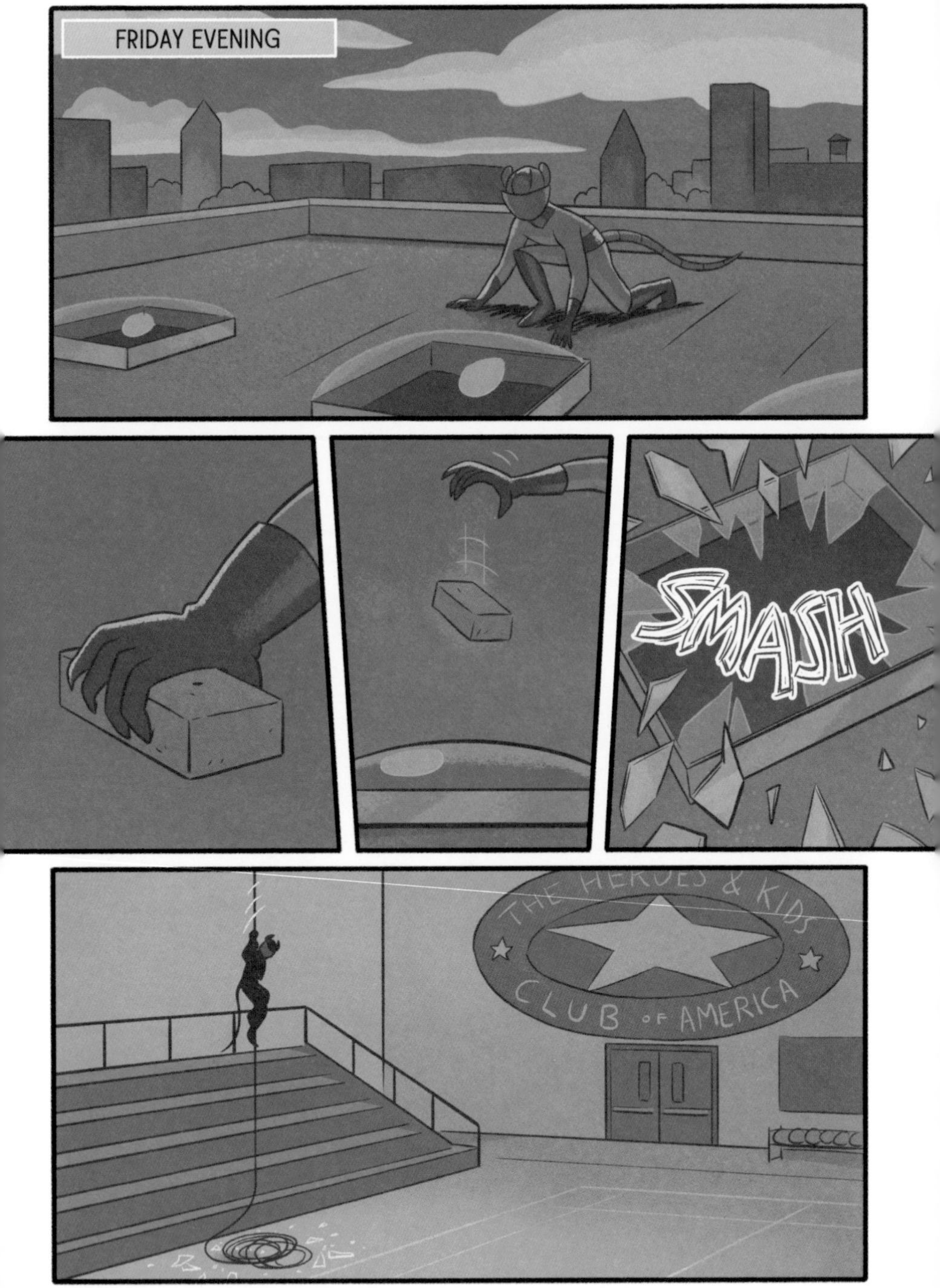
FRIDAY EVENING
SMASH
THE HEROES & KIDS CLUB OF AMERICA

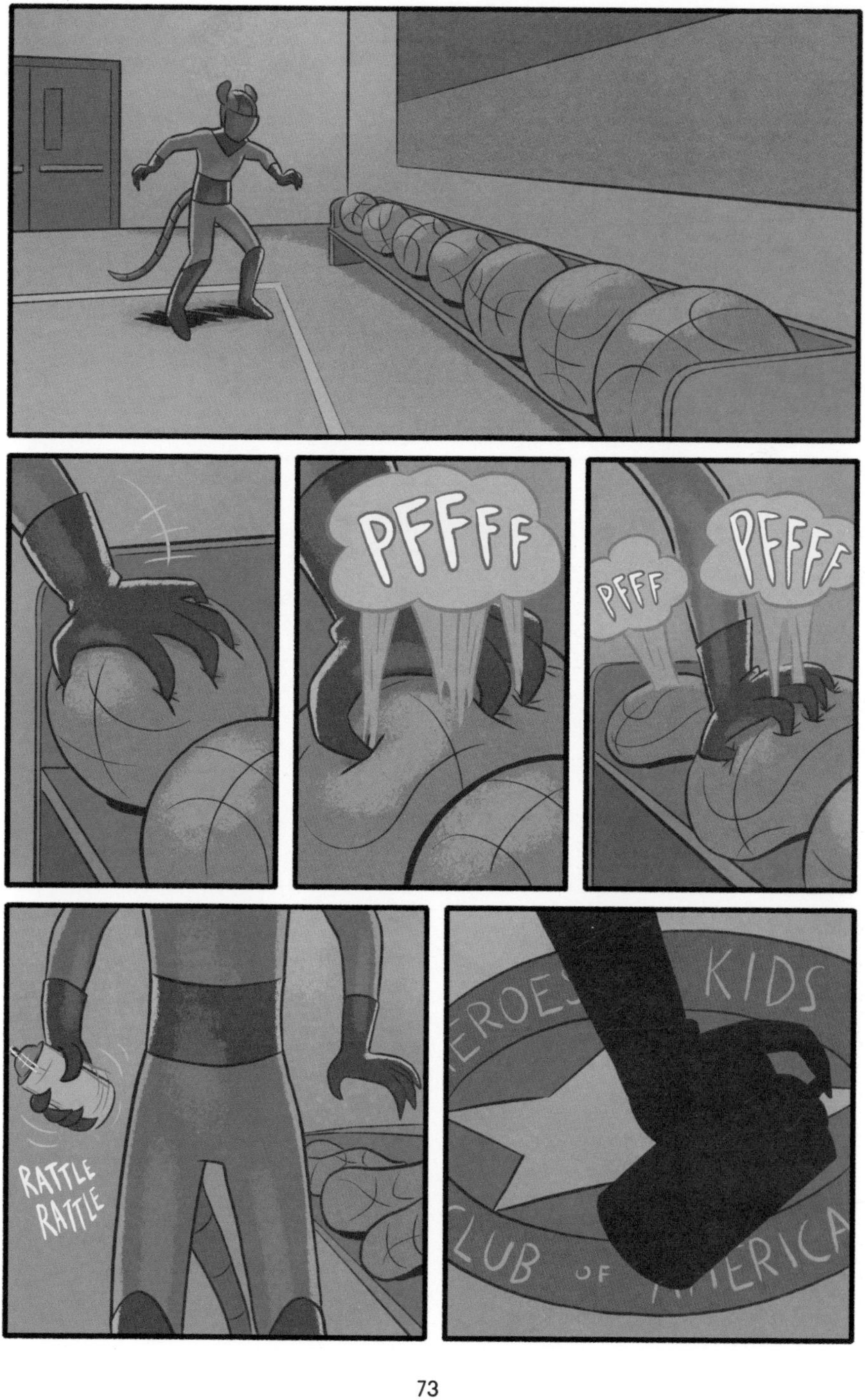
PFFFF
PFFF
PFFFF
RATTLE RATTLE
HEROES KIDS CLUB OF AMERICA

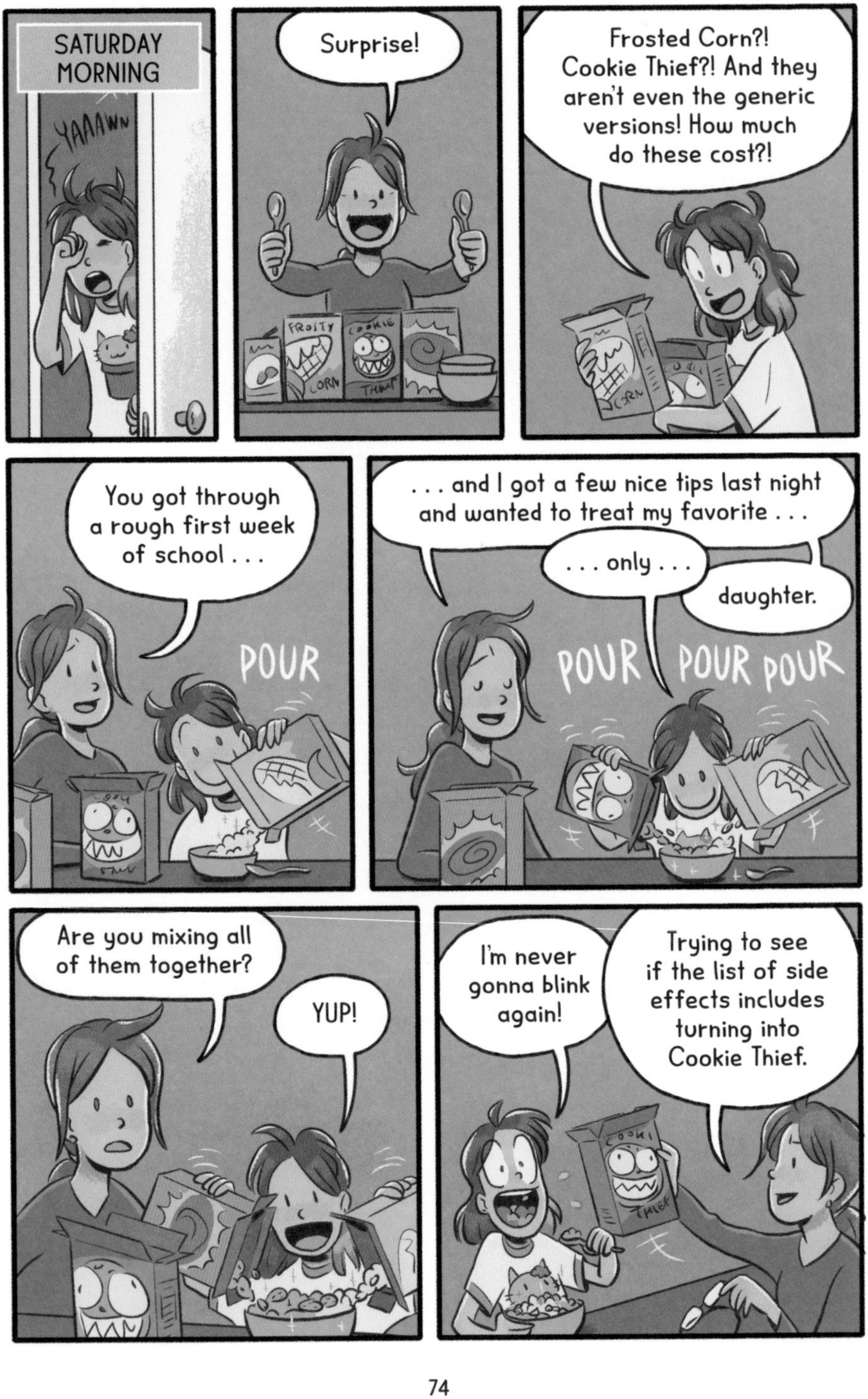
SATURDAY MORNING
YAAAWN
Surprise!
FROSTY CORN
COOKIE THIEF
Frosted Corn?! Cookie Thief?! And they aren't even the generic versions! How much do these cost?!
You got through a rough first week of school . . .
POUR
. . . and I got a few nice tips last night and wanted to treat my favorite . . .
. . . only . . .
daughter.
POUR
POUR POUR
Are you mixing all of them together?
YUP!
I'm never gonna blink again!
Trying to see if the list of side effects includes turning into Cookie Thief.

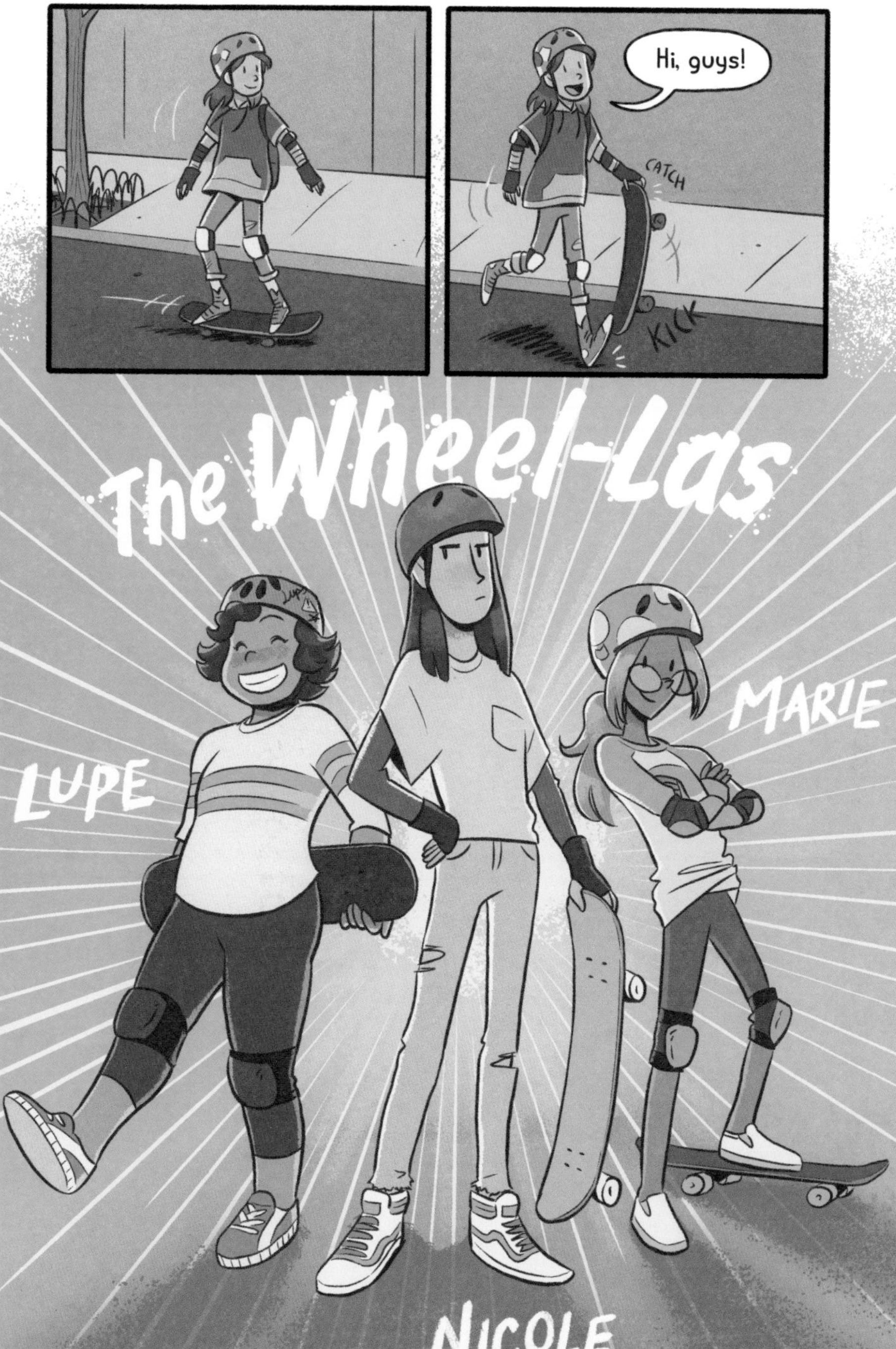
Hi, guys!
CATCH
KICK
The Wheel-Las
LUPE
MARIE
NICOLE

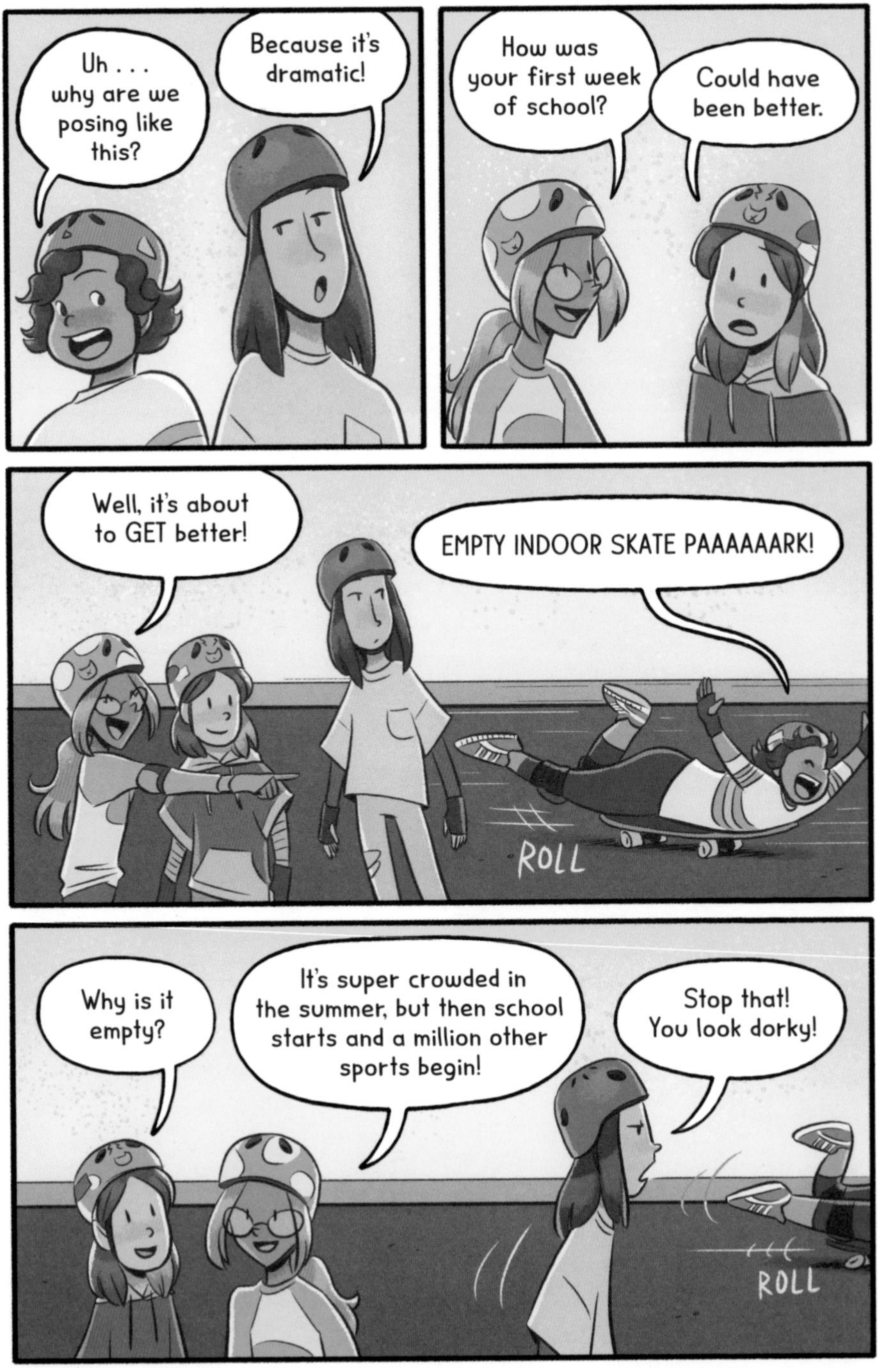
Uh . . . why are we posing like this?
Because it's dramatic!
How was your first week of school?
Could have been better.
Well, it's about to GET better!
EMPTY INDOOR SKATE PAAAAAARK!
ROLL
Why is it empty?
It's super crowded in the summer, but then school starts and a million other sports begin!
Stop that! You look dorky!
ROLL

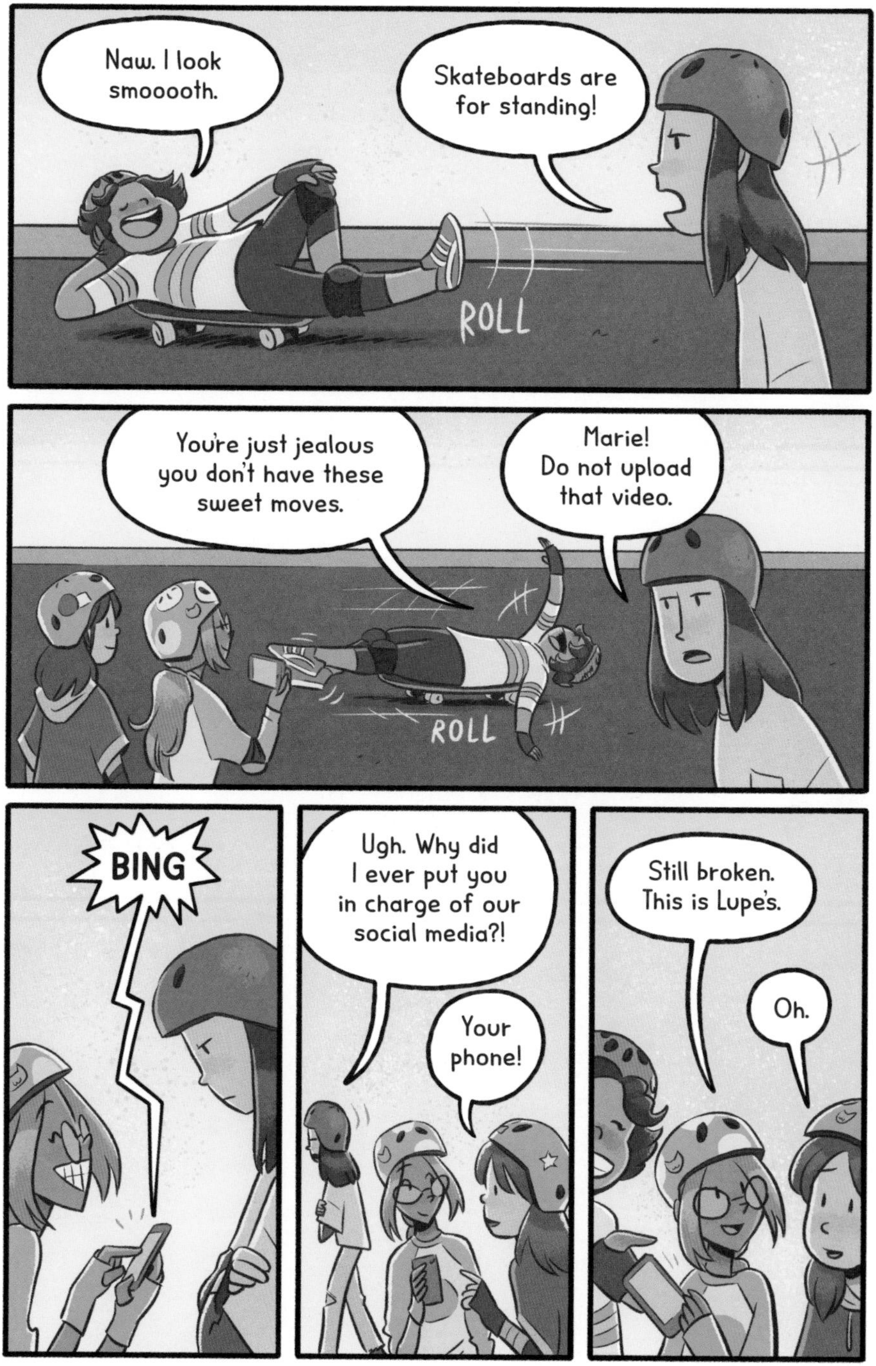
Naw. I look smoooooth.
Skateboards are for standing!
ROLL
You're just jealous you don't have these sweet moves.
Marie! Do not upload that video.
ROLL
BING
Ugh. Why did I ever put you in charge of our social media?!
Your phone!
Still broken. This is Lupe's.
Oh.

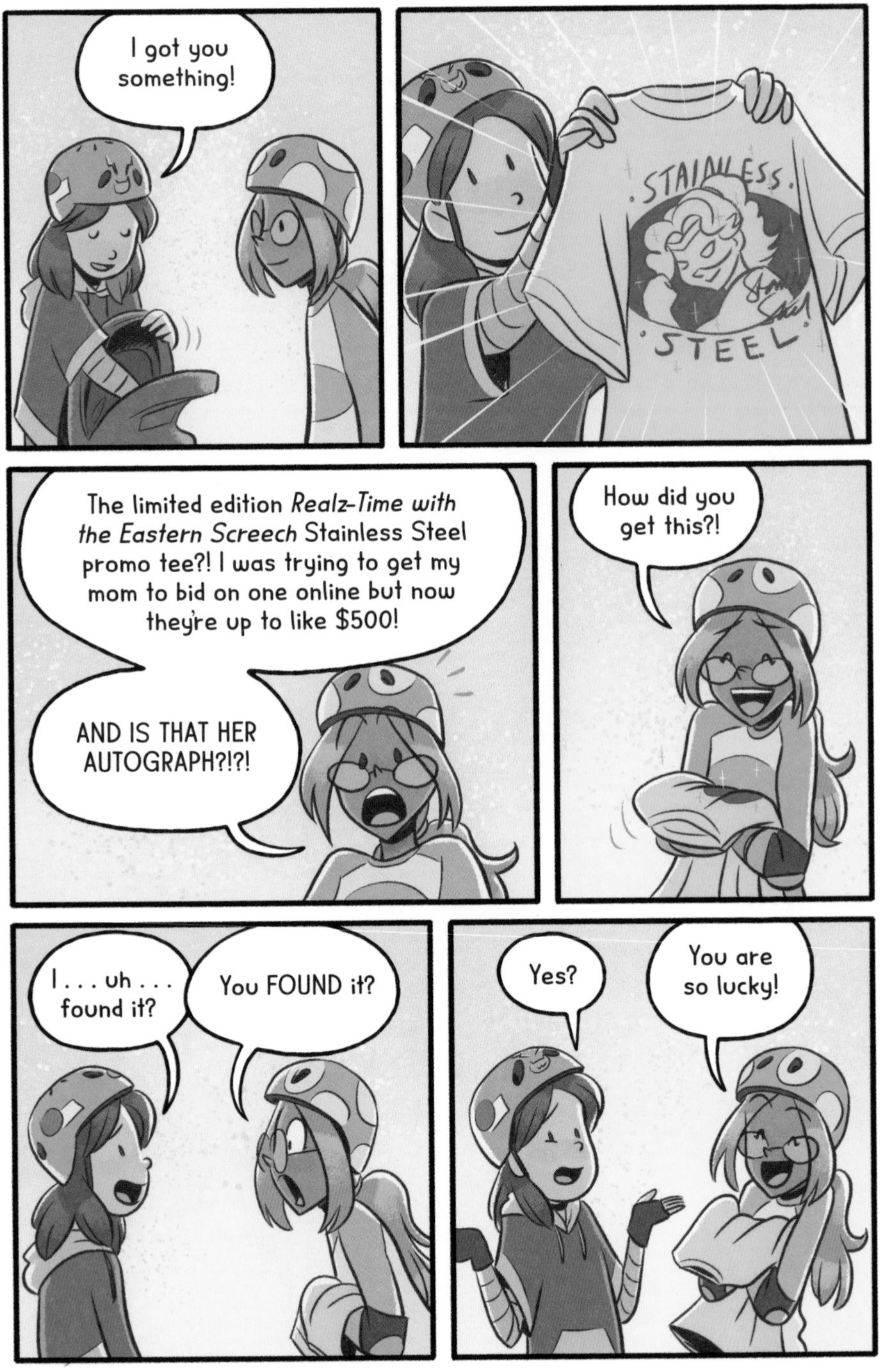
I got you something!
STAINLESS STEEL
The limited edition *Realz-Time with the Eastern Screech* Stainless Steel promo tee?! I was trying to get my mom to bid on one online but now they're up to like $500!
AND IS THAT HER AUTOGRAPH?!?!
How did you get this?!
I . . . uh . . . found it?
You FOUND it?
Yes?
You are so lucky!

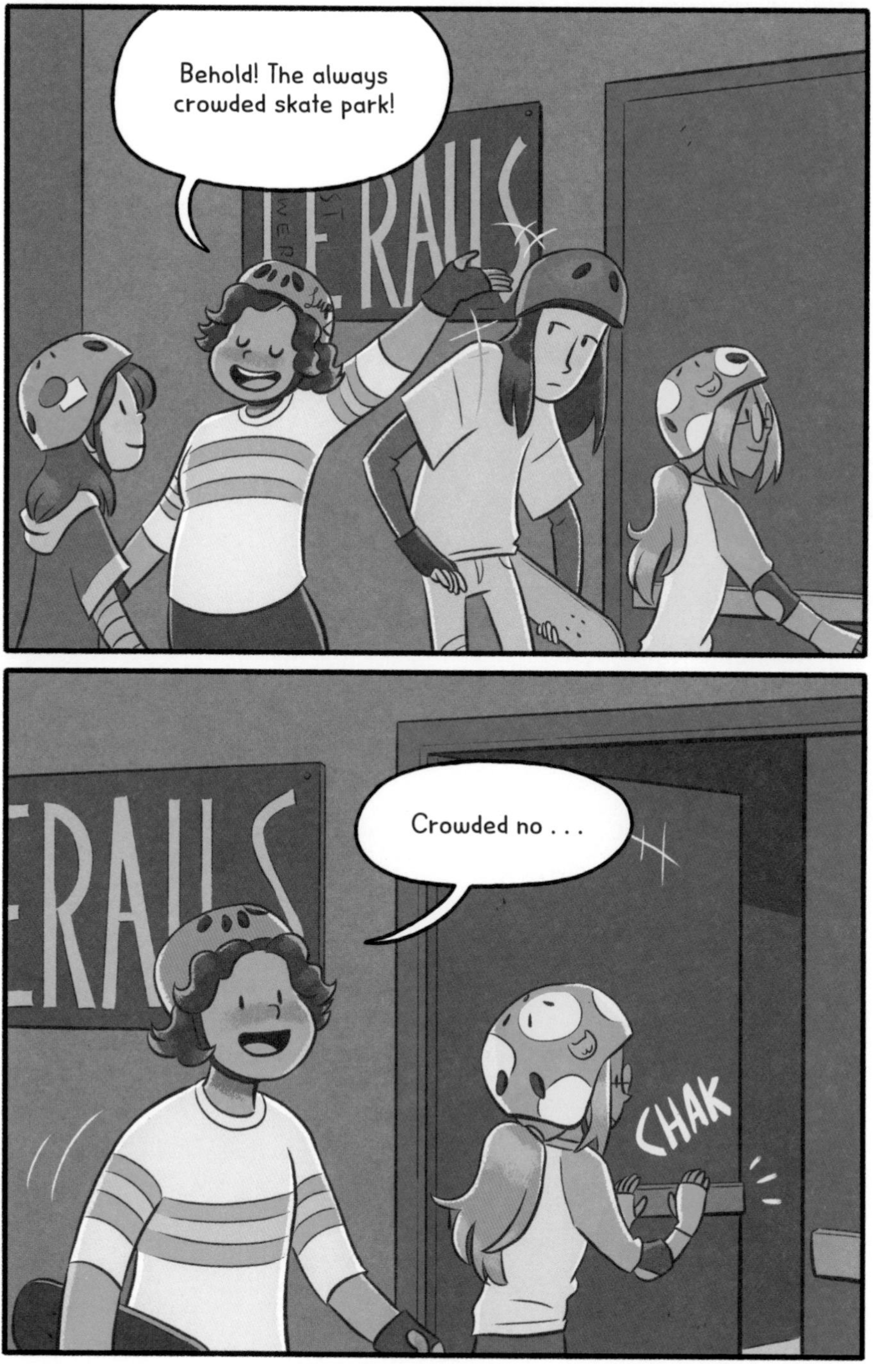
Behold! The always crowded skate park!
Crowded no . . .
CHAK

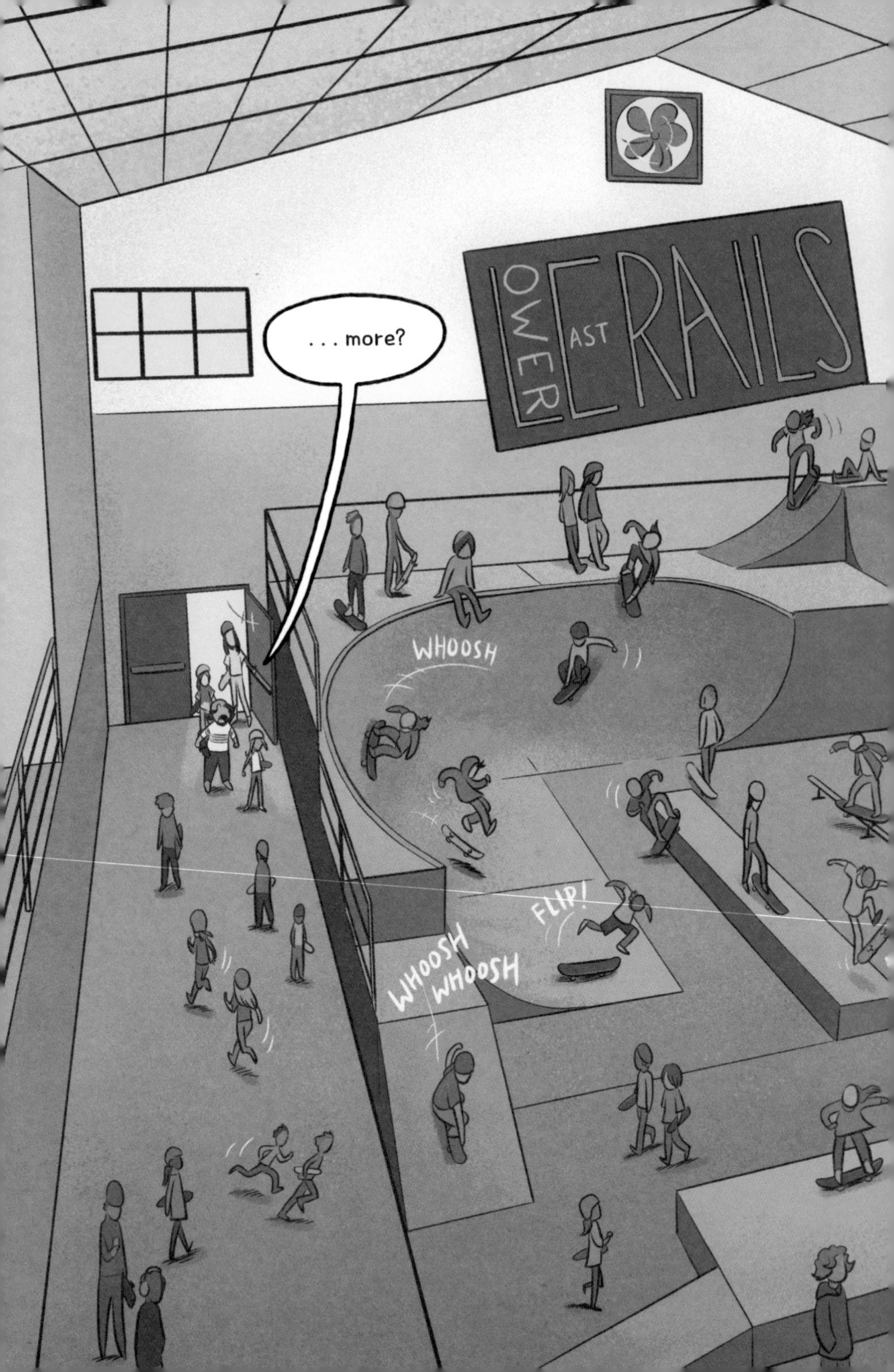
LOWER EAST RAILS
. . . more?
WHOOSH
FLIP!
WHOOSH
WHOOSH

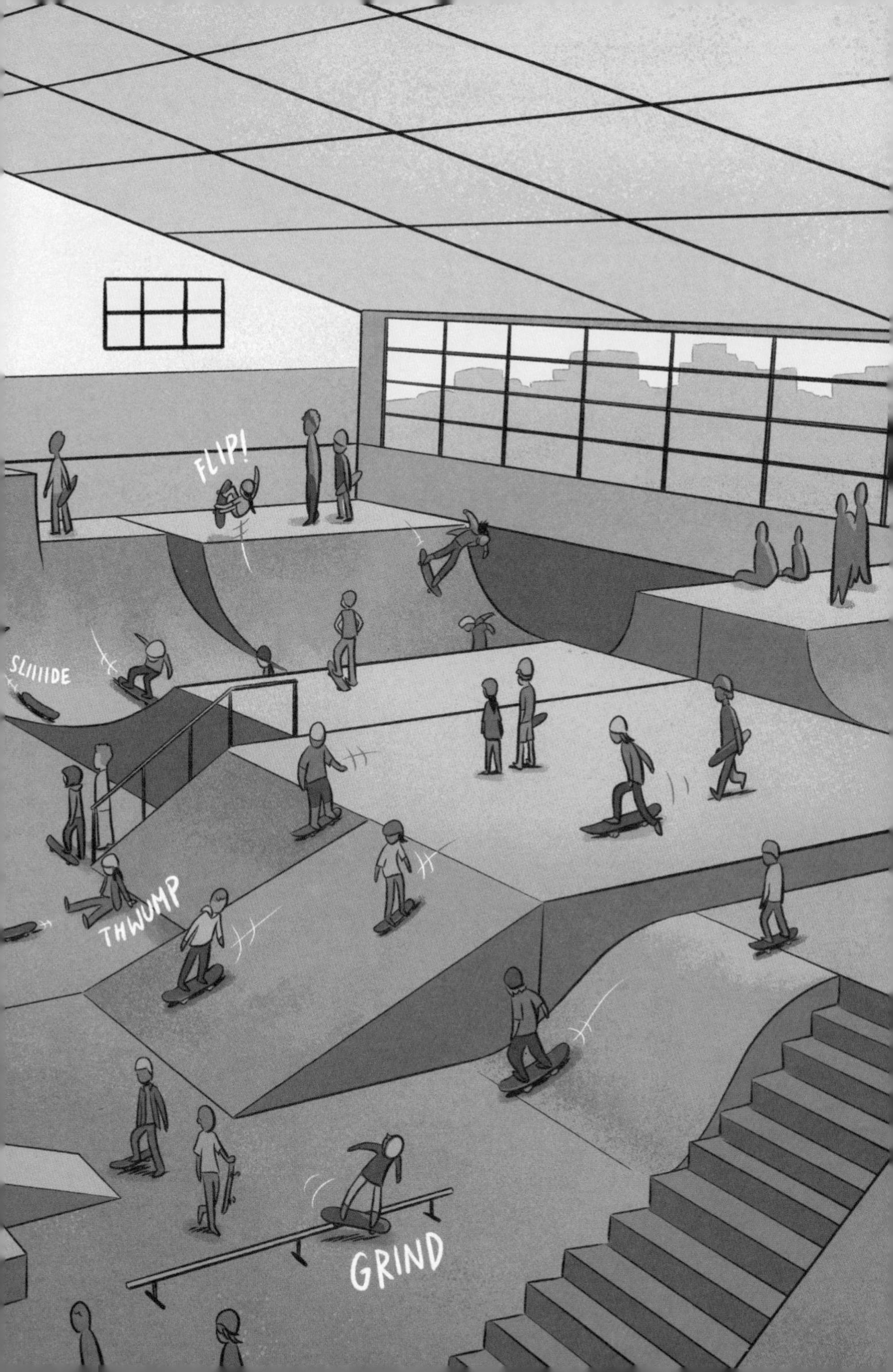
FLIP!
SLIIIIDE
THWUMP
GRIND

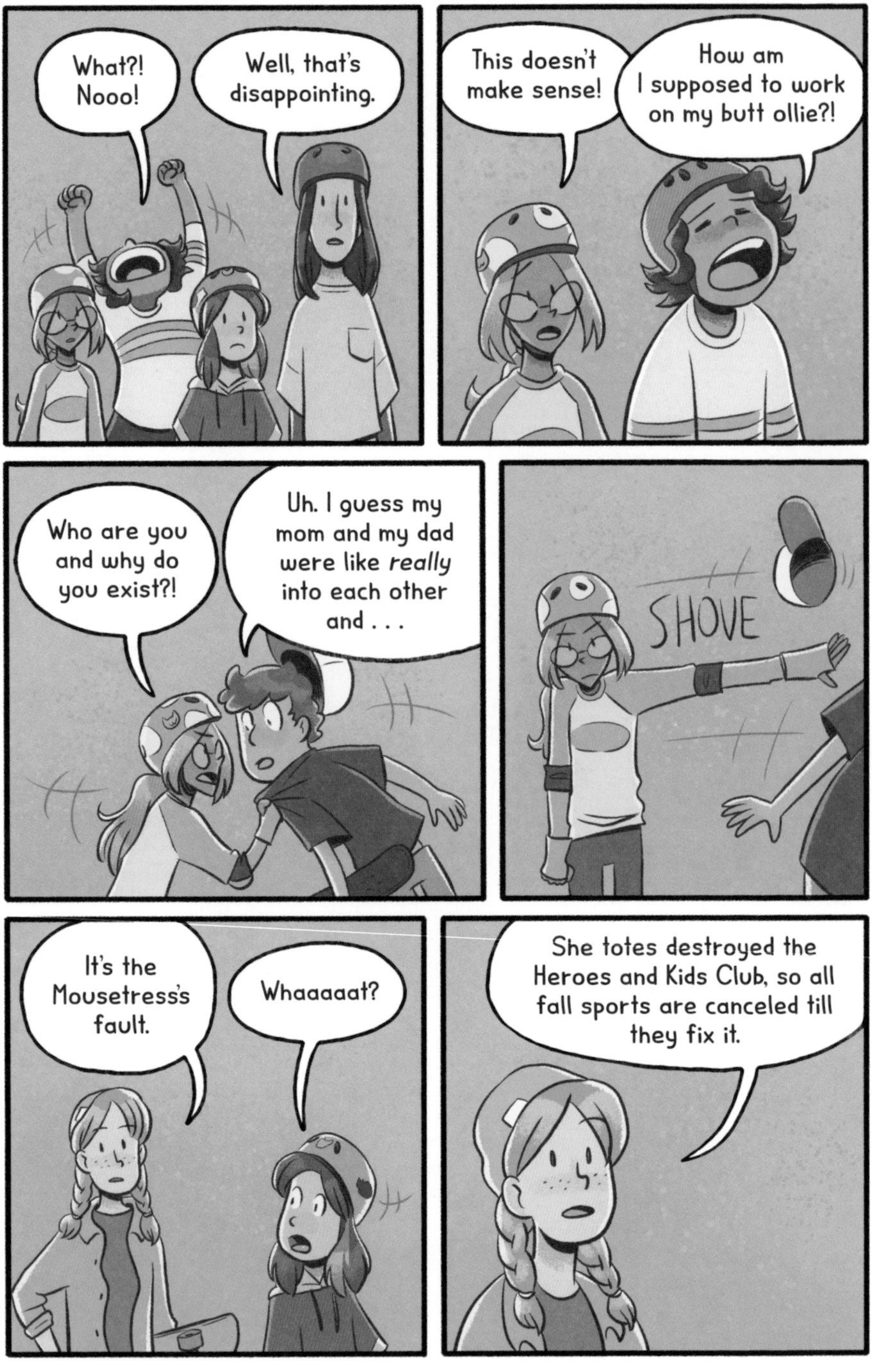
What?! Nooo!
Well, that's disappointing.
This doesn't make sense!
How am I supposed to work on my butt ollie?!
Who are you and why do you exist?!
Uh. I guess my mom and my dad were like *really* into each other and . . .
SHOVE
It's the Mousetress's fault.
Whaaaaat?
She totes destroyed the Heroes and Kids Club, so all fall sports are canceled till they fix it.

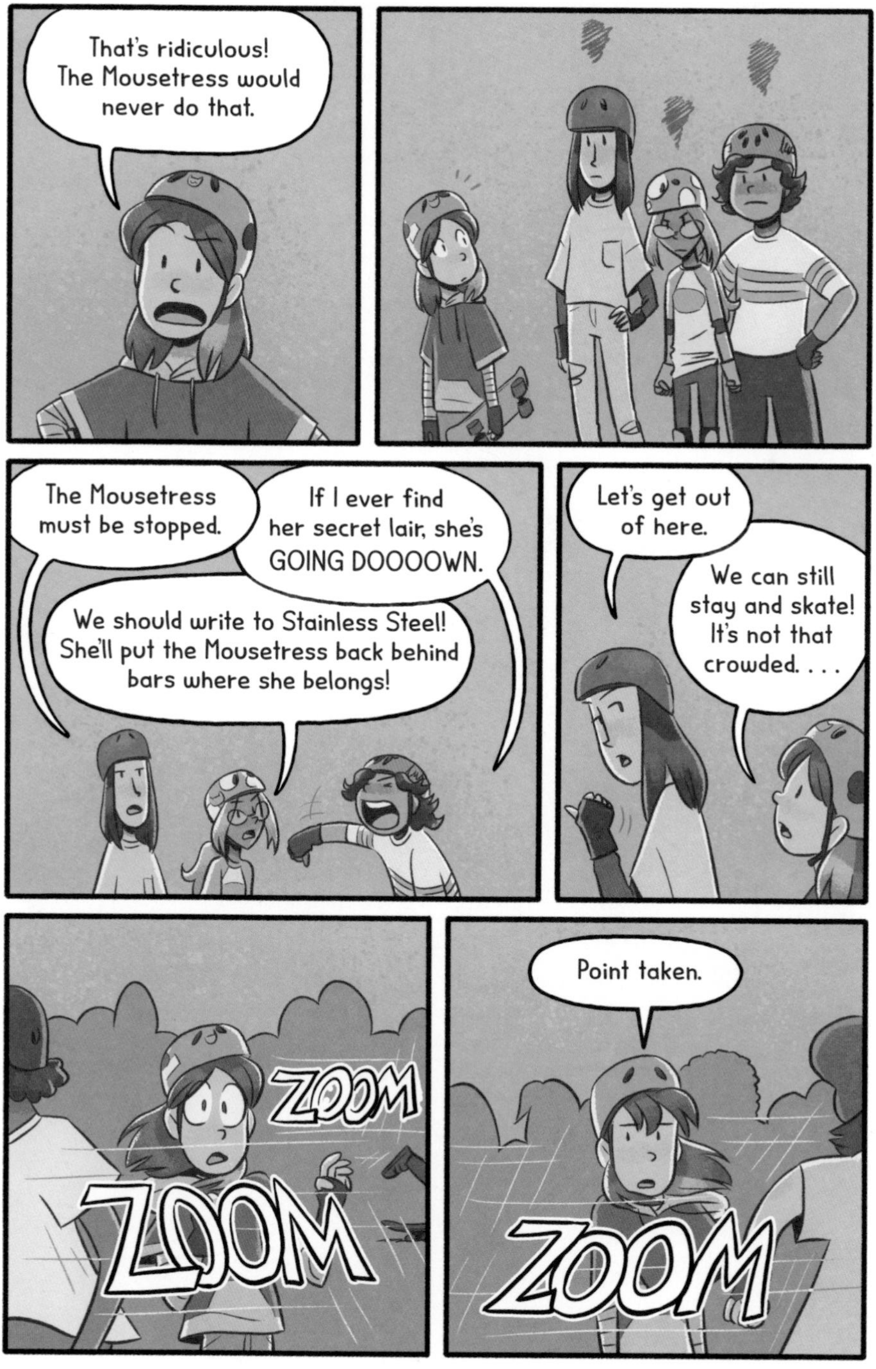
That's ridiculous! The Mousetress would never do that.
The Mousetress must be stopped.
If I ever find her secret lair, she's GOING DOOOOWN.
We should write to Stainless Steel! She'll put the Mousetress back behind bars where she belongs!
Let's get out of here.
We can still stay and skate! It's not that crowded. . . .
ZOOM
ZOOM
Point taken.
ZOOM

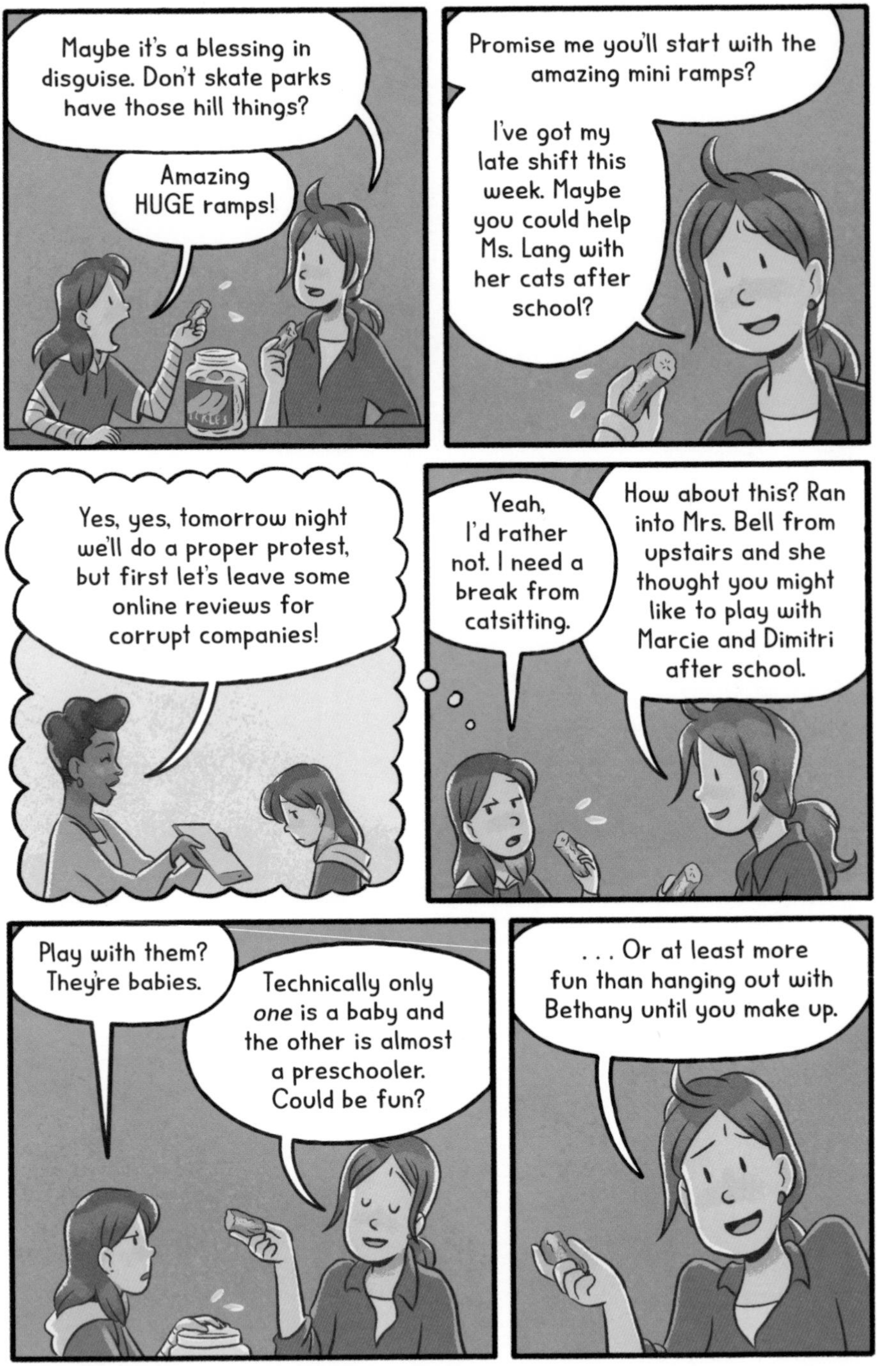
Maybe it's a blessing in disguise. Don't skate parks have those hill things?
Amazing HUGE ramps!
Promise me you'll start with the amazing mini ramps?
I've got my late shift this week. Maybe you could help Ms. Lang with her cats after school?
Yes, yes, tomorrow night we'll do a proper protest, but first let's leave some online reviews for corrupt companies!
Yeah, I'd rather not. I need a break from catsitting.
How about this? Ran into Mrs. Bell from upstairs and she thought you might like to play with Marcie and Dimitri after school.
Play with them? They're babies.
Technically only *one* is a baby and the other is almost a preschooler. Could be fun?
. . . Or at least more fun than hanging out with Bethany until you make up.

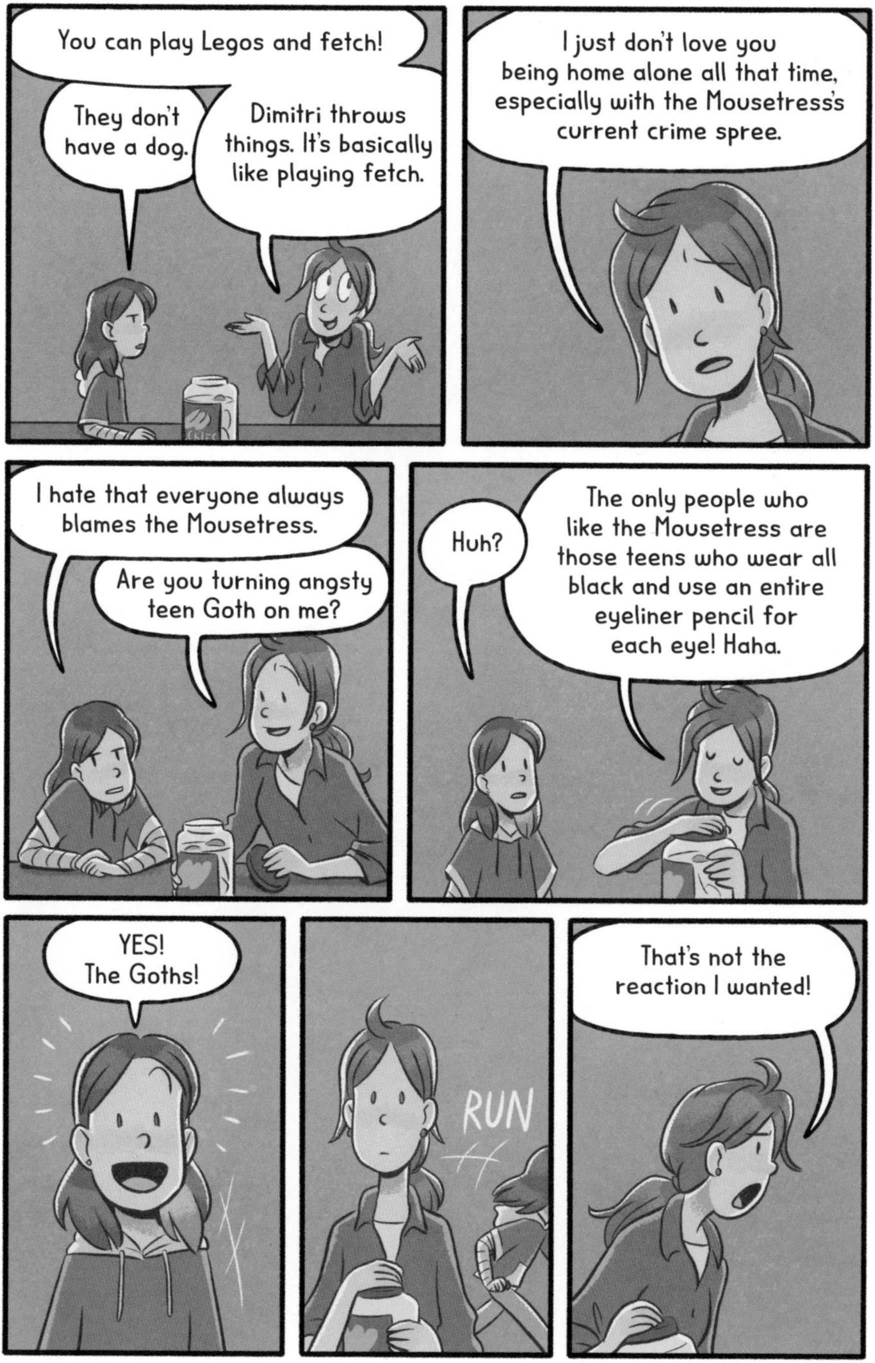
You can play Legos and fetch!
They don't have a dog.
Dimitri throws things. It's basically like playing fetch.
I just don't love you being home alone all that time, especially with the Mousetress's current crime spree.
I hate that everyone always blames the Mousetress.
Are you turning angsty teen Goth on me?
Huh?
The only people who like the Mousetress are those teens who wear all black and use an entire eyeliner pencil for each eye! Haha.
YES! The Goths!
RUN
That's not the reaction I wanted!

CHAPTER SIX

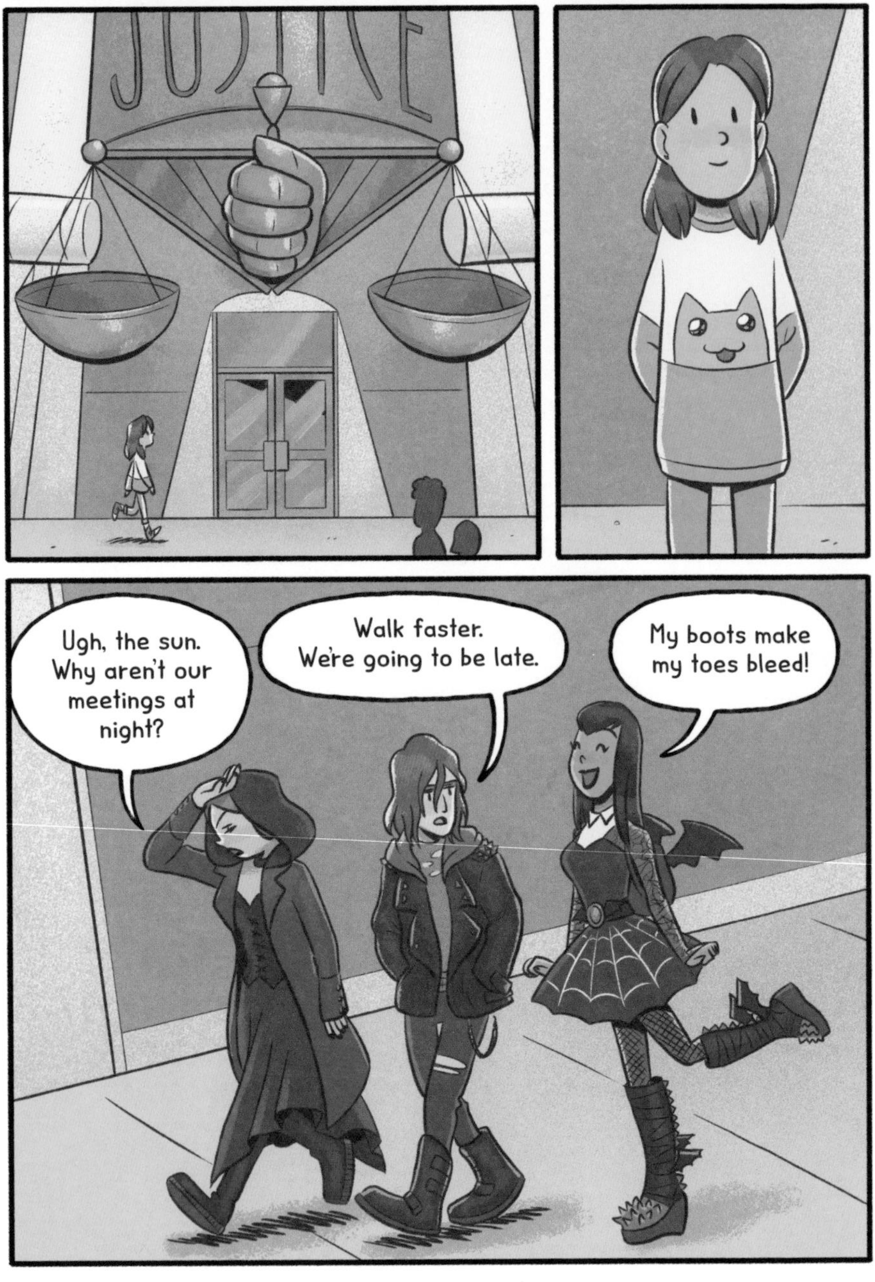
Ugh, the sun. Why aren't our meetings at night?
Walk faster. We're going to be late.
My boots make my toes bleed!

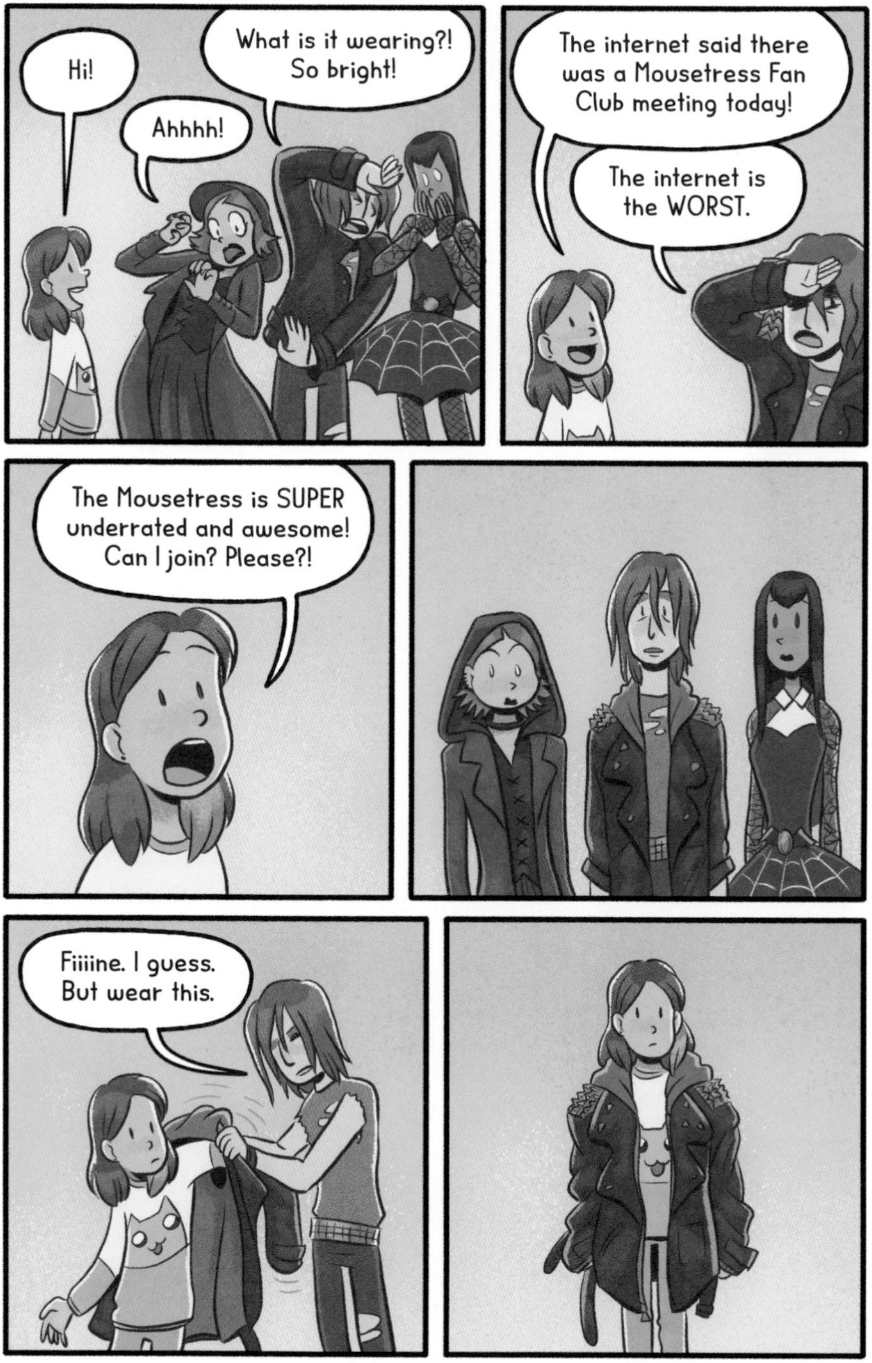
Hi!
Ahhhh!
What is it wearing?! So bright!
The internet said there was a Mousetress Fan Club meeting today!
The internet is the WORST.
The Mousetress is SUPER underrated and awesome! Can I join? Please?!
Fiiiine. I guess. But wear this.

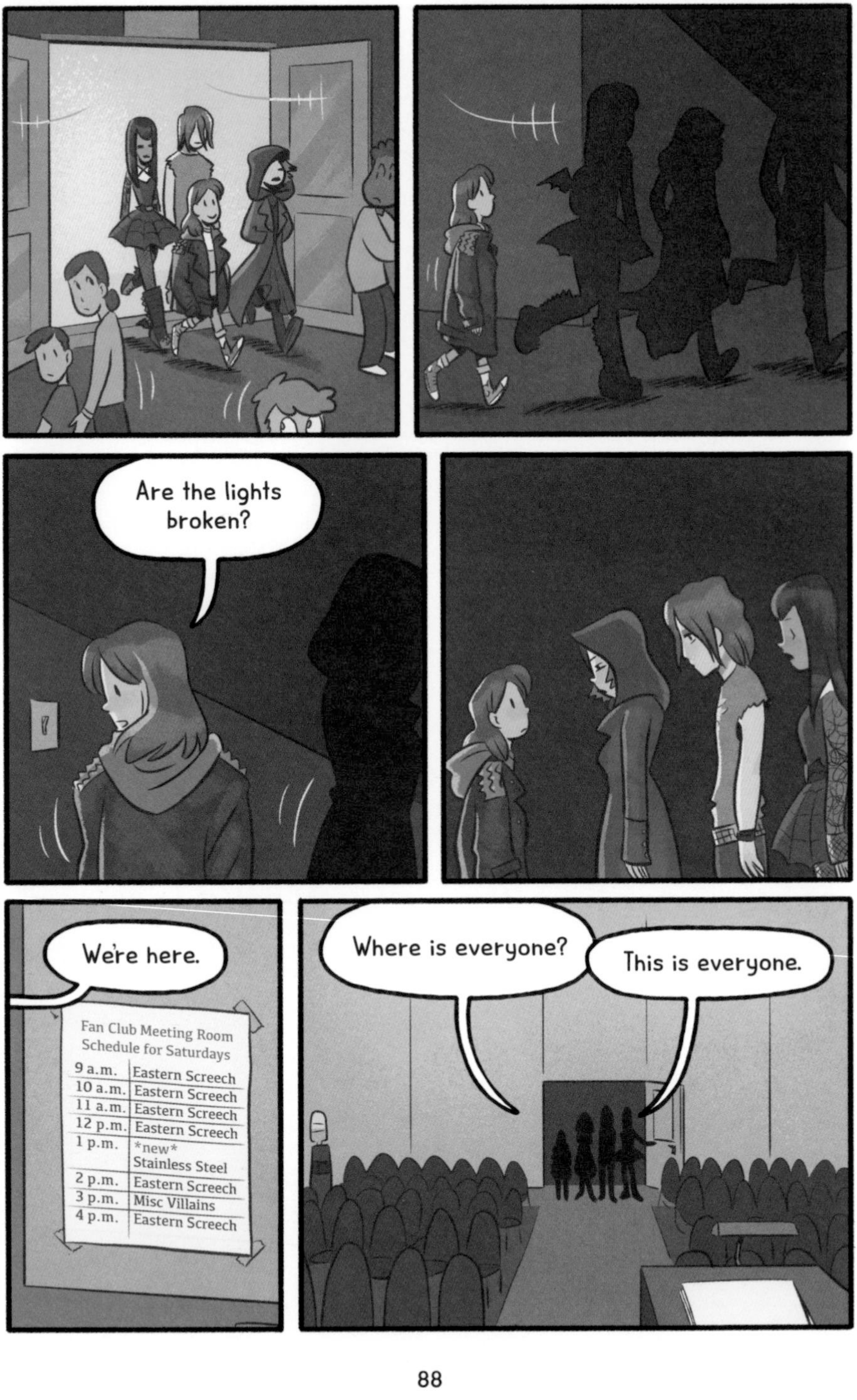
Are the lights broken?
We're here.
Fan Club Meeting Room Schedule for Saturdays
9 a.m. Eastern Screech
10 a.m. Eastern Screech
11 a.m. Eastern Screech
12 p.m. Eastern Screech
1 p.m. *new* Stainless Steel
2 p.m. Eastern Screech
3 p.m. Misc Villains
4 p.m. Eastern Screech
Where is everyone?
This is everyone.

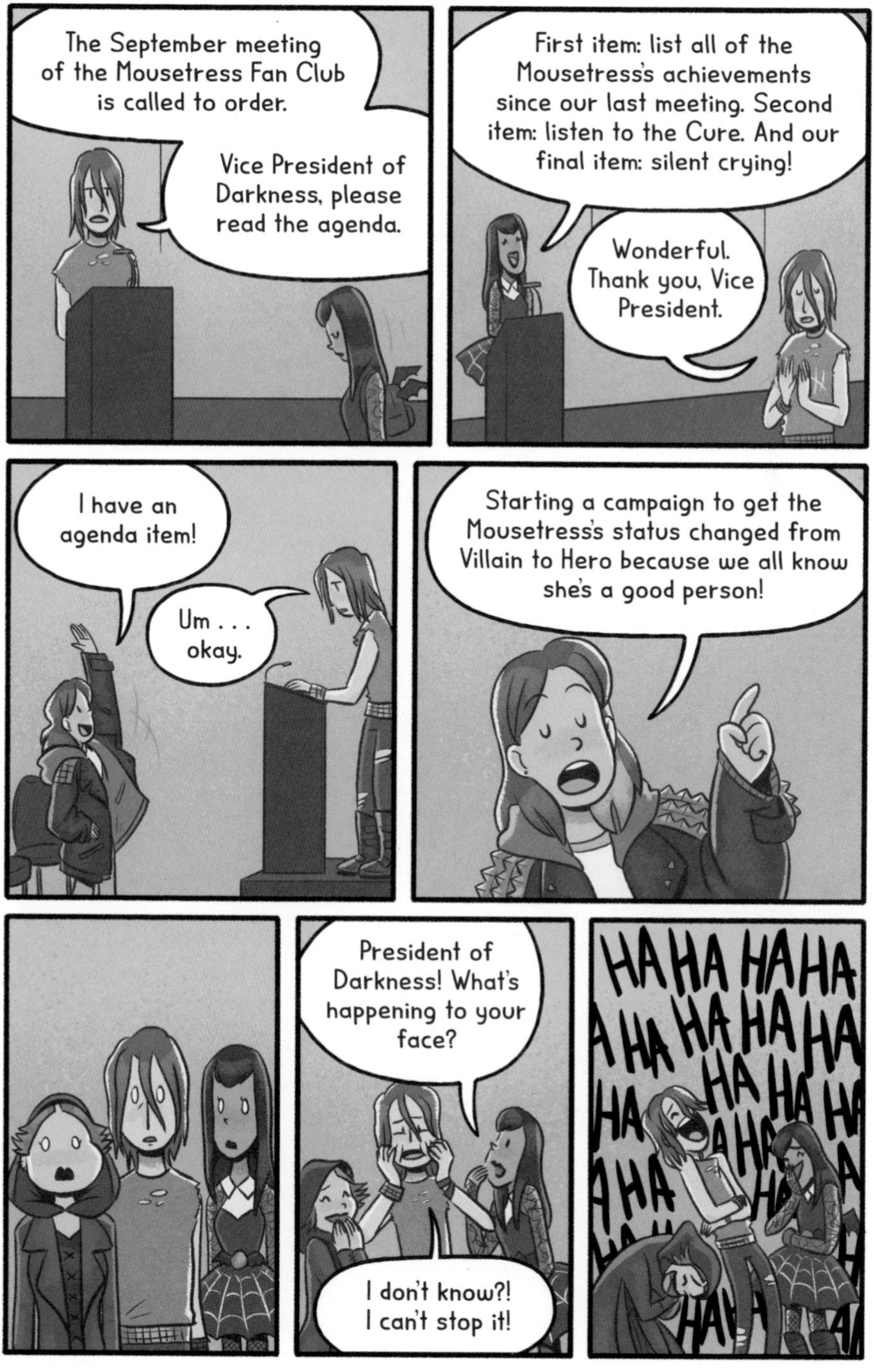
The September meeting of the Mousetress Fan Club is called to order.
Vice President of Darkness, please read the agenda.
First item: list all of the Mousetress's achievements since our last meeting. Second item: listen to the Cure. And our final item: silent crying!
Wonderful. Thank you, Vice President.
I have an agenda item!
Um . . . okay.
Starting a campaign to get the Mousetress's status changed from Villain to Hero because we all know she's a good person!
President of Darkness! What's happening to your face?
I don't know?! I can't stop it!
HA HA HA HA HA HA HA HA HA HA HA HA HA HA HA HA HA HA HA HA

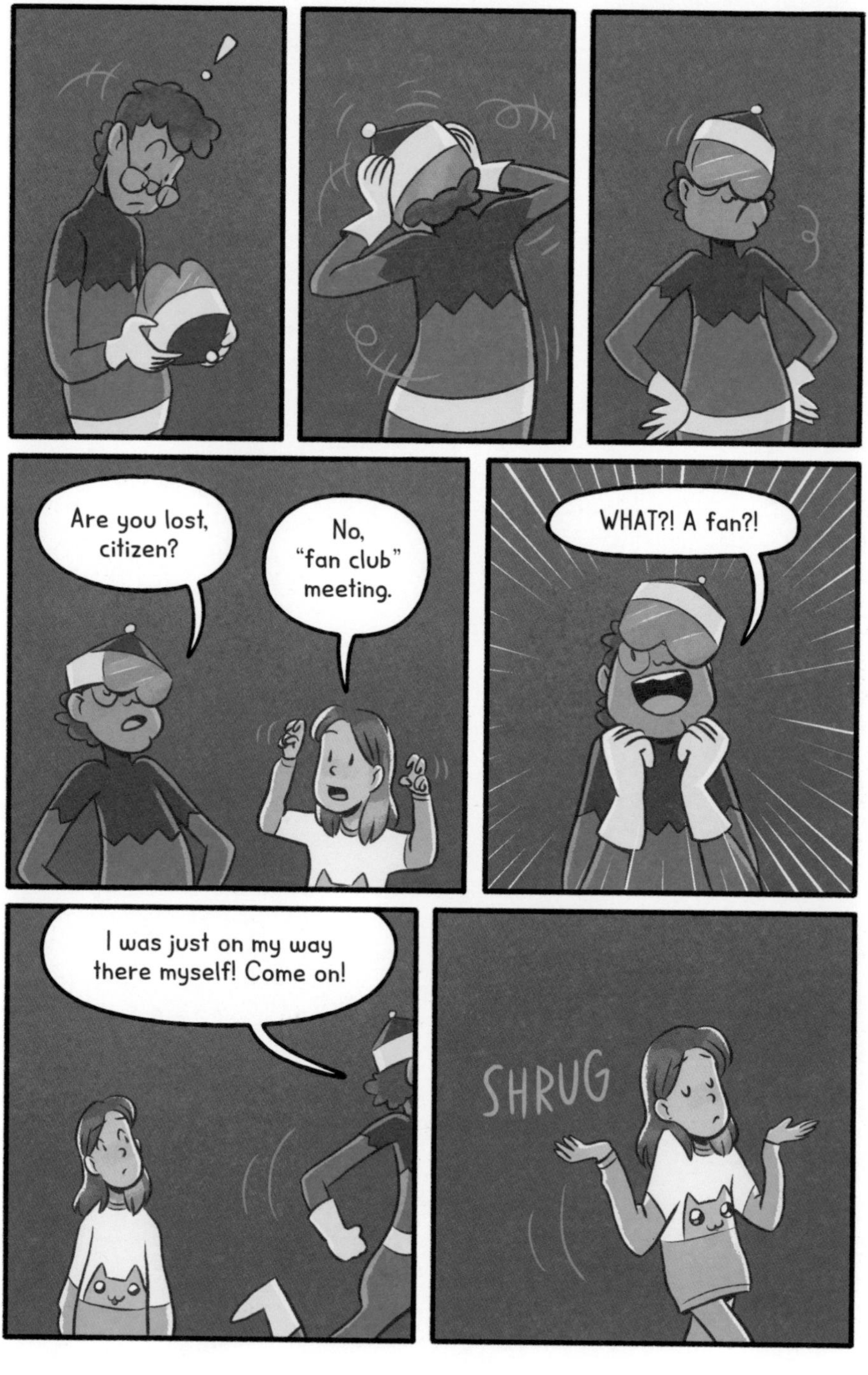
!
Are you lost, citizen?
No, "fan club" meeting.
WHAT?! A fan?!
I was just on my way there myself! Come on!
SHRUG

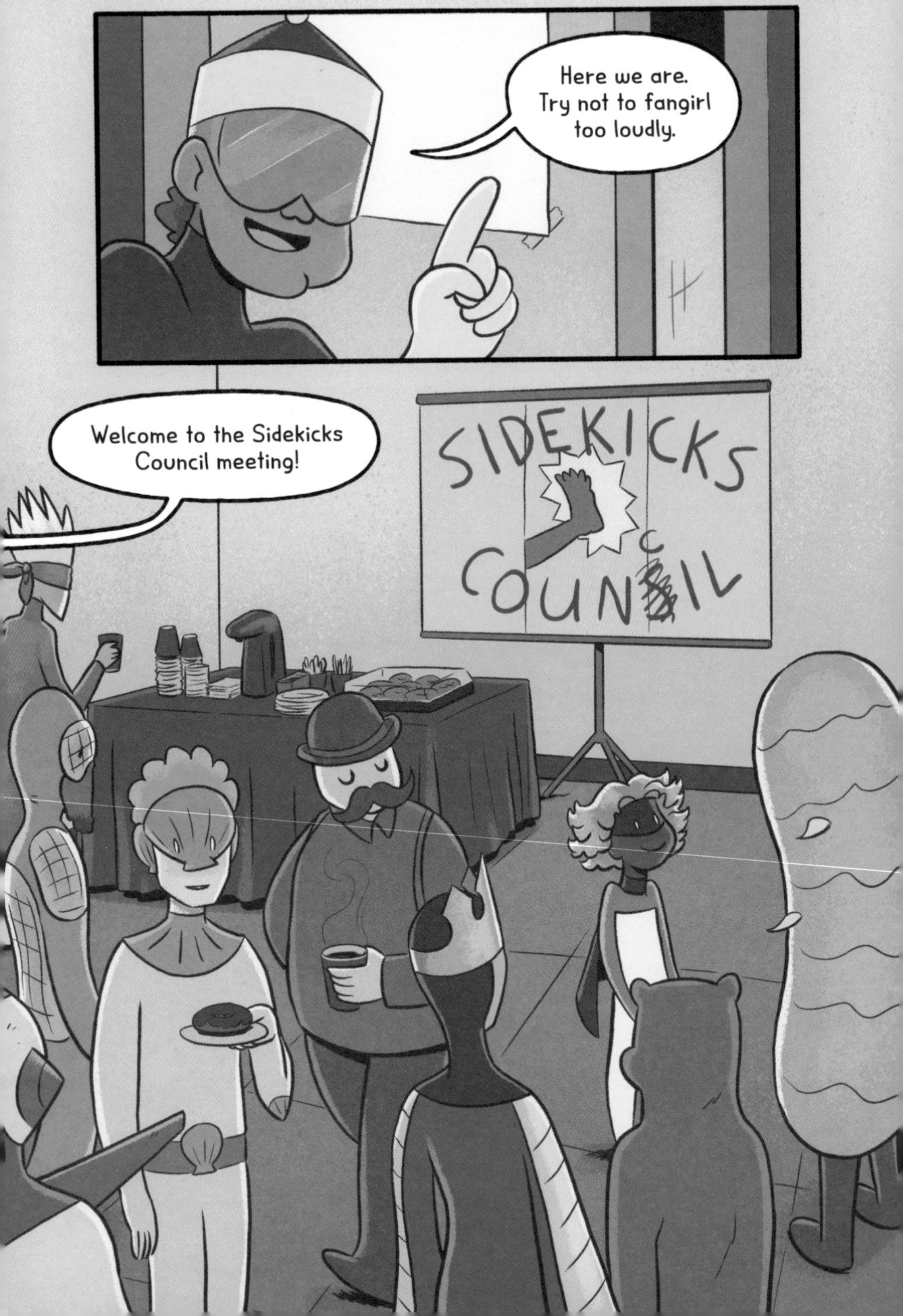
Here we are. Try not to fangirl too loudly.
Welcome to the Sidekicks Council meeting!
SIDEKICKS
COUNCIL

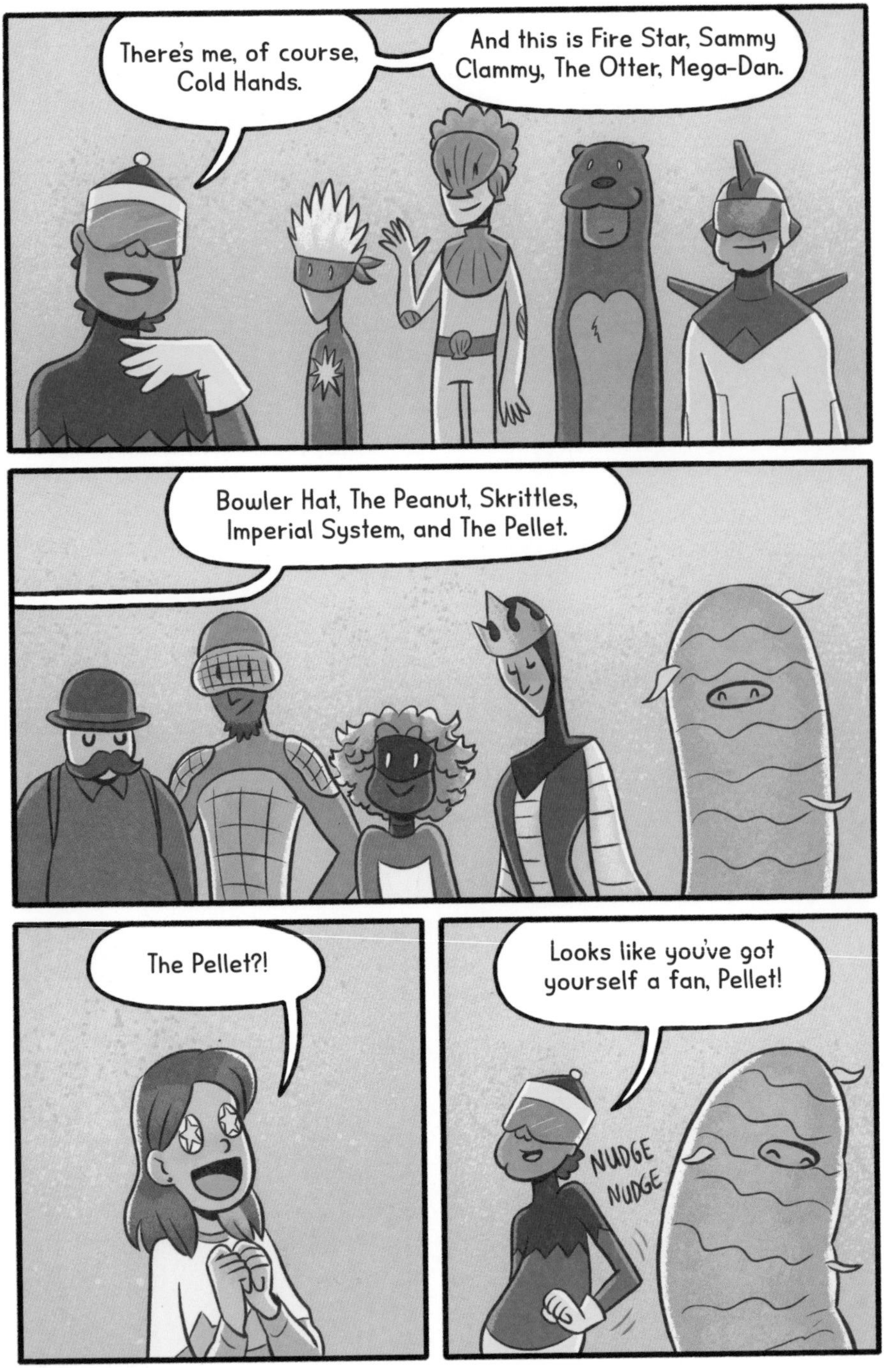
There's me, of course, Cold Hands.
And this is Fire Star, Sammy Clammy, The Otter, Mega-Dan.
Bowler Hat, The Peanut, Skrittles, Imperial System, and The Pellet.
The Pellet?!
Looks like you've got yourself a fan, Pellet!
NUDGE NUDGE

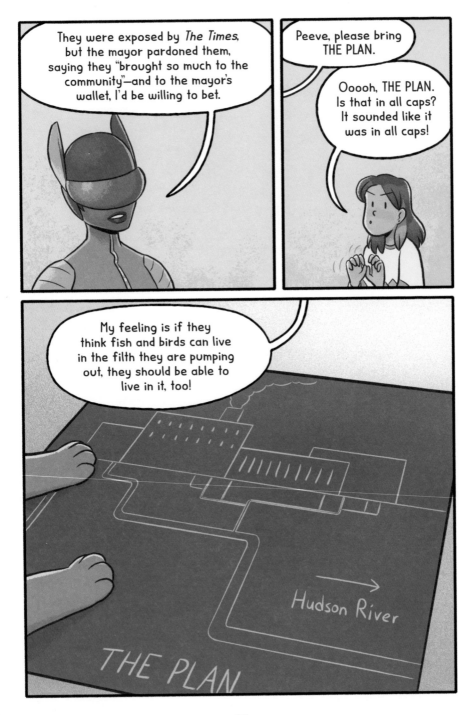

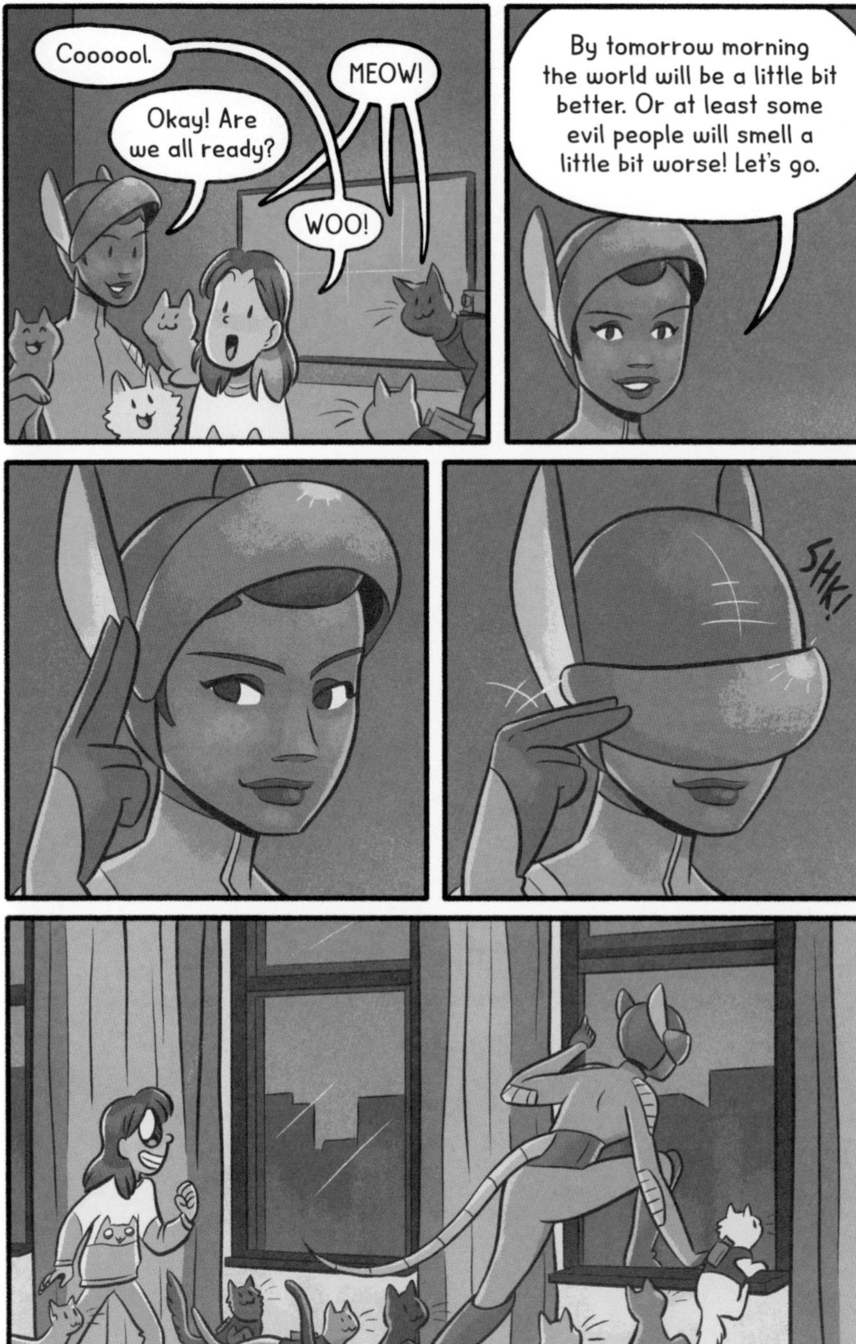
Coooool.
Okay! Are we all ready?
MEOW!
WOO!
By tomorrow morning the world will be a little bit better. Or at least some evil people will smell a little bit worse! Let's go.
SHK!

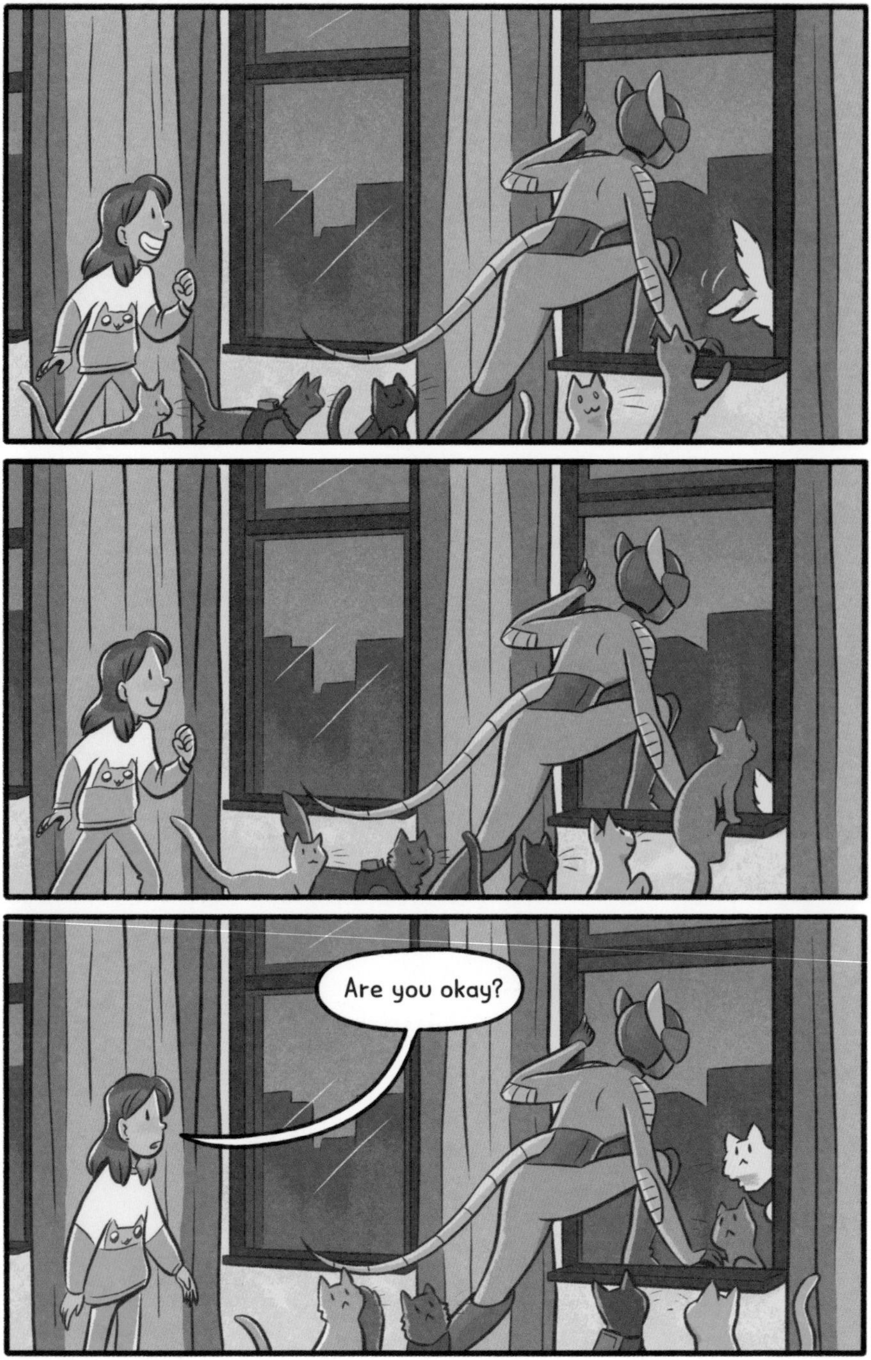
Are you okay?

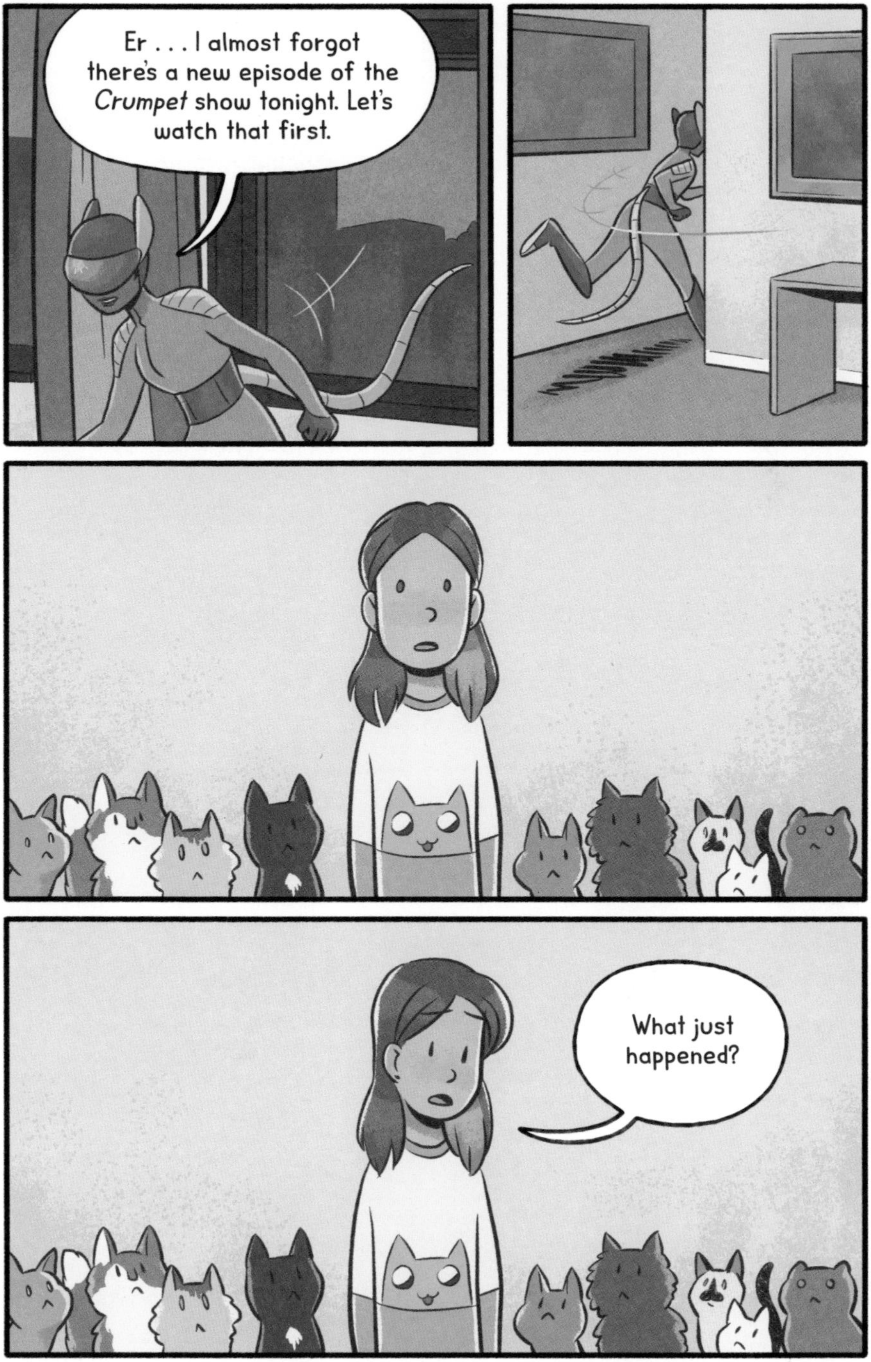
Er . . . I almost forgot there's a new episode of the *Crumpet* show tonight. Let's watch that first.
What just happened?

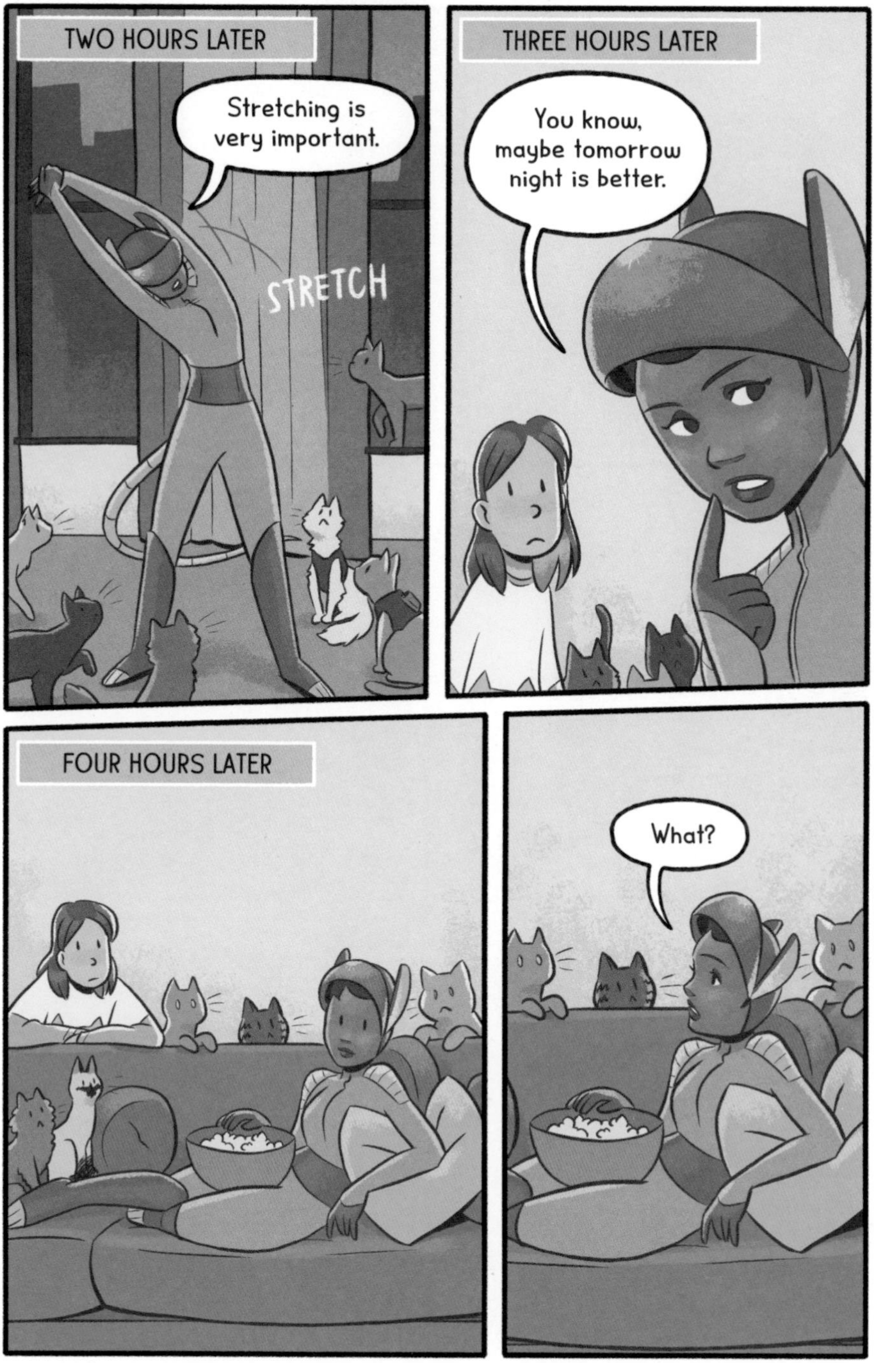
TWO HOURS LATER
Stretching is very important.
STRETCH
THREE HOURS LATER
You know, maybe tomorrow night is better.
FOUR HOURS LATER
What?

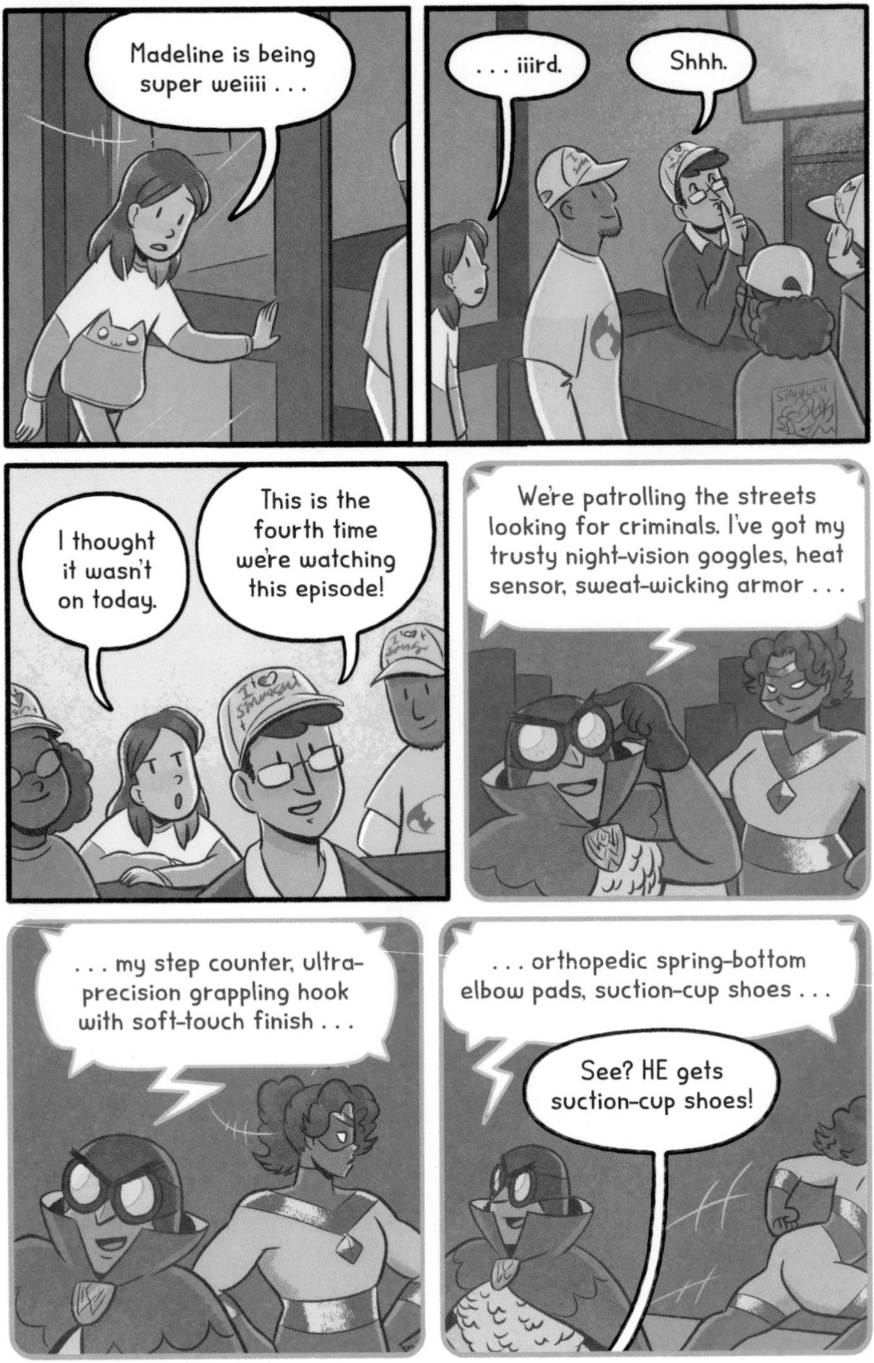
Madeline is being super weiiii . . .
. . . iiird.
Shhh.
I thought it wasn't on today.
This is the fourth time we're watching this episode!
We're patrolling the streets looking for criminals. I've got my trusty night-vision goggles, heat sensor, sweat-wicking armor . . .
. . . my step counter, ultra-precision grappling hook with soft-touch finish . . .
. . . orthopedic spring-bottom elbow pads, suction-cup shoes . . .
See? HE gets suction-cup shoes!

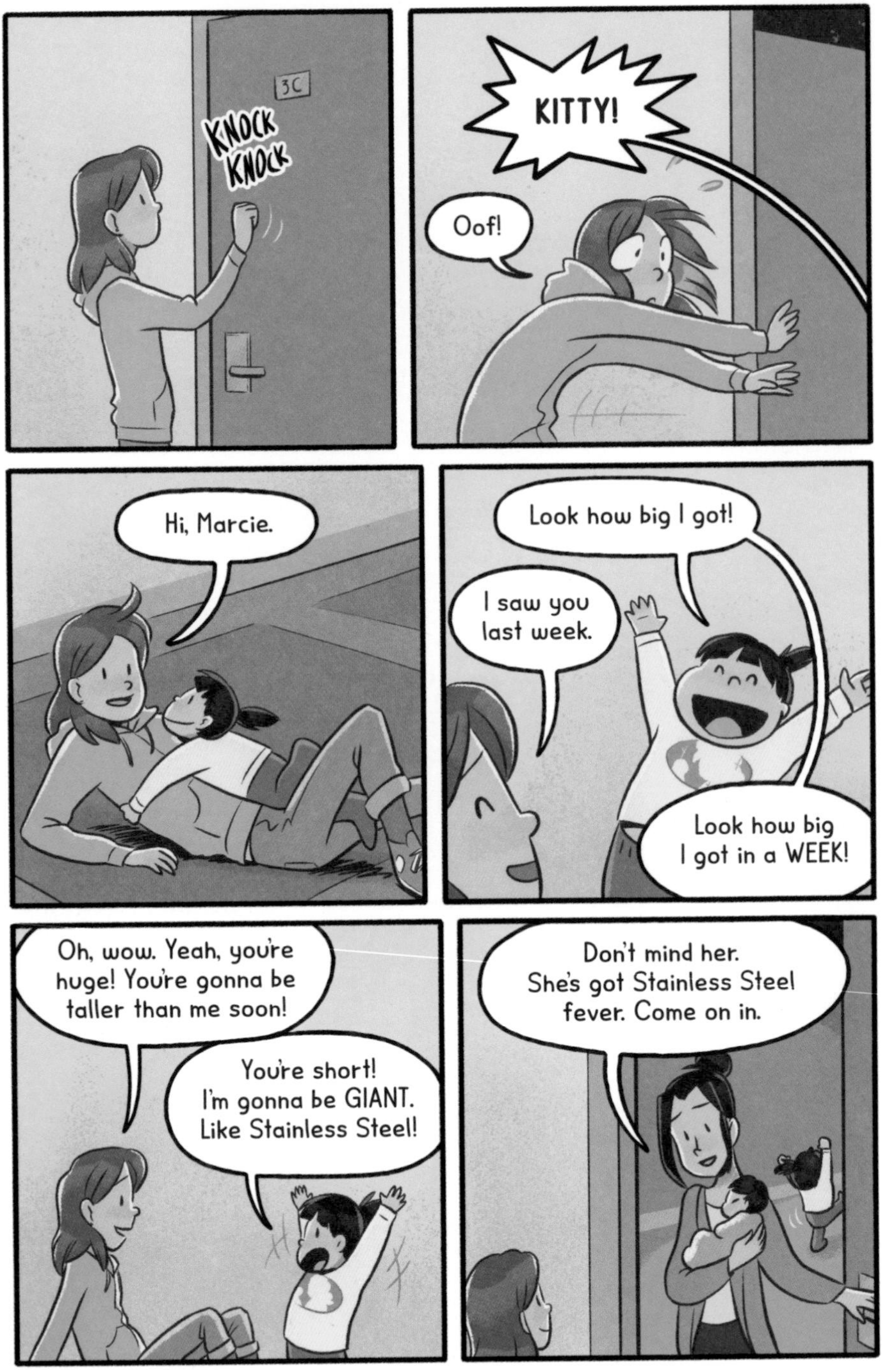

3C
KNOCK KNOCK
KITTY!
Oof!
Hi, Marcie.
Look how big I got!
I saw you last week.
Look how big I got in a WEEK!
Oh, wow. Yeah, you're huge! You're gonna be taller than me soon!
You're short! I'm gonna be GIANT. Like Stainless Steel!
Don't mind her. She's got Stainless Steel fever. Come on in.

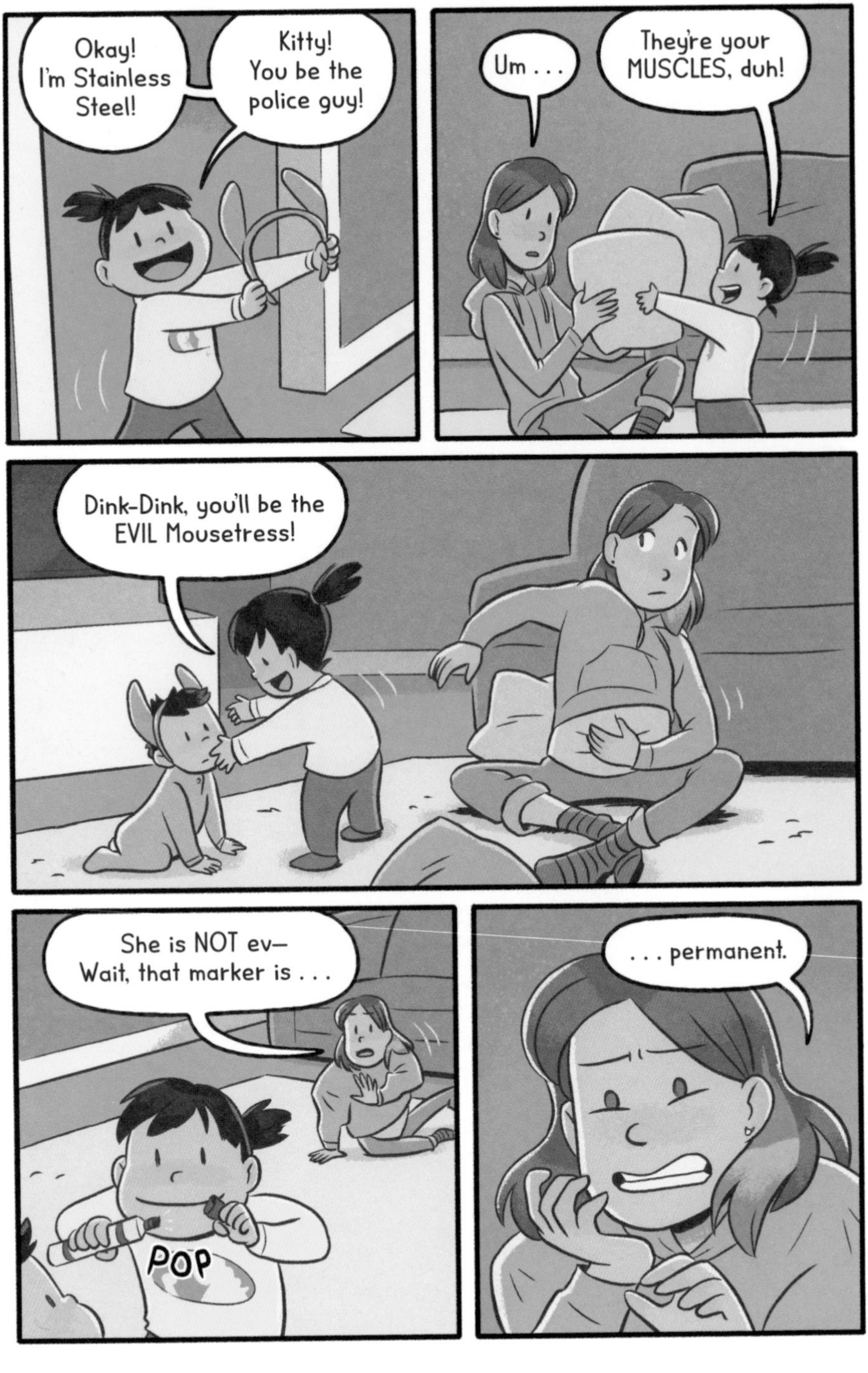
Okay! I'm Stainless Steel!
Kitty! You be the police guy!
Um . . .
They're your MUSCLES, duh!
Dink-Dink, you'll be the EVIL Mousetress!
She is NOT ev— Wait, that marker is . . .
POP
. . . permanent.

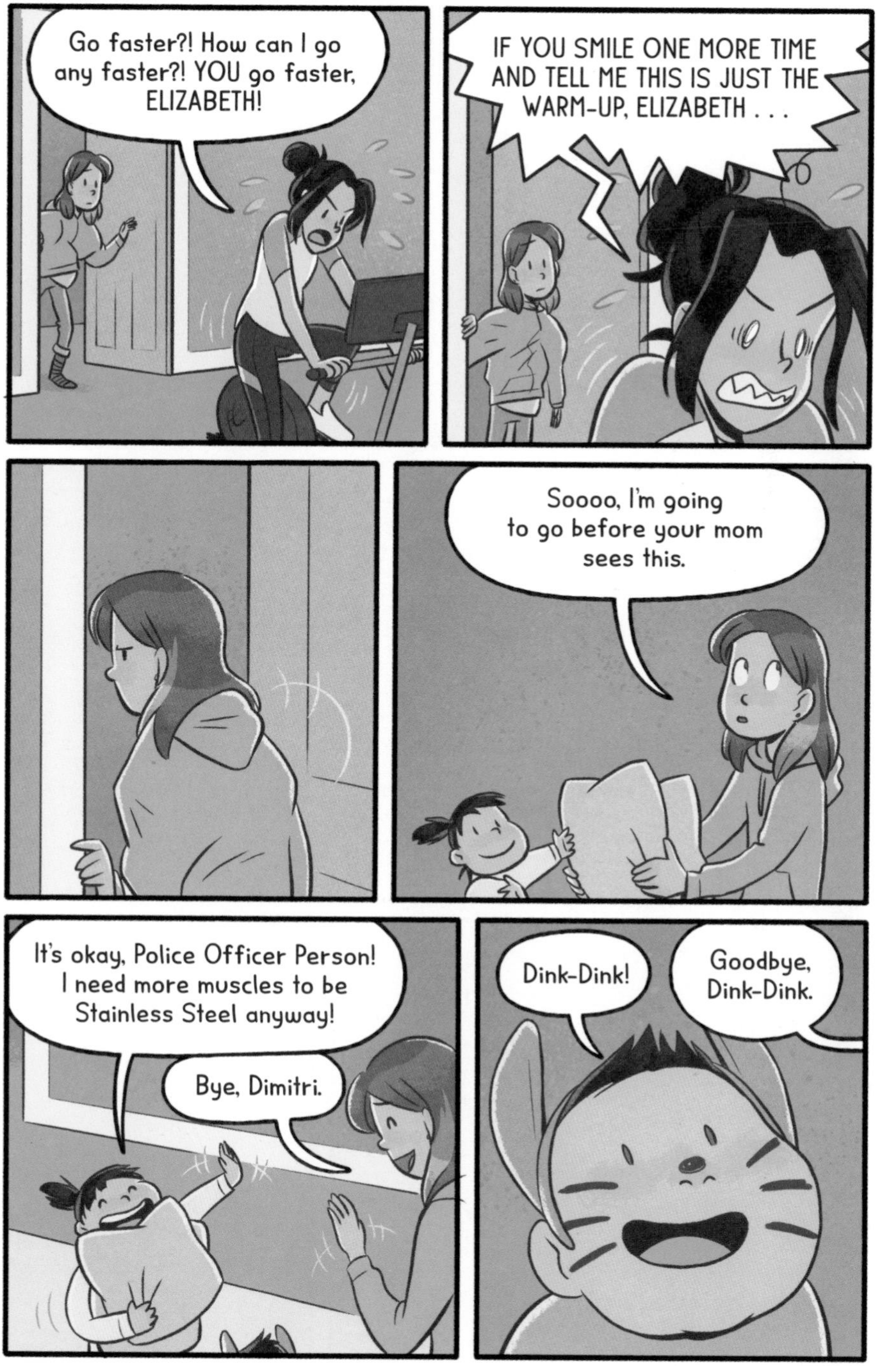
Go faster?! How can I go any faster?! YOU go faster, ELIZABETH!
IF YOU SMILE ONE MORE TIME AND TELL ME THIS IS JUST THE WARM-UP, ELIZABETH . . .
Soooo, I'm going to go before your mom sees this.
It's okay, Police Officer Person! I need more muscles to be Stainless Steel anyway!
Bye, Dimitri.
Dink-Dink!
Goodbye, Dink-Dink.

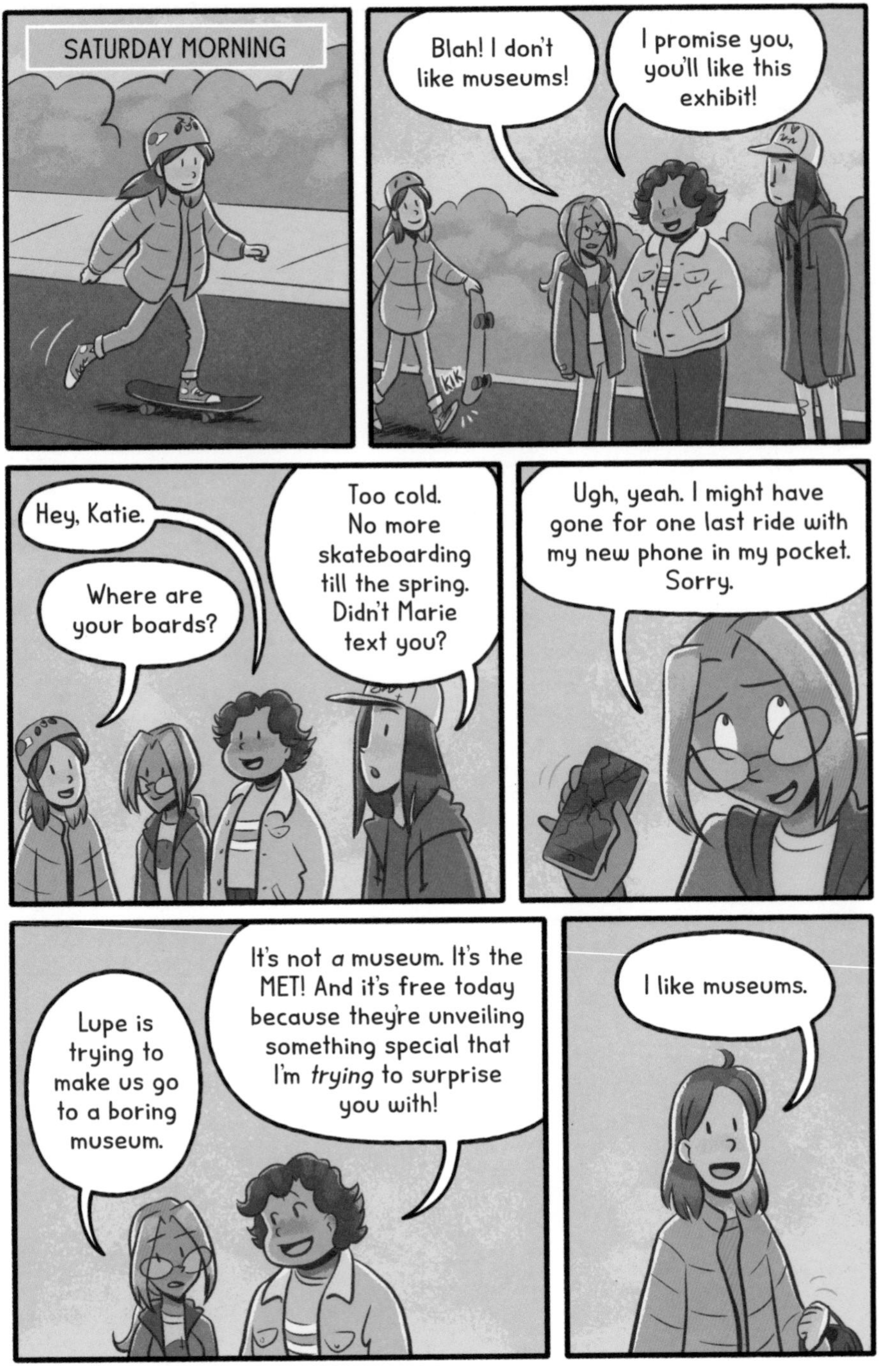
SATURDAY MORNING
Blah! I don't like museums!
I promise you, you'll like this exhibit!
KIK
Hey, Katie.
Where are your boards?
Too cold. No more skateboarding till the spring. Didn't Marie text you?
Ugh, yeah. I might have gone for one last ride with my new phone in my pocket. Sorry.
Lupe is trying to make us go to a boring museum.
It's not *a* museum. It's the MET! And it's free today because they're unveiling something special that I'm *trying* to surprise you with!
I like museums.

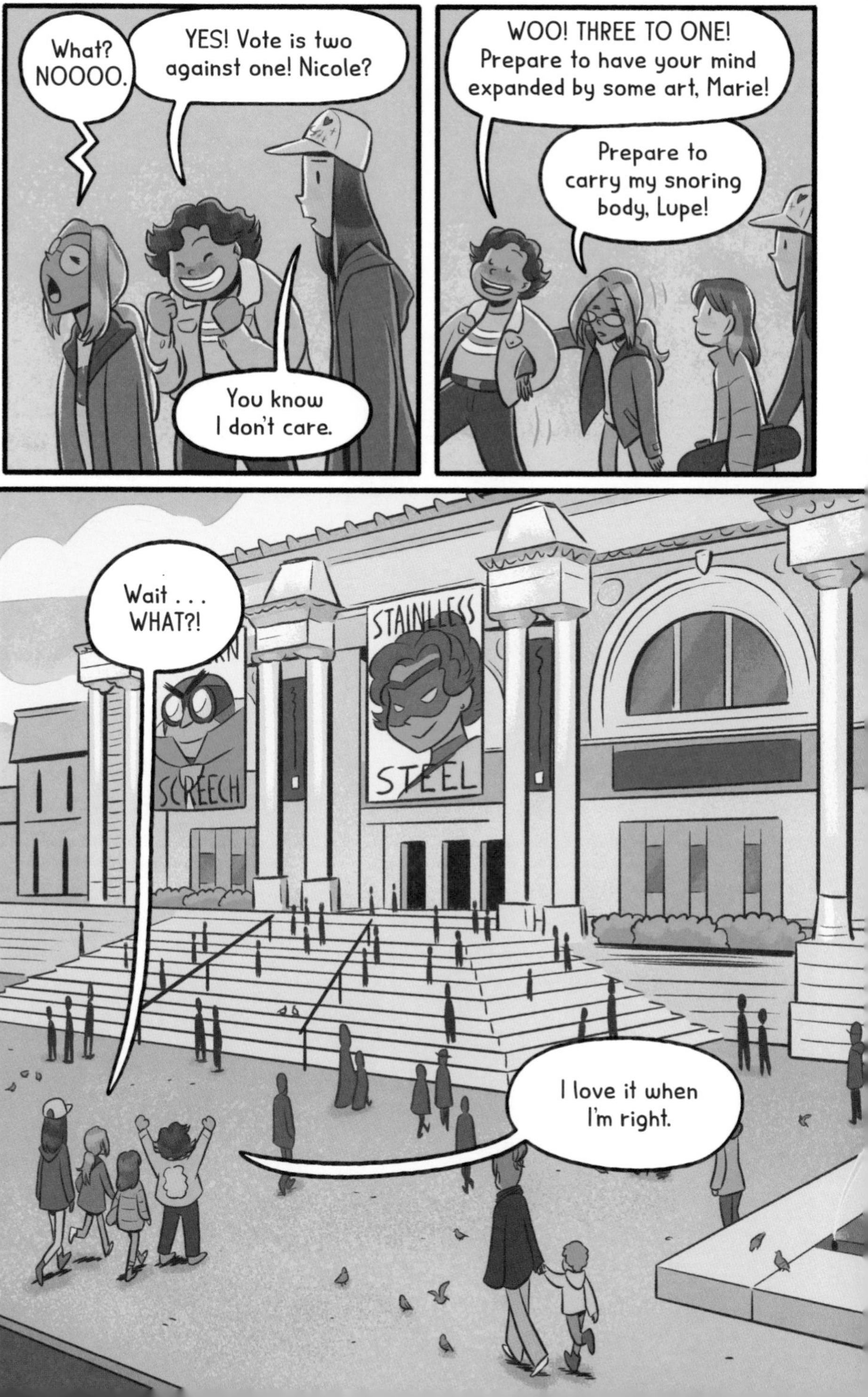
What? NOOOO.
YES! Vote is two against one! Nicole?
You know I don't care.
WOO! THREE TO ONE! Prepare to have your mind expanded by some art, Marie!
Prepare to carry my snoring body, Lupe!
Wait . . . WHAT?!
SCREECH
STEEL
I love it when I'm right.

117

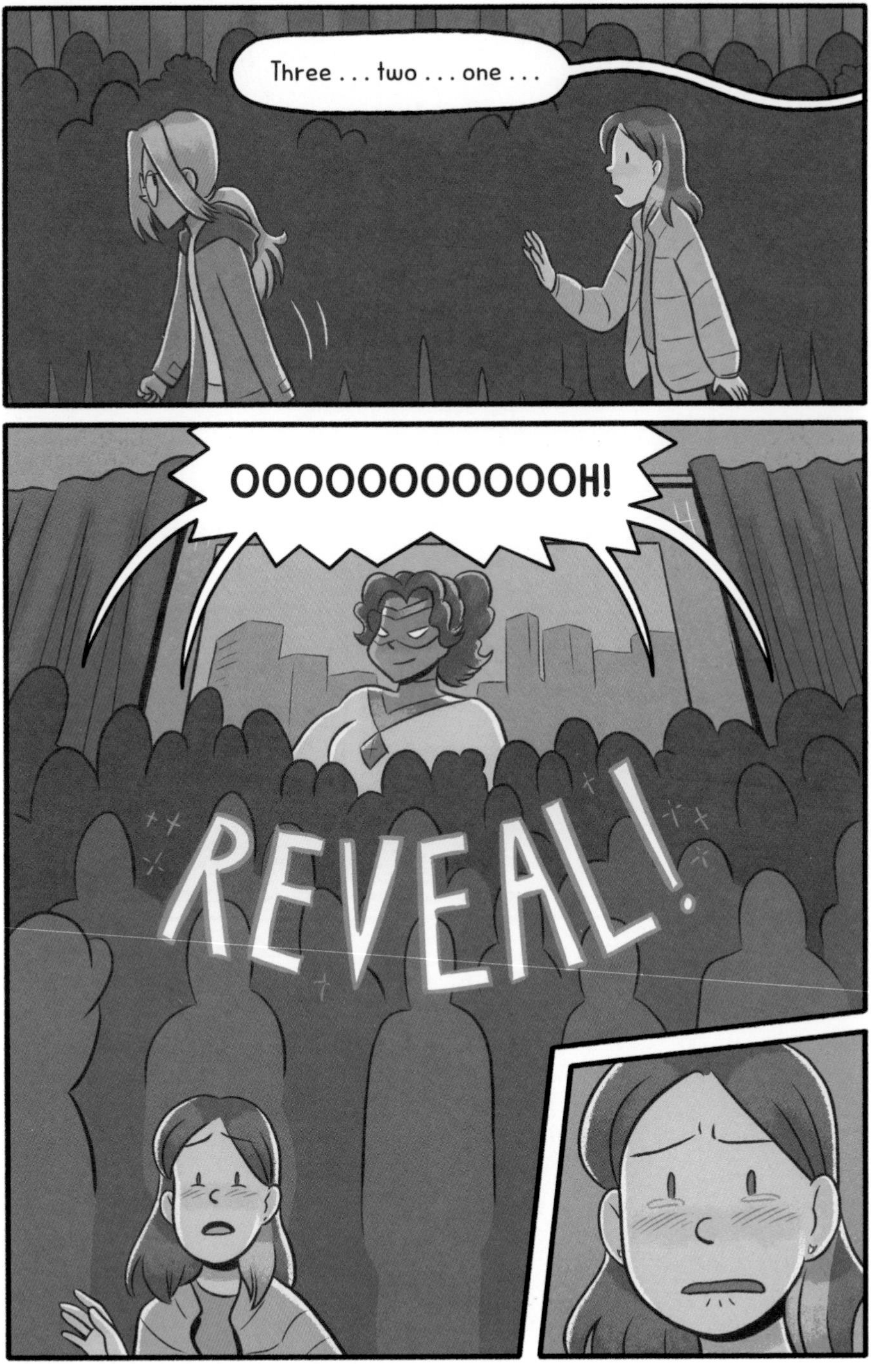
Three . . . two . . . one . . .
OOOOOOOOOOOOH!
REVEAL!

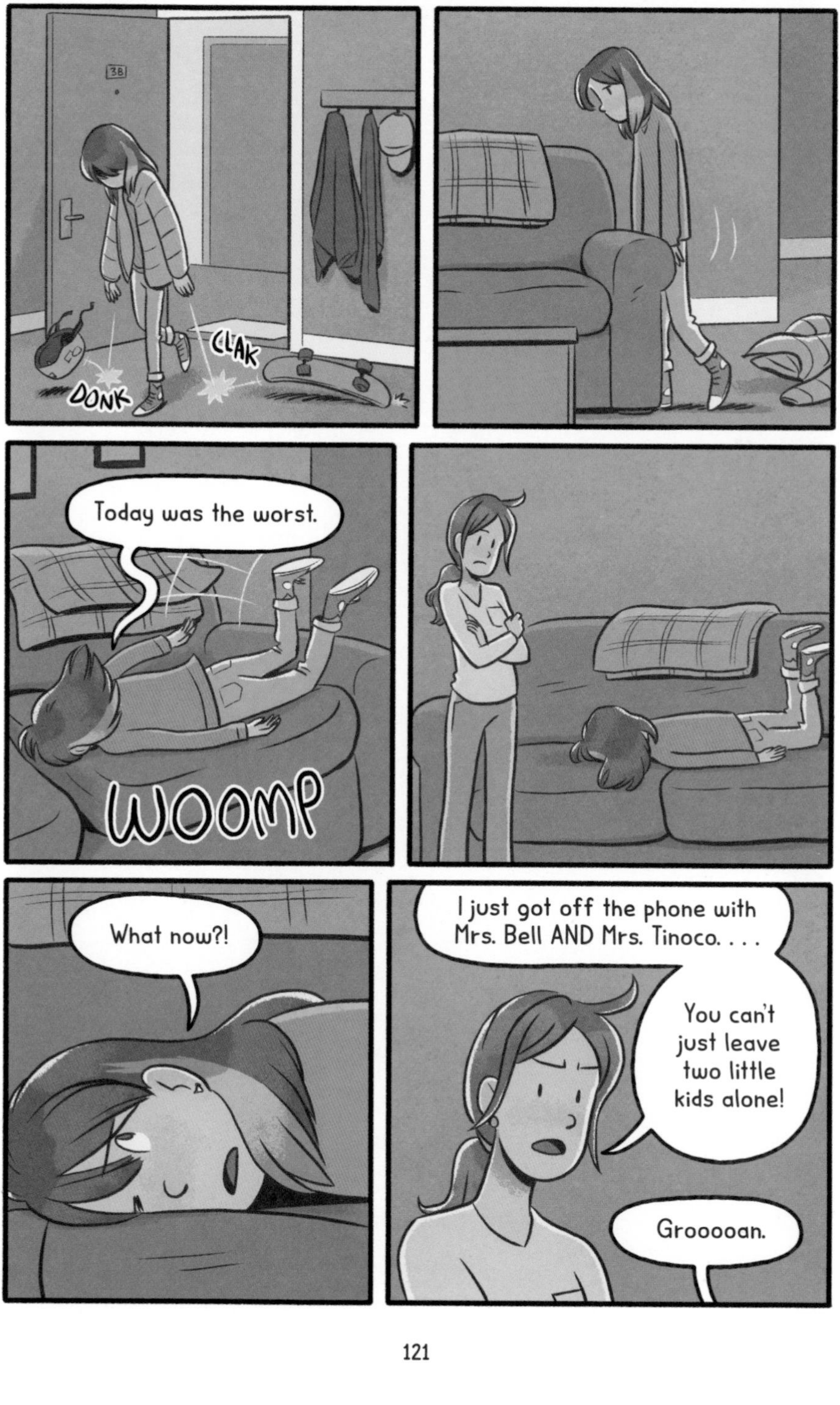
DONK
CLAK
Today was the worst.
WOOMP
What now?!
I just got off the phone with Mrs. Bell AND Mrs. Tinoco. . . .
You can't just leave two little kids alone!
Grooooan.

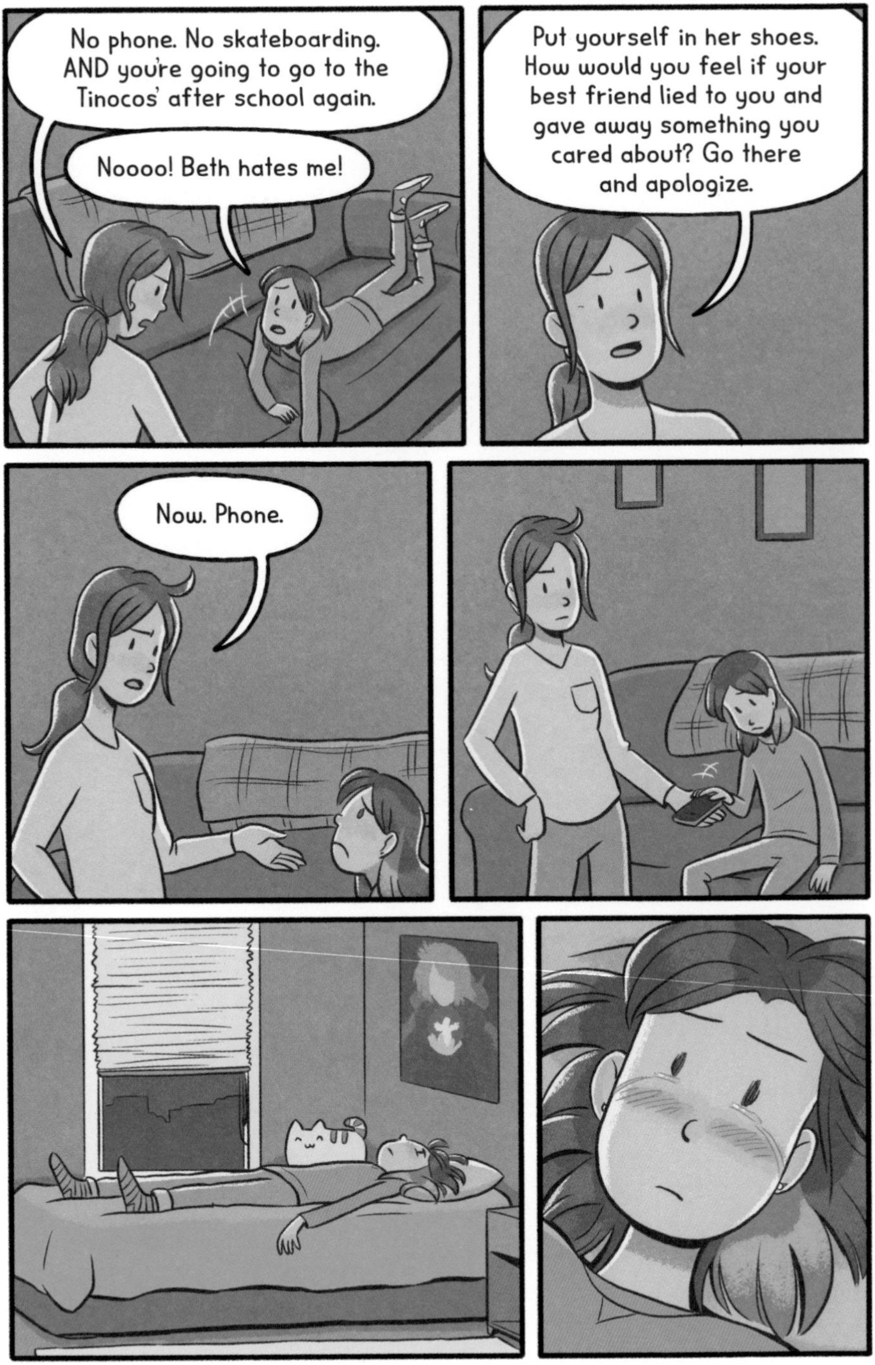
No phone. No skateboarding. AND you're going to go to the Tinocos' after school again.
Noooo! Beth hates me!
Put yourself in her shoes. How would you feel if your best friend lied to you and gave away something you cared about? Go there and apologize.
Now. Phone.

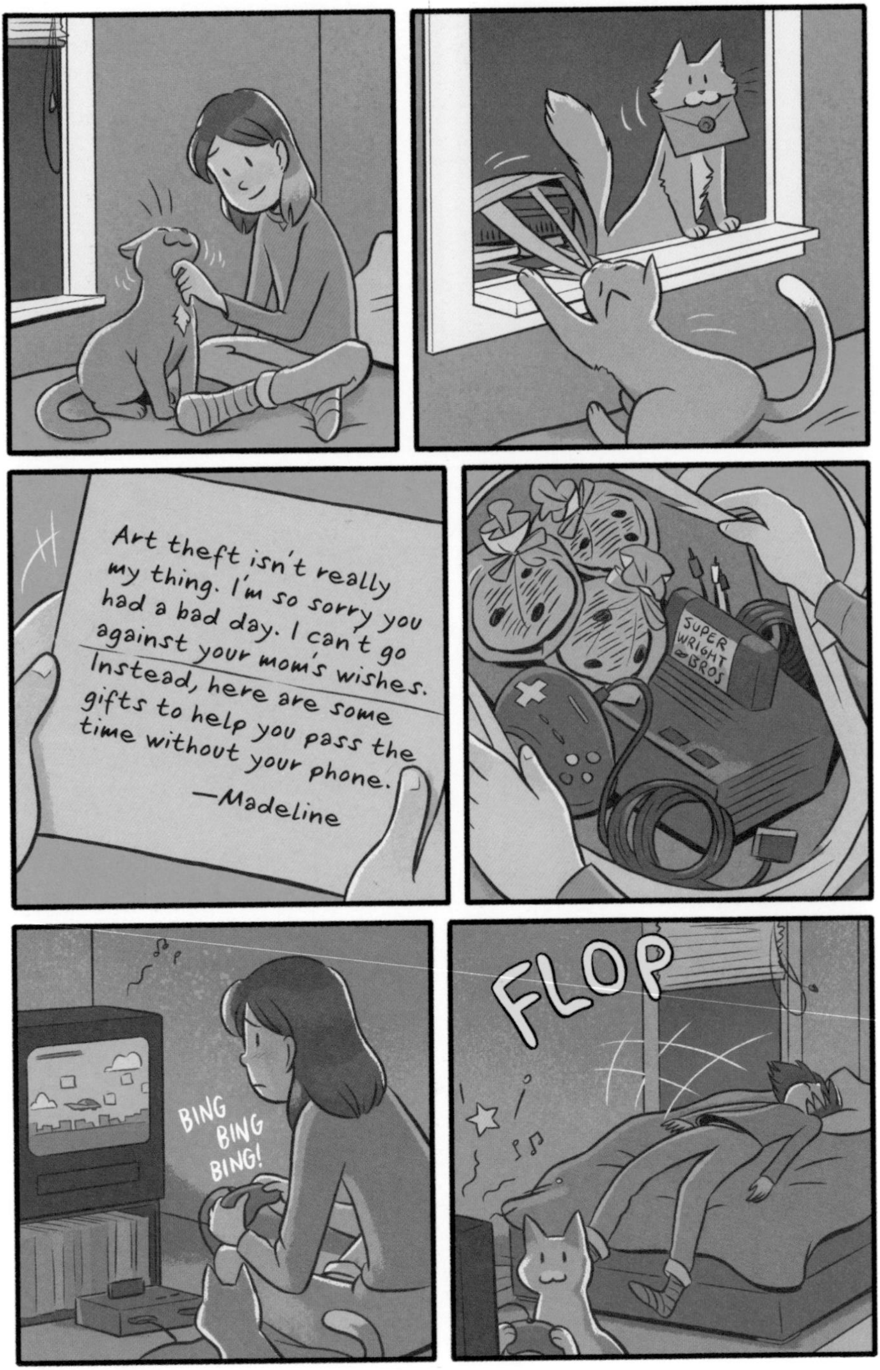
Art theft isn't really my thing. I'm so sorry you had a bad day. I can't go against your mom's wishes. Instead, here are some gifts to help you pass the time without your phone.
—Madeline
SUPER WRIGHT BROS
BING BING BING!
FLOP

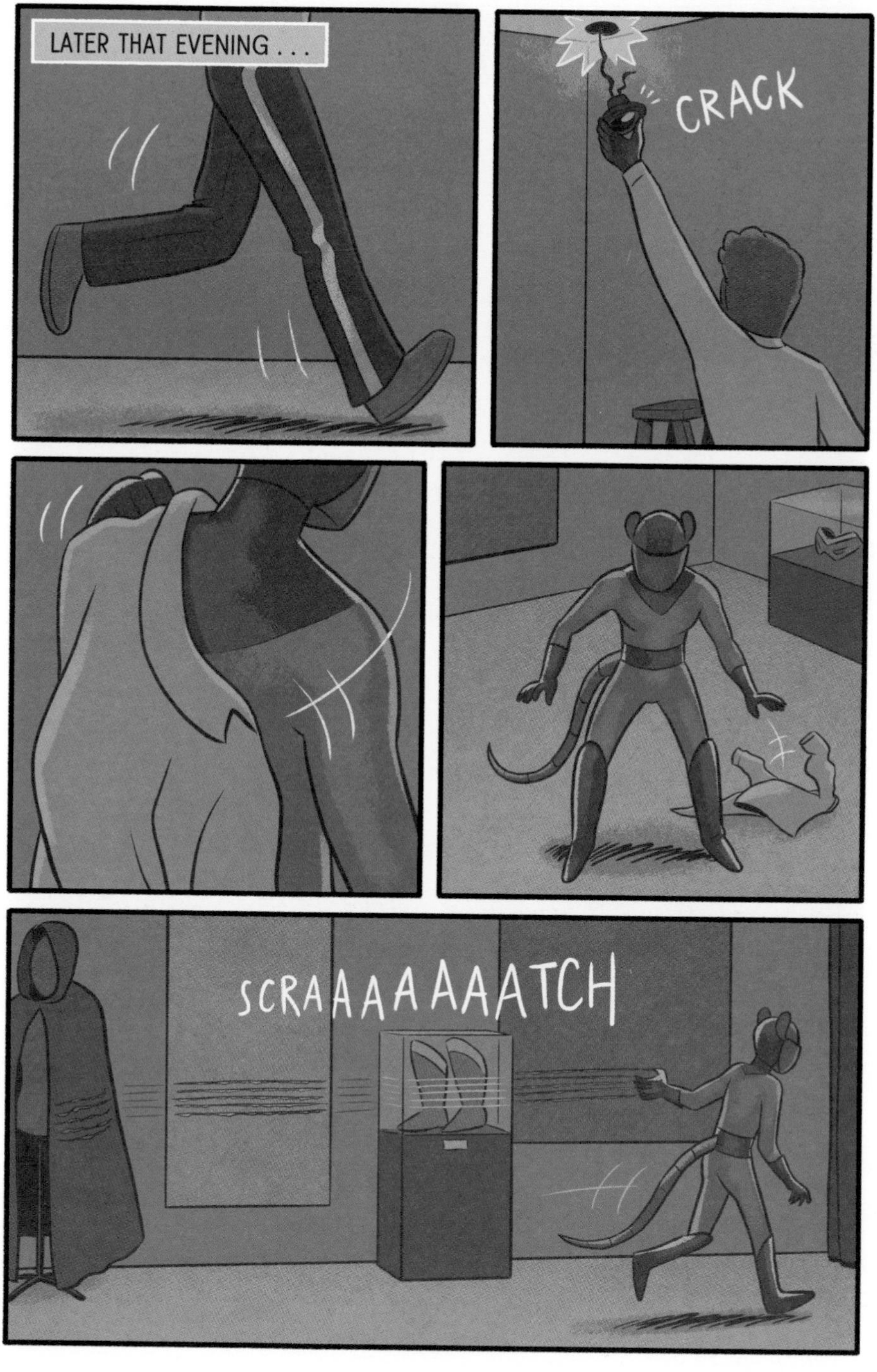
LATER THAT EVENING . . .
CRACK
SCRAAAAAAATCH

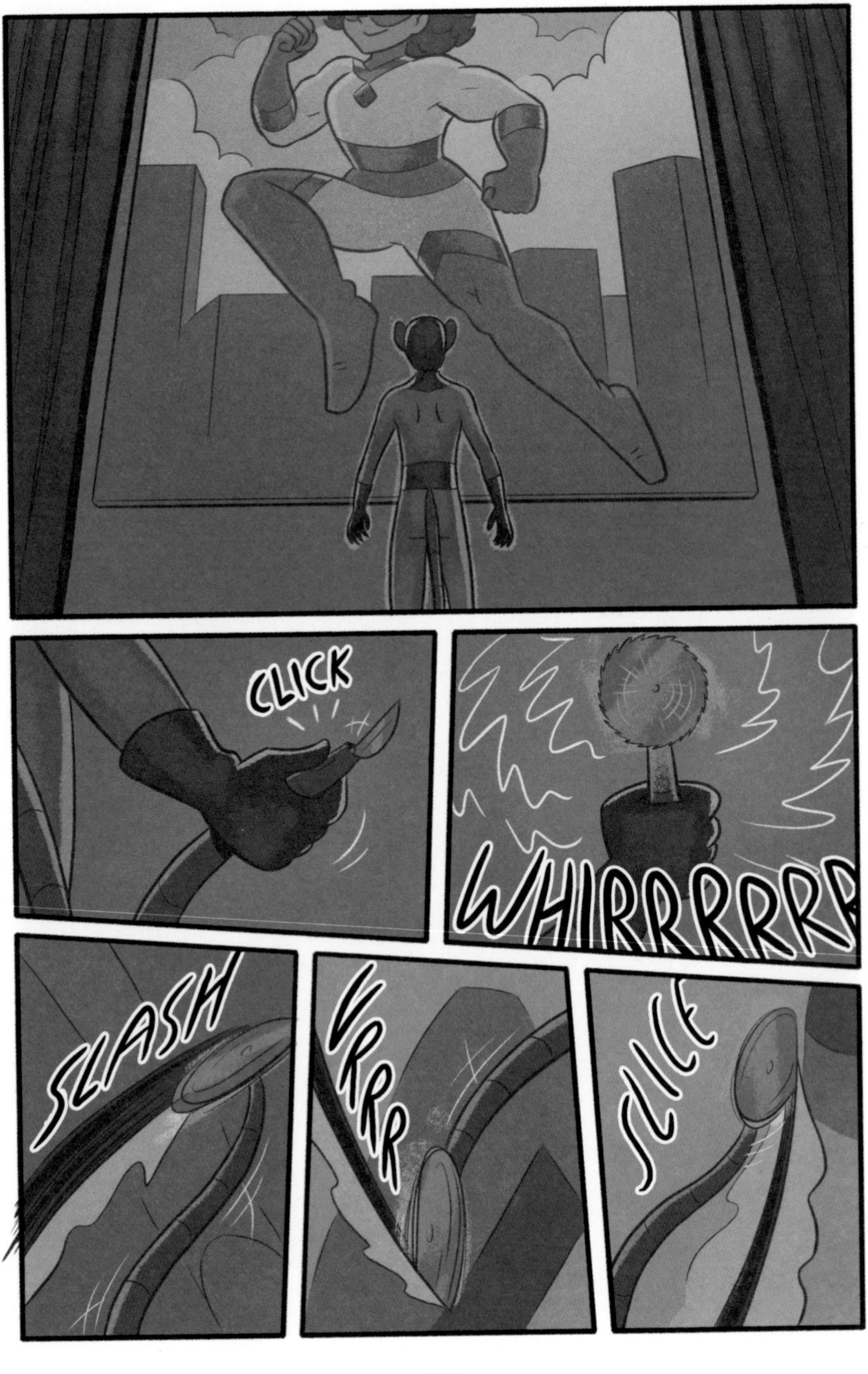
CLICK
WHIRRRRRR
SLASH
VRRR
SLICE

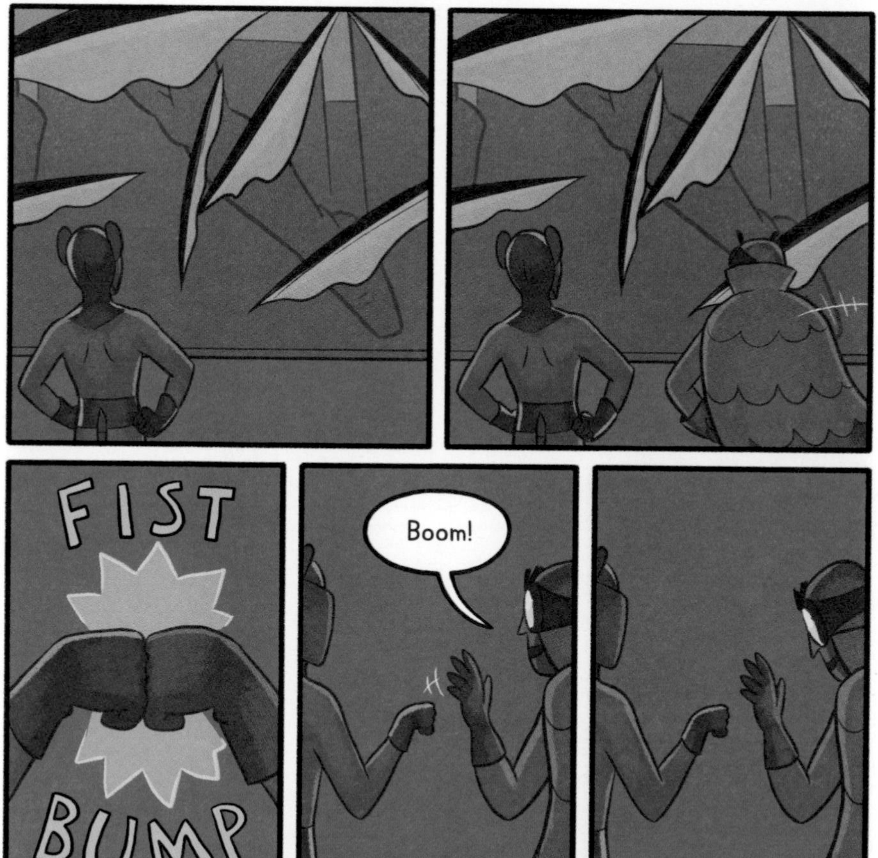
FIST BUMP
Boom!
Whatever.

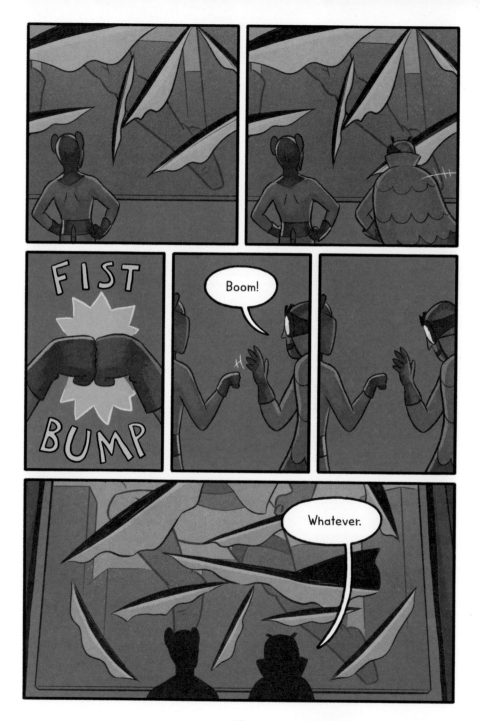

CHAPTER EIGHT

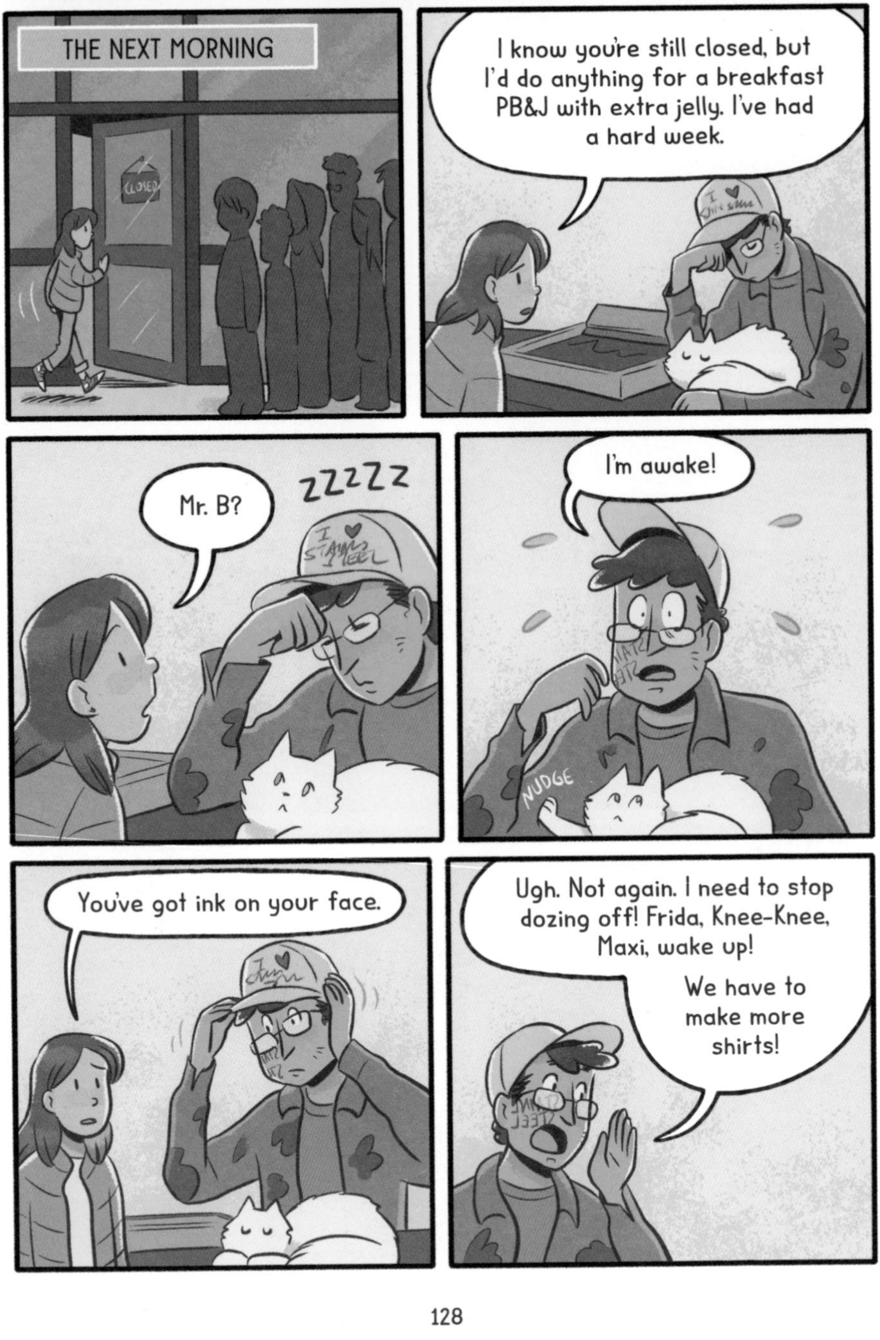

THE NEXT MORNING
CLOSED
I know you're still closed, but I'd do anything for a breakfast PB&J with extra jelly. I've had a hard week.
Mr. B?
ZZZZZ
I'm awake!
NUDGE
You've got ink on your face.
Ugh. Not again. I need to stop dozing off! Frida, Knee-Knee, Maxi, wake up!
We have to make more shirts!

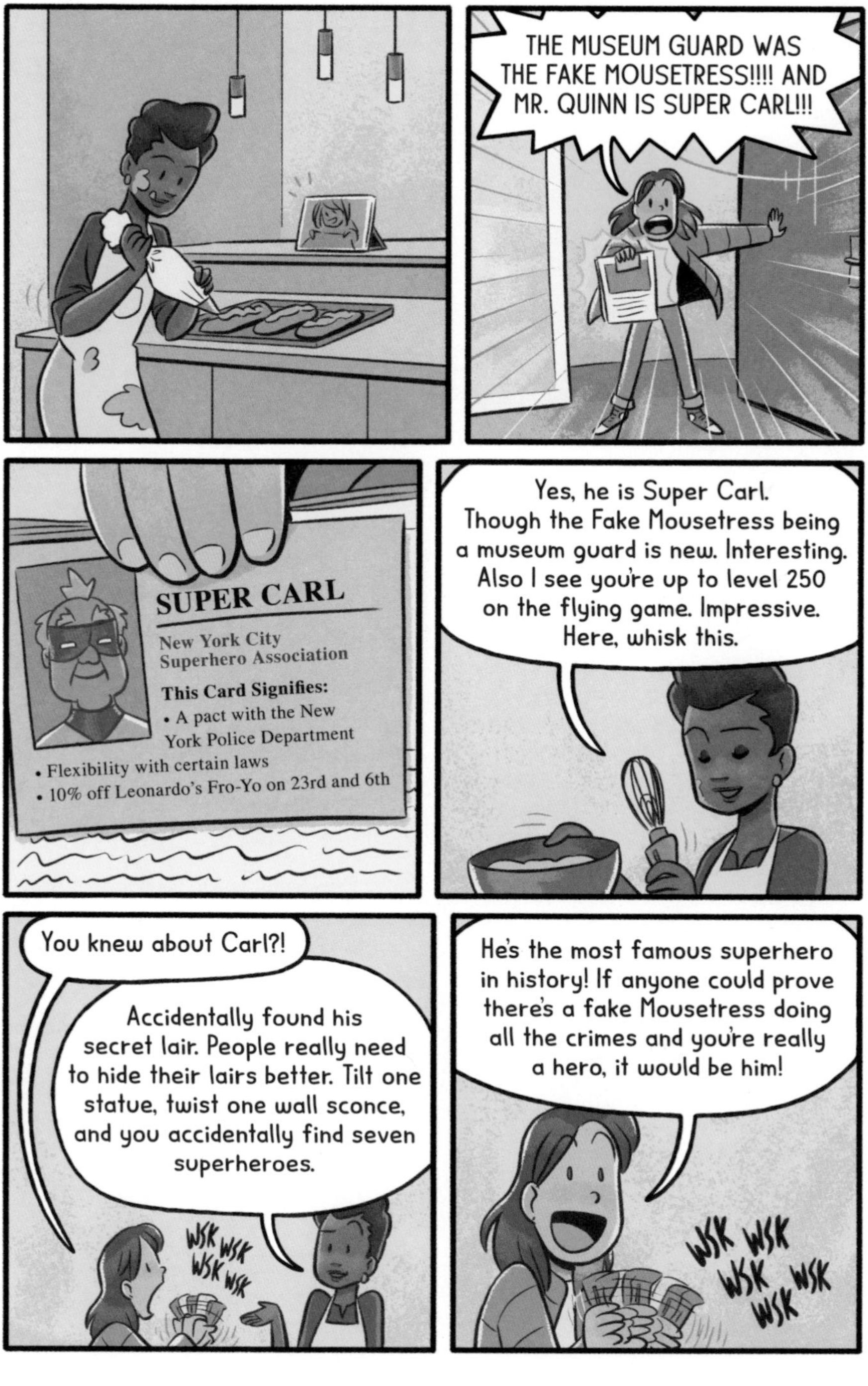
THE MUSEUM GUARD WAS THE FAKE MOUSETRESS!!!! AND MR. QUINN IS SUPER CARL!!!
SUPER CARL
New York City Superhero Association
This Card Signifies:
• A pact with the New York Police Department
• Flexibility with certain laws
• 10% off Leonardo's Fro-Yo on 23rd and 6th
Yes, he is Super Carl. Though the Fake Mousetress being a museum guard is new. Interesting. Also I see you're up to level 250 on the flying game. Impressive. Here, whisk this.
You knew about Carl?!
Accidentally found his secret lair. People really need to hide their lairs better. Tilt one statue, twist one wall sconce, and you accidentally find seven superheroes.
WSK WSK WSK WSK
He's the most famous superhero in history! If anyone could prove there's a fake Mousetress doing all the crimes and you're really a hero, it would be him!
WSK WSK WSK WSK WSK WSK

132

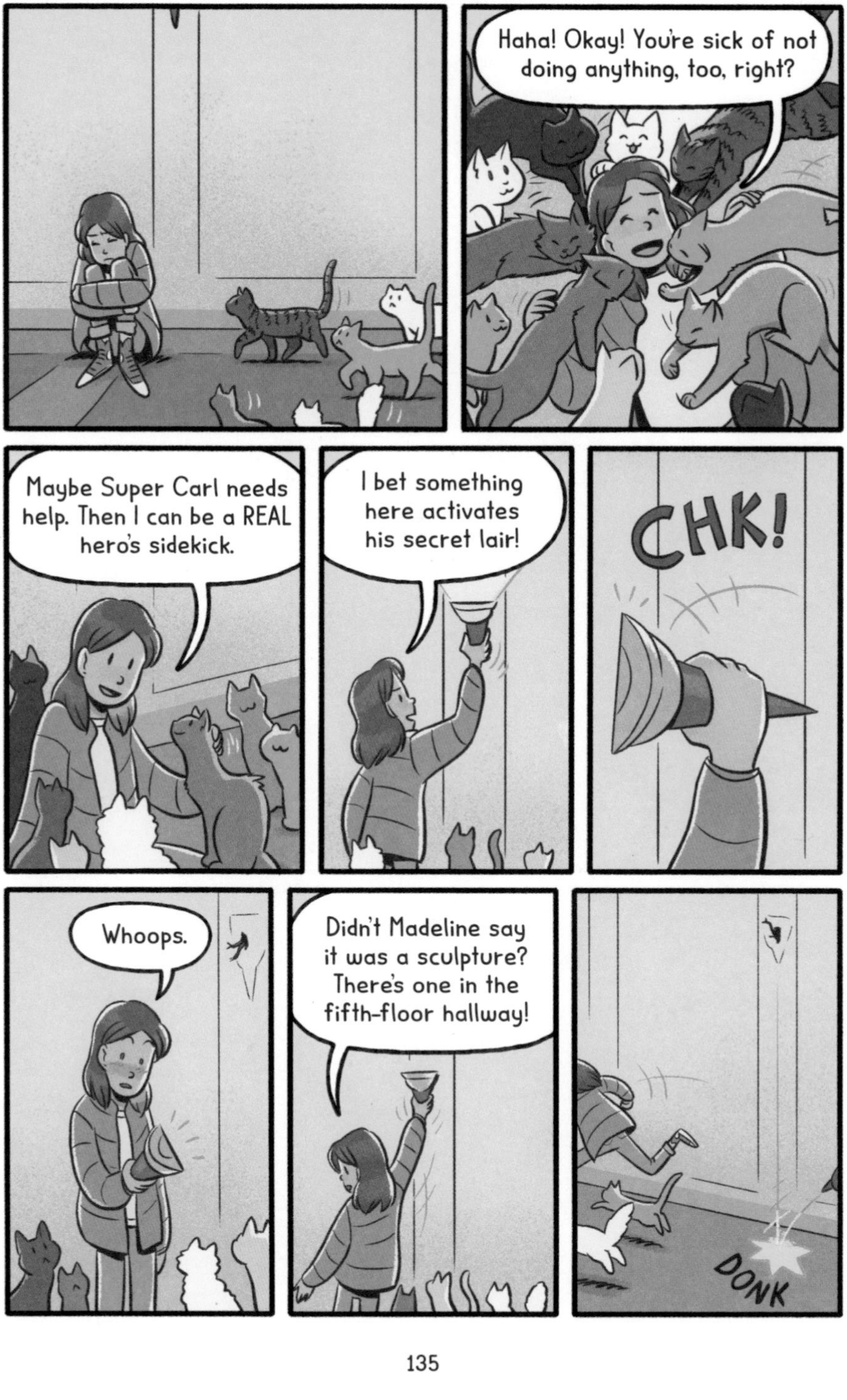
Haha! Okay! You're sick of not doing anything, too, right?
Maybe Super Carl needs help. Then I can be a REAL hero's sidekick.
I bet something here activates his secret lair!
CHK!
Whoops.
Didn't Madeline say it was a sculpture? There's one in the fifth-floor hallway!
DONK

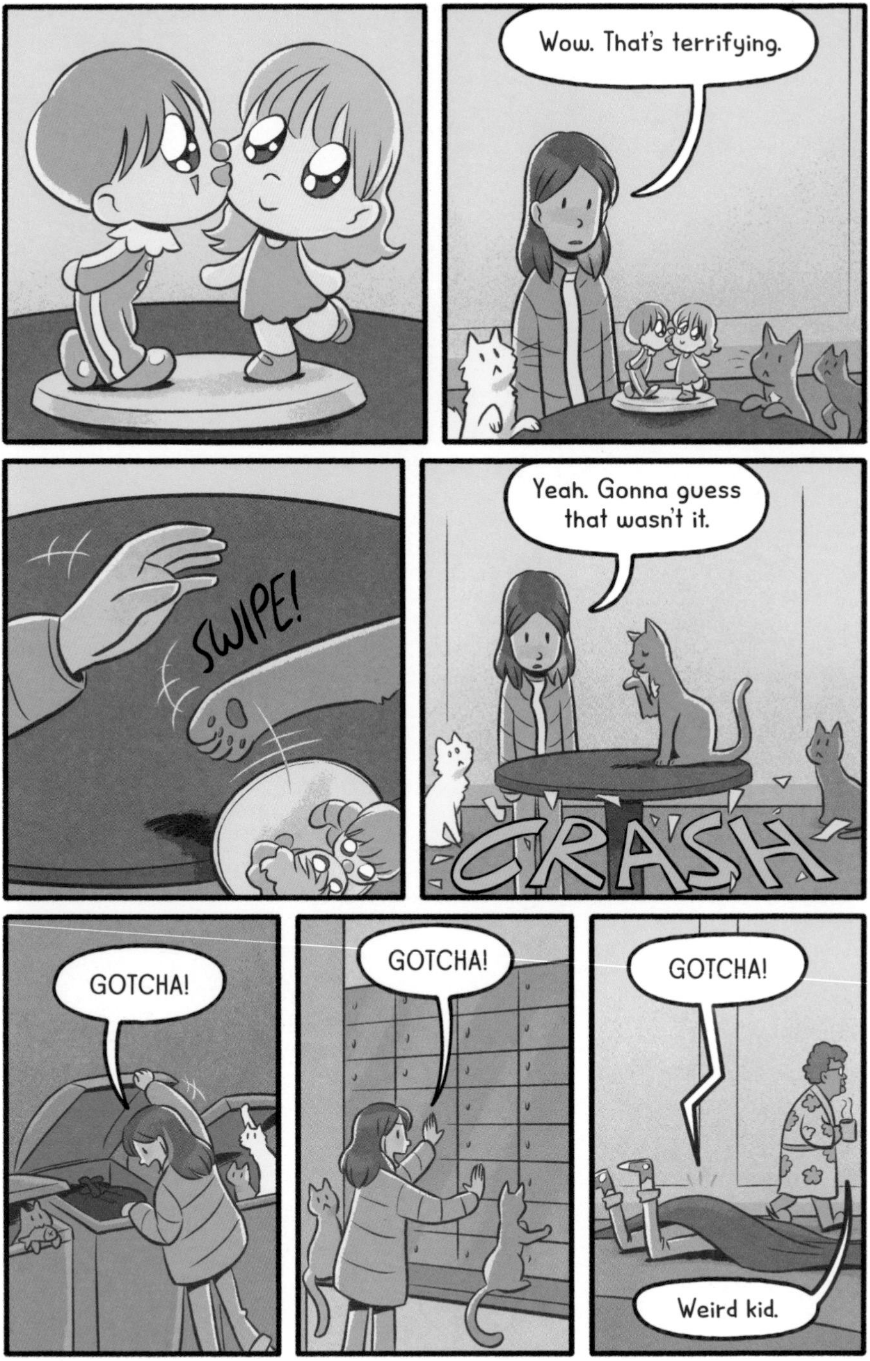
Wow. That's terrifying.
SWIPE!
Yeah. Gonna guess that wasn't it.
CRASH
GOTCHA!
GOTCHA!
GOTCHA!
Weird kid.

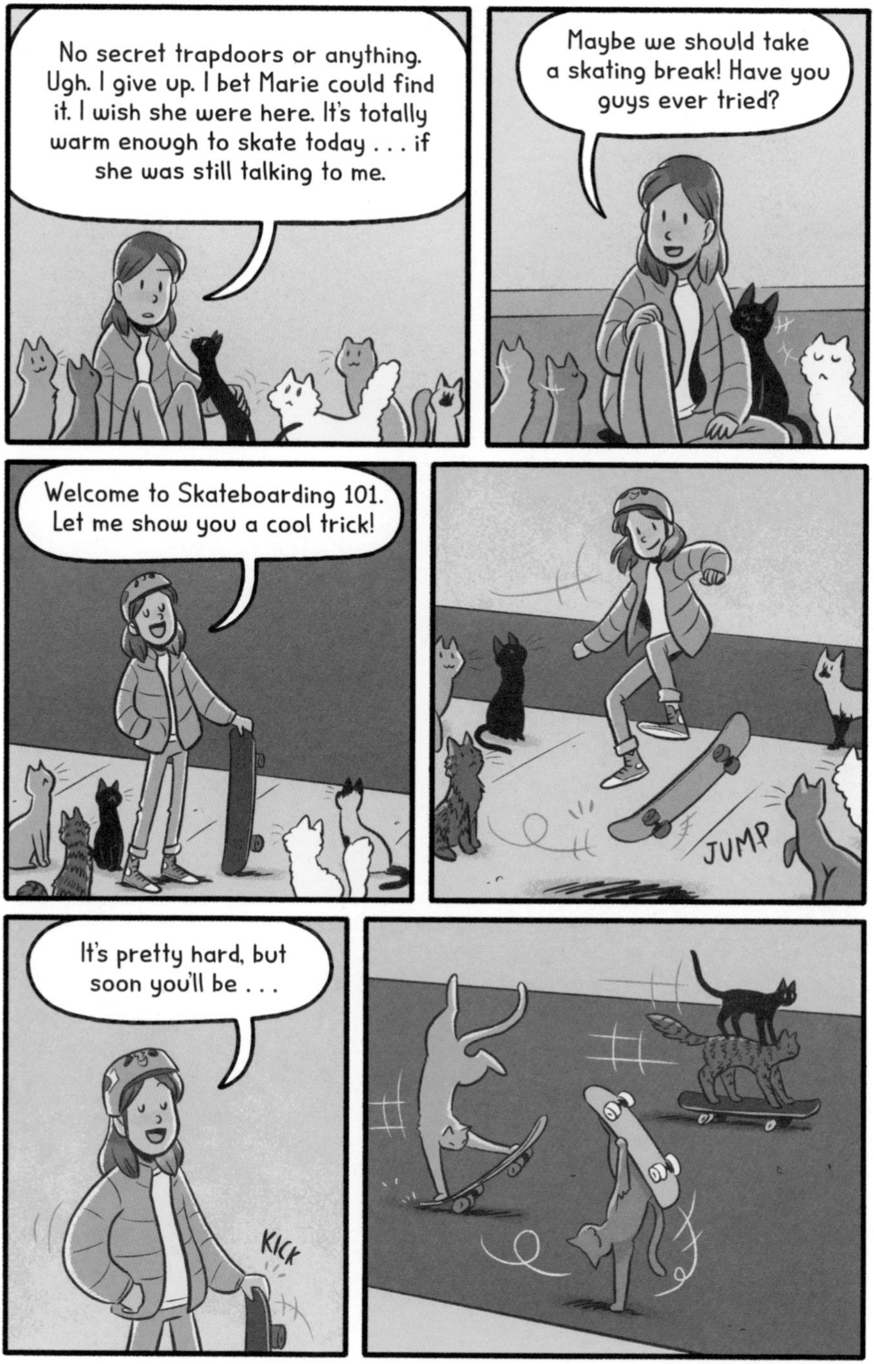
No secret trapdoors or anything. Ugh. I give up. I bet Marie could find it. I wish she were here. It's totally warm enough to skate today . . . if she was still talking to me.
Maybe we should take a skating break! Have you guys ever tried?
Welcome to Skateboarding 101. Let me show you a cool trick!
JUMP
It's pretty hard, but soon you'll be . . .
KICK

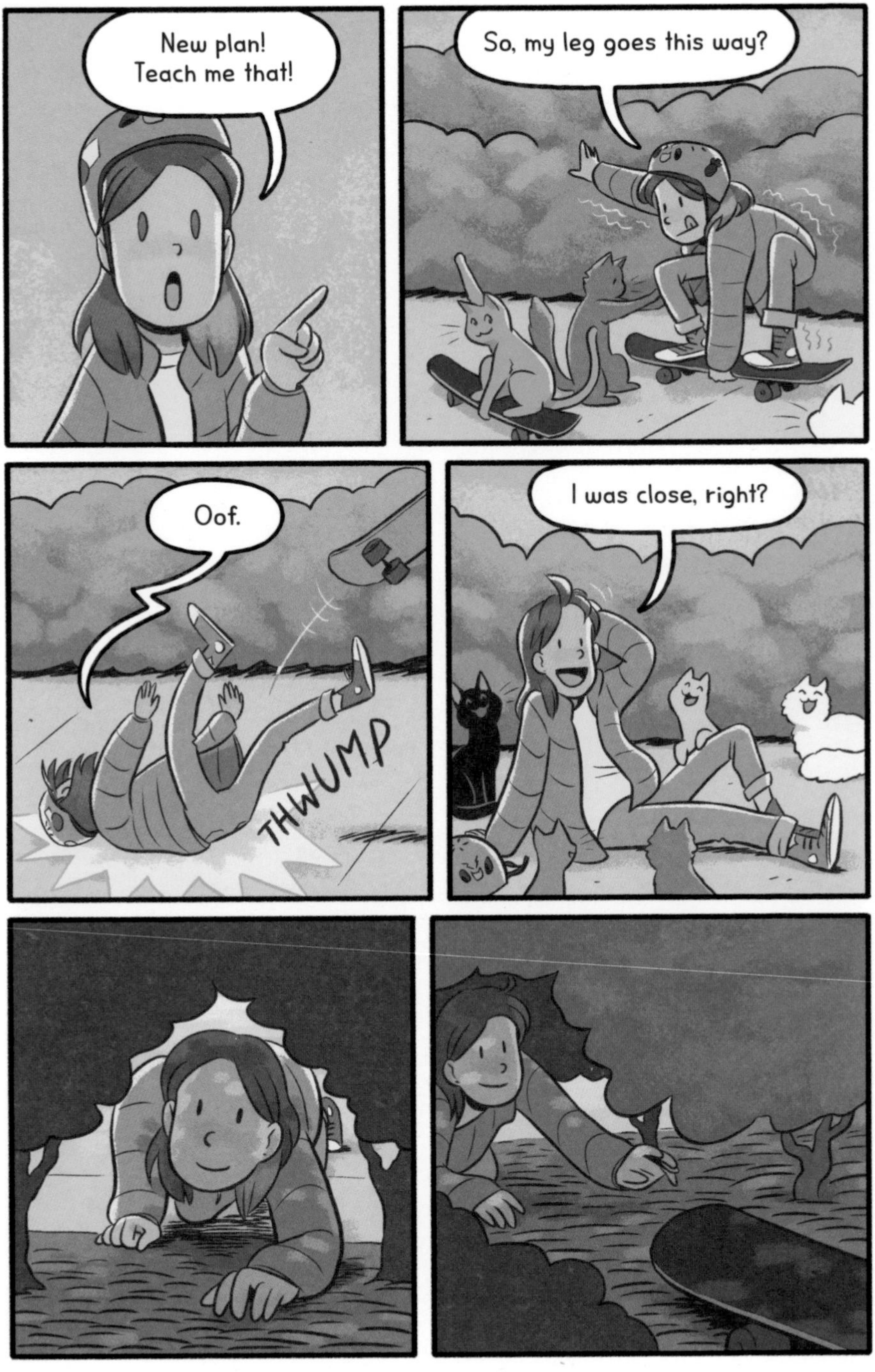
New plan! Teach me that!
So, my leg goes this way?
Oof.
THWUMP
I was close, right?

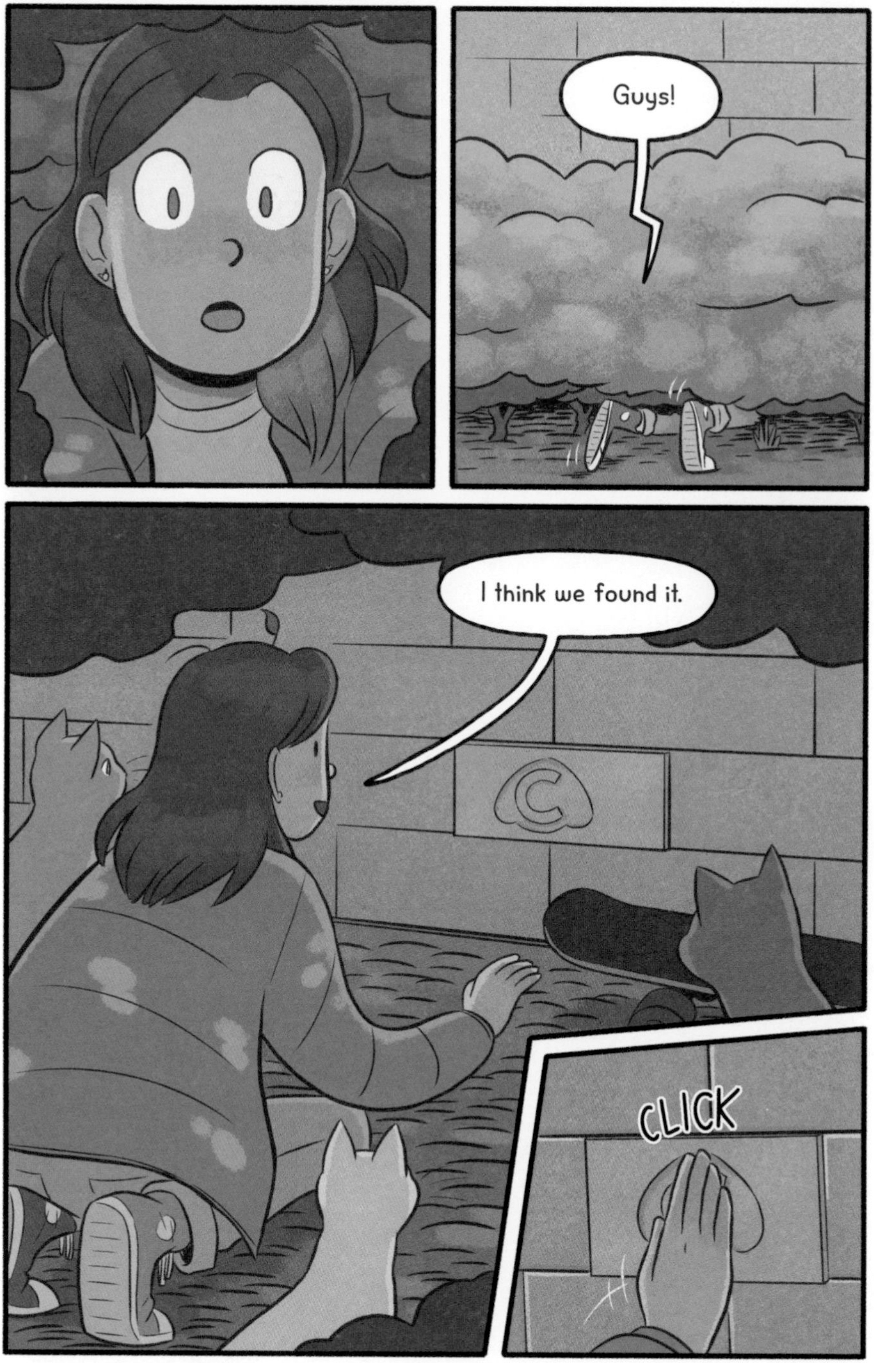
Guys!
I think we found it.
CLICK

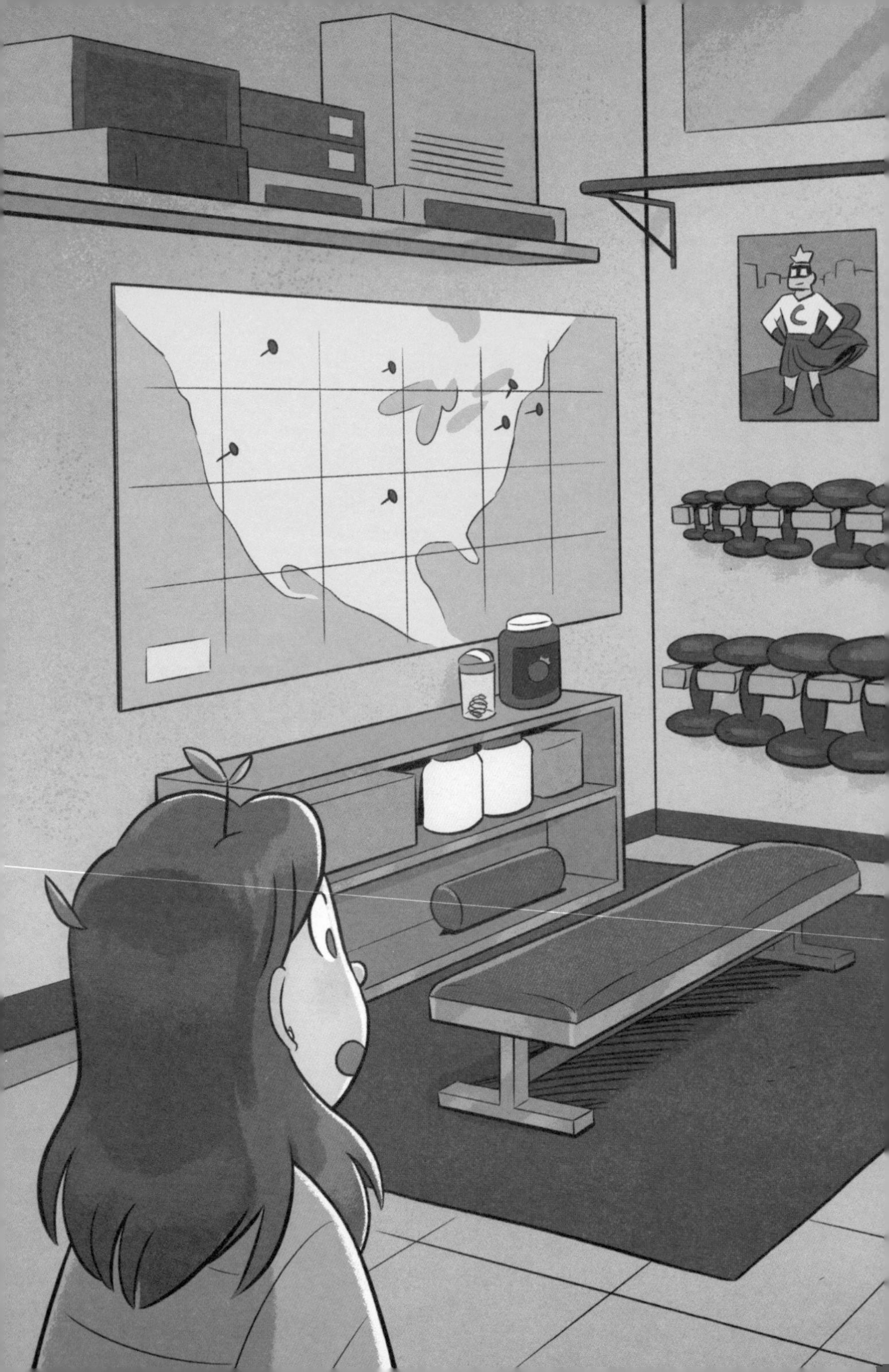

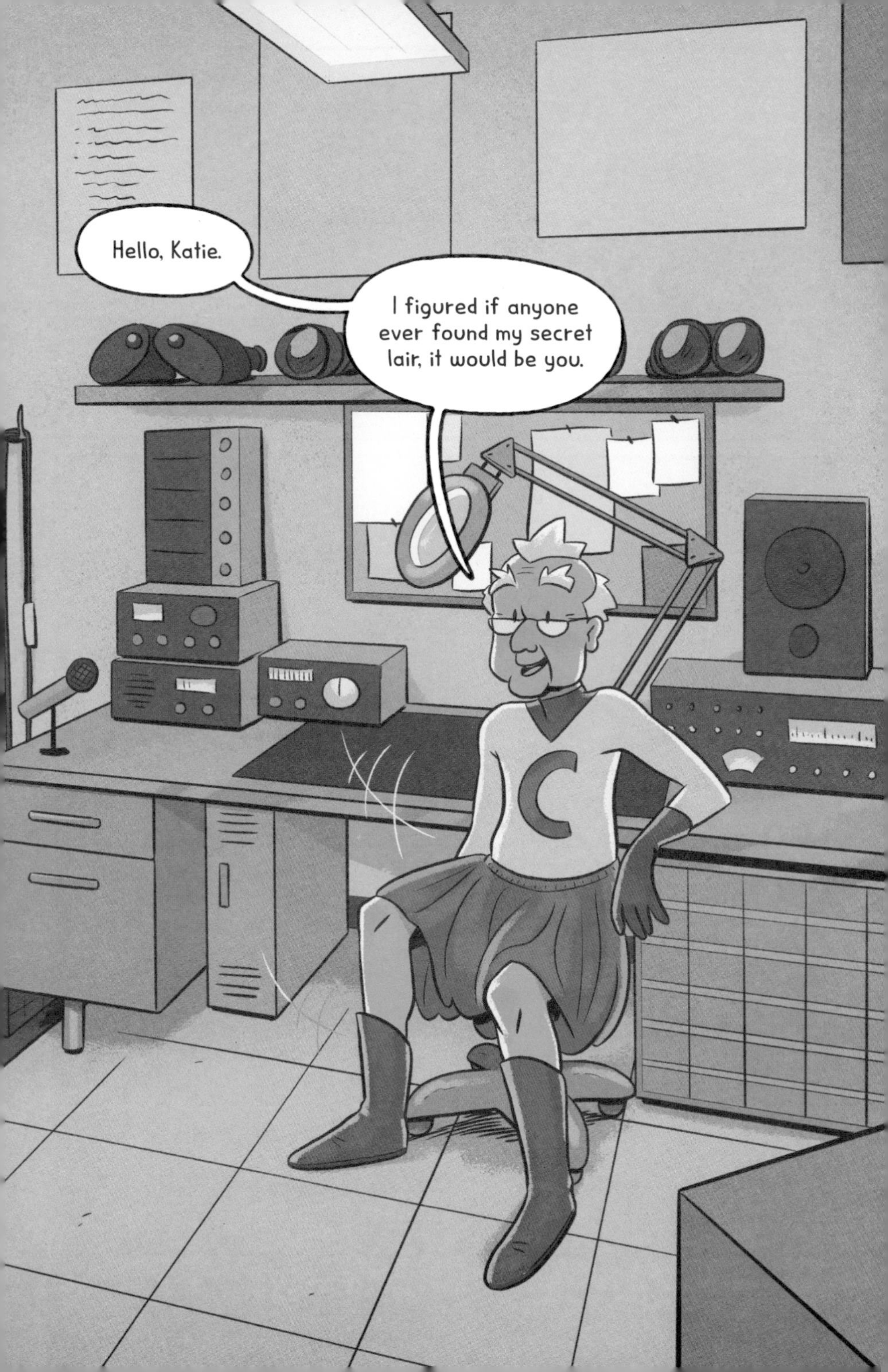
Hello, Katie.
I figured if anyone ever found my secret lair, it would be you.

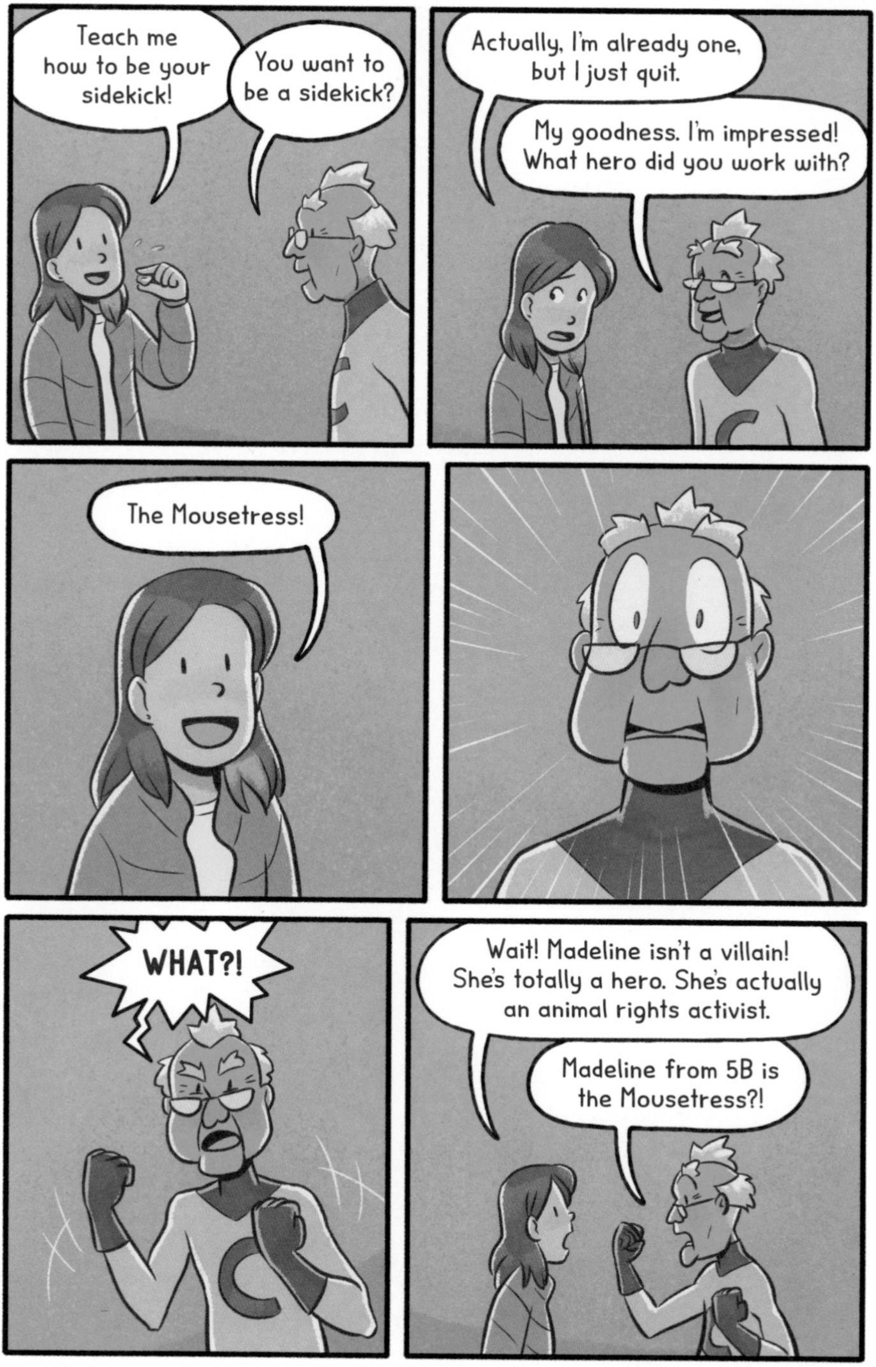
Teach me how to be your sidekick!
You want to be a sidekick?
Actually, I'm already one, but I just quit.
My goodness. I'm impressed! What hero did you work with?
The Mousetress!
WHAT?!
Wait! Madeline isn't a villain! She's totally a hero. She's actually an animal rights activist.
Madeline from 5B is the Mousetress?!

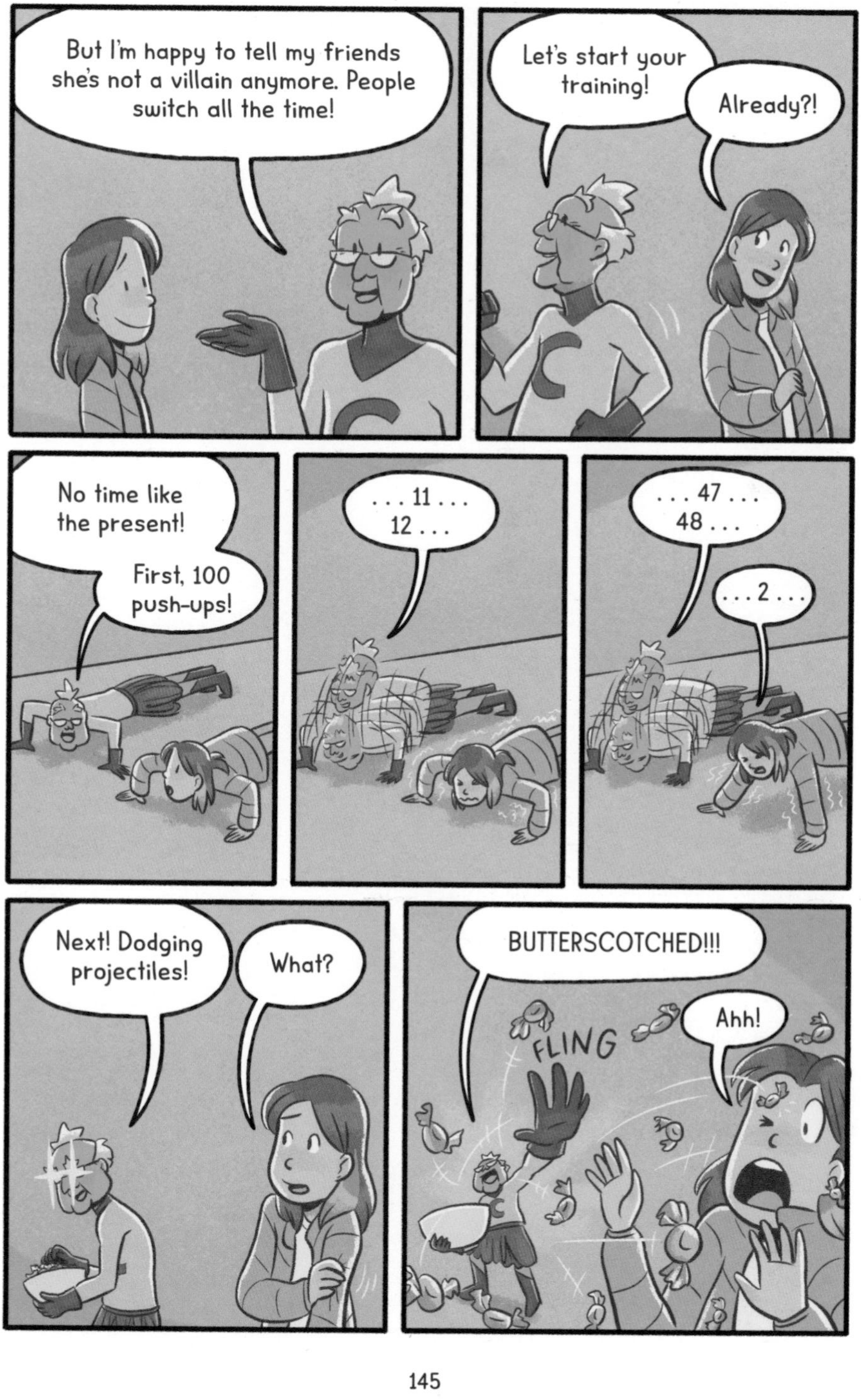
But I'm happy to tell my friends she's not a villain anymore. People switch all the time!
Let's start your training!
Already?!
No time like the present!
First, 100 push-ups!
. . . 11 . . . 12 . . .
. . . 47 . . . 48 . . .
. . . 2 . . .
Next! Dodging projectiles!
What?
BUTTERSCOTCHED!!!
FLING
Ahh!

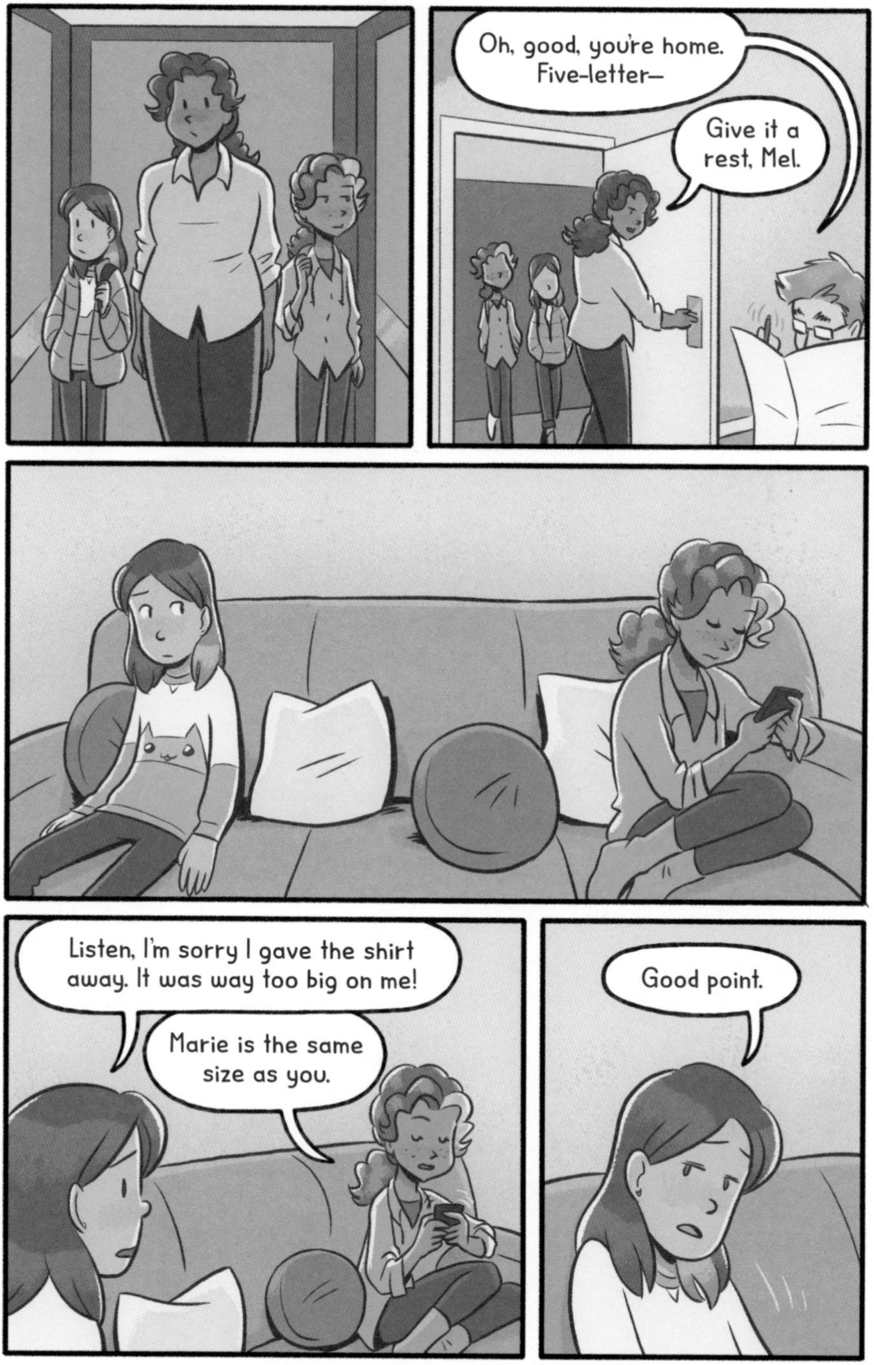
Oh, good, you're home. Five-letter–
Give it a rest, Mel.
Listen, I'm sorry I gave the shirt away. It was way too big on me!
Marie is the same size as you.
Good point.

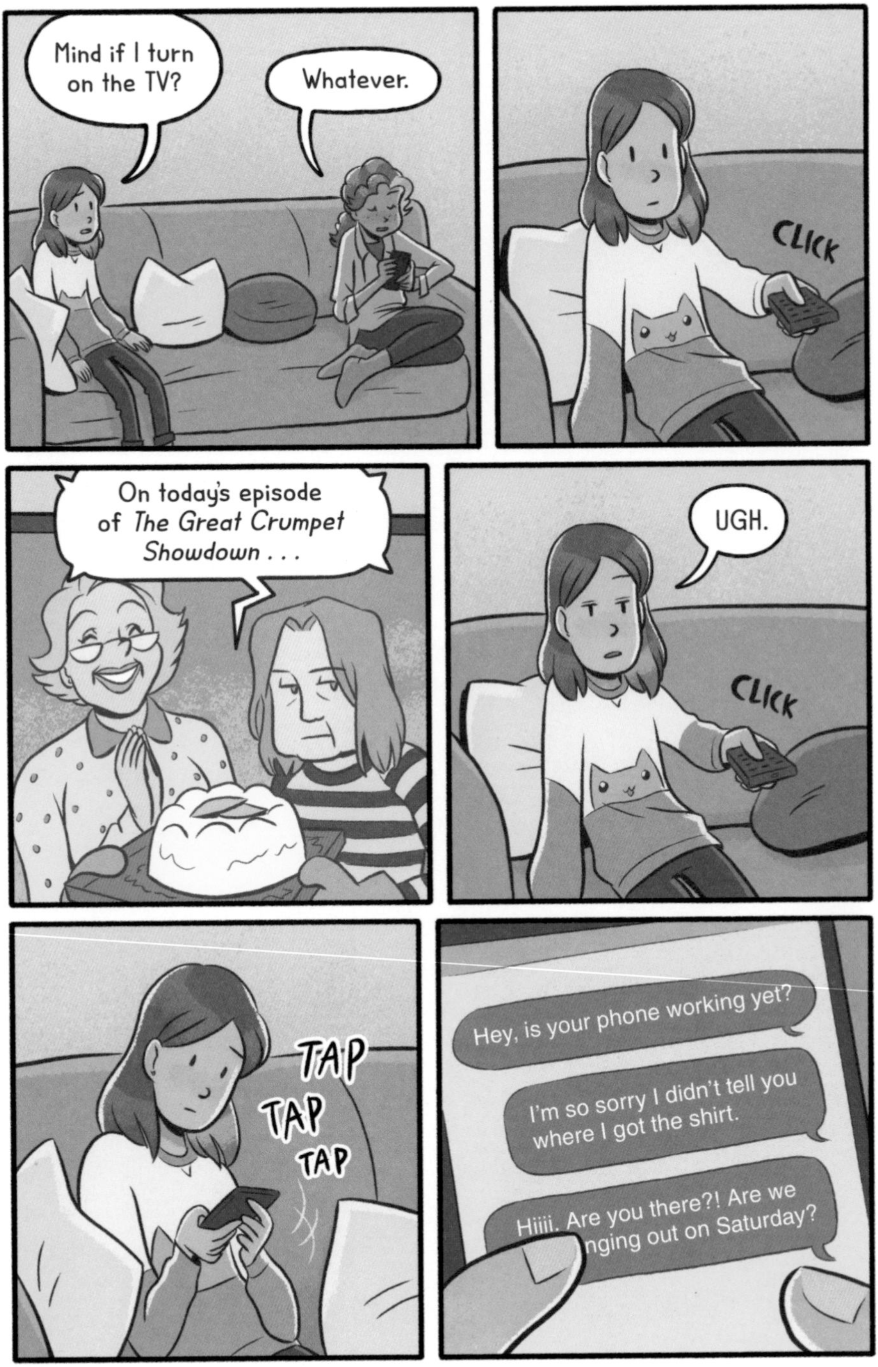
Mind if I turn on the TV?
Whatever.
CLICK
On today's episode of *The Great Crumpet Showdown* . . .
UGH.
CLICK
TAP
TAP
TAP
Hey, is your phone working yet?
I'm so sorry I didn't tell you where I got the shirt.
Hiiii. Are you there?! Are we
nging out on Saturday?

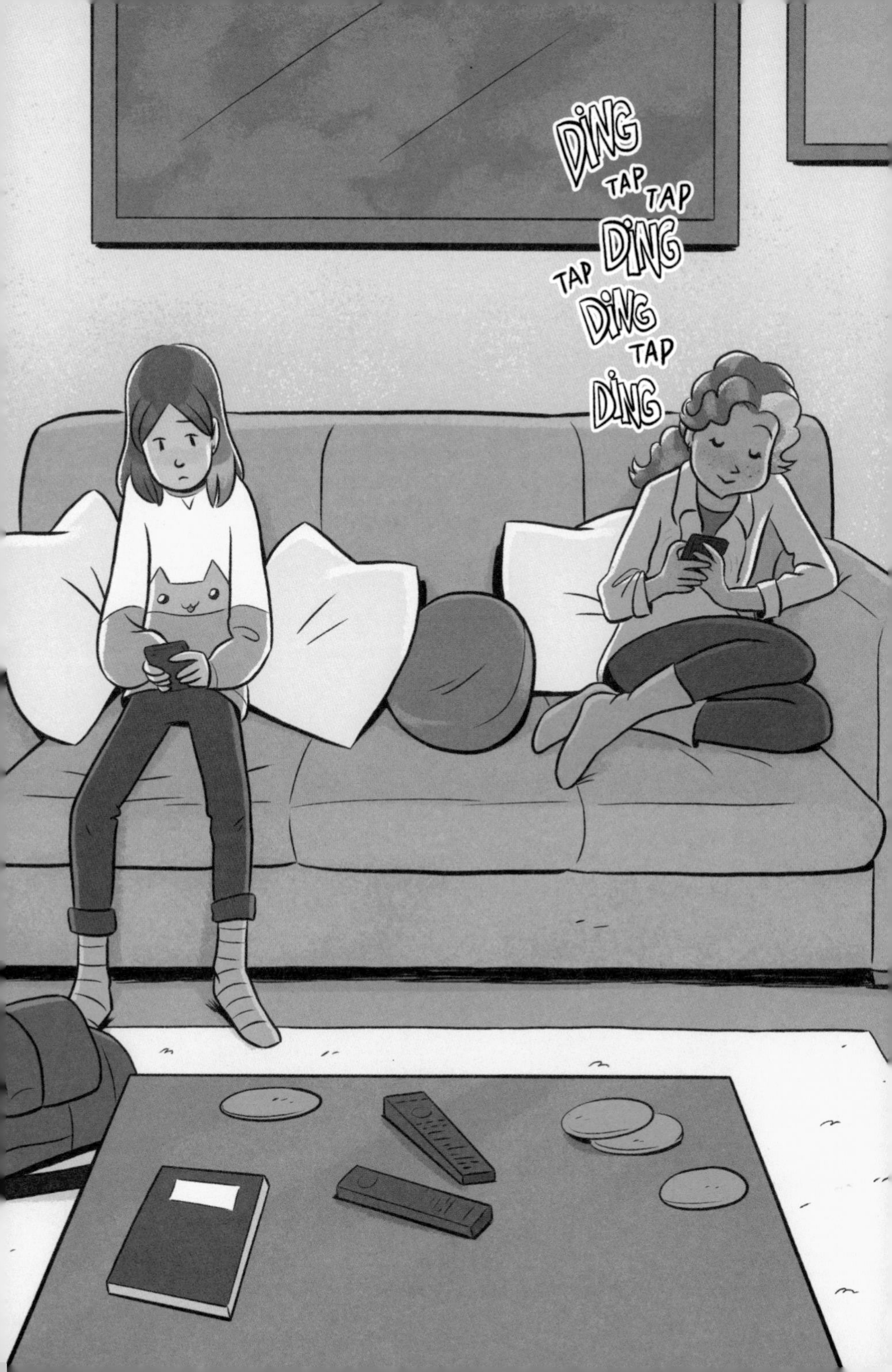
DING
TAP TAP
DING
TAP
DING
TAP
DING

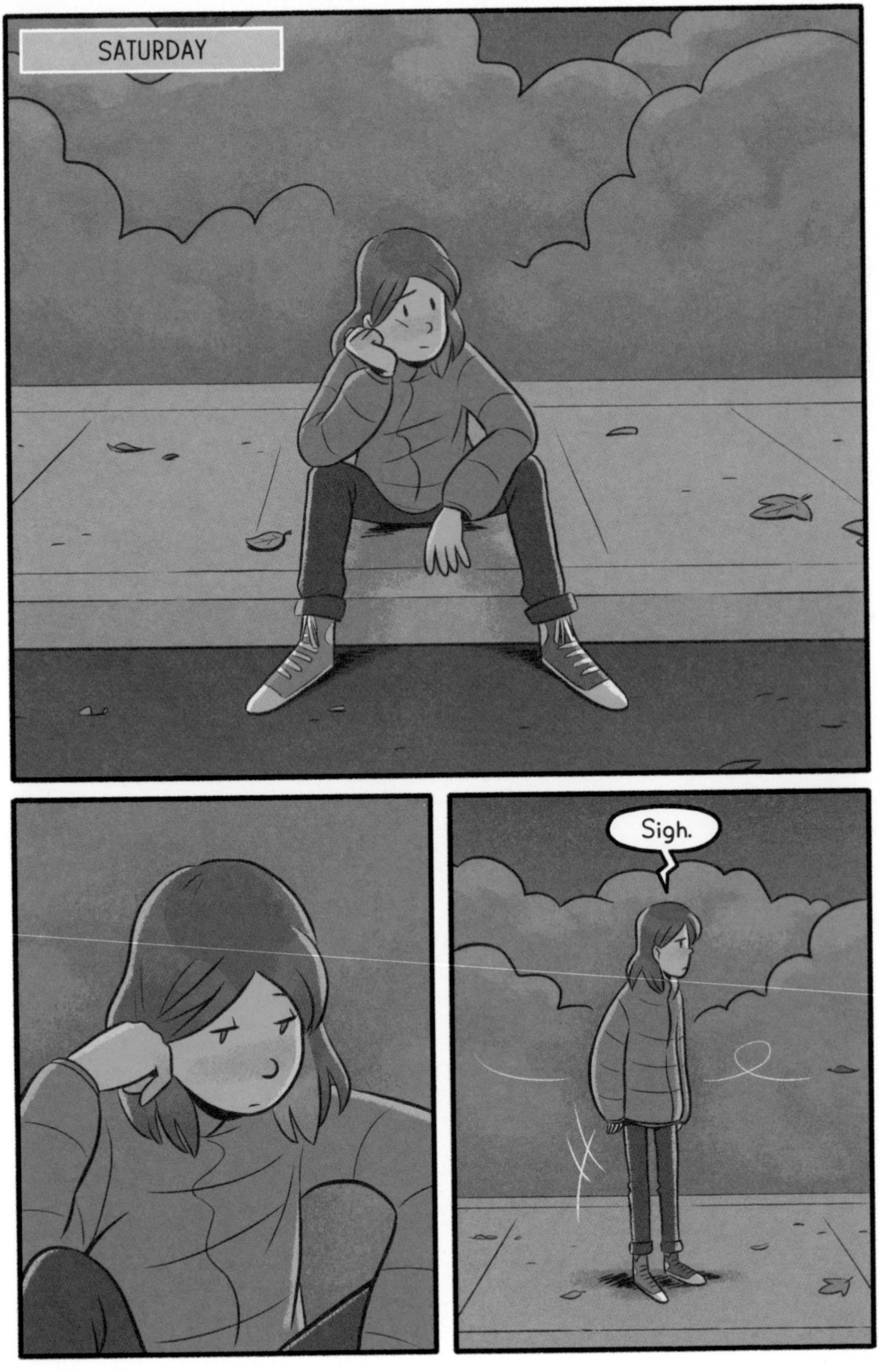
SATURDAY
Sigh.

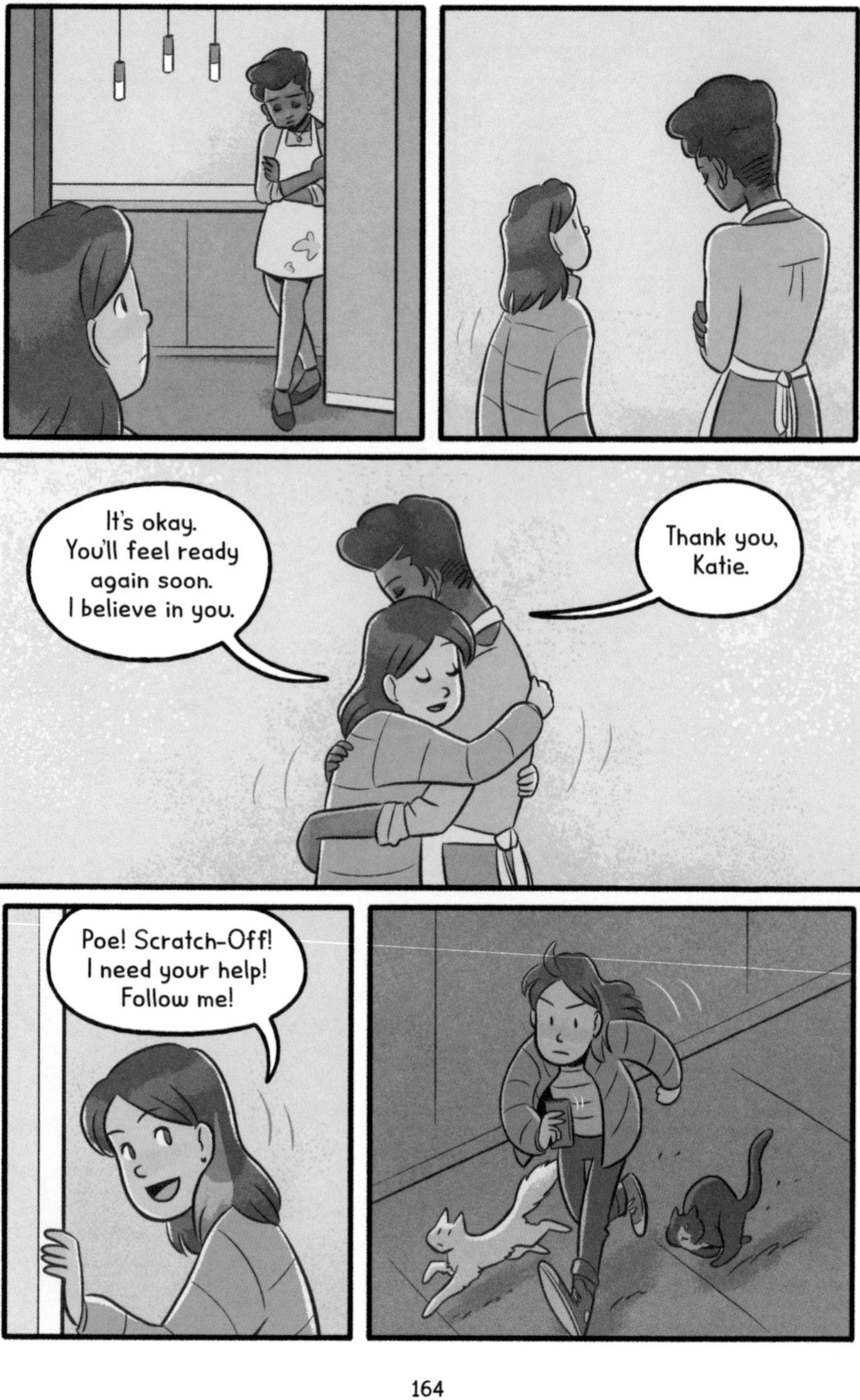
It's okay. You'll feel ready again soon. I believe in you.
Thank you, Katie.
Poe! Scratch-Off! I need your help! Follow me!

CHAPTER TEN

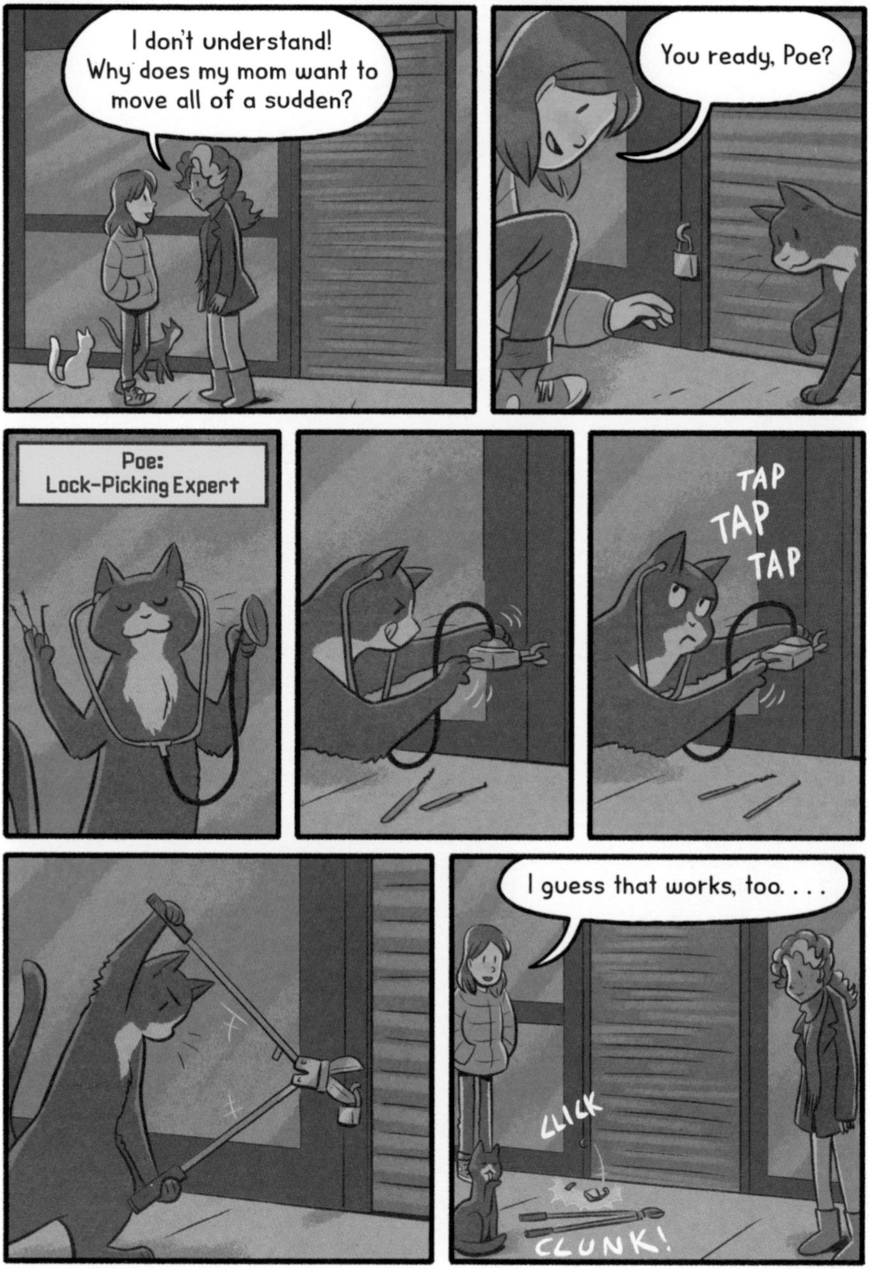
I don't understand! Why does my mom want to move all of a sudden?
You ready, Poe?
Poe: Lock-Picking Expert
TAP TAP TAP
I guess that works, too. . . .
CLICK
CLUNK!

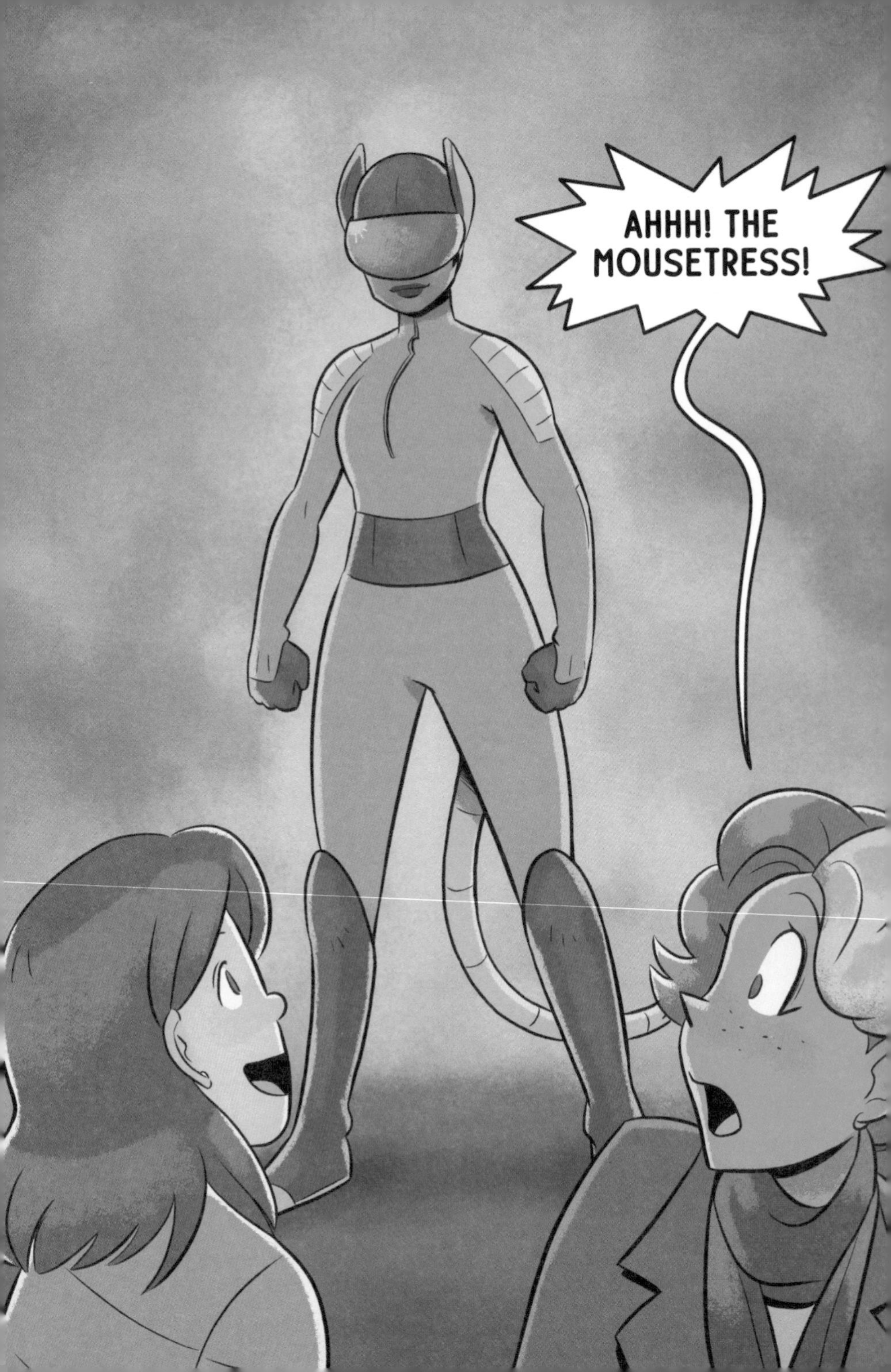
AHHH! THE MOUSETRESS!

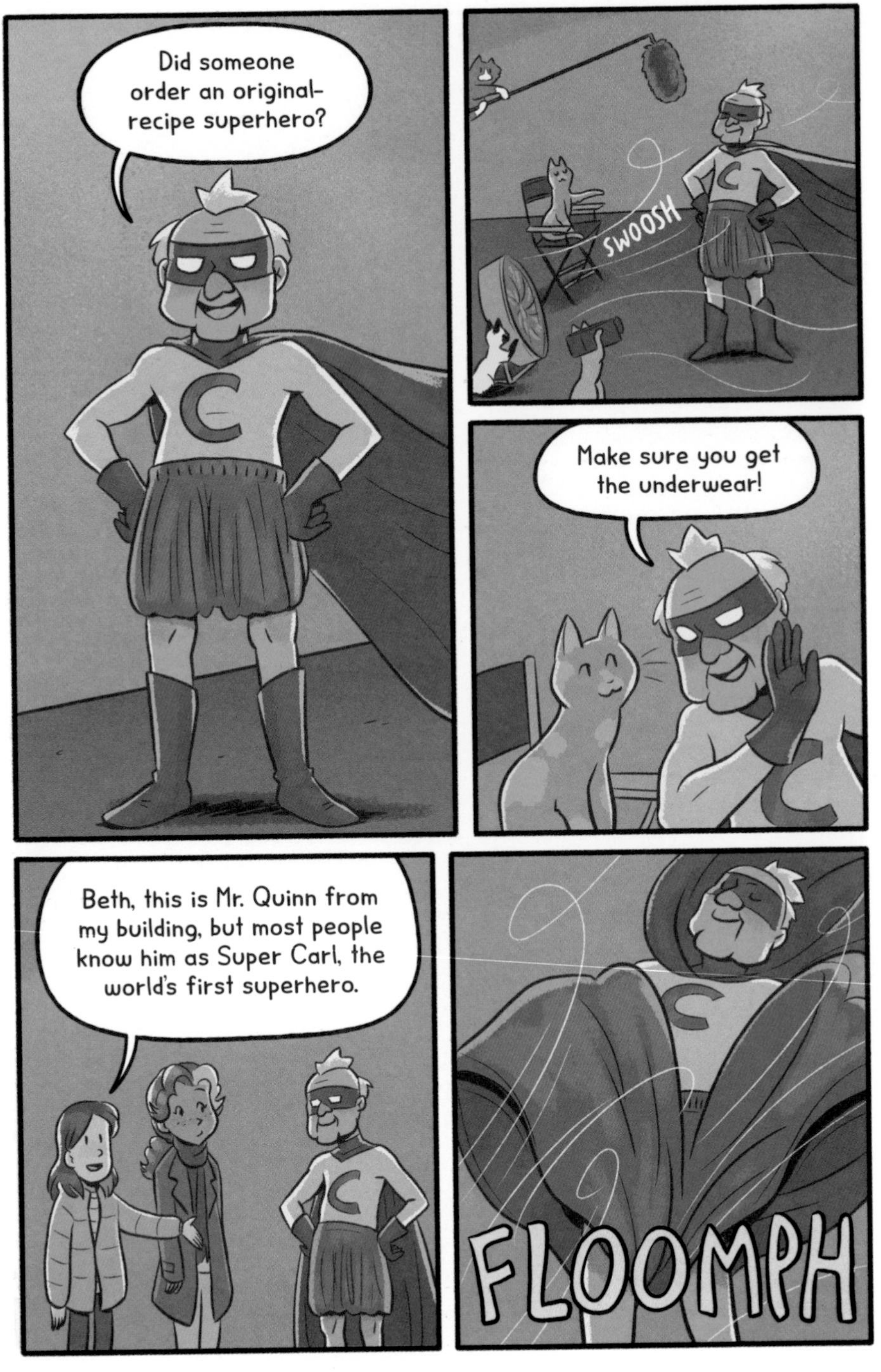
Did someone order an original-recipe superhero?
SWOOSH
Make sure you get the underwear!
Beth, this is Mr. Quinn from my building, but most people know him as Super Carl, the world's first superhero.
FLOOMPH

173

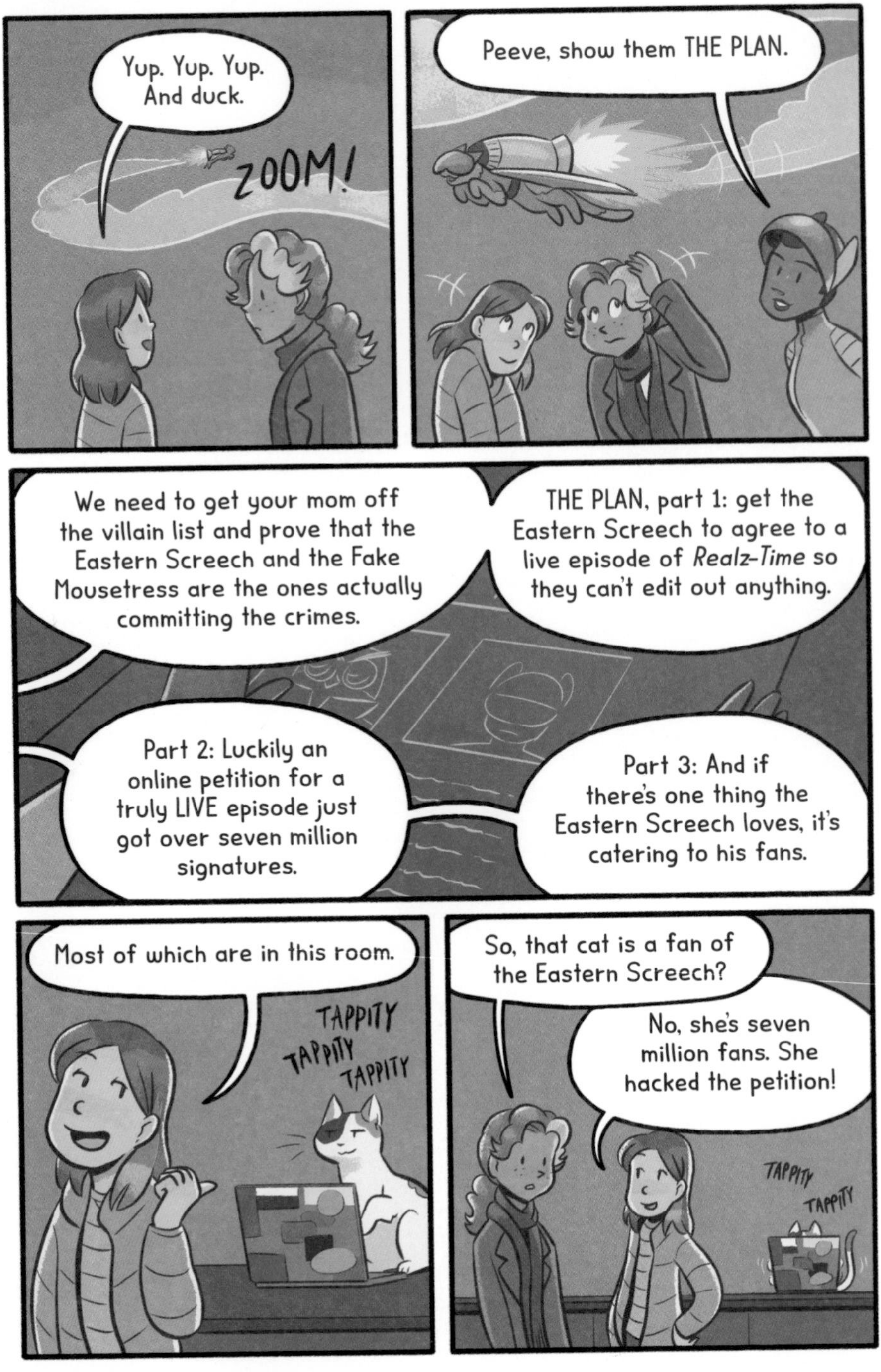
Yup. Yup. Yup. And duck.
ZOOM!
Peeve, show them THE PLAN.
We need to get your mom off the villain list and prove that the Eastern Screech and the Fake Mousetress are the ones actually committing the crimes.
THE PLAN, part 1: get the Eastern Screech to agree to a live episode of *Realz-Time* so they can't edit out anything.
Part 2: Luckily an online petition for a truly LIVE episode just got over seven million signatures.
Part 3: And if there's one thing the Eastern Screech loves, it's catering to his fans.
Most of which are in this room.
TAPPITY
TAPPITY
TAPPITY
So, that cat is a fan of the Eastern Screech?
No, she's seven million fans. She hacked the petition!
TAPPITY
TAPPITY

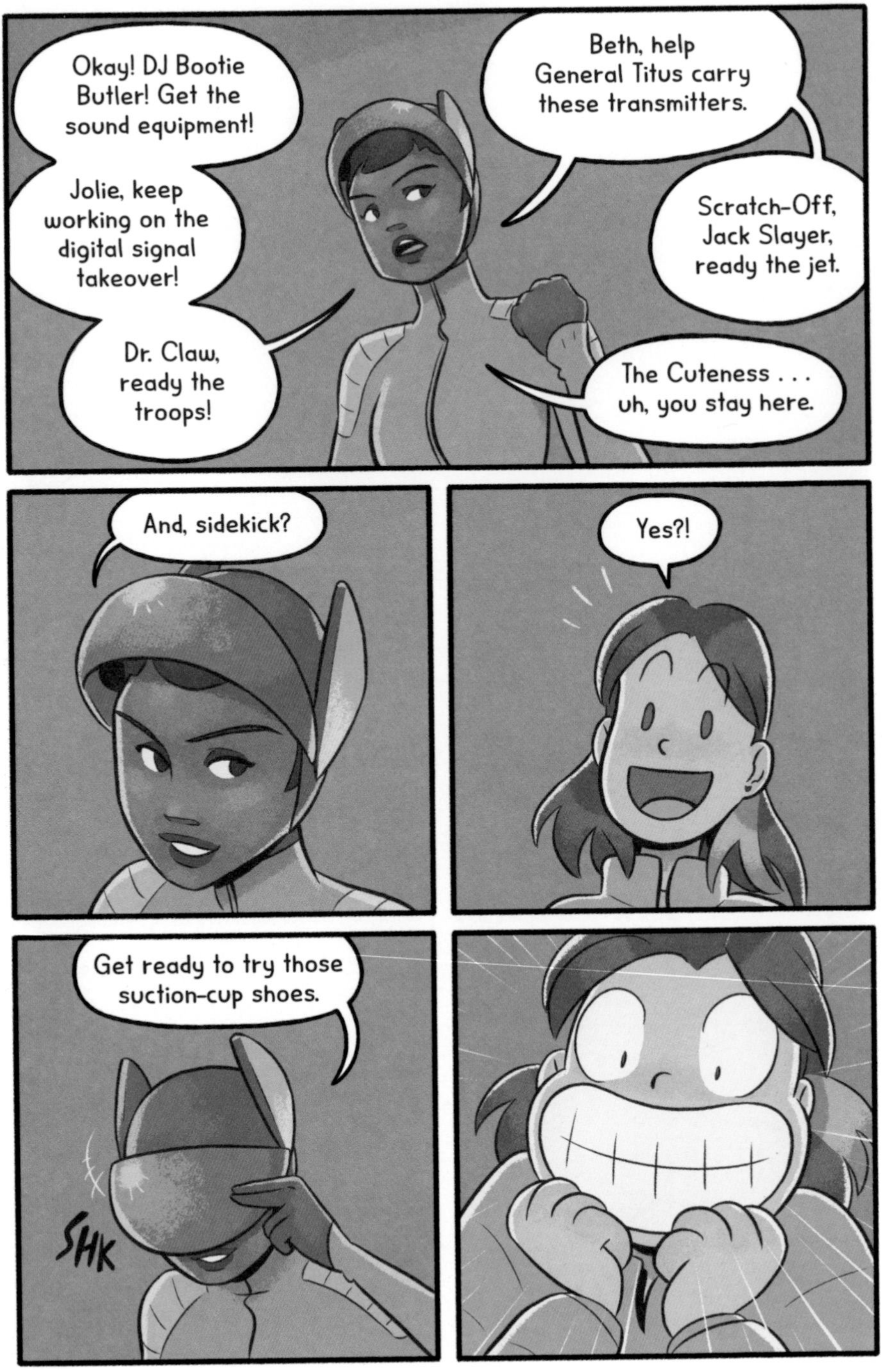

Okay! DJ Bootie Butler! Get the sound equipment!
Jolie, keep working on the digital signal takeover!
Dr. Claw, ready the troops!
Beth, help General Titus carry these transmitters.
Scratch-Off, Jack Slayer, ready the jet.
The Cuteness . . . uh, you stay here.
And, sidekick?
Yes?!
Get ready to try those suction-cup shoes.
SHK

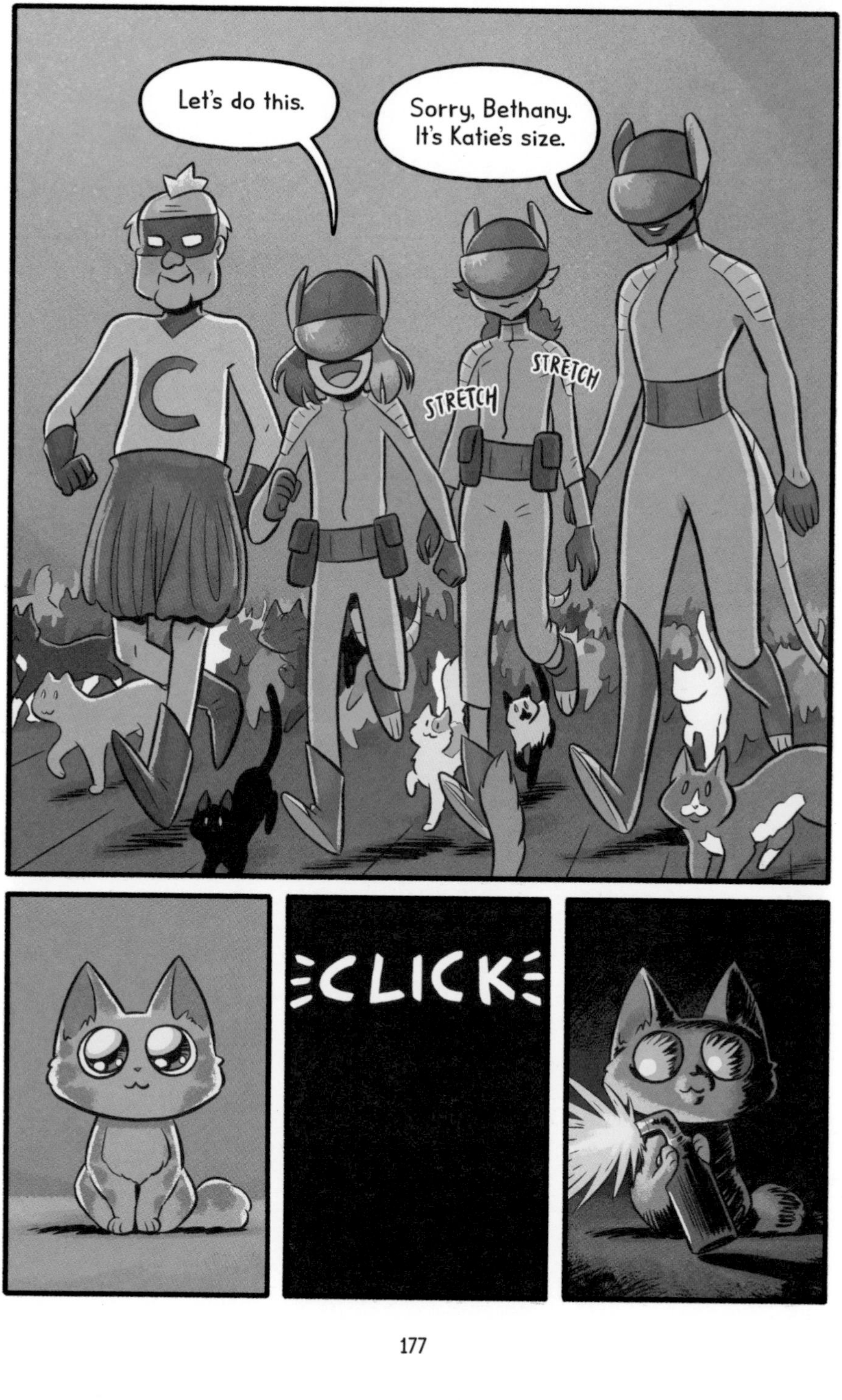
Let's do this.
Sorry, Bethany.
It's Katie's size.
STRETCH
STRETCH
CLICK

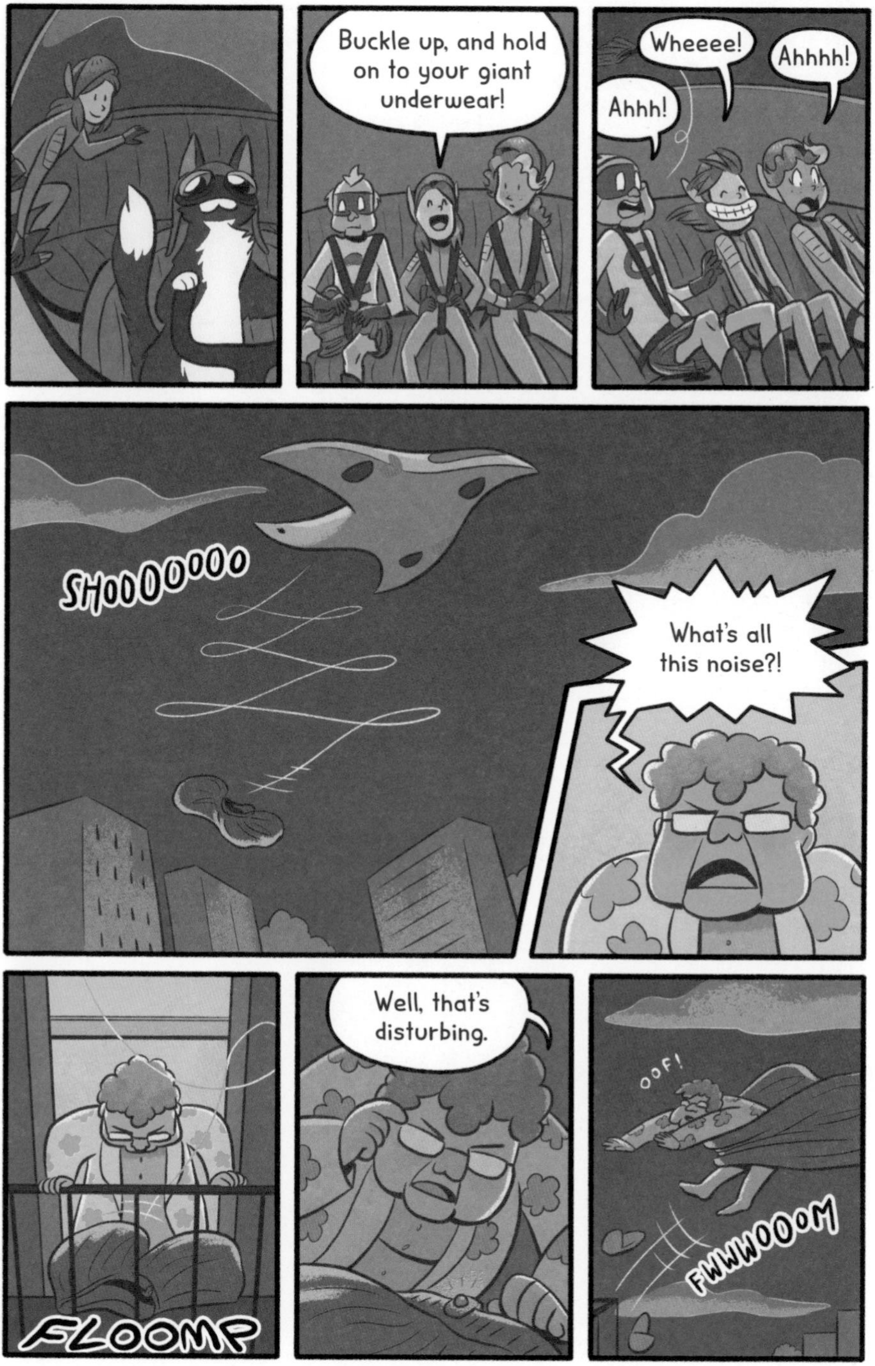
Buckle up, and hold on to your giant underwear!
Wheeee!
Ahhhh!
Ahhh!
SHOOOOOOO
What's all this noise?!
FLOOMP
Well, that's disturbing.
OOF!
FWWWOOOM

181

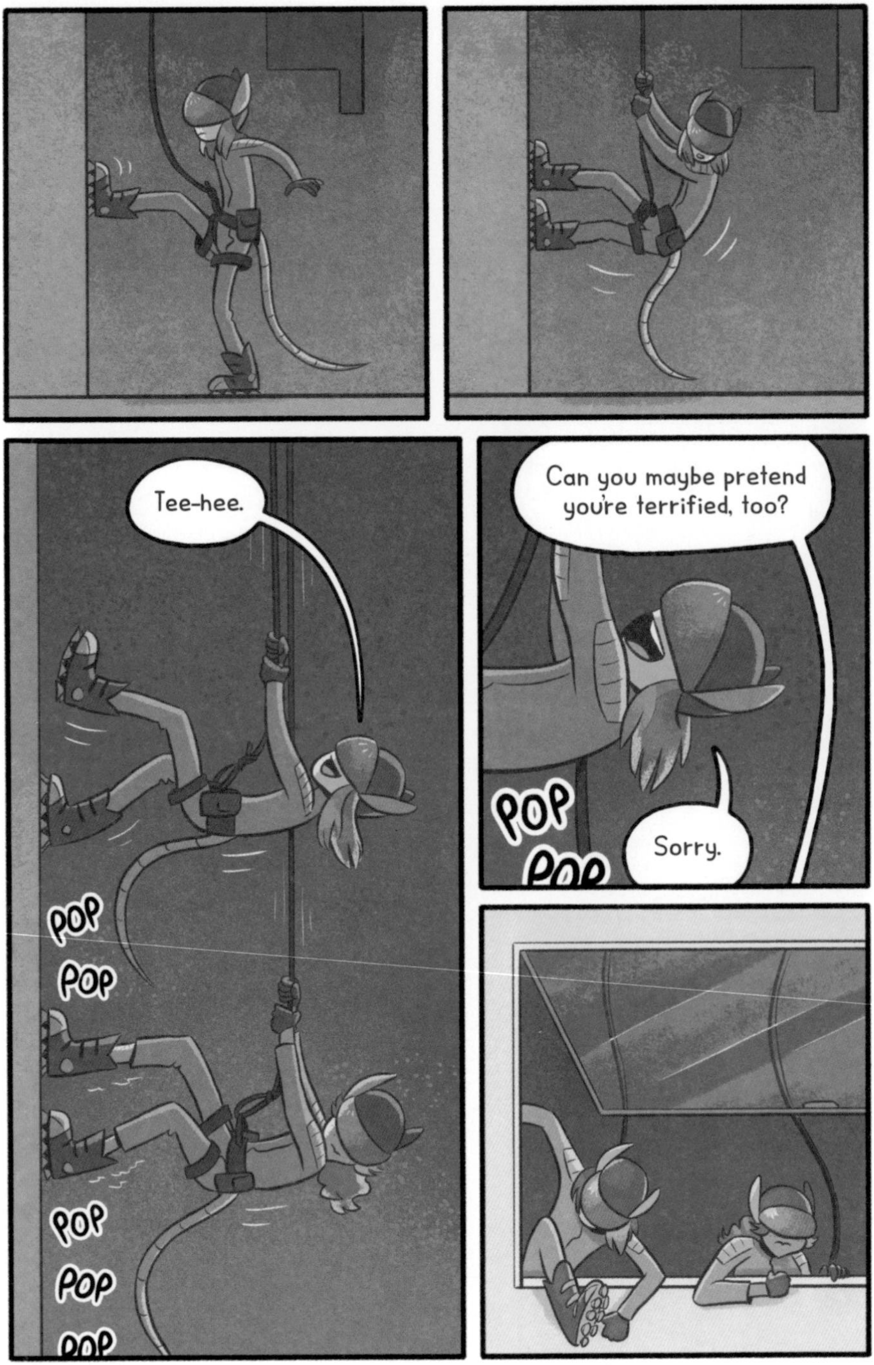

Tee-hee.
POP
POP
POP
POP
Can you maybe pretend you're terrified, too?
POP
Sorry.

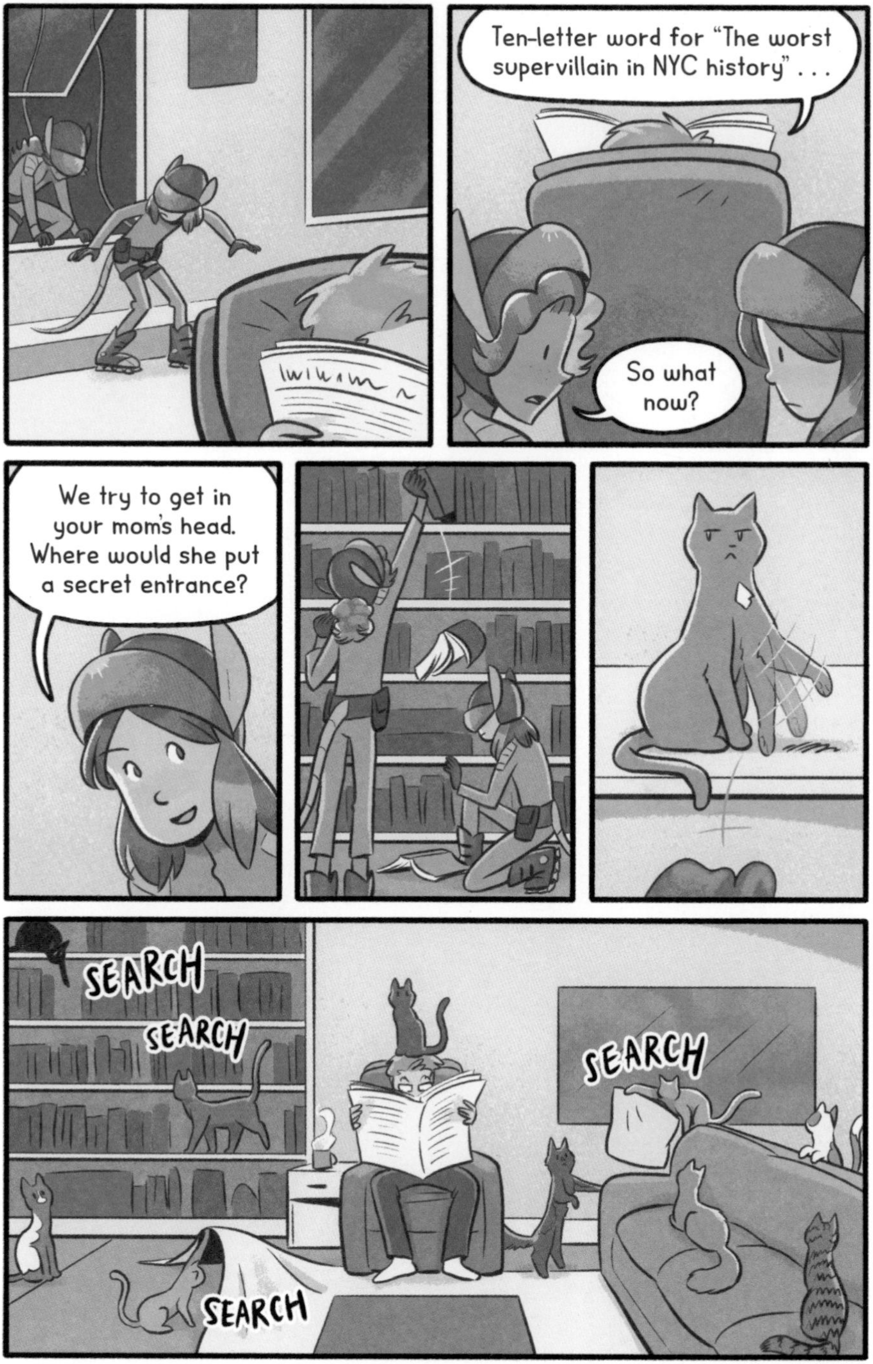
Ten-letter word for "The worst supervillain in NYC history" . . .
So what now?
We try to get in your mom's head. Where would she put a secret entrance?
SEARCH
SEARCH
SEARCH
SEARCH

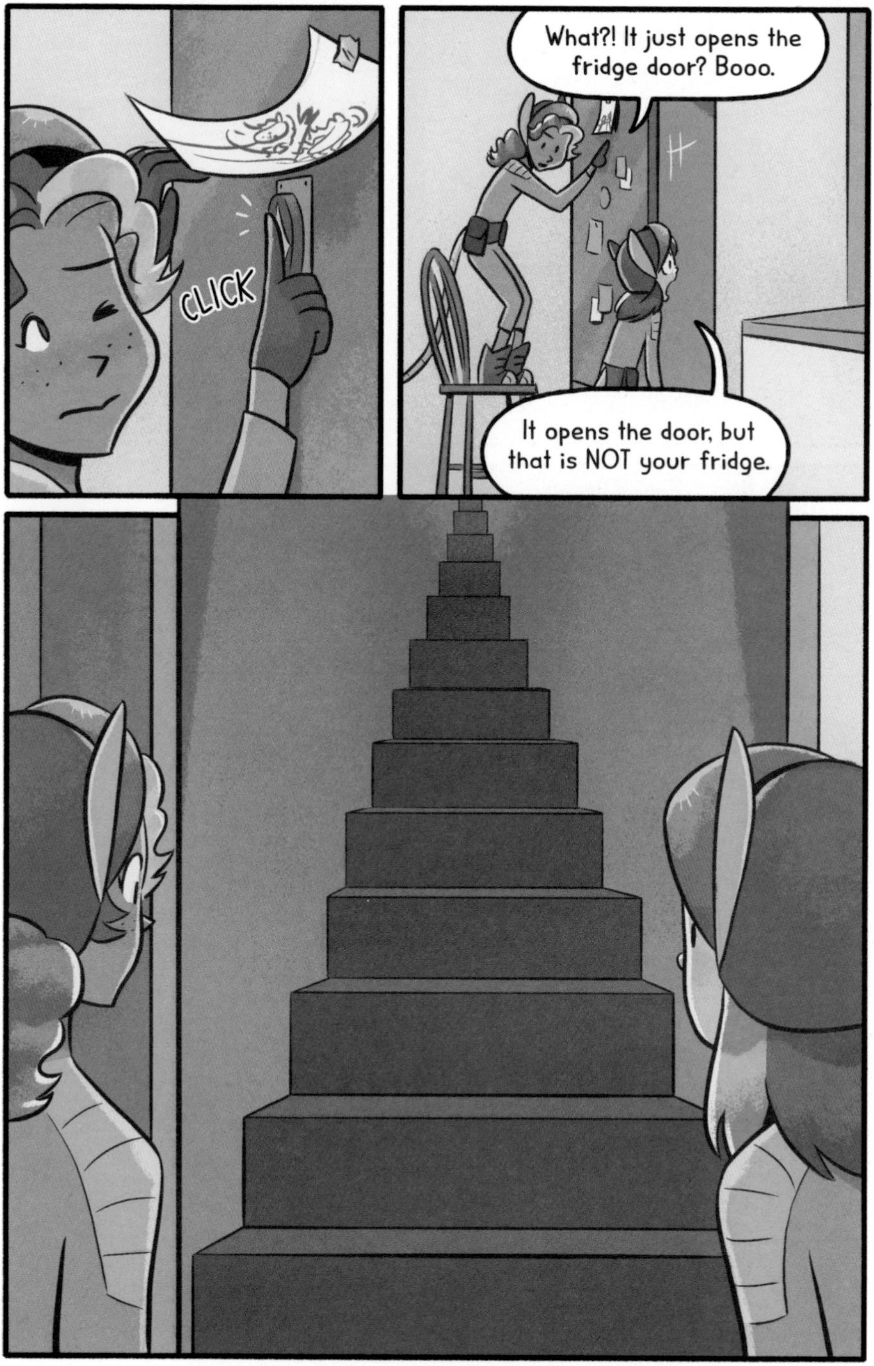
CLICK
What?! It just opens the fridge door? Booo.
It opens the door, but that is NOT your fridge.

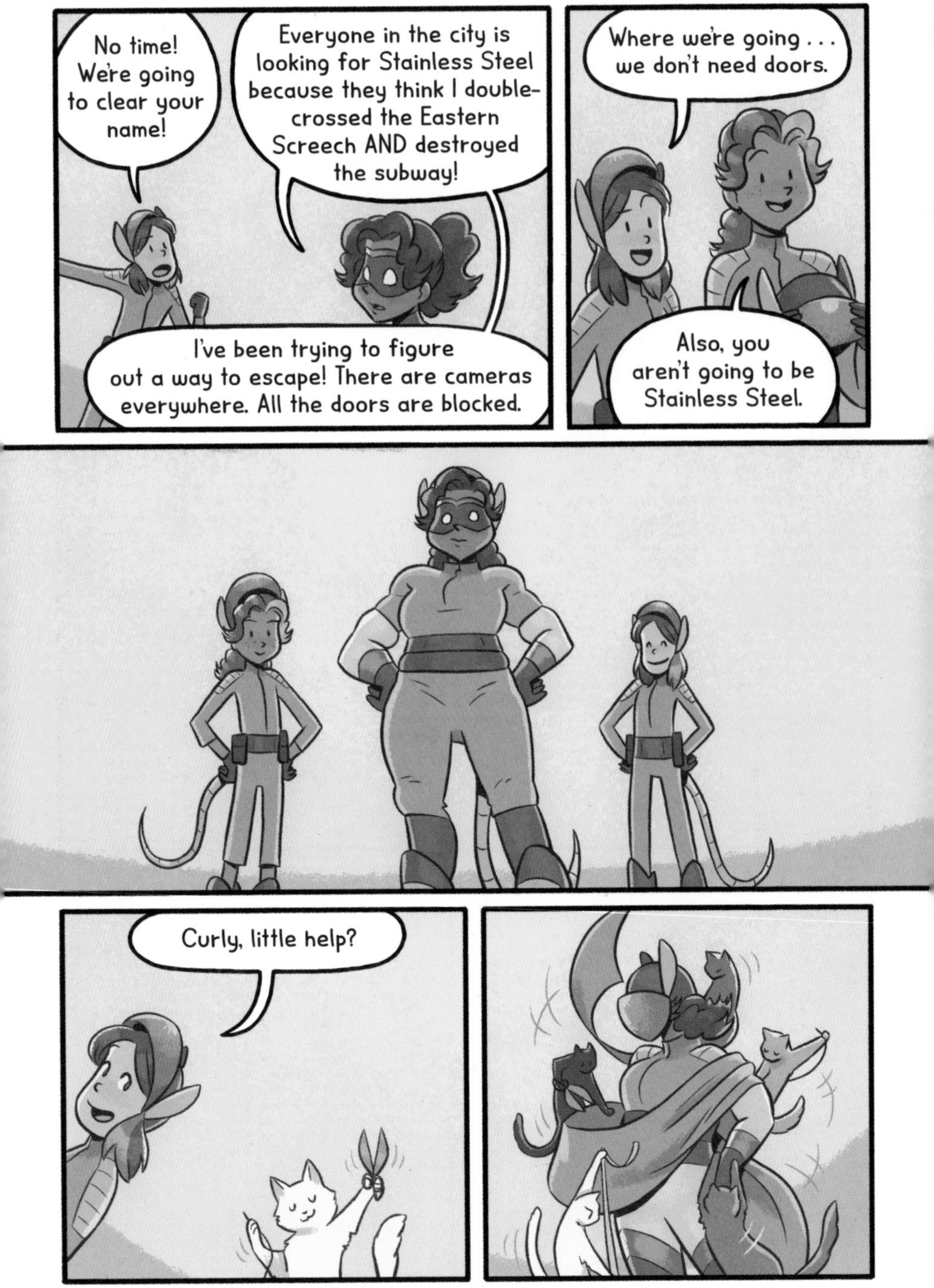
No time! We're going to clear your name!
Everyone in the city is looking for Stainless Steel because they think I double-crossed the Eastern Screech AND destroyed the subway!
I've been trying to figure out a way to escape! There are cameras everywhere. All the doors are blocked.
Where we're going . . . we don't need doors.
Also, you aren't going to be Stainless Steel.
Curly, little help?

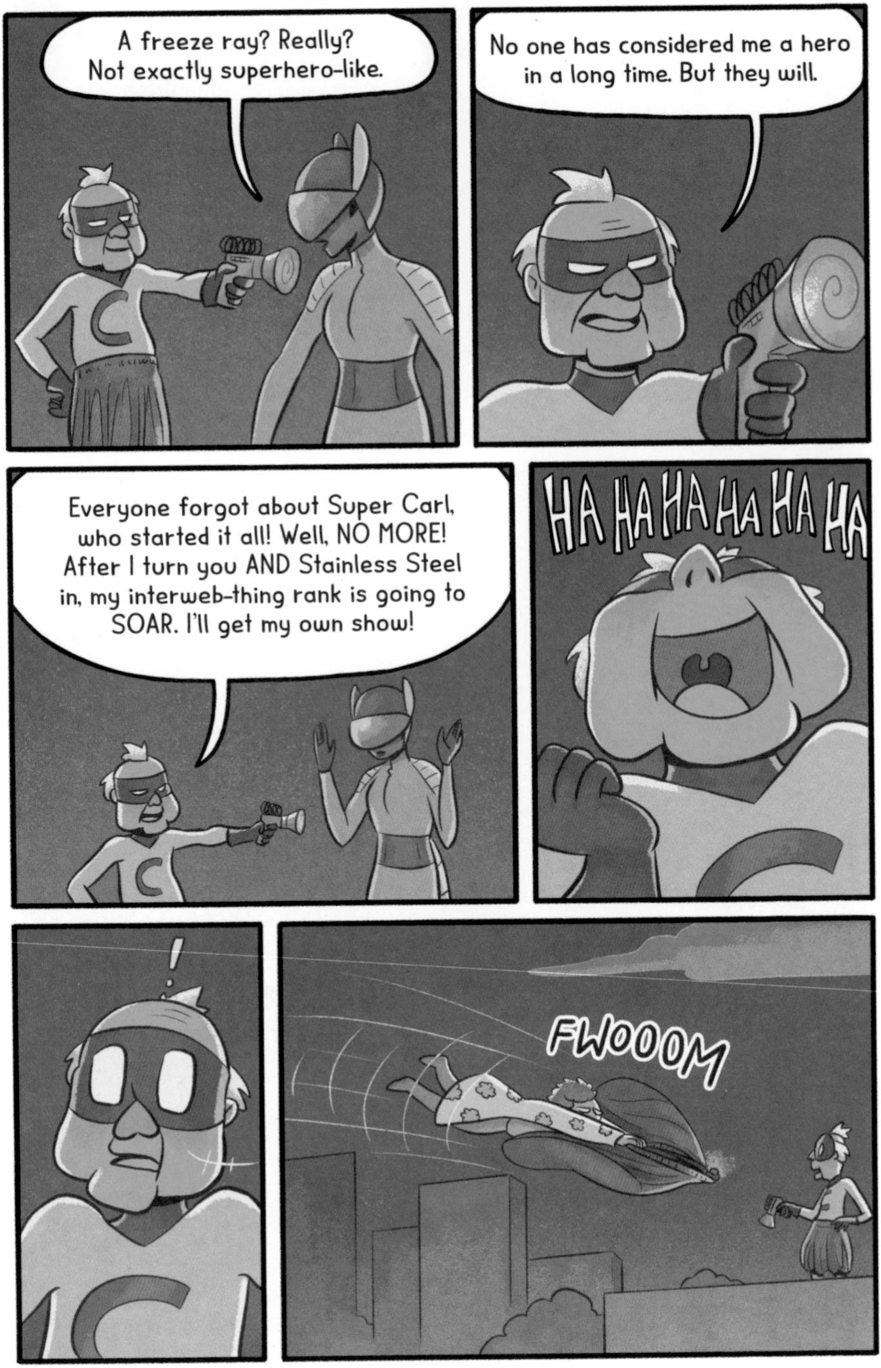
A freeze ray? Really? Not exactly superhero-like.
No one has considered me a hero in a long time. But they will.
Everyone forgot about Super Carl, who started it all! Well, NO MORE! After I turn you AND Stainless Steel in, my interweb-thing rank is going to SOAR. I'll get my own show!
HA HA HA HA HA HA
!
FWOOOM

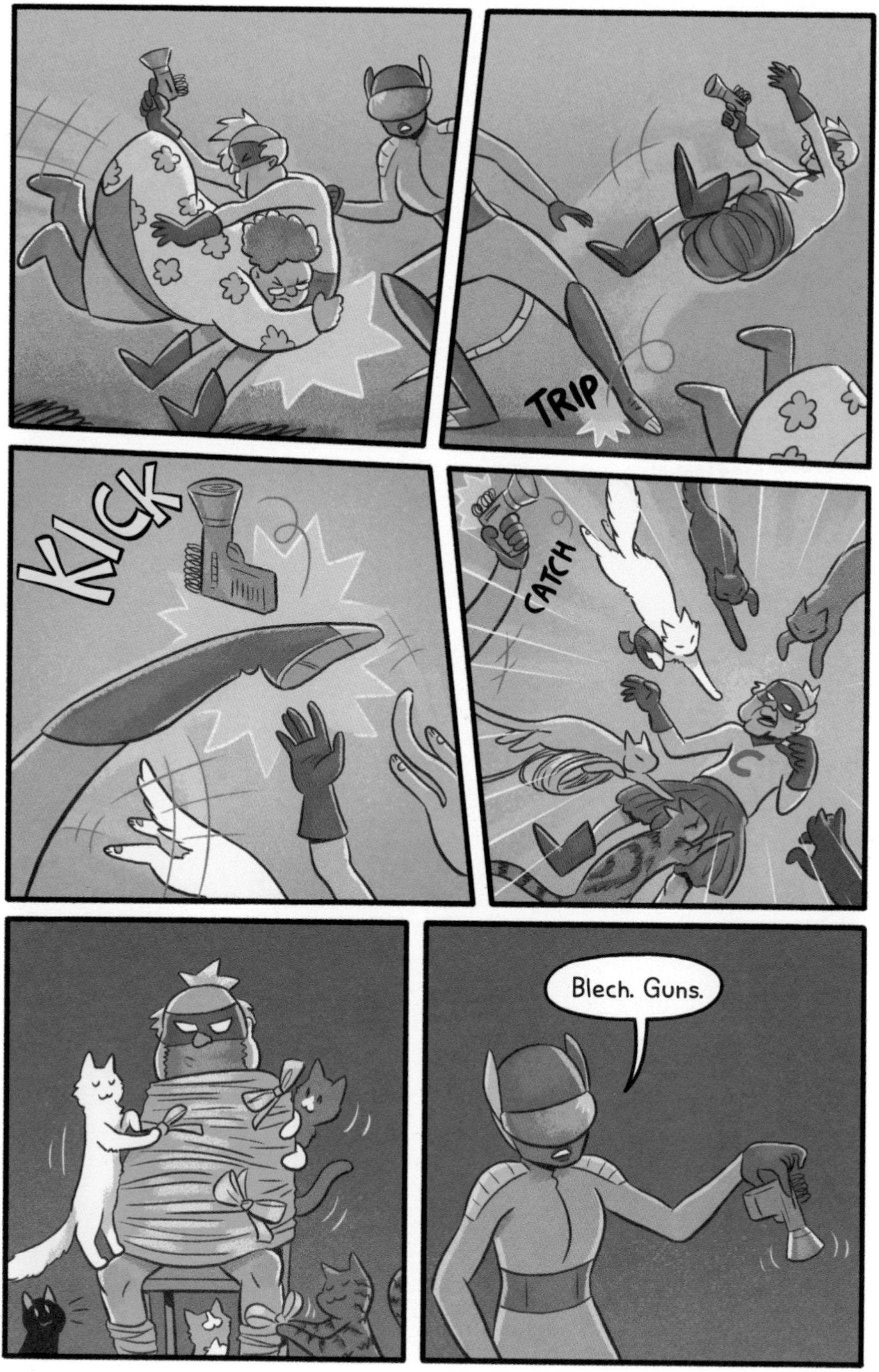
TRIP
KICK
CATCH
C
Blech. Guns.

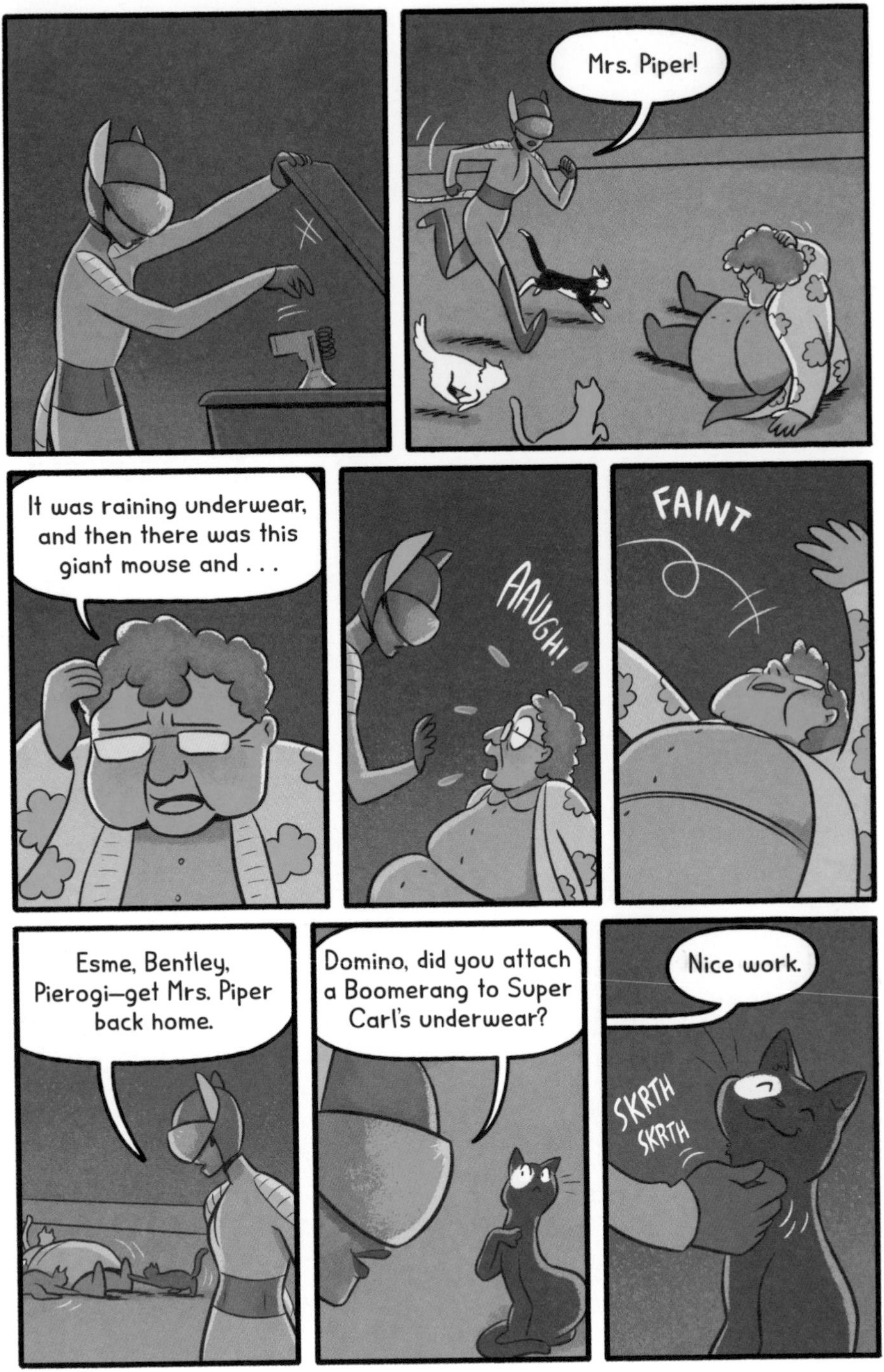
Mrs. Piper!
It was raining underwear, and then there was this giant mouse and . . .
AAUGH!
FAINT
Esme, Bentley, Pierogi—get Mrs. Piper back home.
Domino, did you attach a Boomerang to Super Carl's underwear?
Nice work.
SKRTH SKRTH

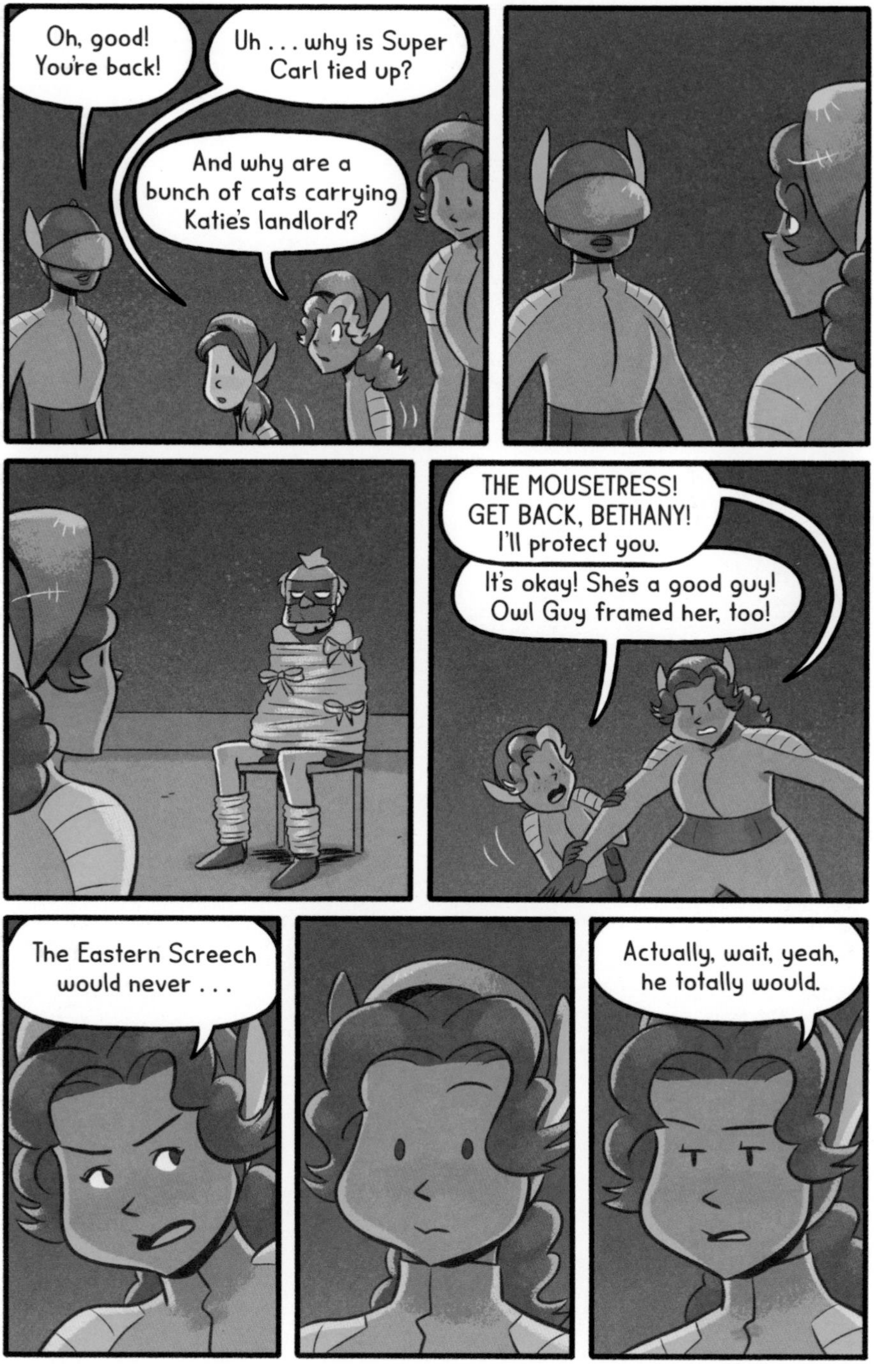
Oh, good! You're back!
Uh . . . why is Super Carl tied up?
And why are a bunch of cats carrying Katie's landlord?
THE MOUSETRESS! GET BACK, BETHANY! I'll protect you.
It's okay! She's a good guy! Owl Guy framed her, too!
The Eastern Screech would never . . .
Actually, wait, yeah, he totally would.

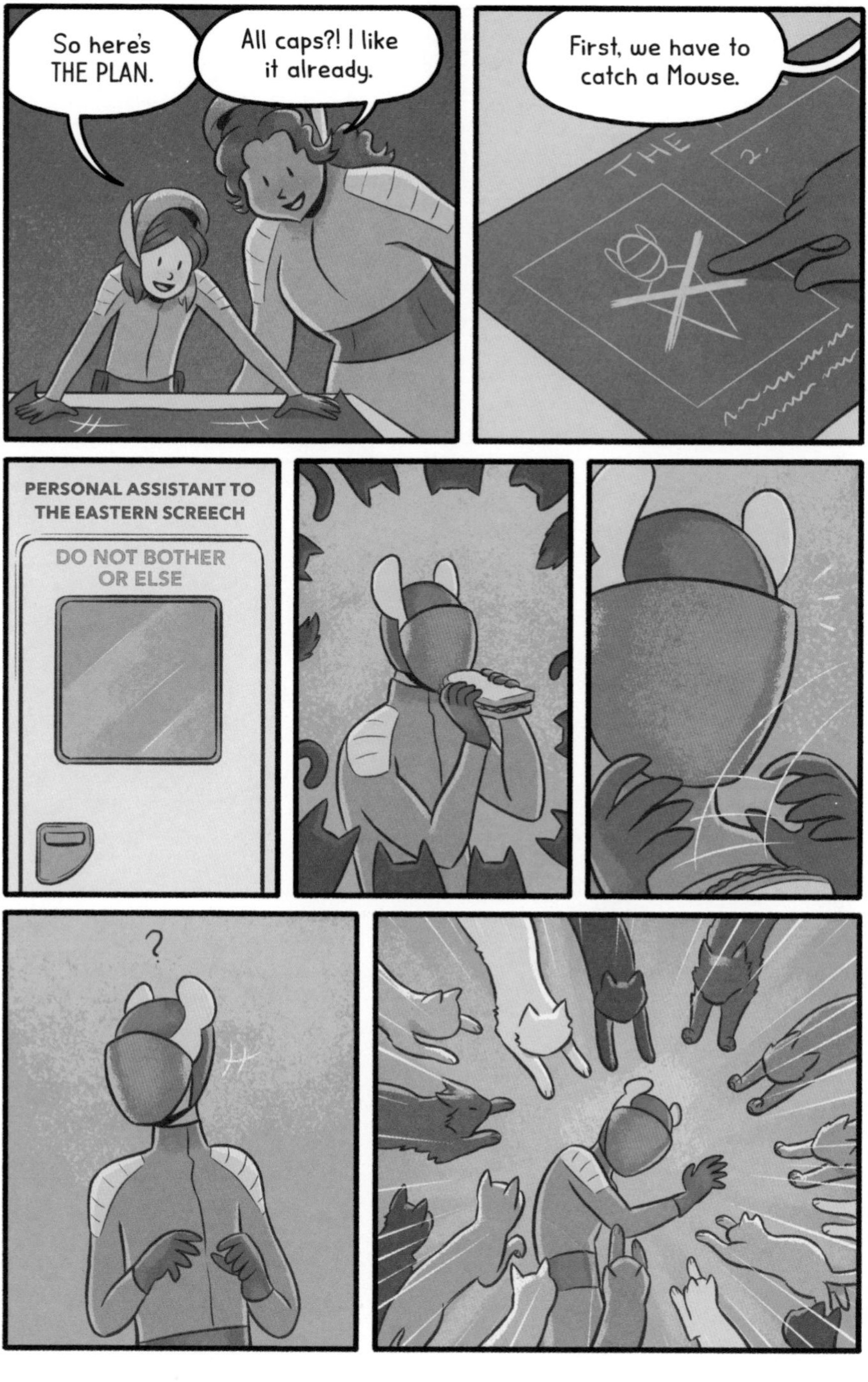
So here's THE PLAN.
All caps?! I like it already.
First, we have to catch a Mouse.
THE
2.
PERSONAL ASSISTANT TO THE EASTERN SCREECH
DO NOT BOTHER OR ELSE
?

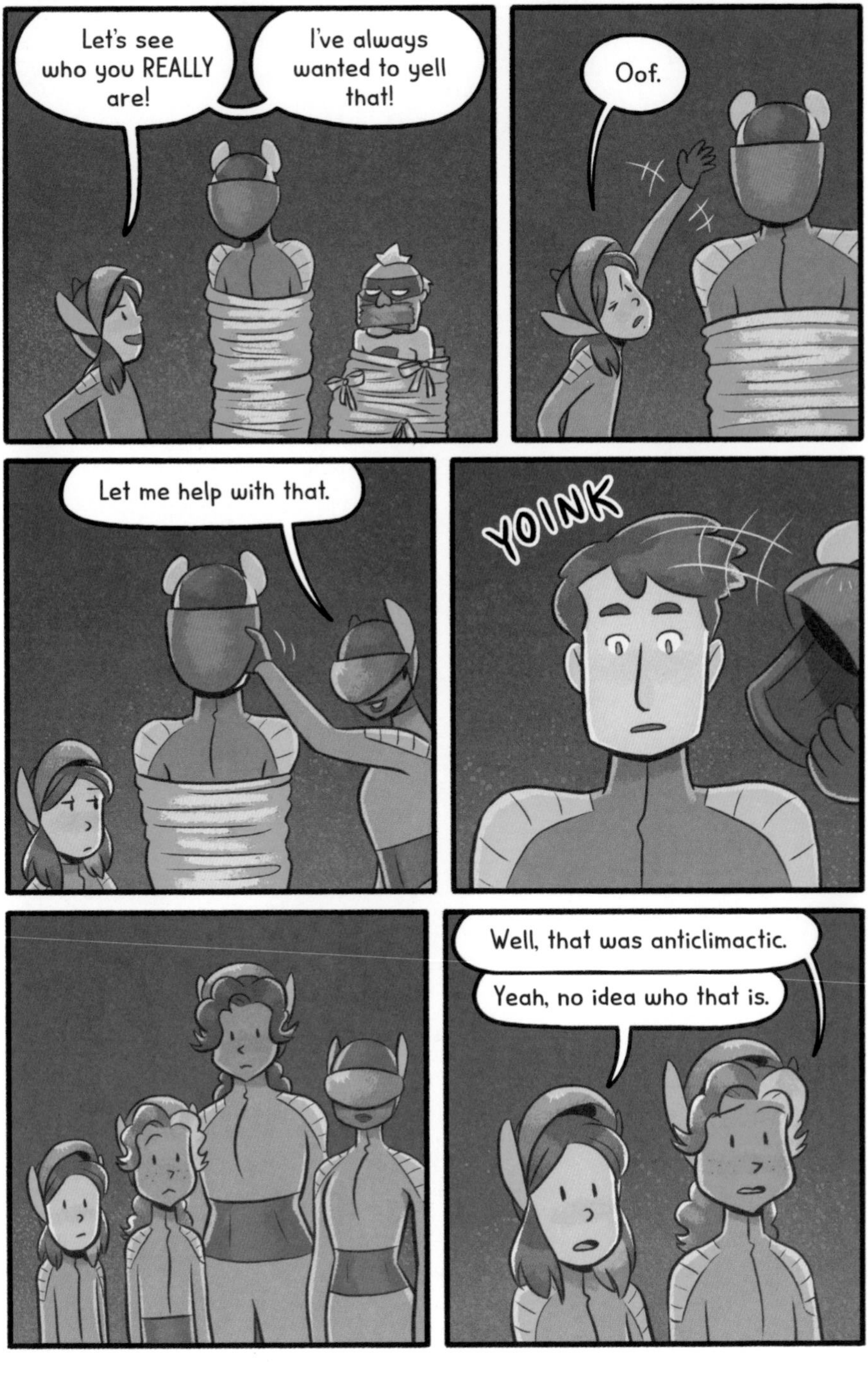

Let's see who you REALLY are!
I've always wanted to yell that!
Oof.
Let me help with that.
YOINK
Well, that was anticlimactic.
Yeah, no idea who that is.

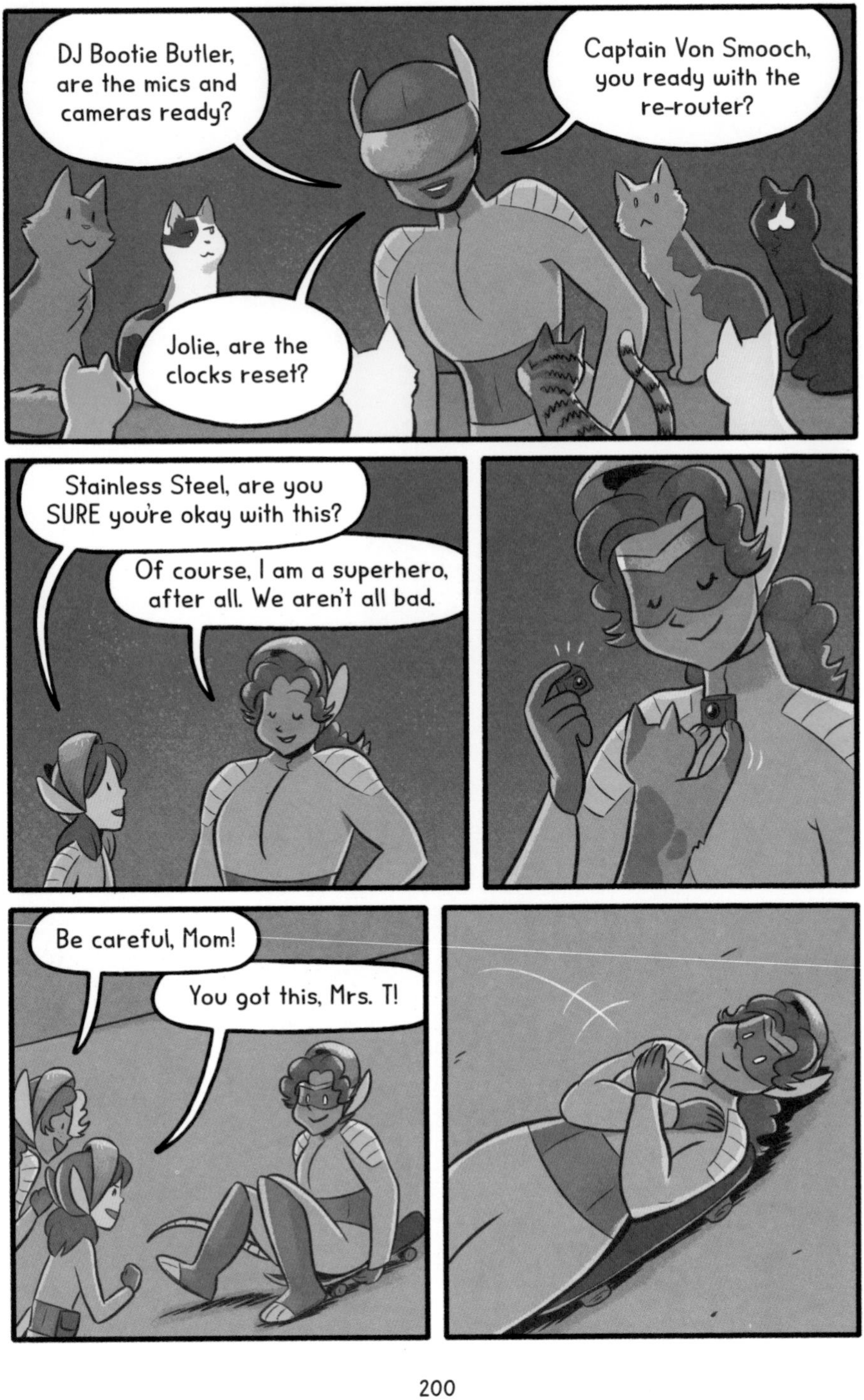
DJ Bootie Butler, are the mics and cameras ready?
Captain Von Smooch, you ready with the re-router?
Jolie, are the clocks reset?
Stainless Steel, are you SURE you're okay with this?
Of course, I am a superhero, after all. We aren't all bad.
Be careful, Mom!
You got this, Mrs. T!

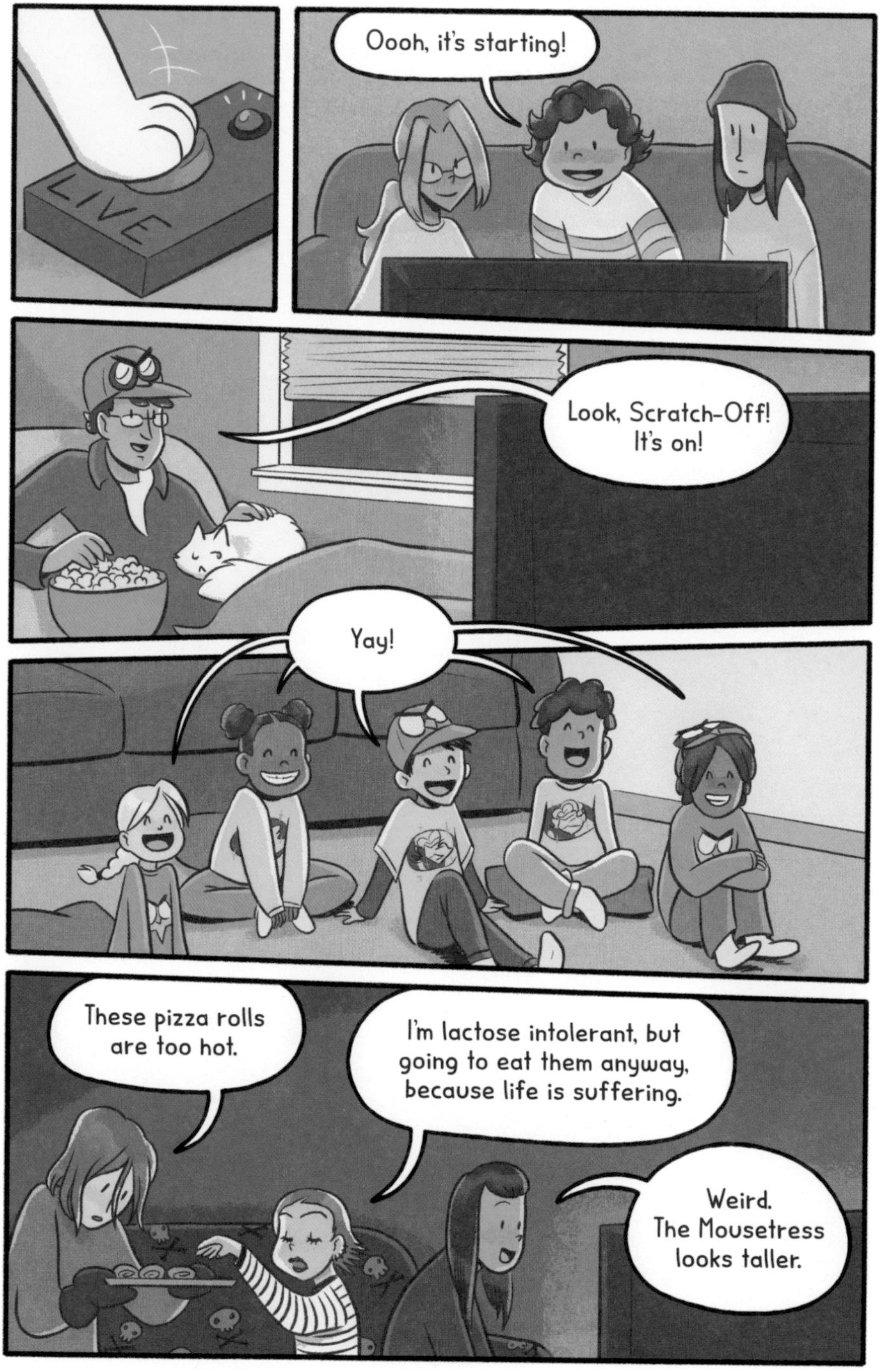
LIVE
Oooh, it's starting!
Look, Scratch-Off! It's on!
Yay!
These pizza rolls are too hot.
I'm lactose intolerant, but going to eat them anyway, because life is suffering.
Weird. The Mousetress looks taller.

207

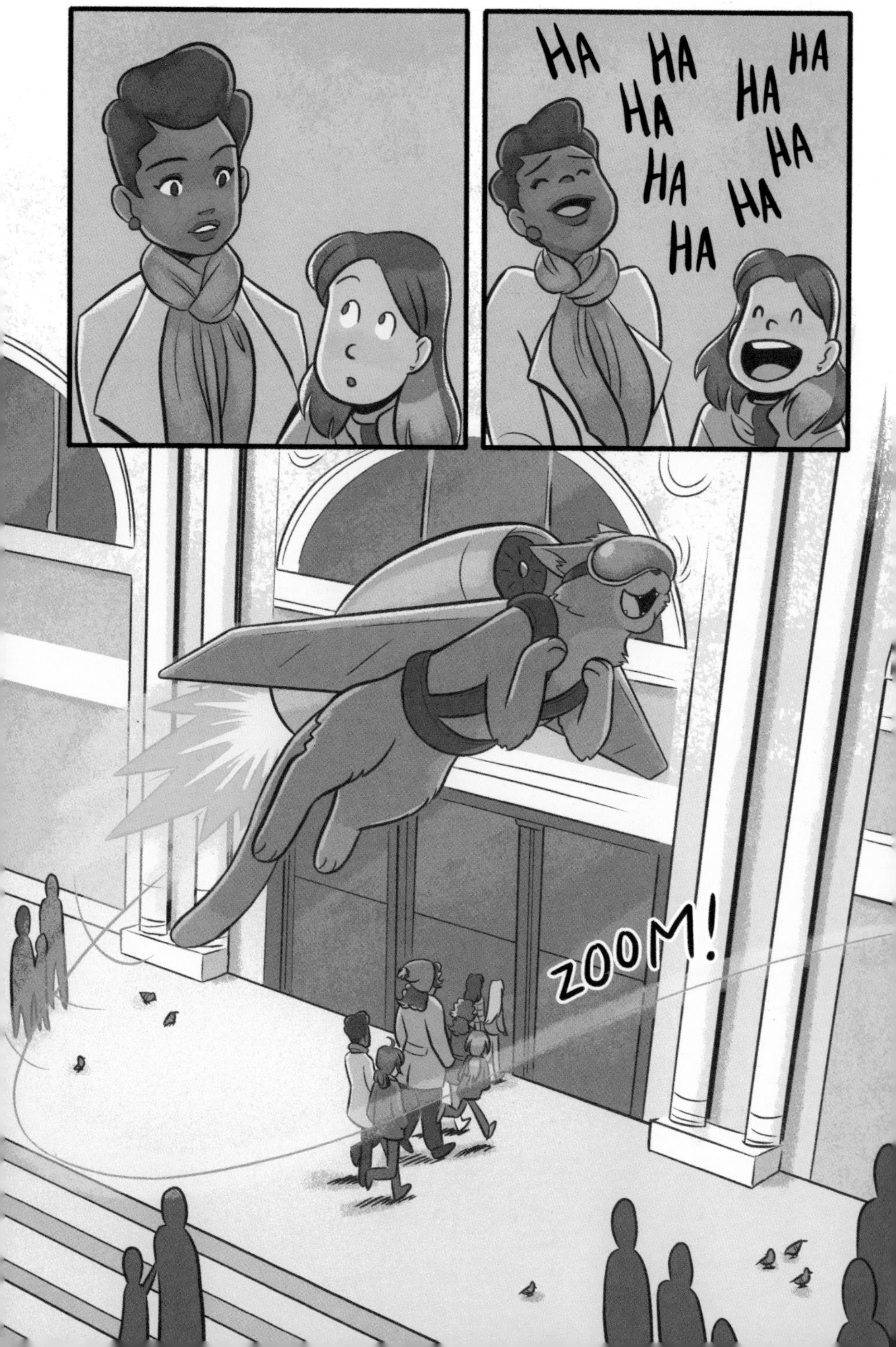
HA HA HA HA HA HA HA HA HA HA
ZOOM!

Some Heroes Have Capes...
Katie Has Cats!

Collect them all!

And don't miss
Katie the Catsitter
The Purrfect Plan
coming in 2024!

TOP 10 HERO RANKINGS
SPONSORED BY KELMOUNT CAPE WAX

"If it isn't Kelmount, it isn't . . . Kelmount? (We need a better slogan.)"

1. STAINLESS STEEL
★★★★☆

"Both of my daughters want to be Stainless Steel when they grow up, and I can't blame them. I think I do, too!"

2. THE ANVILATOR
★★★★★

"The best hero in the city, hands down! (Anvil hands, that is. So rad!) Has a kinda weird sidekick, though, who asked if he could finish my sandwich."

★★★★✦

"Wait, it's 'Angle'? Not 'Angel'? Well, that explains the lack of wings and excessive protractor use."

3. JUSTICE ANGLE

4. VERDE VENCEDOR
(OR GREEN VICTOR)
★★★★★

"Dude! His outfit is like Perrrrrfect green-screen green. Has anyone told him this? Please don't, because I'm having so much fun in Photoshop."

★★★★★

"I got mugged on Saturday, and he showed up to help on Wednesday. I guess I should be mad, but he's SO CUTE."

5. SLOTH-MAN

6. GOWANUS ADONIS
★★★★★

"Strong, powerful . . . no,
I'm not describing his hero skills.
I'm describing the way he smells."

★★★★★

"The F train wasn't running in Manhattan, but he
said I could just take the A to Jay Street and then
it's a super-lazy transfer to the Coney Island
bound. No stairs! You saved me, Subway Saint!"

7. SUBWAY SAINT

8. THE HIPSTER TWINS:
POCKET PROTECTOR AND FANNY PACK
★★★★★

"Will only work in Brooklyn. Truly an
amazing duo, though they sometimes get
distracted from crime fighting to argue
about the best record of all time."

★★★★★

"Tastiest bagels in NY, grapple-
hooked right to your apartment!"

9. CARB CRUSADER

10. THE EASTERN SCREECH
★★★★★

"How is Owl Guy still in the top 10?!
Let's get him off this list and get
more awesome women heroes on it!
Stainless Steel 4 Eva."

TOP 10 MOST-WANTED VILLAINS

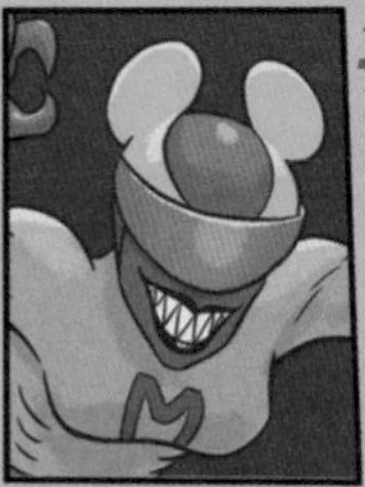

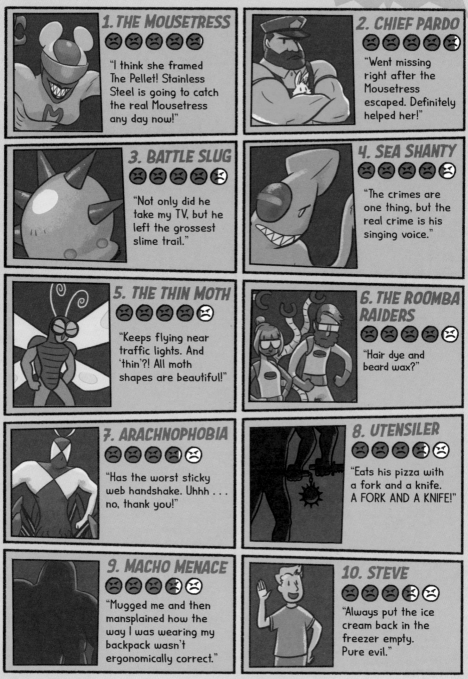

1. THE MOUSETRESS

"I think she framed The Pellet! Stainless Steel is going to catch the real Mousetress any day now!"

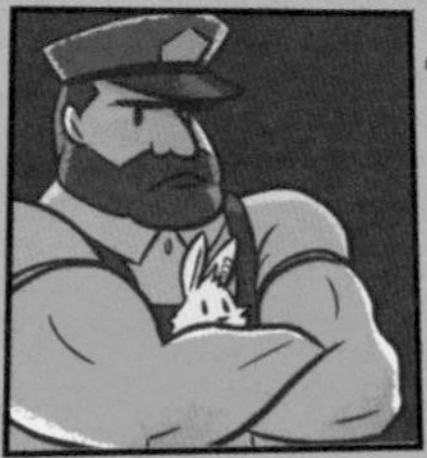

2. CHIEF PARDO

"Went missing right after the Mousetress escaped. Definitely helped her!"

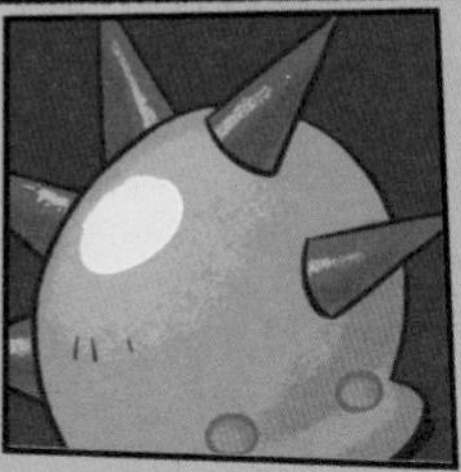

3. BATTLE SLUG

"Not only did he take my TV, but he left the grossest slime trail."

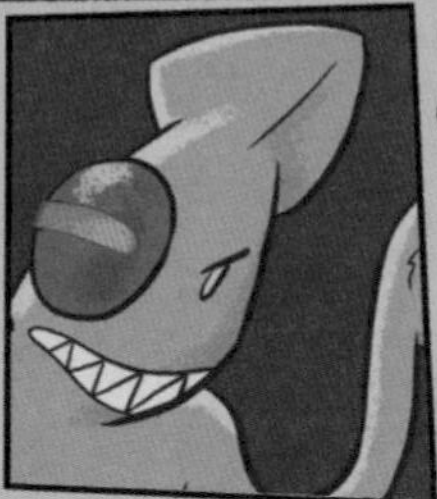

4. SEA SHANTY

"The crimes are one thing, but the real crime is his singing voice."

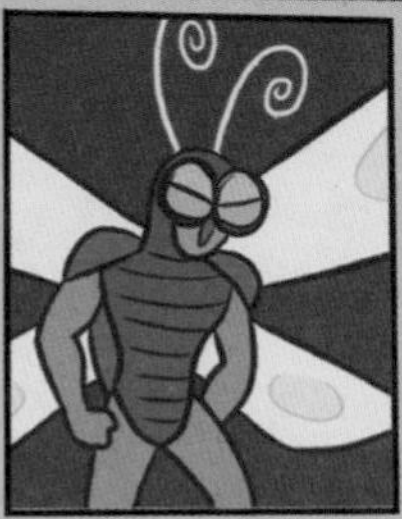

5. THE THIN MOTH

"Keeps flying near traffic lights. And 'thin'?! All moth shapes are beautiful!"

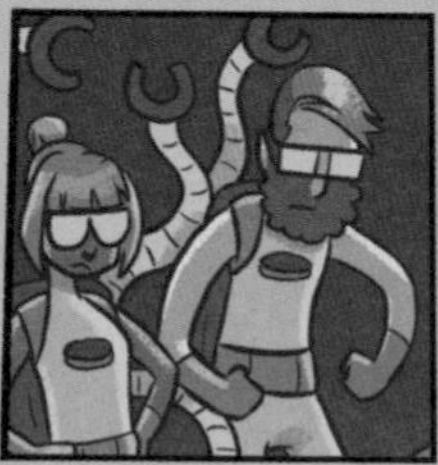

6. THE ROOMBA RAIDERS

"Hair dye and beard wax?"

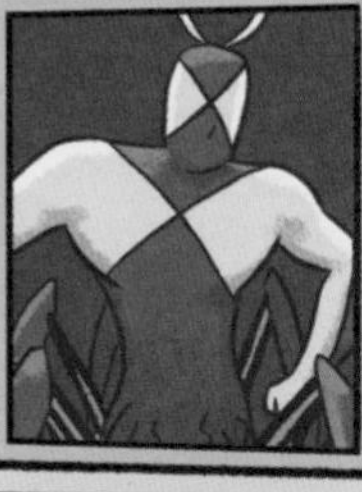

7. ARACHNOPHOBIA

"Has the worst sticky web handshake. Uhhh . . . no, thank you!"

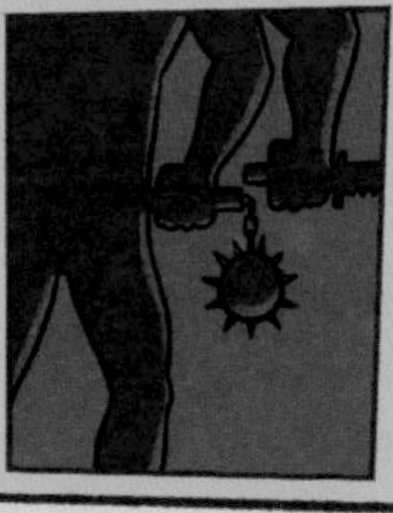

8. UTENSILER

"Eats his pizza with a fork and a knife. A FORK AND A KNIFE!"

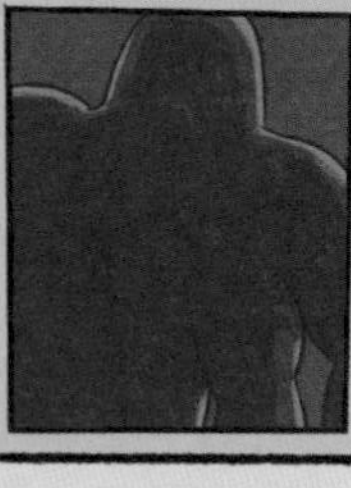

9. MACHO MENACE

"Mugged me and then mansplained how the way I was wearing my backpack wasn't ergonomically correct."

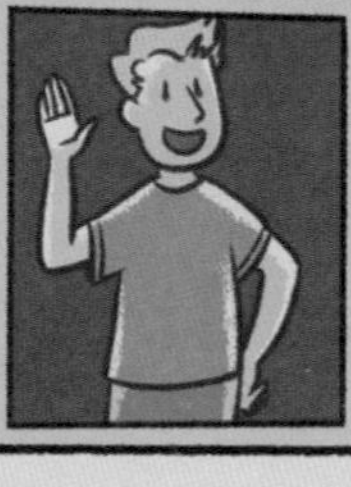

10. STEVE

"Always put the ice cream back in the freezer empty. Pure evil."

MEET COLLEEN!

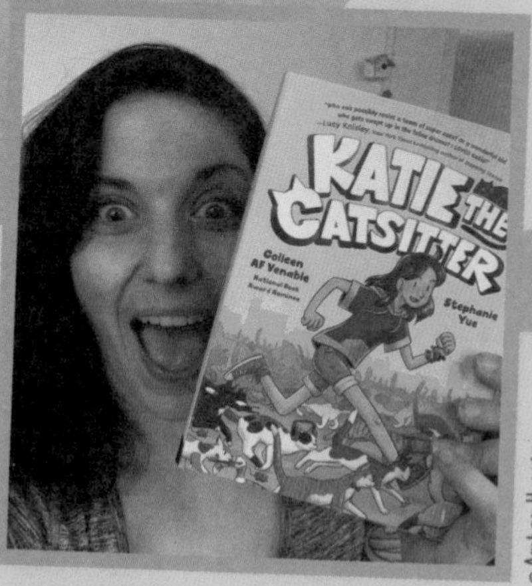
KATIE THE CATSITTER
Colleen AF Venable
Stephanie Yue

© Amber Harrison

COLLEEN AF (ANN FELICITY) VENABLE

grew up in Walden, New York. She's a lifelong comic book fan, maker, and roller-skater, and was the designer for multiple award-winning graphic novels at First Second Books. She is also the author of the Eisner-nominated Guinea Pig, Pet Shop Private Eye series and the *School Library Journal* Best Book *The Oboe Goes Boom Boom Boom,* and was longlisted for a National Book Award for her YA graphic novel debut, *Kiss Number 8.* Colleen splits her time between Brooklyn, New York, and an old house from the 1800s in North Adams, Massachusetts, that she's rebuilding with friends. She's got two bunnies named Tuck and Cher that do NOT like cats but may secretly be cats themselves. Visit Colleen online at colleenaf.com and @colleenaf.

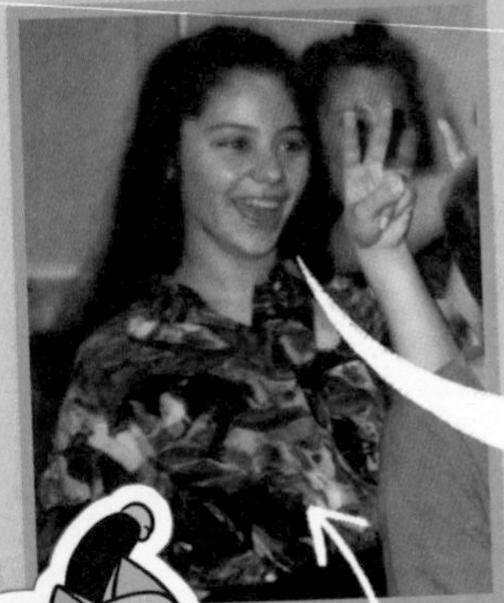

ME AT 12!

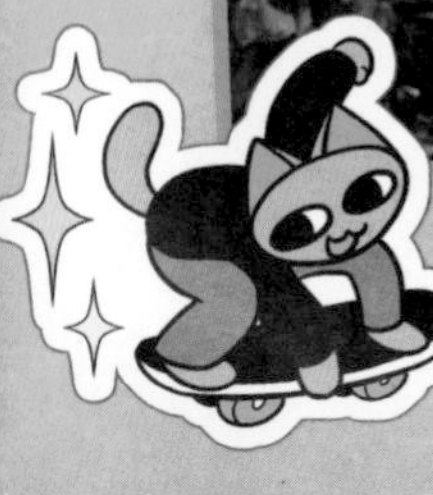

Who in *Katie the Catsitter* is most like me? Hmmm. That's a tough one because they're all little parts of me. For instance, I was a latchkey kid like Katie, with parents who were amazing but had to work a ton to make ends meet. But I was also like Beth. I was the first one of my friends to start putting up pictures of crushes in my locker (and OH BOY did I have a lot). I'm also very much like Lupe: optimistic, quick with a joke, really into sequins and crafting, and much better at skateboarding if I just lie down on the board.

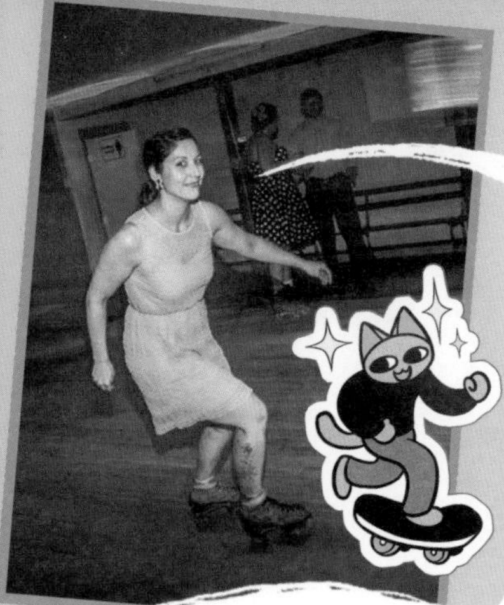

I was also a lot like Marie . . . at least when I tried to skateboard. I tried so hard but could never figure it out! I blame it on the GIANT hill that was next to my house that I was always sure I could accidentally roll down. When I was a kid there were no skate parks. But there were roller rinks! I learned to roller-skate and still skate today. I'm even taking roller-dance classes! Some of the people in my class are over eighty years old and can do fancy tricks! (And are much better than me!)

Did you know that over 200 of the cats in the book are based on real-life cats? There's a real Pierogi and Paw Simon and Dr. Claw and Captain Von Smooch! They belong to my friends! Other cats, like Frida, the artist, were named after people I admire who also had amazing skills. One cat that didn't make the book: my own childhood cat! I named Kitty when I was six, and he lived for almost twenty years!

SOME OF MY EARLY WRITING

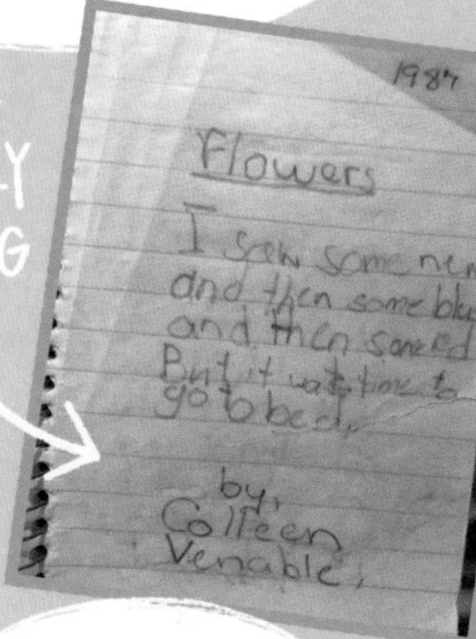

1984

Flowers

I saw some red and then some blue and then some red But it was time to go to bed.

by, Colleen Venable

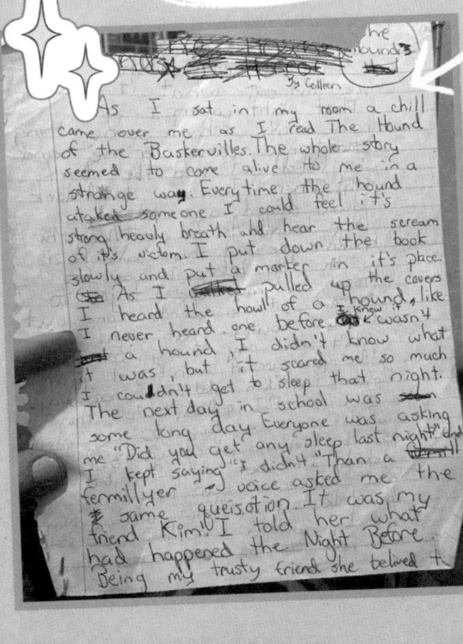

The Hound

By Colleen

As I sat in my room a chill came over me as I read The Hound of the Baskervilles. The whole story seemed to come alive to me in a strange way. Every time the hound ataked someone I could feel it's strong heavy breath and hear the scream of it's victom. I put down the book slowly and put a marker in it's place. As I pulled up the covers I heard the howl of a hound, like I never heard one before. I know it wasn't a hound, I didn't know what it was, but it scared me so much I couldn't get to sleep that night. The next day in school was some long day. Everyone was asking me "Did you get any sleep last night" and I kept saying "I didn't." Than a fermillyer voice asked me the same queisotion. It was my friend Kim! I told her what had happened the Night Before. Being my trusty friend she belived t

When people ask how I became a writer I say two things: Encouragement and Not Giving Up. I loved writing as a kid and wrote all the time. It was in seventh grade that Mrs. Grodin told me she was enjoying my stories and I started to write them for her weekly! She'd put a check in the margin if she liked a line. I once got a check plus-plus-plus! When I grew up, I started to submit my stories to publishers. I wrote over thirty books before I finally got one published! I feel so lucky to be able to share this story with all of you!

MEET STEPH!

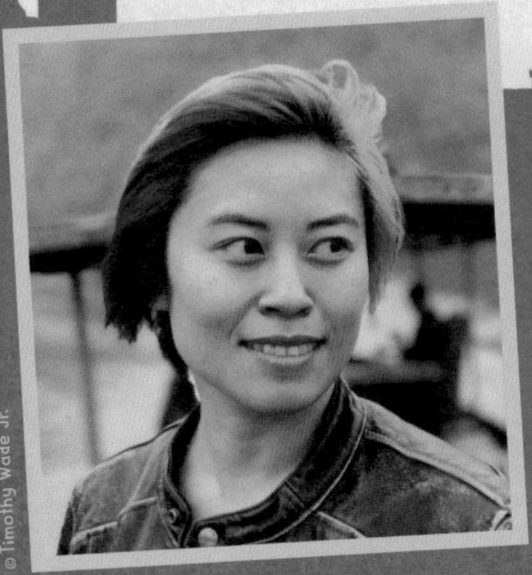

© Timothy Wade Jr.

STEPHANIE YUE grew up in Atlanta, Beijing, and Hong Kong. She's a lifetime comic fan and martial artist (with a black belt in kung fu) and travels the world by motorbike. In addition to Katie the Catsitter, Stephanie is the illustrator of the Guinea Pig, Pet Shop Private Eye series and several picture books and chapter books. She was also the colorist for *Smile* by Raina Telgemeier. Stephanie divides her time between Asia, Europe, and the United States, where she's building a van into a mobile live-work studio and drawing the third Katie the Catsitter graphic novel. Visit her online at stephanieyue.com and on Twitter at @quezzie.

I relate to Katie because when I was her age it felt like everyone else was growing up faster than me. In reality, I was probably more like Marie—athletic, fearless, and 100 percent a superfan of anything I got into, but hopefully a little more coordinated! I rollerbladed everywhere and climbed everything, and I was really into Sailor Moon. If you look closely at Stainless Steel's costume design, her tiara is a nod to my Sailor Moon days.

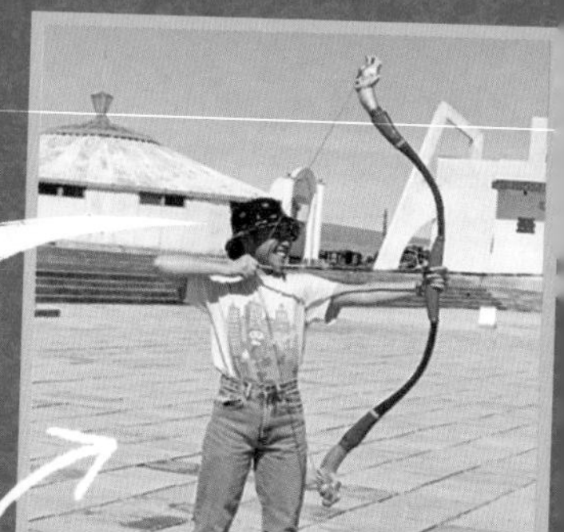

AGE 12, ON A SCHOOL FIELD TRIP TO INNER MONGOLIA

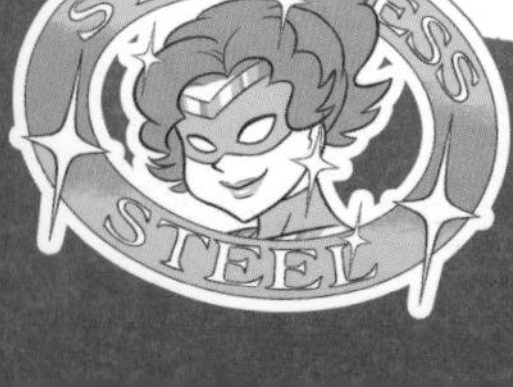
STAINLESS
STEEL

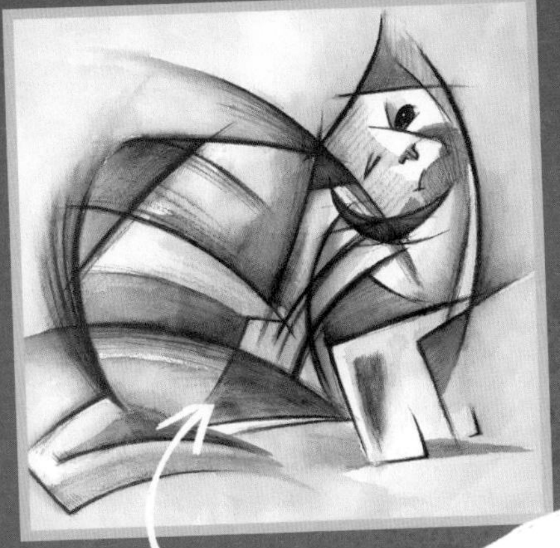

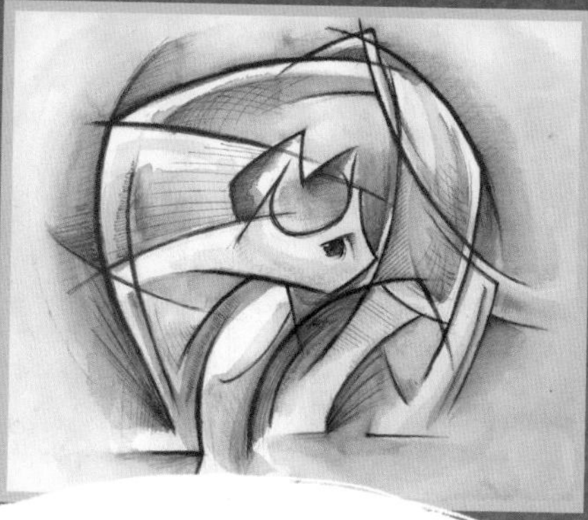

CUBIST / FUTURIST CAT ILLUSTRATIONS FROM MY SENIOR PROJECT IN HIGH SCHOOL. I HAVE A HISTORY OF DRAWING CATS!

Whenever someone asks me how I got started drawing, I tell them I just never stopped! Drawing is a natural way to express yourself, and lots of kids draw. Many adults don't draw anymore, maybe because someone told them they weren't good at it or they should focus on other things. It's a shame because drawing can be such a neat window into how someone else sees the world. Eventually, I practiced drawing so much I went to art school, but you don't have to go to school to draw. Drawing is for everyone. Who cares if someone else thinks it's good or not as long as you're having fun?

Like Katie, I wasn't allowed to have cats or dogs when I was growing up, but I talked my parents into letting me keep a hamster. The pet shop in Beijing didn't carry hamster food and suggested a diet of puppy pellets and fresh vegetables instead. I suspect puppy food is much higher in protein than hamster food because Hammie didn't grow up to be fluffy and round like most hamsters but unusually strong and smart.

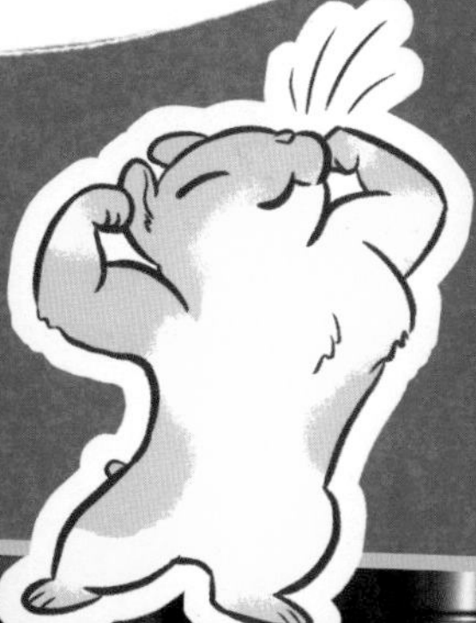

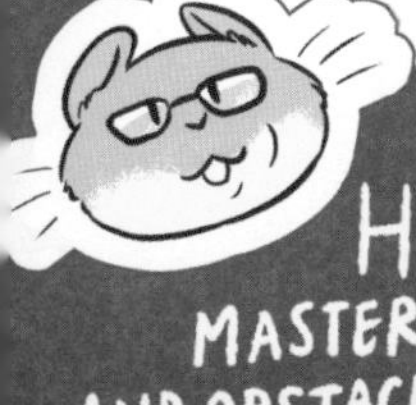

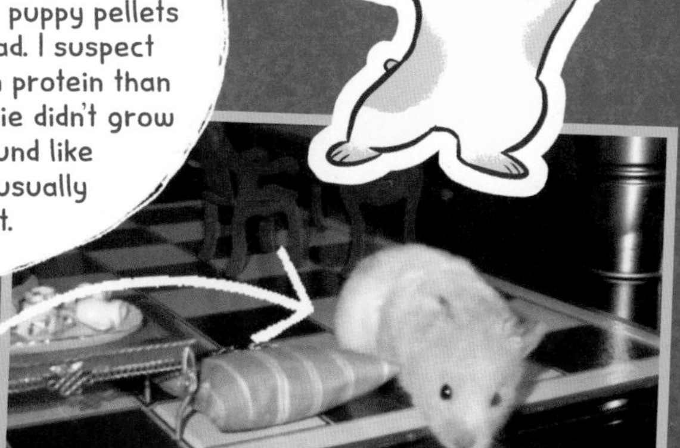

HAMMIE MASTERING CHESS AND OBSTACLE COURSES

How to Draw Moritz in 4 Easy Steps

1. Start with a pencil to lightly lay down the basic shapes. Moritz's head is roughly a circle with two triangles for ears and a tube connected to a squashed circle body.

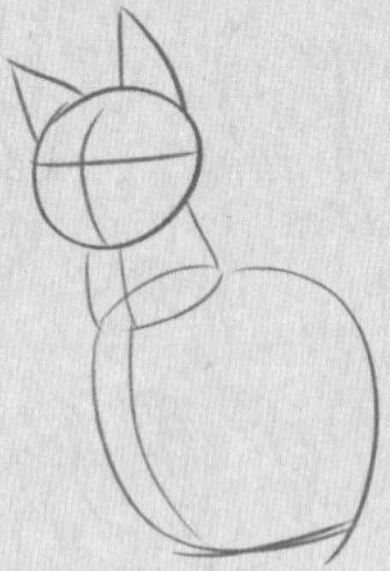

2. Add details like nose, eyes, tail, and attack paw. Moritz's superpower is the counterattack, so he needs a counter and an attack subject.

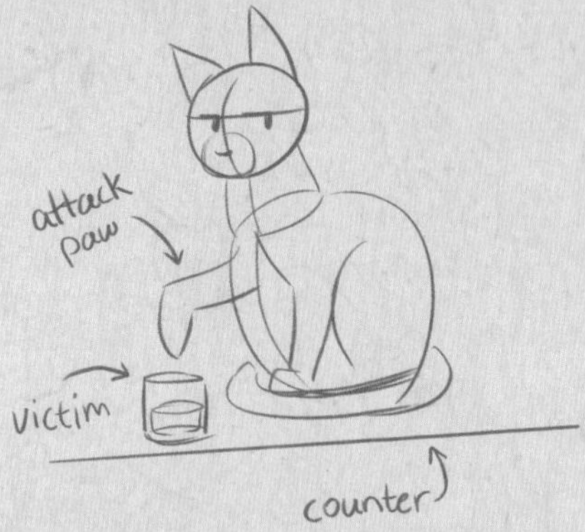
attack paw
victim
counter

3. Draw Moritz in ink over your setup drawing, lightly erasing as needed. Don't forget his personal details, like his white neck tuft, twitching tail, and direct eye contact.

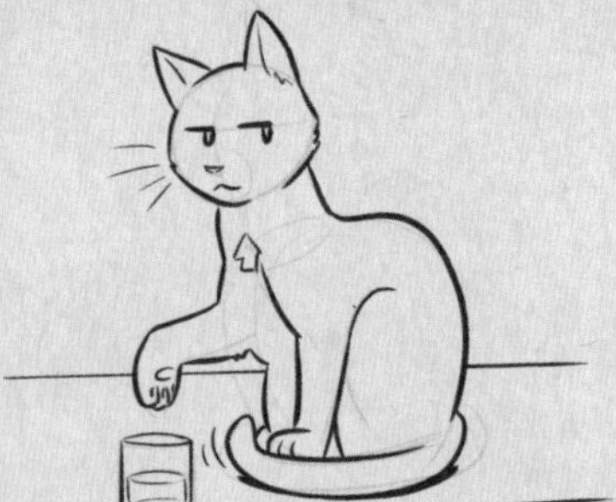

4. Now you can fully erase your underdrawing and bring Moritz to life with some color and a mischievous smile. Oh no! He's already issued a counterattack!

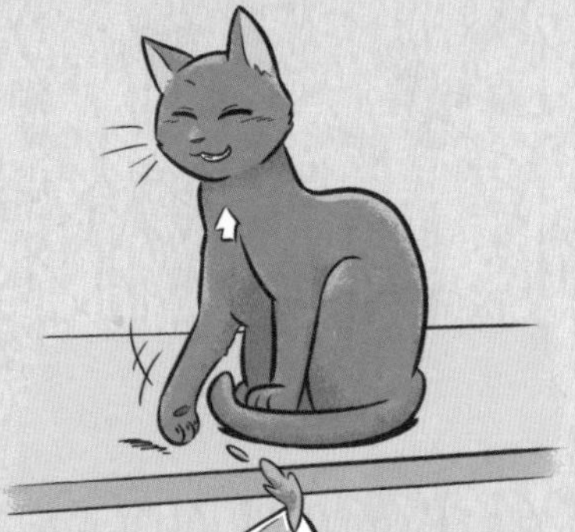